BROKENHEARTED

THE POWER OF DARKNESS

A novel by

Elisa S. Amore

Translated by

Leah Janeczko

WHAT READERS ARE SAYING ABOUT
BROKENHEARTED

"Elisa S. Amore is the undisputed queen of romantic fantasy." —F magazine

"Brokenhearted explodes with the revelation of a huge secret you won't be able to guess: a secret at the heart of everything. This novel exceeds all expectations—you won't be able to put it down!"
—Franci Cat

Intense, exciting, thrilling. A journey through impossible worlds, full of revelations, crises, and blood feuds. The story of a love that can withstand anything." Coffee&Books blog

"A truly epic battle between good and evil in which nothing is as it seems."
—Elena Serboli, R. Fantasy blog

"Elisa weaves many genres together in this special, unique story— fantasy, romance, gothic horror. She's created a masterpiece." –
Valentina, Goodreads

"An astounding novel. I am blown away by the intricate plot."
—Paola, Goodreads

"From the first page to the last, I was breathless with suspense. I cried, laughed, felt desperate."
–Maria Cristina, Goodreads

"An amazing plot line, like nothing I've ever read before."
–Damiana, Goodreads

"It's a complex, perfectly woven tapestry of magic, action, myths, legends, and overflowing love."–Kaiko, Amazon

"Your heart will be destroyed, and just when you finally see a glimmer of hope, you'll be catapulted into a completely foreign, terrifying world." –Damy C.

"Elisa S. Amore is a jewel of contemporary literature."
–Roberta Volpi, editor

"For once a book exceeded my expectations!"–Georgeta, Goodreads

"With this third volume, the author will amaze the reader with the many twists and turns of the plot."–Giuliana, blogger

"Beautiful! I really hope to see Gemma and Evan on the big screen soon!"
–HarmonyaLove, blogger

"Heartfelt thanks to Elisa for creating a world in her Touched saga where true love can change fate."
–Alessandra, Amazon

"The author has a dramatic ability to describe her characters' emotions. You'll feel them all in your heart!" –AC, Goodreads

"Brokenhearted is the most beautiful book yet in Elisa's saga."–Ilaria, blogger

"The entire novel is a nonstop parade of emotions and mind-boggling events that will keep you riveted until the very last page, set against a backdrop worthy of Dante." –Alessia, author

"Elisa gives me hope!" –TheBookworm

"Once you understand what's happening to the characters, you want to shout out to them and warn them of what's coming! You'll be caught up in the story's ever-increasing tension until you won't be able to put the book down!" –Silvia, blogger

"Such a sweet, intense story leaves an indelible mark on you." –Sonja, Goodreads

"Gemma is a fearless heroine who defies Hell in the name of love." –Germana, Goodreads

Death has never been so close . . .

"But the Lord God called to the man [. . .]
And He said, [. . .] "Have you eaten from the tree
that I commanded you not to eat from?"
The man said, "The woman you put here with me—
she gave me some fruit from the tree and I ate it."
Then the Lord God said to the woman,
"What is this you have done?"
The woman said, "The serpent deceived me, and I ate."
Genesis 3:9-13

PROLOGUE

"Get a blanket-anket-anket . . . We need to warm her-er-er!"
Ginevra.

Her voice reached me from afar, like an echo distorted by the wind. I thought I saw figures scrambling around me. They left pale wakes behind them like objects moving through water—or maybe it was my body that was immersed in a murky, cold, corrosive liquid.

With effort, I recognized Simon's voice. It had the same tinge of desperation as Ginevra's. "She's still alive. Her heart is still beating-ing-ing . . . My God, she's burning up. We've got to help her-er-er!"

"She's in shock-ock-ock . . . Do something, Simon!"

"It must be the poison. I can't counteract it!"

"It's making her blood boil. Here! Quick, let's get her onto the table!"

A metallic noise drowned out their voices, the sound of thousands of nails crashing to the floor—I felt them being driven into my skull. Something cold pressed against my back. An even more piercing chill gripped my stomach. But the pain in my chest . . . it left me breathless. I was trapped in its coils of darkness yet I couldn't remember what had caused it.

"Gemma-emma-emma. You've got to respond-ond-ond! Gemma, please! Open your eyes-eyes-eyes . . . Simon, do something!"

"I'm trying! Damn it!" His frustrated growl filled my head.

Suddenly, all the noise stopped.

"Gemma . . ."

The whisper reached me like a caress. The voice was clear this time, crisp.

"Evan . . ." The impulse made its way from my heart to my lips.

I opened my eyes but found only Simon and Ginevra. I was in a bed. Dazed by the nightmare, I tried to remember how I had gotten there. My eyes finally met Ginevra's and glimpsed the anguish that flashed through them. Reality hit me like a jolt of electricity.

It wasn't a nightmare. A wail of desperation escaped me as a knot gripped my stomach and kept me from breathing. *Evan.* Panicking, I bolted upright and my gaze shot from one side of the room to the other.

"Gemma, stay down." Ginevra tried to calm me, but I couldn't hear her voice any more because a louder, more painful sound had filled my head. It took me a minute to realize it was coming from my heart. "You're not ready to get out of bed yet."

I tried to escape her firm grip but I was too weak and gave in. Still confused, my head throbbing, I looked up. "Evan . . . Where's Evan?" I asked, my voice hoarse with desperation and my eyes pleading for an answer I knew would never come.

Their silence struck me full in the chest, like a stab to the heart. My eyes darted back and forth between them, but neither Ginevra nor Simon could bear to look at me. I closed my tear-filled eyes and turned my head away as the pain washed over me and I abandoned myself to its icy coils, letting it drag me deeper and deeper into an abyss I'd never known before, wanting only for that black whirlpool to swallow me up.

Simon interrupted my tormented thoughts. "It's been six days. The poison you ingested left you with a high fever. It didn't kill you, though. You're still alive, Gemma."

"Your parents came to visit you every day," Ginevra said. She'd read in my mind that I didn't care whether death had spared me. "I told them you would be staying here until you recovered—or for as long as you wanted."

"She convinced them it was best for everyone," Simon added.

They continued to talk to me but I couldn't hear them. Their words made no sense. I was alive while *Evan was dead*. Why? Why was I still alive? Why had the poison taken everything from me, giving me no choice but to look on like an empty shell?

It wasn't fair. There had to be some kind of divine justice I could appeal to. I yanked off the covers and climbed out of bed, barefoot and dressed only in my underwear. Simon tried to bar my way but I was already out the door.

"Let her go." I barely overheard Ginevra's voice from the top of the stairs.

The air was bitter cold but I didn't care. Though I had on only thin white cotton underclothes, the night chill was nothing compared to the freezing pall that clung to my skin. Nothing could affect me compared to the pain that was tearing me apart inside. The wind lashed at me, freezing the tears on my cheeks and taking my breath away, but it didn't matter any more. All I wanted to do was run, afraid that if I stopped, the phantom of that nightmare would reach me. I couldn't let that happen; I knew the burden would be unbearable. I had to run—away from everything. I wasn't strong enough to face reality.

The snow-covered trees darted by as swiftly as ghosts. They tried to grab me but I didn't fear them. Part of me hoped they would snatch me up into their grim world, into the arms of Death, who would ease my suffering, where it wouldn't hurt so much.

Death. I had spent so much time trying to deceive her, and now, in a bizarre twist of fate, the queen of darkness I had so feared was eluding me. Why didn't she send out her loyal shadows to claim me? I wasn't afraid any more, because there could be no place darker than my heart.

I ran across the damp ground with its lingering patches of snow. My legs were numb but I continued to run as the pain inside me grew, swelled, consumed me with every cursed breath. Raindrops mingled with the tears that streamed down my face, washing away the salty streaks left behind by the wind.

I flung myself onto the cold, wet ground, barely registering it, my knees and palms pressed against the earth as my body spasmed in the fits of pain that gripped my chest. I stayed there, trembling, my head drooping like a now-dead part of my body.

I clenched my fists until they hurt and squeezed my eyes shut as a desperate scream rose from my chest. "Noooooo! *Whyyyyy?* I was supposed to die, not him!" I shrieked at the sky. "It was my fate, not his! Evaaaaan!" The pain was uncontainable. It hurt. It hurt unbearably and tore my heart in two.

I wished the earth would swallow me up, that I could just lie there in the hope that the snow would soon arrive to bury me. I let myself fall to the ground, allowing the rain—mocking consoler—to stream over my skin. Finally, I slipped into blackness, weary from the devastating torment I was certain would never end.

When I opened my eyes, snow framed the surface of the lake like a silvery halo while the sun beyond the horizon barely illuminated the dawn. Exhausted, I pushed myself up onto my side and dragged my body to the shore. I curled up and hugged my knees to my chest. I felt emptied. *Evan . . .* Tears returned to fill my weary eyes.

"I knew you would be here." Ginevra crouched down and sat beside me on the damp ground.

I lay there without moving, staring at the ripples on the water. "Why am I not dead?"

Silence lengthened the distance that separated me from her—that separated me from the world.

"We don't know. You ran a high fever for days and you were delirious the whole time. There were times when we thought you weren't going to make it." Ginevra fell into a strange silence, reliving the memory.

"Kill me," I hissed. Ginevra turned quickly toward me. "Look what I've done to your family—first Drake, and now . . . Evan." Uttering his name drove the knife that was lodged in my heart deeper into my flesh. "Kill me. Please." I turned to look at her, blinking as two teardrops escaped my eyes and slid down my cheeks. "I'm begging you, Gwen."

Ginevra reached out and stroked my belly. "Aren't you forgetting something?" She drew me toward her, cradling me in her arm, and I rested my head on her shoulder.

"It hurts too much. I can't—I can't breathe." Ginevra looked at me helplessly. "I didn't tell him. I didn't have time to tell Evan about the baby."

Unable to ease my pain, she said nothing. I lost myself in the somber silence. "He asked me to marry him," I confessed after a moment.

"I know. I always knew it, from the day he realized he loved you. He was just waiting to ask you until you were ready."

More silence.

"I destroyed everything. I don't deserve to live. It doesn't make sense any more. Kill me, I beg you."

"It wasn't your fault, Gemma. It was a trap. *They* kept him away! The Màsala knew he—"

Sobs shook my chest and I couldn't hear what she was saying. "How can I bear all of this? I . . . I can't do it."

"I don't know," she whispered into my hair, "but we'll face it together." She held me tighter as hot tears streamed down my cold face.

I stared at the rippled lake in front of me, my gaze lost between the blanket of fog and the horizon where the first rays of light reflected off its mirrored surface. It was daybreak, yet no light could ever free me from the darkness that imprisoned me. Outside, the sun was rising. Inside me, it had set forever.

Far away
where nothing speaks of you,
where everything tastes bitter,
where memory makes no sense,
it is as cold as ice
that knows not how to melt.
Where the silence of things deafens:
the darkness, the tick-tock of a sweet memory.
Far away, even farther than echo;
where those who think weep,
where every dream is the same color.

From the book of poetry written by my father,
Giuseppe Strazzanti

COMFORTING PROMISES

Mechanically putting one foot in front of the other, I walked down the steep path. In the dense, snow-covered woods, nature displayed her stark winter beauty as she always did. The forest was filled with a thousand sounds, but I could barely hear them. It was astonishing how the world went on, ignoring the suffering inside me, ignoring the rubble of my heart as it splintered into shards day after day and everything crashed down on me again and again. The sun went on rising and setting. Even my own body went on breathing—as if it too were mocking me.

I reached the water's edge, sat down cross-legged, and let the chilly morning air lash at my face. I closed my eyes, forcing myself to dam up the river of tears that constantly waited behind their lids to ambush me.

Each day at the same time my heart led me to that spot as it had the night I awoke from that horrifying dream. With a never-ending pain in my chest I watched the moon's melancholy attempt to reach the sun that eluded her every time. There on the lakeshore, in that spot where the memory of us twisted around my heart like barbed wire, the moon's desperate message touched me. I felt the burden of her sorrow as she watched her beloved sun from afar with her pale light before vanishing after her long journey. I imagined their forbidden desire to meet. Just one day. Just one time. A single moment together.

But no one could ever grant their wish, just as no one could ever again bring back my Evan. My life would remain an endless, bitter-cold night of darkness, devoid of light. My beloved sun had disappeared forever.

Months had passed since Evan's death—or had it been only weeks? I couldn't remember. Time didn't matter any more. I just wanted to disappear, to dissolve in the water like sunbeams at sunset. Instead I went on living. Walking. Breathing.

But every single breath burned my chest.

Unable to explain the actual how or why of Evan's death, Ginevra had told everyone he had driven off one night and never been seen or heard from again—that, worried something terrible had happened to him, we had searched for him high and low, but no one had found him. Other people murmured about a "missing person," but my parents realized the truth. They even offered to take care of the funeral arrangements, when they thought I couldn't hear them, but they'd been dissuaded since a body hadn't been found.

So there had been no ceremony, no funeral—it was as if it hadn't happened. Like it was all just a nightmare. The worst I could ever have imagined, but just a nightmare all the same, which the morning could have taken away. But every day the sun rose without him. I would wake up in his bed and feel like I was dying all over again. I would lie there clutching the covers without opening my eyes, as though I were dead too. Then the dark pit would rise up to fill my chest, brutally reminding me that it was all true, and I would curl up in the sheets and let it swallow me whole as I buried my sobs in his pillow. Evan was gone. Never again would I hear his voice breathe sweet nothings into my ear, never again would I feel his hands caress me, never again would I blush at his penetrating gaze after catching him staring at me with those little creases beneath his eyes. Never again would he tease me . . .

My devastating need for him made me long to die. Instead, I had no choice but to keep going, my heart shattering into a thousand pieces over and over, moment after moment, every single day.

I had lost everything.

The days dragged by, each more painful than the last. At school I would occasionally respond to my friends' worried looks by forcing a smile, but the second I looked into their compassionate faces my eyes would well up and my lips would quiver and I would have to press them tightly together to stop the tears. Feeling naked and fragile, I would run off before my heart fell to pieces right there in front of them. I couldn't let anyone get close to me—I was too vulnerable. Besides, no one could understand how desperate I was inside. It felt like a piece of me was missing, like someone had violently, unexpectedly ripped out a part of my body, an essential part without which it was too painful to go on living.

"Hey . . ."

I rested my head on my knees as Ginevra's calm, caring voice guided me back to reality. "Hey," I whispered.

"Time to go to school," she reminded me gently.

"I don't feel like going." I met her eyes and she understood. She sat down beside me and for a while we stared at the lake in silence. "You keep coming here," she said softly.

"I can't help it," I said, my voice weary. "It's like I need to experience the pain again, let it explode inside, to punish myself."

"Gemma . . ."

The torment I felt was inconsolable and somehow she sensed it as though it were her own, as though there was some sort of connection between my heart and hers. I stared at a colorful hot-air balloon drifting all alone across the sky and remembered when we had all taken part in the Adirondack Balloon Festival, a local event, rising into the air together with hundreds of other balloons before breaking away from the group.

"He wanted to stay," I said aloud, since Ginevra would have been able to hear my thoughts anyway.

After the battle on the frozen lake, Evan had received an execution order. He'd decided to stay by my side to protect me but I'd forced him to go. As we shared our last real kiss, I'd promised to give him another one when he returned, but it was with that kiss—when I'd thought it wasn't actually Evan but an impostor—that I killed him. If only he hadn't left in the first place . . .

"It was my fault. He didn't want to leave me, but I insisted."

"Because it was the right thing to do. You did it for him. You thought it was best for your future together."

"What future? Evan and I don't have a future together any more."

"You had no way of knowing he wouldn't be back before—before the kiss. Come on." Her voice was a barely audible whisper. "Let's go home, at least. It's freezing out here." I nodded, letting Ginevra wrap her arm around me and lead me to her black BMW X6.

Simon rushed up to us the moment we walked through the front door. "She did it again?" he asked Ginevra, as though I weren't standing right there. She nodded. "Gemma . . ." There was concern in his voice. "Gemma, I can help you. Why won't you listen to me?"

I shot him a fiery glare. "Don't come near me!" I threatened, shuddering internally at the idea. "If you can't undo the wrong I've done, I'll pay for my actions. You can't take away my pain too," I cried, partly in despair, partly as a warning. I didn't want Simon to erase my memories of Evan—that would have been unbearable.

"I would never do it against your will," he said, trying to reassure me, "but why won't you let me help you?"

"I never want to forget anything about him." Trying to sound determined, I fought back the tears, losing myself in a silence all my own. "Not a single second, not a single breath he took. Not ever. Not even if the pain kills me."

Ginevra rested her hand on my shoulder. "I know it's too soon, but sooner or later you'll forget Evan and your heart will open up to someone else. You can fall in love again. It happens all the time at your age. Life isn't over for you, Gemma." Encouraged by my silence, she went on. "Peter's a nice guy. Maybe with time you might give him a chance."

I looked at her with an expression that was as stunned as it was angry. How could she say something like that? Could she really think that?

"He's still in love with you. Don't let his love fade away while you're thinking about someone you can never have back."

"Could you ever forget Simon if something happened to him?"

"That's different," she said with a mix of obstinacy and compassion. "I'm not a human, I'm a Witch. We love differently from you mortals."

"Then I guess I'm not human either, because I know I'll never forget Evan. My heart will never have room for anyone but him."

Ginevra was about to say something but changed her mind when she saw the determination in my eyes. I didn't know about her, but as far as I was concerned the discussion was over.

"Gemma, right now it might not feel possible, but you'll get through this," Simon assured me.

"You're wrong, you're all wrong!" I took a breath, trying to keep my voice down. "I . . . I feel like I'm being crushed. I can't breathe."

"Simon's right. You've got to take your life back into your own hands, Gemma. You're still alive!" Ginevra insisted as though she could convince me. "Incredible as it might be, the poison didn't kill you. Faust didn't kill you. Neither did that other Subterranean who passed himself off as Drake! You should be happy; why don't you realize that?!"

I shot her a look, totally offended. How could she even think I might be *grateful* to fate for taking everything from me? It was inconceivable. How could she not understand? It no longer mattered if

I was dead or alive. "How can I go on living when I already feel dead inside?" I stared at her intensely, tasting the poison in my words.

Ginevra leaned over and hugged me. "You're not dead, you just need to realize it. The fever is gone. I think it would be best if you went home."

"No!" I couldn't believe it. Was Ginevra actually kicking me out?

"Gemma, you can't go on hurting yourself like this. Living here is too hard on you. You'll never get over it if you keep refusing to let him go!"

A sob escaped me. What was she trying to tell me? I didn't want to let him go. I wanted to cling to him, to his memory, to his scent, which still lingered on his pillow. Losing that too would be too much for me to bear.

"Maybe we should leave town," Simon whispered, but I heard him.

"NO!" The desperate cry burst from my chest. "No, please! You can't! You can't leave me! It would be like dying all over again, I wouldn't be able to take it!" I felt like I was slipping into a chasm.

"Shh. Gemma, calm down. We're not leaving," Ginevra said softly, shooting Simon a reproachful glance. "I would never leave you. You're my sister and nothing can ever change that."

Simon nodded silently, seeing the truth in it. I forced myself to breathe to ward off a panic attack. "Swear it," I pleaded, looking at her, devastated. She let me go and looked at me for a moment. "Swear it!" I insisted.

"I swear it," she said firmly, stroking my hair. "I could never leave you. Besides, you're not safe yet. There's no guarantee they won't attack you again." She looked at Simon for a long moment. "It's up to us to protect her now. For the time being, I know what you need, Gemma. Follow me."

"Where are we going?" I asked hesitantly.

Simon gave her a nod of agreement. Ginevra turned to look at me, her hand on the door leading to the garage. "You could use a reminder that you're still alive."

THE VOICE OF CONSCIENCE

Ginevra's Lamborghini Reventón shot out of the garage with a feline bound as I tried to banish to a dark corner of my mind the memory that continued to surface whenever my eye fell for more than a few seconds on the leather-and-Alcantara-suede upholstery. The last time I'd been in that car was with Evan. After we'd spent the evening in the garage fixing it, he'd pulled me down onto the seat with him and things had quickly heated up. Time had slipped away unnoticed that night as we hid from reality . . . until my dad had called. It felt like years since then.

I slid my hand into the neck of my red sweatshirt and pulled out Evan's dog tag. I hadn't taken it off since he'd torn it from his neck and put it into my hand a moment before vanishing. I clenched it in my fist until it hurt.

"It'll get easier with time, you'll see." Ginevra was looking at me out of the corner of her eye. She could hear all my thoughts but I didn't care. It had been a while since I'd given up trying to censor them. It was pointless. Besides, it didn't matter any more. I didn't answer. She knew herself it was a lie. "I swore to you we wouldn't leave."

I turned to look at her, alarmed. I hoped she didn't want something in exchange. She couldn't force me not to suffer. She couldn't force me to forget.

"No, Gemma, I don't want you to forget Evan. I wouldn't want it for myself either. But you have to at least make an effort. Try to get a grip." I hung my head, acquiescing, though I didn't know how to go about it. "One step at a time, okay? Evan wouldn't want to see you like this. He fought so that you could live. Don't throw away the gift he wanted to give you." Staring out the window, I bit my lip and tried to swallow the knot in my throat. "Try to take your mind off things at least a little, just for today. Would you? For *me?*"

I gave a small nod, still staring at the trees as they raced past on the other side of the glass, their naked black branches seeming to reach skyward in supplication. "Where are we going?" I managed to ask, making an effort to indulge her. I couldn't repress the pain weighing on my chest, but I could at least force myself to camouflage it, to hide it from the others and keep up appearances. I didn't want Ginevra to have second thoughts and decide to leave me. I wouldn't be able to bear it. Ginevra could read my mind, but she would never be able to fully understand the pain and grief I was experiencing. Those emotions were all mine. I just had to force myself to ignore them for a little while, to push them deep down in my heart so Simon and Ginevra wouldn't leave me.

"I'm taking you to New York City," she said with a sincere smile. "A change of scenery for a few hours will do you good."

"Why isn't Simon coming with us?"

Ginevra laughed. "Guys aren't cut out for this kind of thing."

"*What* kind of thing, exactly? What's your plan?" I asked warily.

"Don't worry, it won't be anything horrible. We'll hang out for a while—you know, girl time. Just you and me. We can do whatever you want. Go shopping, walk through Central Park, admire the view from the top of the Empire State Building, check out the neon signs in Times Square—"

"No stores, please," I was quick to say.

"Whatever. In any case, Lake Placid is too sleepy, too quiet. You need to be somewhere that doesn't give you time to think, at least for a while."

I tightened my lips, not so sure it would be enough.

The cold, gray air of New York City welcomed us only four hours later. It usually took six to get there, but Ginevra had burned up the accelerator. When I got out of the car thousands of sounds hit me, almost throwing me off balance. Ringing phones, footsteps, honking horns, hundreds of voices fused together into a single, constant, incomprehensible buzz. I looked around and took a deep breath just as a hot trail of smells wafted by: hot dogs mixed with smog. My stomach twisted, unsure whether or not to listen to my hunger.

"Welcome to the Big Apple!" Ginevra's face was lit up with excitement, her eyes lost among the shop windows and the thousands of blinking lights. Suddenly a giant plasma screen filled with her image: a blond goddess with breathtaking curves and emerald-green eyes. "I've always loved this place!" she exclaimed, pulling me along by the hand as I rolled my eyes at her narcissism.

The passersby all seemed to be in a hurry, as though each had a specific destination, a direction. I, on the other hand, wanted only to fade into the crowd that packed the street, to lose myself among all the people . . . to forget who I was.

Every so often we stopped at one of the shop windows and each time it took a lot of effort to persuade Ginevra she didn't have to buy me everything I laid eyes on. I would inevitably end up resigning myself and waiting for her on the sidewalk until she came out again with yet another package.

At one point something caught her attention and she stopped so abruptly I almost walked right into her. "Oh. My. God!" she exclaimed, her eyes bulging.

"What is it?" I asked, alarmed. I was almost afraid to turn around and find out what she had seen.

"That dress is amazing! It's breathtaking!"

I followed her gaze to the shop window and saw what she was talking about. "Um, sure, if you live in the eighteen hundreds," I shot back on impulse, but then it dawned on me that Ginevra might actually *have* lived during the Victorian era. Frowning, I looked at her and realized I'd never asked her. "How old are you, anyway?"

A huge smile lit up her face. "You never ask a girl her age, hasn't anyone ever told you that?"

I blinked. "It doesn't count if it's another girl asking. Don't dodge the question."

Ginevra's smile widened into a grin. "Old enough," she replied as she dragged me into the store. Once inside, she squeezed my hand, excitement filling her voice. "Pinch me. I'm in heaven! There are so many of them!" A wave of memories made her eyes sparkle and she lost herself in a world all her own, stroking the fabrics and skipping from one dress to the next. All at once she stopped in her tracks. Her gaze darted around the room like lightning and finished on mine. I started shaking my head in alarm. I could guess from the light in her eyes what she had in mind.

"No way," I said. "Forget it."

"Come on, you promised you would make an effort. Besides, this dress is perfect for you!" She pulled me encouragingly toward a red gown.

"Gwen, I have no intention of buying this dress. I wouldn't know what to do with it."

"Nobody said you had to buy it." Ginevra motioned to the sales clerk who took the dress off the mannequin and handed it to her. She held it out to me, wielding her most persuasive smile. "Aw, try it on. I'm sure you'll look enchanting in it!" I rolled my eyes. "You promised you would humor me!"

"Actually, I never said that," I shot back huffily.

"Like you needed to." With a shrug, she turned to the clerk and pointed at the dress in the window that had caught her eye, then winked at me and disappeared into a changing room before I could respond. I took a deep breath and forced myself to go along with it.

The changing room was spacious—it had to be, otherwise no one would have been able to move around in there wearing one of those hot-air balloons. The curtains and furniture were also done in Victorian style. It was like going back in time.

With a resigned sigh, I took off my clothes, put on the fluffy gown, and smoothed the fabric with my hands. It really was gorgeous, I had to admit. I pulled on my ponytail and a soft wave of dark brown locks tumbled onto my back. For a second I let my guard down and allowed myself to get into the role.

"Miss, do you need any help?" The clerk had come to my dressing room. Her voice was muffled by the thick fabric of the curtain.

"I can't do up the corset." I opened the curtain just as Ginevra appeared opposite me. We stared at each other for a long moment, smiles appearing on our faces. Stunning in her white gown trimmed in gold, she took a step toward me, asking the clerk with a glance to leave us alone. As though she had received an order, the young woman obeyed without hesitation.

Ginevra stepped behind me and laced up the back of my dress so tightly I could barely breathe. I wondered if the clerk was curious as to how Ginevra had managed to lace up her own gown without any help. My eye fell distractedly on the microscopic price tag that dangled from the waist. The gown cost a fortune.

"You're a vision, *chérie*," Ginevra whispered behind my ear, continuing to tug and lace.

"You speak French now?" I said, grinning, as my cheeks turned red at the sight of my reflection in the mirror. I had never fantasized about what it must be like to live in an era totally different from my own, yet

Evan must have been used to seeing girls walking around wearing luxurious gowns like this one. My heart skipped a beat at the thought of Evan just as Ginevra squeezed my shoulders.

"Aren't they amazing?" she asked in an attempt to distract me.

"I can't deny it. They're simply beautiful and you look like a princess."

Ginevra smiled happily, checking herself out in the mirror. Leaving her to admire her reflection, I wandered around the boutique, checking out the accessories and running my finger over the fabrics. My gown swished, dancing across the floor. On display on a small inlaid-wood table were elbow-length gloves grouped into different colors and materials. Another table showed off parasols in linen and lace.

I turned toward Ginevra. Her long blond hair flowed down her back in a golden cascade, curling at the ends. Smiling at her enthusiasm as she contemplated her reflection in the mirror, I turned back to study the store, then glanced out the window. The smile died on my lips and my heart turned to ice as my eyes met his.

Evan.

I rushed outside, desperately looking for the spot where I'd seen him, but the crowds seemed to be increasing. I hurried along, pushing my way through them until I found myself running. Everything around me began to spin, as though the hurrying multitude wanted to sweep me up into its vortex.

It was him. I had seen him. It wasn't a ghost. It was Evan *in flesh and blood.* His eyes of ice had found mine through the window. I'd glimpsed them for only a second but it was long enough for them to absorb all the other colors and turn everything else black and white.

I looked for him among the faces of the passersby, but he had disappeared. Why was he hiding? Had he *chosen* to leave me? Or had he been forced to go and couldn't come back? Utterly confused, I ran a hand over my forehead and grabbed my hair, clenching my fists. I felt like I was on a carousel spinning out of control.

A sinister sound stirred the air right behind my ear. I spun around in alarm. People steered clear, casting nervous glances at me. There came another breath of air on the opposite side that seemed to drift in on an ominous wind. I spun around again, trying to follow it. I felt like I was losing my mind. A cold shiver made my hair stand on end. The malevolent breath of wind seemed to be hovering nearby like a ghost. Then the infernal whisper crept into my mind:

Murderer.

Clutching my hair with both hands, I began to shake my head convulsively. I didn't want to hear it, but the voice continued to torture me: *Murderer. Murderer. Murderer.*

I sank down against the wall with my knees pressed to my chest, squeezed my eyes shut, and covered my ears as the tears battled to come out.

No. No. No!

"Hey, hey . . ." Someone touched my arm. A familiar voice, very close to my face. I raised my head and looked into her big green eyes. "Everything is fine." Ginevra was beside me, squatting on the sidewalk.

The sounds from the street suddenly returned, hitting me loud and clear, like someone had just unmuted the world. People hurried along the sidewalks and cars zoomed down the streets. I looked around, feeling like a frightened animal. I had no idea what had just happened or how I had gotten there—it felt like I had just lived through a nightmare. Was my desperation actually verging on insanity?

"Everything is fine." Ginevra continued to talk to me as I tried to convince myself I wasn't crazy. I nodded and rested my head on her shoulder. I must have been a strange sight, wearing a Victorian gown and sporting a pair of Nikes. People glanced at me, then ignored me and continued peacefully on their way. I, on the other hand, was in shock.

"Well? Want to tell me what happened?" Ginevra asked, her voice concerned and comforting. I shook my head, not sure I knew myself. "You ran out of the store. I looked everywhere for you but I couldn't block out the thoughts of all the other people to track down yours."

Suddenly I remembered everything. "Evan," I whispered, my voice breaking from the lump in my throat.

"Gemma." Ginevra sighed with exasperation and turned to look me straight in the eye. "Evan is dead. Do you understand what I'm saying?"

I frowned. I felt like I wasn't really there, but rather, suspended between the present and the insane moment I had just experienced. In my head I was still trapped in Evan's gaze. "I saw him," I whispered in a barely audible voice, not looking at her.

"That's impossible." Ginevra took me by the arms. "You *thought* you saw him. Your mind projected his image. You're still upset about what happened." But I wasn't listening, because another memory had made my blood run cold: the chilling accusation carried by the wind.

Murderer, it had said. I trembled as Ginevra held me tight. "I killed him. I killed Evan. I'm a murderer. I deserve to die."

"Gemma, you need to stop feeling guilty about what happened. It was an evil scheme *plotted out from beginning to end*."

The tears returned to slide down my cheeks. "I should have known. I should have known it wasn't him." I looked at Ginevra desperately, my lips quivering. "I didn't recognize him!"

Ginevra lifted my chin as though I were a child. "Listen to me: there's no way you could have known! We fell into our own trap. It wasn't your fault. That Subterranean tricked us all right from the start."

I looked away, unable to let Ginevra's words in so they could touch my broken heart. Nothing could convince me it wasn't my fault. *I* had killed Evan. Death had come to him by my lips. I had taken his life with a kiss cursed by fate. The chilling whisper I had heard in my head was my own conscience screaming its reproach, reminding me of what I'd done.

We walked on for a few blocks. My fit of madness had driven me pretty far away. I felt incredibly awkward with my Nikes and the gown flowing imperiously over the rough asphalt. I lifted the skirt to avoid ruining it.

"What do you say we stop off somewhere to eat?" she asked in a considerate tone.

"I'd rather go home, if you don't mind."

Ginevra made a vague gesture and shrugged. I realized that if she went without food she risked turning grouchy, but I felt vulnerable and wanted to get home as soon as I could. "Besides, we need to take this dress back," I reminded her, though I could already see the gray of Ginevra's car in the distance.

"No need." A smile escaped her. "I bought it."

I blinked and shot her a disapproving glance. "You said you weren't going to!"

"No, I said *you* didn't have to buy it." The smile on her lips turned into a grin. "I never said I wouldn't buy it for you."

Resigned, I shook my head and carefully gathered up the skirt of the gown so I could sit down in the passenger seat. The Lamborghini took off, drawing only a few stares. In Manhattan it was easy to go unnoticed. We certainly weren't in Lake Placid, where all eyes were always trained on the five of us.

The three of us, I forced myself to remember.

"I can't wait to see how you manage to change now!" Ginevra smiled, trying to lift my spirits.

"Very funny! You know I have no intention of spending four whole hours in a car suffocating in this thing. Where are my clothes?"

She pointed at the hood of the car. "In the trunk, of course."

"What??"

She shrugged, her smile spreading into a grin, then gave in. "Don't worry, just kidding. They're right there under your seat."

"Would you help me?" I asked, pointing at my dress's laces. "I can't undo it on my own."

While Ginevra kept her hands on the steering wheel and her eyes on the road, the long laces began to float through the air and undo themselves, sending a tingle down my back. I slid off the gown and folded it up in the bag that had contained my clothes.

"Ah . . . at last!" Slipping on jeans and a sweatshirt felt like a dream. "Is your offer of food still good?"

"Forget it." Ginevra glanced at me. "Absolutely not."

"Come on!" I begged her. "You can't let me starve to death just to avoid getting a few crumbs on the floor mats! It'll take us hours to get home!"

She glanced at me and caved. "Oh, all right. What are you hungry for?"

"A burger and fries?" I asked, looking at her hopefully.

"You're disgusting," she shot back, jutting her chin toward the glove box in front of me.

When I opened it, two hamburgers and two sides of French fries almost tumbled out onto my lap. I looked at Ginevra. "For both of us? Didn't you just say I was disgusting?"

She shrugged it off. "Seemed rude not to keep you company."

"Yeah, right." I smiled to myself and picked up a bag of fries. She reached out, took one and popped it into her mouth.

Halfway home I fell asleep, switching off my mind for what felt like no more than an instant. I woke up with a start, feeling like I was drowning, just as Ginevra pulled through the gates at home. Groggy, I mumbled, "We're back."

The garage door closed behind us and the engine went silent. Simon rested his hands on the roof of the car and leaned down to greet Ginevra with a kiss. Lately they'd been careful not to overdo it with the PDAs when I was around, worried I would sink back into a pit of longing for Evan.

Simon headed to the front of the car. "How much stuff did you buy?!" he exclaimed in shock when he saw the number of boxes Ginevra had managed to fit into the Lamborghini's storage compartment.

"It's not for me. That's all hers," she said with a nod and a wink in my direction.

"I had nothing to do with it, I swear," I told him, raising my hands defensively.

"That's what I figured." Simon shot me an understanding look. "What is this?" he gasped, almost horrified by Ginevra's gown from the 1800s that was peeking out of its bag.

"Don't ask me." I pressed my lips firmly together, not wanting to get involved.

"My God! I was so happy when these things finally went out of fashion! Is she doing it to torture me?"

With a shrug, I followed them toward the living room door. Out of the corner of my eye I glimpsed the black motorcycle in the darkest area of the garage. The previous summer, in a race spawned by sibling rivalry, I'd gotten onto that bike with Ginevra and—who knew how— we'd won. The next day Ginevra had started to teach me how to drive a bike, but when Evan got back from the mission he'd been on he'd replaced her as my teacher. He'd said later he planned to buy me my own motorcycle so I could join in the races.

I stared at the spot beside Evan's bike—a spot that would forever remain empty.

"I'll pay you back sooner or later," I promised Ginevra, sitting on her bed as she put her purchases away in her walk-in closet. I had no idea how I would manage that, but I would find a way.

"You don't owe me a cent," she was quick to reply.

"That dress cost a fortune, not to mention all the other things! I told you not to buy me anything, but you never listen."

"You'll be thanking me soon enough when you don't fit into those any more," she said with a grin, pointing at my hip-hugger jeans.

"Hey!"

Ginevra laughed, but her eyes quickly filled with warmth. "You're still one of us. That hasn't changed," she said to convince me she didn't want me to pay her back. To judge from her words, she seemed to be avoiding letting Evan's name slip. "What's our is yours. You can take all the money you like whenever you need it."

"Don't be ridiculous. I could never take your money."

Ginevra's only reply was to turn and walk into her closet. From what she'd told me, her collection was nothing in comparison to the typical wardrobes of Witches, who liked to wear a different outfit for each occasion. "Third drawer down," she said abruptly.

I looked around, wondering if she was mad at me. "Huh?"

"Open it."

Puzzled, I went to the dark wooden dresser. "Do you need something in partic—" I froze when I pulled the drawer open. It was full of stacks of hundred-dollar bills. "What the hell?"

Ginevra appeared in the doorway. "Go ahead, take some and put them in your backpack. You never know when they might come in handy!"

"Ginevra, are you crazy? They're going to think I robbed a bank! I can't take your money!"

She strode over in a huff. "Empty it," she ordered me.

"Huh?! What for?"

"Go on, empty it!" she insisted.

"Why? I don't get what you're trying to pr—"

Before I could finish, Ginevra moved between me and the dresser. "Fine, I'll do it myself." In a flash, she dumped the contents of the drawer onto the floor, forming a pyramid of bills.

"What are you—"

She waved her hand over the money and before my shocked eyes the bills burst into flames, warming my face.

"Whoa-whoa-whoa! Wait!" I tried to stop her, but in the blink of an eye the fire carbonized all the money. I stared at the pile of ashes in shock.

Ginevra's laughter snapped me out of it. "It's only paper, Gemma!"

"Sure, go tell that to all the people who wage wars for centuries for some of that 'paper.'"

With a flick of her hand, the now-empty drawer slammed back into the dresser, making me jump. "Go ahead, open it again."

"You're kidding, right?" I turned to look at her, but my hands unconsciously opened the drawer. It was full of money again.

"That's how it works for us." I stared at her, floored, and blinked as a giant smile spread across her face. "It's a treasure chest," she explained, looking pleased.

"A *what*?" I still couldn't believe what I'd just witnessed.

"I've tried to convince Simon that times have changed, but he still insists on calling them that. There are several of them throughout the house. Once they were filled with gold coins, but now"—she leaned over, picked up a stack of bills, and waved it in front of my face— "it's only paper. Do you get it now? You can use the treasure chests whenever you want. I don't need to be present. They respond to anyone and will give you whatever world currency you want. Consider it a private—and bottomless—bank."

"It's like the leprechaun's pot of gold at the end of the rainbow," I murmured.

"What?"

"Never mind." I sat on the bed and Ginevra went back to focusing on what she'd been doing. I was still stunned, but also relieved there was no need to pay her back all that money after all. "I'm going to go draw a hot bath," I said, raising my voice so she could hear me from the closet.

"You just relax. I'll take care of the rest. Oh, and . . . I hung up your dress in my closet in case you feel like putting it on again."

I walked out the door with a smile, definitely doubting that would ever happen.

A CRY OF REMORSE

The spa in their house was like an oasis of peace. In the hot tub, the water burbled on the surface like little geysers emitting spirals of steam.

After my bath, I really needed to call my parents. I knew I had disappointed them over the last few weeks, so I'd decided to stay on at Evan's house and try to avoid them as long as I could, partly out of fear of facing them and partly because I didn't think I would be able to bear their pity. It wasn't fair—I knew that—but I couldn't help it. Ginevra had explained to them that something had happened to Evan, that he'd disappeared. Her powers of persuasion had come in handy in convincing them not to insist, to let me detach myself from Evan gradually. They had respected my decision and stepped aside. I couldn't imagine how much my mom must have suffered.

The truth was Ginevra wanted to keep an eye on me and study the effects the poison had had on my body—or rather, the effects it *hadn't* had; for some bizarre reason, it hadn't killed me. Maybe it was because of the baby. My mortal blood combined with Evan's Subterranean blood had probably generated something different, something stronger, that had protected me. No matter how many explanations came to our minds, nothing had solved the mystery.

Even so, Ginevra was right: I couldn't stay there forever. It was time for me to go home. I sank into the boiling-hot water, shivering at its contrast with the bitter cold in my heart. The memory of Evan's gaze as he stared at me through the shop window was like a needle stuck in my brain. How could it possibly have been only my imagination? Was I so tormented that my brain was responding to my heart's desperate need by generating hallucinations?

It was like living a nightmare. Part of me still cherished the hope that at any moment someone might wake me, but it never happened. I had fallen into a dark pit. Every day I sank deeper and deeper; the ground continued to cave in and I was farther and farther from the light—from my Evan. I felt like a fire deprived of oxygen that was gradually dying, condemned to be reduced to nothing but ash.

The heat of the water was so comforting it alleviated some of the chill I felt inside. All I had to do was let myself sink. Driven by that desire, I slowly slid down and the heat on my neck sent little tingles of pleasure through my body, caressing me in waves. I needed it so badly. If only that heat could reach the ice in my heart . . .

I slid farther down until my head was submerged. The surface of the water closed above me and I was swept up in a sensation of infinite peace, a sweet oblivion that enveloped me like a warm velvet blanket. It cradled me and gently rocked me in its warmth.

Evan.

His eyes smiled at me. There, in that dreamy, sleepy state I saw nothing but his face. He was waiting for me. The soft curve of his lips moved slightly, mouthing something in slow motion.

Jamie. He was calling to me. *I love you.*

I felt tears sting my eyes but no longer felt any pain as I glided toward him, finally feeling him so close again. I wanted to cry out that I loved him too, that we would be together again, that soon I—

All at once something tore me away from him. Someone was clutching me. I opened my eyes and struggled to breathe as water streamed out of my nose, freeing my lungs.

"Gemma! What on earth were you doing?!" Horrified, Ginevra shook me. "My God. Are you out of your mind?! I was keeping an eye on you and all of a sudden I couldn't hear your thoughts any more!"

Only then did I become aware of where I was. "I—"

"Come here," she whispered, and squeezed me tight. Her embrace was the key that unlocked all my pain. Sobs suddenly wracked my body and a torrent of tears streamed from my eyes.

"I miss him," I whispered, my voice barely audible.

"I know." Ginevra stroked my hair.

"I don't . . . don't know how to live without him." She held me tighter. "I can't breathe. Without Evan, it's like I'm suffocating. I just want to die so I can be with him again. Help me, please."

"I'm here," she whispered comfortingly in my ear, trying to calm me. "I'll always be here for you."

"Sometimes I just want to disappear. "

"Look at me." She took my face in her hands. "You can't give up now. It's hard, I know, but you have to fight."

My chin quivered as more tears filled my eyes. "What sense is there in fighting? Don't you get it? Evan is dead! *Dead*. He's dead, and my will to fight died with him. Let them take me," I cried. I struggled to keep my voice steady, but the sobs returned to shake me and the pain to grip my chest, overwhelming me. "Why doesn't anyone come looking for me? Why don't they kill me so I can join him?"

"You wouldn't join him anyway."

"I pray for death to come free me from this living hell."

"You can't say things like that! You have to do it for Evan. Gemma, he sacrificed everything to keep you alive. You can't do this to him. If you gave up now, his death would have been in vain." Ginevra stroked the water with her hand.

Though I wanted to nod, nothing she had said eased my pain. Her eyes came to rest on my belly. She caressed it as though the gesture concealed a thousand words.

I sat up, trying to compose myself. "I'm not even sure it's there," I blurted. "It's been over three months but my body hasn't changed. I don't feel *anything*." It was a relief to finally admit it out loud. I had taken several pregnancy tests, but the total lack of symptoms had left me in doubt. Still, it wouldn't have been a good idea to see a doctor to confirm the pregnancy, let alone have sonograms done; none of us knew what a Subterranean's seed might generate, and Simon and Ginevra couldn't risk exposure that way. Day after day I would look at my belly, expecting it to grow, but it never did. There was nothing about my body that suggested I was pregnant except that I hadn't had any periods—but then again, major stress could make women skip periods.

Ginevra continued to stroke the surface of the water, gliding her fingers through the foam, swaying slightly as she traced wide lines. Her face wore an absorbed look. She raised her head and our eyes met. "It's there." She smiled at me. I stared at her in silence, bewildered by her confidence. I wanted to ask how she could be so sure, but words weren't necessary. She covered my belly with her hand and looked me in the eye. "I can hear its little heart beating," she whispered.

Her voice was like a caress. Something hit me right in the chest. An emotion. I sat there, dazed and silent as the echo of Ginevra's words made its way through my heart. Instinctively I raised my hands to my abdomen and the whole world seemed to stop. He was *really* inside me? I was stunned, as though just discovering it.

A part of Evan was growing inside me. I couldn't risk losing him.

As the unexpected certainty sank in, I looked up at Ginevra and we smiled at each other. I let out the breath I'd been holding and hot tears slid down my face uncontrollably.

"It might be a girl; I can't be sure," Ginevra said.

I slowly leaned back in the tub and considered Ginevra's comment. Suddenly her expression darkened, alarming me. She nervously pushed some foam aside with her fingers, as though searching for something beneath the surface.

"What's wrong, Gwen? Why are you looking at me that way?"

"How did you get that scar?" she asked, pointing at the wispy, silvery streaks on my abdomen.

"What, that? It's nothing, just a birthmark," I was quick to reassure her. "My grandmother used to tell me that in some parts of the world there's an old wives' tale that says that when you're pregnant, if you have a craving but don't satisfy it, the baby will end up with a birthmark in that shape on its skin. Ridiculous, isn't it? The funny thing is, it seems my mom was always asking for coconut or something like that when she was expecting me."

Ginevra blinked and looked at me again with a strange light in her eyes. It looked like . . . *concern*?

"What is it?" Did she not believe me? Suddenly I remembered when Evan had also noticed it the first time we made love. I struggled not to sink into the abyss. I hadn't even had the chance to tell him about the baby.

She composed herself and gave me a smile that looked forced. "Are you okay now, or do you want me to stay here with you?" Ginevra looked distracted, focused on something I couldn't grasp.

"No, no. Go back to Simon. I think I'll stay here a little longer."

"You sure?"

"Sure."

Watching her walk out the door, I tried to get a grip and banish the sadness. I cupped some water in my hands and rinsed away the dried tears that had left my skin tight.

I can hear its little heart beating. My heart trembled at the memory of Ginevra's words. I really *was* expecting a baby—Evan's child. Who knew why my body wasn't showing any visible signs yet. My belly was the same as it always had been. And none of us knew how things might turn out. Sooner or later I would have to start researching to find out if there had been other cases like mine. Would the baby be human? Or would it have powers like its father? A thought struck me like a lightning bolt: would he have to serve Death as an Executioner? I didn't want to think about it.

A strange sound outside the door put me on guard. I got out of the tub and wrapped a towel around me. Steam seemed to be seeping out through the gap under the door, drawn into the hall by some sinister power. I opened the door a crack and peeked out. There was an unearthly silence. An eerie one. I took a cautious step forward, groping for the light switch. I could barely see a thing.

In the utter silence, an ominous whisper drifted through the air and into my ear. A chilling whisper, like someone praying under their breath. A door slammed behind me. I spun around and jumped: a figure stood at the end of the hall. My heart racing, I squinted and tried to make out the face. His gaze came to rest on mine and when I recognized him my heart thumped and went still.

Evan.

My eyelids fluttered and a tear slid down my cheek. "Evan!" I cried, rushing toward him. In the spine-chilling silence of the dark hallway, my voice resounded off the walls, returning to me in a twisted echo. Before I could reach him, though, his face suddenly filled with terror and he pulled back, flattening himself against the wall.

"Evan!" I froze. I'd seen that fearful look before.

Jamie . . .

I reached him and tried to take hold of him, but he staggered and collapsed to the ground. I leaned over him, wracked with sobs as his body jerked from the spasms caused by the poison.

No! Not again, no!

"Evan, I'm begging you, don't die. Don't leave me, please." Tears flooded my eyes as he shuddered, sprawled on the floor. It was happening again: the past had sucked me into its vortex of pain and I could do nothing to stop it. I couldn't keep Evan from dying.

"Evan!" I grabbed his head in both hands and continued to weep, drowning in desperation. I wanted time to stop. I wanted to keep him there with me, even at the cost of giving my life for his. His lips moved, his voice barely audible. Trying to understand what he was whispering to me, I stared at his lips forming the words and my heart turned to ice.

Murderer.

An explosion inside my chest left me shattered. I knelt there in shock as a breath of wind brushed my ear, sweeping past like a ghost. Following it with my eyes, I turned toward the dark hallway and started with fright. A little girl wearing a white petticoat stared at me, hidden in the shadows. Very slowly, she began to drift toward me. I stifled a shriek of terror and turned to look at Evan, but the spot where he had been lying was empty. I couldn't breathe.

The girl came to an abrupt halt. A single shaft of light barely illuminated the hallway and through the gloom I finally saw her face. I tried to scream but no sound came from my throat, my words frozen in terror at the sight. It was me at age five, but her face was pale as a ghost's. She had deep, dark rings under her black eyes and her hair hung loose to her waist. The sinister whisper filled my head once more as the little girl raised her arm and pointed at me. An accusation. She was *accusing me*.

I put my hands over my ears to block out the whispers, but it was no use: a thousand voices were murmuring a single spine-chilling word: *Murderer. Murderer. Murderer.*

I felt I might lose my mind. An icy wind lashed my face. My eyes shot up and found the girl right in front of me. Her eye sockets were empty and pitch black. I cringed and my heart leapt to my throat when her lips moved, joining the voices inside my head: "*Murderer.*"

A shudder rattled me down to my bones. Then, in the distance, another voice: "Gemma! Gemma! Wake up, damn it!"

I found myself sprawled on the floor, trembling, feeling like I had fallen from an incredible height. Simon and Ginevra were at my side, shaking me. I looked up at them in shock, my body still quivering.

"What happened?" I murmured, so softly I wasn't sure I had actually uttered the words.

Simon and Ginevra exchanged a glance. "Everything's fine now. We're here."

"Evan . . ."

Another fleeting glance. Was I going insane? "I think you had a hallucination. It was like you fell into a trance. I couldn't hear your thoughts again."

What Ginevra said shocked me. What was happening to me? Was one single moment of relief from my guilt enough for my conscience to wake up and fling accusations at me?

"No, Gemma." Exasperated, Ginevra forced me to look at her as though I had forgotten every word she'd told me, as though I had lost my senses. "Evan is gone," she said cautiously, without hiding her compassion.

"Maybe you should lie down for a while," Simon suggested, his gentle voice betraying his concern. "A little shuteye would do you good."

I couldn't disagree. Nodding, I let Ginevra help me dry myself off. As I got under the covers I felt like an automaton—a dry, empty, useless husk on the verge of cracking.

"Want me to stay here until you fall asleep?" I nodded again, or at least I thought I did. I was so tired. "Simon called your parents to let them know you're okay." She squeezed my hand. "You'll see, tomorrow you'll . . ."

Ginevra continued to talk, but I couldn't hear her any more.

THE EMPTY ROOMS OF THE HEART

Drake's cheerful face came into focus against the blurred backdrop of the lake at sunset. "You still here, sunshine?" When I turned toward him, I found him leaning over me and holding out his hand. "Why don't you come with us? We found an amazing place beyond the woods!" His smile was an invitation to follow him, so I took his hand.

"Finally," Evan's warm voice whispered in my ear as he slid his arm around my waist. "I couldn't wait any longer without you." His lips touched my hair and I trembled, shaken by a strange sensation. Something was wrong.

Drake's harmonious laughter rang through the trees as I followed Evan and him into the woods. Given their cheerful, perfectly calm expressions, it seemed there was no reason for me to be worried, but still, a vague presentiment nagged at me. From time to time Evan squeezed my hand. As though by magic, his touch banished my every fear. Even so, the treetops grew denser with each step we took, blocking the sunlight, and the air grew colder and colder. "Evan, what—"

"Shh. Don't be afraid." Suddenly the woods gave way before us, revealing blocks of worn stone that looked as old as the world itself.

"You can't change fate." Evan's voice touched my ear as gently as a breath of warm air. Still, something wasn't right. All at once I experienced a terrible feeling of loss, and when I spun around I was shocked to discover they were gone. I was alone, surrounded by the darkness. Even the woods had vanished. Fear filled me and it took all my strength to gulp down the lump in my throat that threatened to suffocate me. I moved through the rubble, trying to figure out where I was. All at once, there among the stones, I saw the entrance to a cave. I looked around, unsure of whether it was a hiding place or a trap. In the end I decided to risk it and ventured inside. The air was damp and a golden glimmer danced over the rock walls.

Trailing my hand over the craggy stone, I advanced slowly, my steps hesitant and my heart racing. In the distance I heard a faint lapping noise: there must have been water there. I raised my eyes. Thousands of glittering stalactites hung from the ceiling—a magnificent sight.

Suddenly I tripped and found myself sprawled on the cold rock. As I ran a hand over my forehead I noticed something on the ground—a strange groove. I traced it with my fingers and quickly brushed aside the dust, revealing a symbol carved into the rock. I stared at it. It looked familiar. Had I seen it somewhere before?

Something made me look up. Eyes. Jade ones, like Ginevra's. I flinched, but then realized they were kind. They belonged to a beautiful woman who was leaning over me, her hand held out. She had gorgeous, wavy, chestnut-brown hair that flowed over her breast and a braid around her head that framed her face, making it even more radiant. There was something in her eyes—something elusive yet familiar.

"Did I frighten you?" Her voice penetrated my bones with its harmonious sweetness. A strange power emanated from her. She laughed at my fear, the most beautiful sound I'd ever heard. "How silly. You shouldn't be afraid of me. Come, I'll help you up."

Concealing my uncertainty, I complied and took her hand. "Who are you?" I asked.

"My name is Anya."

"I'm—"

"Gemma."

"How did you—"

Her graceful laughter rang through the cave, which meanwhile had changed. It was as though the walls before us had pulled back to make room for a small, shimmering body of water. *The same color as her eyes . . .* Curiosity banished every thought: all I wanted was to go to the water's edge and admire the varied hues that dappled its surface. I had never seen anything like it. The little pond seemed enchanted.

Drake's words returned to my mind. Was this the amazing place he wanted to show me? "What place is this?" I asked Anya.

"You'll love it, you'll see!" she replied, her enthusiasm tinged with a trace of sensuality, like an enchantress. Did she want me to follow her?

In the blink of an eye Anya was on the opposite shore. I was left breathless by how swiftly she'd moved. She teased me, her harmonious laughter echoing through the cave again, then turned solemn. "You have to come with me," she announced. "You can't change your fate. Sooner or later you'll have to realize that."

Something in her firm tone sounded wrong to my ears. She materialized at my side again, making me jump, but then smiled at me. "Come. I want to show you something."

She took my hand and I let her guide me. I couldn't resist; my body was ignoring my instincts and obeying only her. But once we reached the water's edge I stopped, momentarily steeling myself against Anya's power over me. Just as I slipped out of her grasp, something glimmering beneath the surface caught my attention. When I recognized him I dropped to my knees and gripped the lake's rocky border, driven by renewed desperation.

"Evan . . ." The water was deep but I could make out his shape. He was chained to the bottom, his face turned up toward the surface as though he had heard my voice.

"EVAN!" I screamed, gripped by an uncontrollable impulse. I plunged my arm into the water to grab him but jerked it back when excruciating pain seared my flesh. The water felt corrosive. I desperately scanned the ripples in search of his face but could no longer see the bottom of the pool.

"What does it mean?" I asked Anya, trying to hold back my tears. "Where is Evan?" Was my mind playing tricks on me? Was it Anya, toying with me? "Who are you?" I shouted, trembling.

Anya slowly shook her head. "That's not the right question." She stared at me for a long moment. "Come with me, Gemma." She held out her hand and stepped barefoot into the water.

I looked into her eyes, my heart pounding. There was something buried deep within me that yearned to follow the woman, certain she could reveal mysterious secrets to me. Yet there seemed to be a threat in her invitation, making part of me rebel against that ancestral call. She emanated an aura of power like an alluring siren, and I was willing to follow her into the abyss like a sailor enchanted by her sweet voice.

I murmured Evan's name. For some insane reason, I thought following her would lead me to him. Driven by that desire, I reached out to take Anya's hand but my heart balked. Heeding its warning, I immediately pulled back.

"You have to come with me, Gemma," Anya insisted. "It's your destiny. It always has been, right from the start."

I blinked, entranced both by her gaze and the water, whose lure continued to magnetize the part of me unable to resist.

"You belong to us," she repeated more slowly, in a persuasive whisper.

I reached toward her. "I belong—"

"Gemma! Gemma, wake up!" The voice dragged me away from that enchanting place. I found myself staring into Ginevra's worried eyes in the semidarkness of Evan's room as the first light of dawn peeked in through the curtains.

"Ginevra." I stared at her, confused. "What happened? Why are you shouting?"

She heaved a sigh of relief as Simon appeared in the doorway, agitated. "It's been a hellish night." She cautiously rested her hand on my forehead. "You were delirious. You kept mumbling the weirdest things." Another concerned sigh. "You started screaming and we came running, but nothing could wake you. You had a really high fever again and we were afraid you were slipping back into that state of unconsciousness."

"Do you think it's because of the poison, still?" I asked.

Simon went over to Ginevra and took her hand to calm her. "Her body should have purged it from her system by now."

"We can't be sure," she said. "Something's wrong. I've never seen anyone survive such a high fever and wake up like nothing happened."

"I . . . I'm fine," I tried to reassure them. I touched the back of my hand to my forehead: it was beaded with sweat, but cool. When I met Ginevra's worried gaze, it felt like she was hiding something from me, but I immediately banished the thought. "Honestly. Everything's fine. Don't worry, guys."

"We'll stay here with you," Simon offered.

"Really," I was quick to reply, "there's no need."

"No, Simon is right. Besides, it's almost morning. We can go downstairs if you like," Ginevra suggested. "Unless you want to sleep a while longer."

For some reason, I had the impression that Ginevra wanted me to get up, that she actually thought my going back to sleep was a bad idea. *She was afraid it would happen again.*

"Fine with me," I said. "I wouldn't be able to fall back asleep anyway."

"Perfect," Ginevra murmured, not taking her eyes off me.

I distractedly tucked my hair behind my ear, embarrassed by her unusual look of concern. She seemed to be studying me. "Gwen, are you worried about something?"

My question seemed to startle her, but her expression remained calm. "No," she said casually. "Why should I be? You said you were okay, didn't you?" She got up from the bed, crossed the room, and leaned against the doorframe.

"Yeah," I said, finding her behavior a little perplexing.

"Perfect!" she exclaimed with a bit too much enthusiasm to be believable. She nodded to Simon. "Go prepare the TV. I'll take care of the food while Gemma is getting ready."

I bit my bottom lip, staring at Simon as he left the room. Ginevra followed. Before the door closed behind her, I called. "You're sure everything's okay?"

She wavered, showing her hesitation. "Everything is under control."

I couldn't see her face, but her calm, calculated tone betrayed how hard she was trying to hide her true emotions. As the door swished shut an uneasy tingle crept over my skin.

What was Ginevra hiding from me?

The second I walked into the kitchen their whispering abruptly ceased. "Hey!" Ginevra welcomed me aloud so Simon, whose back was turned to me, would know I was there.

The impression that they were hiding something from me was taking root in my mind. "Hey," I replied without much enthusiasm. I slipped my thumbs into the back pockets of my jeans and rocked back and forth to ease the unusual awkwardness.

Simon came over and pulled out a chair at the table for me. "Called your parents already?"

"Yeah. I promised to have lunch at home with them. We've been spending so little time together lately, I couldn't bring myself to say no. This whole situation must be really hard on them." Simon and Ginevra exchanged fleeting glances, confirming my suspicions. "Is there something I should know?" I asked. Their hesitation convinced me to insist. "Gwen, what were you two talking about before I walked in?"

Ginevra looked unperturbed but for a split second Simon's eyes wavered.

"Simon?" I pressed him.

"They found Evan's car." A blade pierced what was left of my heart. "It happened last night."

"This isn't good for her. She doesn't need to hear it," Ginevra said.

"Yes I do," I said. "I want to know."

Ginevra nodded, her eyes fixed on mine. "The police are dragging the lake for him. They think they'll find his body there. We saw helicopters and the chief of police stopped by when you were in the shower."

"He asked us some questions. Wanted to let us know he would keep us posted if they find him."

I gripped the back of the chair. Hearing someone refer to Evan as a corpse made my stomach churn. "He didn't want to talk to me?"

"Simon made him uninterested in you."

It took a few seconds for her meaning to sink in. I knew how easy it was for a Subterranean to influence humans' minds however they pleased. Simon could manipulate people's memories, so he must have made the police chief forget all about me.

"Maybe you shouldn't go to school today," Ginevra suggested.

"No, I could use the distraction."

"They might ask you all sorts of questions. I don't think being around people who feel sorry for you will be good for you."

"It won't be very different from what I'm already going through. I can handle it," I said, determined. For some reason, the thought of staying home scared me. I didn't want the nightmares to come back and haunt me. Besides, nothing could make me feel worse than the burden already weighing on my heart.

"I told Evan to get rid of that car! He must have forgotten, damn it!"

Simon's comment hit me straight in the heart. I stared at him, shocked by his irritable remark. How could he talk about Evan in that tone?

Ginevra sensed the indignation in my thoughts and rested her hand on Simon's wrist to make him understand. "It's better this way." It was incredible how she managed to keep her cool in every circumstance.

"She's right," I spoke up, drawing their glances. "They wanted an explanation. Now they've got one. At least they'll have something new to talk about." My voice sounded distant to my own ears. It felt like I was in a parallel dimension where nothing made sense, as if I were living someone else's life, one that didn't belong to me. A life that was bizarre, meaningless. Painful. Or maybe it was my refusal to accept having lost Evan that made it so unreal. I left my slice of buttered toast on my plate and grabbed my backpack. I felt drained of all emotion, and my appetite had disappeared as well.

"I'm going to school," I announced, walking quickly away from the table.

"Wait! I'll go with you!" Ginevra exclaimed. Simon held up his hand to say goodbye and I nodded at him.

Minutes later, Ginevra and I were walking through the school doors. I tried to keep my head down to avoid all the compassionate looks, but with every step I heard the other students' murmurs. Everyone's attention seemed directed solely at me.

"Gemma!" Jeneane and Faith caught up with me as I was pretending to put some books away in my locker.

"I heard what happened on the news," Faith began shyly. I hung my head, unable to look them in the eye.

"You have no idea how sorry we are. This must be awful for you." Jeneane put her arms around me and hugged me.

"I can't imagine what you're going through," Faith added. "If you need anything at all, day or night, we're totally here for you."

"What she needs is to avoid thinking about all this," Ginevra said, looking at them sourly, "and this attitude certainly doesn't help."

"Gwen!" I said with annoyance. "Take it easy. I'm not a child." I turned to my old friends. "Everything's fine. Actually, I already suspected something like that had happened, but I really appreciate your support. Maybe someday soon we could hang out."

"That's not a bad idea," Ginevra agreed.

"Count on it," Jeneane said while Faith nodded in silence, tears in her eyes. "Just let us know when."

"Thanks. See you in class." I shut my locker, thinking of how I had avoided everyone over the last few months and wondering how they could possibly still be willing to talk to me. Peter was silently waiting for me to be the one to start up our relationship again. Meanwhile, my parents always let me know when he stopped by to ask how I was. He also glanced in my direction whenever he thought I wouldn't notice. He always knew what I needed.

For some strange reason I found it comforting that everyone now thought Evan was dead, as though sharing an infinitesimal part of my pain gave me the strength to pretend I was all right when they looked at me. The news had formed a sort of shield—admittedly a fragile one full of cracks—around my heart that helped me hide my anguish from the world. But despite everything, beneath that shield the pain still burned and nothing could ever make it subside.

The hours dragged by as I watched the snowflakes perform a slow dance outside the window. The teacher's voice paused from time to time and I was almost sure his gaze had followed mine out the window, but I was too apathetic to find out.

"Hey." Ginevra tugged on my sweatshirt to grab my attention and tapped on some papers she was holding. "Check these out." She slid them onto my desk.

There was no need to look down for me to know what they were. Just to be nice, I thumbed through them but then gave a grunt of disinterest. "I don't want to go to some stupid college."

"At least give them a look!"

"What makes you think they would accept me in my condition?" I protested, trying not to raise my voice.

"No need to worry about that." Her tone softened, making me look her in the eye. "I'll be there to help you. We'll do it together, all four of us."

"Four?"

"The three of us and the baby. It'll already be born by then."

"Oh, right."

"We can babysit while you're out. Simon loves babies. He had a little brother. It was hard to leave him when he enlisted. If you don't want to go someplace far away, you could apply to Nazareth College in Rochester. Your grandparents live around there too."

"Gwen, I'm not even sure I'll be able to finish high school. Yale, Dartmouth, Boston? They would never accept me." My voice faded at the thought of how I'd used to dream of going to a prestigious university. It had been a sand castle that the wind had swept away, leaving behind only ruins. "In any case, I don't deserve to go to them any more. My grades would have done a nosedive if you hadn't insisted on doing my homework for me. Speaking of which, like I've already told you, you've got to stop doing it."

"Only when you feel ready to take your life back into your own hands. Until then, I'm not letting it fall apart."

"I'll never be ready," I mumbled, tears welling in my eyes.

"Yes you will." Her whisper was barely audible, but I heard it. "I promise."

I returned to my thoughts of Evan and the darkness in which my soul dwelled without his light to illuminate my path. If I closed my eyes I could almost believe for an instant that he was still there with me. I looked out the window as though he might reappear at any second. But the emptiness that had taken up residence inside me reminded me it would never happen.

I walked down the hall with Ginevra and realized for the first time how hard it was not to think of my pain when everyone around me did nothing but remind me of it. Despite her attempts to distract me, every look, every gesture, every whisper brought back the memory of what I had lost.

"Jeremy Lloyd is still head over heels for you," I whispered as we walked into the cafeteria.

Jeremy was a brawny sophomore who couldn't take his eyes off Ginevra. She was constantly teasing him. When he struggled to hide his shyness by acting cocky she would have fun turning the tables on him with little witcheries. Once in a while Jeremy dared to ask her out, to at least give him a chance, but she would just toy with him by making something fall to the ground between them so he would trip over it and look ridiculous.

"Looks like he's been working out, don't you think?"

"He's coming this way," I warned Ginevra under my breath, noticing she was hiding a sly smile. "Don't do it again, please?" I begged her, but her smile grew brighter and before I could stop her Jeremy tripped over a chair, probably wondering how it had gotten there.

"How you doing, Jer?" she asked with a smile he would never forget.

I rolled my eyes and held out my hand to help him to his feet, but he got up on his own, looking at Ginevra with adoration. "Always great, when you're around," he said, moving closer. "Still convinced you don't want to go out with me?" he asked point-blank, seeming unconcerned about coming on too strong. "Consider it an open invitation," he insisted, raising an eyebrow.

Ginevra moved dangerously close to him. "You know what, Jeremy? I would love it if you . . ." She whispered something in his ear. I could see he was having trouble staying on his feet with all the excitement that had to be running through him.

"Absolutely," he murmured, under her spell.

Ginevra smiled and turned her back on him. "Who knows? I might just give you a chance." She was only teasing him, but Jeremy's face instantly flushed. "Once you've learned how to walk without falling over yourself, that is." Her answer left him speechless as, amused, she wielded her most dazzling smile.

"And I bet you'll never let that happen," I muttered. "Give it up, Jer. She's already got a boyfriend." I pushed her away, exasperated by her sadistic game. "Ginevra, you really are unbelievable! This is insane! Your magnetism is surreal. All the guys hang on your every word. I'd love to know how you do it."

Ginevra raised a malicious eyebrow. "That's one of the advantages of being a Witch. You know, how you look isn't important, because everybody has their own personal taste when it comes to appearances. What counts is your allure, the energy you emanate. It's like a love potion that we give off with every glance. If you can feel the electricity, rest assured he feels it too. You just need to learn to use that power to your advantage. It's your attitude that makes the difference. Everything in life is seduction. If you know how to wield it, the world is in your hands. We Witches have complete control over our pheromones. It's lots of fun." She smiled.

"It's hard for me to agree, seeing how *you're* the only one who had any fun just now."

"That's not true. The whole cafeteria laughed when Jeremy fell." She grinned and patted my shoulder. "Don't get so bent out of shape about it. Besides, at the moment I have a mission to accomplish, so humor me."

"What would that be?" I cast her a glance as she sat down at a secluded table.

"Making you smile!" She winked at me and I stifled a laugh. "I managed, didn't I?"

As I shook my head, my eyes came to rest on a table in front of us and my smile vanished as quickly as it had appeared. Peter had just left his lacrosse team and was sitting there alone, frowning and looking glum.

Before I could open my mouth Ginevra had guessed my intentions. "Go talk to him," she said with an encouraging nod, probing my mind.

"I'm not sure that—"

"He's waiting for you," she assured me, knowing I was afraid he wouldn't want to speak to me any more. "He's been choosing to sit alone for a while now, hoping you'll feel ready to talk to him, hoping you know he's there for you—that he always has been. Don't be afraid, Gemma. Not with him. Fear is just an obstacle, and until you get past it you'll never know what's waiting for you on the other side."

Peter had probably heard the news too. It wasn't hard to imagine he felt bad for me. Though I'd known him my whole life, his sweetness continued to amaze me.

"It's time for you to go talk to him, don't you think?"

Giving a little nod, I stood up before I could change my mind. I walked over slowly, studying Peter's profile. He hadn't noticed me yet. "Talking to yourself?" I asked.

Peter raised his melancholy eyes for only a second and then stared blankly at the table again, as though convinced I was just a figment of his imagination. "There's no better company than yourself," he said. His tone was vaguely bitter but also defeated. I was sure he was referring to me, to my absence in his life.

"Sorry, I'm bothering you," I murmured, turning to go.

"No, wait." I stopped without turning around. There was a long pause. "How are things?" he asked.

The simplicity of his question defused my tension. I pulled out a chair and sat down facing him, grateful he hadn't mentioned Evan's car being found. We looked at each other without saying anything, tacitly trying to determine what remained between us. We hadn't seen each other for a long time, but shouldn't friendship be able to survive anything? Where would we pick things up? Would we act like nothing had happened? That was impossible—I had set off on a journey toward the universe and my world had crumbled too many times. The Gemma he'd once known was gone, even if part of her was still trapped in the ashes of a star that had exploded inside her.

"Seen the news?" I asked, my gaze wandering to his tray.

"I haven't been watching much TV lately," he said without asking what I was referring to.

"Never mind." When I looked up into his face I felt a strange, terrible sensation. We had become strangers. From the way his eyes wavered almost imperceptibly, it was clear that he'd realized it too. I could never have imagined it might happen to us.

"I heard you've been asking about me over the last few weeks."

"I shouldn't have, probably," he said after a moment of silence.

"No, I'm happy to know"—I struggled to find the words— "that you don't hate me."

His face lit up and his eyes shot to mine. "Why would I hate you?"

"Well, because . . . because of how things went."

"I could never hate you."

I rubbed my hands together, completely on edge, and glanced at Ginevra. She was looking out the window but I was sure she was listening to us. "I was afraid you would. Hate me, I mean." Peter frowned, surprised. This time, when our eyes met, they exchanged a bit of the affection that used to warm us. "You could call me sometime if you feel like it," I suggested.

"I've wanted to," he admitted, his tone still sad. "I dialed your number lots of times . . . stared at it, but in the end I didn't make the call."

"Why not?"

"You were holed up in that fortress. Sometimes I wondered if you were hiding from me." He smiled to himself but immediately grew serious again. "The truth is I was afraid you weren't ready. You certainly didn't need anybody else feeling sorry for you. Besides, I was sure you knew that when you were ready, I would be there."

A lump rose in my throat. My chin trembled and I tightened my lips to avoid crying, but a solitary tear escaped anyway. Peter reached his hand toward mine in a silent gesture of comfort—the only kind I could bear.

"You're right." I smiled through the tears. "You've always known what I need." I squeezed his hand. "Now I know how much I missed you."

Peter smiled at me tenderly as the bell rang for a long moment, our eyes locked the whole time.

"There she is. You see her talking with Turner again in the cafeteria?"

"They've always been *close*, Peter and her. He's the baby daddy, if you ask me. The other guy found out about them and ditched her."

As I listened to the two girls gossip in the hall, uncontrollable anger built up inside me. Ginevra squeezed my hand but I was about to erupt like a volcano.

"Great theory. Shame he crashed afterwards." The two girls laughed.

It was seriously too much. I rushed at one of them and slammed her against the lockers. She cried out and I looked her in the eye. "Don't even *think* of talking like that about him," I snarled right into her face. "Because next time I'm gonna rip your tongue out."

"Oh my God, did you see that?"

"What is she doing?"

"She's crazy, the poor thing."

Hearing the whispering behind me, I slowly came to my senses. "Gemma," Ginevra called. She hadn't tried to stop me. She'd probably wanted to shut them up too when she heard them insulting Evan. "That's enough. Let's go."

I released my grip on the girl, whose eyes filled with tears. Minutes later I heard my name over the PA system. I was being called to the principal's office. I let out an exasperated groan. Wasn't I going through enough already?

"Don't worry. I'll take care of it," Ginevra assured me.

I opened the door to the office and saw the girl I'd attacked, along with her friend. When I walked in she backed up like she was terrified of me. I rolled my eyes. I hadn't hurt her that badly—certainly not as badly as she'd hurt me with her poisonous words. Still, it came as no surprise; Mallory Gardner was in Jeneane's drama class. She was just putting on an act for the principal.

"Miss Bloom, is it true you assaulted Miss Gardner?"

"Yes, Mr. Reynolds, but she said—"

"What she said is irrelevant!" he bellowed, leaving me mortified.

"Mr. Reynolds!" Ginevra sat down facing his desk and crossed her legs. "Don't you think 'assault' is a bit too strong a word? All Gemma did was give her friend a great big hug."

"Whaaa?" Mallory sputtered. "She slammed me against the lockers! You saw it for—" Ginevra shot her a piercing glare and Mallory choked back the rest.

"Miss Gardner, have the courtesy to let her finish. What is it you were saying?" The principal was putty in Ginevra's hands.

"I was saying it might be better to consider the issue resolved. After all, Gemma is going through a terrible time. More stress wouldn't be good for her."

"But Gemma attacked her!" Mallory's friend said. "Mr. Reynolds, you saw the scratches for yourself!" She pulled the top of the girl's shirt down to bare her shoulder and I flinched at the sight of the red marks my nails had left. Had I actually been the one to make those?

My eyelids fluttered as they disappeared before my eyes.

"What the— They were right here!"

"She's making it up. She must have rubbed her skin to put on this little charade. She's the one who attacked Gemma with her gratuitous insults!" Ginevra snapped. "Mr. Reynolds should punish the two of you for your lack of moral support."

He considered Ginevra's words. Another glance from her, and he succumbed to her powers of suggestion. "She's right. You shouldn't have been so cruel to your classmate, especially in light of what she's had to endure recently. A one-day suspension will help you reflect," he said sternly, filling out two slips of paper.

"What? That's insane!" the two girls whined.

"Are you questioning our principal's judgment?" Ginevra asked, feigning innocence.

The two scowled at her. She smiled as they walked out the door carrying their suspension slips, then stood up and took me by the hand. "Mr. Reynolds, we're really grateful for your understanding. It would be better if Gemma's parents didn't learn about this little misunderstanding."

"Of course. No need to alarm the family over something that never happened."

Ginevra was unbelievable. Without my saying a single word, she'd turned the tables in our favor in a matter of minutes and had the girls *I* attacked be suspended. Actually, they deserved it. I smiled too, savoring our little victory.

As I stood up to follow Ginevra, who was already at the door, an old photo of a little girl on the principal's desk struck me. Noticing that it had drawn my attention, he seemed to shake himself free of Ginevra's spell, breaking the connection between them. "My little Caitlin," he said, his face growing sad.

The girl was on a bicycle and looked very sweet. "She's adorable."

"Gemma, we'd better go now," Ginevra said.

"Who's the boy next to her?"

"Gemma, I told you, let's go." She sounded nervous, but I didn't listen to her. I couldn't take my eyes off the photograph.

"It looks like he really cares about her." I reached out, uncontrollably drawn to the photo, but the principal snatched it away and stared at me like I was crazy. "What boy? Are you pulling my leg?"

Confused, I looked at him and turned back to the photo. "The boy squatting down next to her, in the green shirt. I was just saying that, from his smile, he looks really affe—"

"There is no boy in this photograph." A shiver ran down my spine. What was he saying? "This is the last memento we have of Caitlin. She died minutes after this picture was taken, hit by a car," the principal said, his eyes filling with tears.

I looked more closely at the picture. Was he kidding me? There was a boy right there! He had incredibly light eyes and long blond hair tied in a ponytail, and was crouching beside her as though . . . as though waiting for her.

As I stared at the photograph, stunned, it dawned on me: the principal couldn't see him because he was a Subterranean, there to claim little Caitlin's soul. "I don't—" I wanted to apologize but had no idea what to say.

How was it possible that I could see him? It was just a photograph!

Ginevra rested a hand on my shoulder. "Gemma, we should go now. Mr. Reynolds, as I mentioned, Gemma has been going through a very difficult time . . ."

"I'll write her a pass to go home," he agreed, still upset. I watched his hand as it moved across the slip of paper, but I wasn't actually there. I was lost—lost in doubt, in strange thoughts. Lost in my madness.

I dropped Ginevra off and parked the BMW in my parents' driveway. Before getting out, I took a deep breath. They must have already heard the news about Evan's car being found. Mom's suffocating hug confirmed my assumption. "Honey, we heard what happened. You have no idea how sorry we are." I looked at her, unable to speak. "I know you haven't wanted to talk about it, but Ginevra told me Evan unexpectedly disappeared and that no one knew where he was. She also told me the search led nowhere and that—that you suspected he was dead. But none of us could have imagined something like this."

Maybe out of egotism, I had never talked to my parents about Evan's death. How could I have confessed to them that I'd been the one to kill him, when not even I could accept it? "I know, Mom, but the news doesn't change anything. He was gone before and he's gone now, and there's nothing anyone can do about it."

"She just can't get over it," my dad murmured from the other room, disheartened by my mood.

"Honey, thank God . . . I'm so happy you weren't in the car with him," Mom added.

Her remark chilled my heart and my body reacted by freezing. I pulled away from her, furious. "Thank God for *what*?" I hissed. "You don't know what you're talking about. It was all my fault! I'm the one who should have died! Not Evan!" But Mom could never understand that. It was true: she simply didn't know. "I'm sorry." I fought back the tears, horrified with myself.

"Honey, it's not your fault. You're still shaken," she whispered, stroking my hair. But her words just twisted the knife stuck in my heart by reminding me of what I had done. She had no idea how wrong she was. It was *all* my fault. "You're still upset."

I pulled back and wiped away my tears. "No, I'm fine. It's just that I skipped a few meals, so all I want to do is eat, if that's okay with you," I lied, wanting the moment to end.

"Of course. Everything's ready."

"How's Iron Dog doing? I have to admit I kind of miss the little monster," Dad said, sensing my desperate need to change the subject.

"Couldn't be better. Ginevra loves him. Besides, their yard is a lot bigger than ours."

"I wish you would come home," Mom said softly, letting all her grief show. "But I realize that with work and everything else, you wouldn't get the attention you need right now."

"Simon and Ginevra are good people," I reassured her.

"I know, and I have no doubt they'll take good care of you. I've seen how much they care for you. Still, it's important for you to know that whatever you need, we'll always be here. You do know that, don't you? Please tell me you do," she begged.

"I know, Mom. Of course I do."

She had always felt guilty about the time she denied me because of work, and now her concern was off the charts. But there was nothing she could do. It was a good thing Simon and Ginevra had used their powers to convince her to let me stay at their place, otherwise she would have felt even worse. I was kind of sorry, but knew it was for the best.

"Besides, next year you would have left us anyway to go to college," Dad reminded me. Or maybe he'd said it for Mom's benefit. I took a sip of soda and looked down. "I mean, you still want to go to a good college, don't you?" Dad asked.

"Of course," I forced myself to say. I didn't want to disappoint them yet again, and the sigh of relief he and Mom drew made it clear that any other answer would have done just that. "Ginevra already got me some application forms." I just hoped the principal didn't change his mind and tell them what had happened at school. He probably thought I was crazy now too.

"Good. You know how much it means to us. You've worked so hard and it would be a shame to waste all the effort you've put in over the years."

"You're right," I lied again. "That's not going to happen."

I wondered how they would accept the truth when I didn't end up going to college after all. I decided that for the time being it didn't matter; I would cross that bridge when I came to it. For now, it was like I was watching my life through a fogged-up window. I couldn't see through the glass. I couldn't imagine a future without Evan.

Lunch lasted longer than usual, as though my parents didn't want to let me leave because they were afraid they would never see me again. They looked sad as they watched me go upstairs to my room, where I holed myself up for a little while.

I leaned back against the door and waited until I heard only the silence that told me they'd gone. Then, moving slowly around the room, I studied every detail carefully: the walls, desk, books, bed . . . Everything was just as I'd left it, but nothing was like it had been before. Every surface, every detail was filled with the memory of Evan, his scent, the sound of his laughter in my hair—

"Gemma?"

I jumped. "Mom! I thought you'd already left."

"Without saying goodbye?" She shut the door, stood behind me and rested her hands on my shoulders. "If I ask you how you are, will you tell me the truth this time? It's just me and you, like it used to be."

I looked at her. I always tried to avoid crying in front of others, to hide my pain, but that made it accumulate behind the door to my heart until it crushed my chest. So sometimes the door burst open, which was exactly what I felt was about to happen. "I'm not the same person I used to be, Mom."

"Of course you are. You might feel lost, but you'll find your path again, you'll see."

"Sorry, but there's no path for me any more," I confessed.

"Gemma, not all is lost. You have to have faith. Pessimism is an easier road than the tortuous one that leads to hope. Not everyone has the courage to walk that road, but you've always been a fighter. It might look like the end of the world to you right now, but that will pass. And when you fall in love again, Evan will be only a mem—"

I jerked away from her, feeling the rage build up inside me. "I realize it's not the end of the world. The world doesn't give a damn about me—it just keeps moving along like I don't exist, like none of this is important. But I know for sure it's the end of *my* world. I'll never have anyone else in my life."

"Honey . . ."

"Leave me alone, Mom! You can't understand."

"Don't hold back your tears. Not in front of me, please. Don't keep your emotions from me. I was just trying to encourage you. You can't give up hope—it's the only light we have left when life darkens our path. Without hope everything turns dark, and I don't want that for you."

"It's *already* dark, Mom! *Why can't you understand that?!*"

"*You're* the one who doesn't understand. You've got your whole life ahead of you. You can't destroy everything because of one boy! I know it's hard, but you'll come out of it, I promise."

"Don't promise me things that are out of your control." I moved away, desperately wanting to distance myself from her, from those words. "You once told me life is like a mountain: you only reach the top when you give up and stop climbing. When you think there's nothing left but to descend. Well, I'm there. I give up, Mom. I can't do it."

"Of course you can. You're going through a rough period, but one day everything will make sense again. You're only seventeen! You'll go to college, meet lots of other boys, and fall in love ag—"

"It's not going to happen, Mom!" I shouted in frustration. Why wouldn't she go? Why wouldn't she leave me alone?! I wished she would disappear. I wished they would all disappear forever.

Mom smoothed my hair behind my ear. "I'll try to explain it using an analogy you understand really well: love is like a book. When one story ends, you can't just lose hope. You close one book but you can open others—as many as you like. You're the one who chooses whether to reread the same book over and over or to move on."

I sighed. She was always ready to dole out advice, to preach from the pulpit of her perfect life. But mine wasn't perfect—just the opposite! Why couldn't she see that? "No, Mom. Let me tell you how things are. It's true, a love story is like a book you loved, but even when it ends you can always hide away in the pages of your memories whenever you want. That's enough because you know no other story could ever offer you the emotions it made you feel."

"No one can erase those emotions, but that doesn't mean you can't experience other, *different* emotions when you fall in love again. You can discover new stories, Gemma. If you close yourself off, you'll never know what new adventures await you."

"I'm not going to go out looking for another boyfriend or a father for my child. I'm raising the baby on my own," I stated, adamant. I had given Evan the keys to my heart and no one else would ever be able to unlock it.

"Gemma, the love we hold inside is precious. It's a little fire that keeps us alive. We need to watch over it, hide it sometimes, maybe, but never give anyone else the power to extinguish it."

"How *dare* you tell me something like that?! You, of all people, who raised me spewing your *stupid* theories about eternal love!" I could see my words had hurt Mom deeply. The tears built up inside me. "I'm sorry," I mumbled, feeling horrible. "Please, I need some time alone."

She clasped me to her and turned to go, stopping in the doorway. "Keep climbing, Gemma. Your peak is still far away."

I clenched my fists once she'd closed the door, feeling like everything inside me was on the verge of exploding. All at once I couldn't hold it in any more. Blind rage took over and with a shriek of frustration I let its fury rush through me. Gnashing my teeth, I hurled everything on my desk to the floor, picked up every object I could get my hands on and smashed it against the walls. I wanted to destroy everything. Taking a framed photograph from the shelf, I shattered it against the door.

The sound vibrated inside me, reminding me that I too was made of fragile glass. I fell to my knees and picked up the frame, not caring if I cut myself. Behind the shards, my image smiled, wrapped in Evan's arms. The moment was clear in my memory: we'd been on a boat, my feet dangling in the water. Evan had surprised me by sitting down behind me and pulling me close between his outstretched legs. I still remembered the thrill that contact made me feel. Evan had stroked my cheek with his nose and Ginevra had captured the moment. Running my finger over my smile, a smile I would never wear again, I wept. This time I didn't even try to stop the tears. I felt terribly alone. Empty. Robbed.

Torn apart.

"Evan," I murmured almost inaudibly. The room was blurry through my tear-filled eyes. "I miss you . . . You promised. You promised you would never leave me," I told him, sobs breaking my voice. "You said you would always be there. Please, give me a sign, be it a light or a shadow."

Silence. Deafening silence.

I tried to stifle my sobs, but all I could hear was the echo of my pain as it washed over me again. Suddenly a gentle breeze came through the window and caressed my skin, sending a shiver through me. My chin quivered as I remembered when it had been Evan who arrived in silence with his warm, penetrating gaze. I closed my eyes and let the tears stream down my face as, with trembling lips, I whispered to the wind, hoping it would carry my words to him: "I miss you to death. I don't know how to go on without you."

But when I opened my eyes, the room was empty. It had been all along. For the millionth time, I felt alone. My room had never seemed so big before—or maybe it was just me feeling the emptiness of being without Evan.

FRAGILE

From time to time I took one hand off the steering wheel of the BMW to wipe my eyes so I could see the road. The short drive from my parents' house to Simon and Ginevra's must have gotten longer somehow, because it felt like I would never get there. The snow had stopped falling, leaving the air damp and the streets slippery. Fluffy white patches had accumulated on the branches that raced by like ghosts outside the window, projecting me into a surreal landscape. Inside the car, Lana del Rey's melodious voice cradled me in my own dark paradise. The words seemed to have been written just for me. *There's no you, except in my dreams tonight . . .* It was getting harder and harder to ease the pain when it wrapped me in its thorny embrace. My guilt was killing me. I couldn't accept the fact that my lips had taken Evan's last breath.

I had always considered my own death the most terrible scenario of all—it was impossible to imagine a worse torment. Ever since I'd learned about the Subterraneans and the fate that had been written for me, it had occupied my mind. I'd learned to live with the awareness that each moment might be my last. It had never once occurred to me that I might be the one to go on living, without Evan. But now I was condemned to a fate worse than death; losing Evan so unexpectedly was a pain I would never learn to live with.

Fate had mocked us to the very end. I felt like I was living in an ironic fairy tale. In the silence of the car—Lana's song had ended—I answered my own thoughts out loud: "Yeah, but unlike with a book, you can't peek at the final pages of your life to see how things will end up. You can't rewrite the ending if something goes wrong." I sank into silence again, ruminating. The pages of your life turned all on their own, day after day, and all you could do was look on. I had ruined everything, and the pain, the guilt, the memories of Evan and everything we had lost—*the life I had torn away from him*—were driving me insane.

I wiped my eyes with the sleeve of my sweatshirt and the memory of his voice swept over me.

"You planning on eating the whole thing?" Evan gestured at my sleeve, which I had distractedly raised to my mouth. My sleeves were always too long for some reason, and when I was nervous I sometimes chewed on them without realizing it. "Won't be easy to digest." His mouth widened into a grin. "Don't be nervous. There's no need."

"You're not the one who's in danger of losing everything," I reminded him.

He stifled a cheerless laugh. "What would be left for me if you died? I'm not going to let him touch you ever again, Gemma. No one is going to hurt you. And I'm not doing it just for you—I'm doing it most of all for myself. I would be lost if I lost you."

I would be lost if I lost you.

I would be lost if I lost you . . .

A breath of air brushed my neck. My eyes flew to the windows, but they were all rolled up. I pulled my sleeves down over my hands to protect myself from the cold—or maybe from the chill the memory had left behind. Though I turned up the heat, another shiver swept over me. This time a strange noise accompanied it—an eerie, evil hiss—and the wind seemed to whisper directly in my ear. Alarmed, I glanced into the rearview mirror to check the back seat, but nothing was there. When I returned my eyes to the road my heart leapt to my throat: two eyes of ice stared at me from the center of the street.

Evan.

I slammed on the brake, scant feet from him, and the car came to a halt so abruptly I hit the steering wheel. Trembling and on the verge of tears, I raised my head. The road was deserted. I turned off the engine, got out, and looked around, my breathing ragged. A car zoomed past, but my heart was so swollen with disappointment I didn't even flinch. Even the wind mocked me, howling all around me.

"Evan . . ." I whispered, devastated. Hanging my head, I forced myself back into the car and allowed desperation to flood through me, clenching the steering wheel until my fingers were numb.

"Miss?" A rap on the window made me jump. I quickly dried my tears and struggled to compose myself before lowering the window.

"I'm sorry, miss, I didn't mean to startle you. Are you all right?" asked the man standing beside the car.

I'd never seen him before, but judging from his accent I guessed he was a tourist. Lake Placid was full of them year round. In winter it was a perfect destination for people who loved skiing or snowboarding. Not only because of the Adirondacks, but also because we had hosted the Olympics not once but twice—in 1932 and 1980—and attractions like the Olympic Center and the Olympic Jumping Complex were open to anyone looking for a thrill.

"Thanks, I'm just a little tired," I managed to say, but the forlorn expression on my face must not have convinced him, because he insisted.

"You're really pale. Want me to take you home?" he offered in a kind tone.

"No, there's no need," I was quick to reply, forcing myself to hide the fear creeping up inside me. After all, the road was secluded and the man gave no sign of leaving. He could have been anyone.

"You sure you're okay to drive? And don't worry—my wife is with me, back there." My eyes followed his thumb to the side of the road, where a young woman waved to me from a car. I stifled a sigh of relief. At least he wasn't some maniac. "Thank you . . . really, but I'm fine. I'm already feeling better."

The man gave in. "All right, but take care, okay?"

Nodding, I started the engine. I watched his car pull away, then lowered the sun visor to look at myself in the mirror. A scream burst from me: Evan was in the back seat. I whirled around but there was no one there.

Sitting there, breathless, I buried my face in my hands. What the hell was happening to me? Was I descending inescapably into madness? With trembling hands I lowered the mirror again, gasping for air, my heart in my throat. This time it reflected only me. I slumped back into my seat. There had never been a reflection—unless my guilt, which had decided to torment me, had created it.

I quickly drove back to the house, trying to compose myself.

Irony trotted up to me, tail wagging. Ginevra was reclined in a regal position on the red couch while the vacuum cleaner danced back and forth to the rhythm of the music. In spite of how terrible my life was, the scene got a faint smile out of me.

"Why am I always the one who has to clean the house?" she called. I tossed my keys onto the entryway table, shaking my head at Ginevra's complaint.

"I'm not talking about *you*, of course," she said in a low voice as I passed her.

"You say it as if it took you effort."

"At least I managed to make you smile!" In my mind, Ginevra's words almost sounded like a reproach but she was quick to ease my sense of guilt. "Gemma, it's okay for you to smile every once in a while. Don't feel bad about it. Evan wouldn't want to see you this way."

Hearing his name threatened to drag me back down into the abyss, but Simon rescued me in the nick of time. "Hey! You'd better move or you might be involved in an accident," he warned me from the kitchen. Only then did I realize the vacuum cleaner was moving straight toward me as though possessed.

I went to join him. "Thanks, I'm not insured against that kind of thing."

"Well? How did it go with your parents?"

"Just like I expected." I sat down on a chair across from his.

He nodded, solemn. "I can imagine. And at school?"

"You should have seen her! She showed her true colors!" Ginevra said from the next room. "I liked how you acted this morning. We really can do it, if you want. Rip her tongue out, I mean."

"I think the suspension is enough. Besides, those *aren't* my true colors. Anger made me overreact, that's all."

"I'm almost afraid to ask, but . . . what happened?"

"Gemma taught a lesson to two girls who were dissing Evan."

"Seriously?"

"Yes. I'm so proud of her! C'mon, don't feel bad. They deserved it," she said to me.

"Yeah, maybe they did."

"I warned you that you were going to deprive her of her innocence," Simon teased his girlfriend.

"Malicious people only understand malice. Talk to them using other language and they won't understand a word you're saying."

"Nice theory," he said, rolling his eyes.

"You bet it is," Ginevra shot back.

"If you hadn't sweet-talked the principal, he definitely would have punished me," I pointed out, disproving her logic.

"But that didn't happen, and those two will think twice before saying anything like that again. Just remember: my offer is still good."

"We're not ripping out their tongues, Gwen."

"All right, all right, it was just a suggestion!" she said defensively, still sprawled on the couch.

"So how do you feel?" Simon asked me, turning serious again. I was about to answer him but when he saw the frustration on my face he quickly changed the subject, winking at me instead and nodding in Ginevra's direction. "I bet she broke some hearts, as usual?" Judging from his expression he wasn't the least bit worried.

"It's not my fault!" Ginevra called from the next room, loud enough to be heard over the music. "It's that Jeremy kid who just won't give it up!"

With an embarrassed shrug, I stared at my hands, unsure what to say. "I keep telling her to cut it out, but she thinks it's fun to fry his neurons." Simon burst out laughing. "You're not jealous?" I asked, lowering my voice in amazement.

"I don't have the slightest doubt about Ginevra's feelings for me." He smiled calmly. His words aroused a distant yet warm memory in me of the feeling of security I used to get when I looked into Evan's eyes. "Supernatural love—be it a Subterranean's or a Witch's—isn't like human love," he explained, his tone sweet.

"What do you mean?"

"How can I put this? Let's say that for humans, love is like the moon: fickle and inconstant. Its pale glow warms their lives that otherwise would remain in total darkness. Our love, on the other hand, is like the sun. Its light illuminates everything, turns everything into an explosion of colors. It's fiery. It's eternal—until it dies along with us."

I listened to him, wordless, fully aware that though I was human, my love was also like the sun.

"You were the only thing that mattered to Evan," Simon added, getting straight to the point. "He would have done anything to keep you alive."

"Even die?" I retorted bitterly.

"Even die. You know that. Just like I'm sure your love for him goes beyond normal human limits."

Grateful he understood me, I nodded and got up from the chair before the armor I had managed to build around me could fall to pieces in front of him. "I'm going to rest for a while, if you don't mind. I'm pretty tired." I left the room, secretly afraid of what I might be about to face.

I had no idea what was happening to my body or my mind, but something was definitely wrong. Sometimes it was like my brain hid away in a world all its own, a world where Evan still existed and the pain was only a memory, and when that happened nothing could snap me back to reality. But the illusion lasted only moments and then reality would hit me full force right in the chest, stoking the fire of my desperation, and my heart would end up bleeding even more. I hadn't spoken a word to anyone about my millionth hallucination, but I was sure Ginevra had already discovered everything while silently probing my thoughts.

I went upstairs to Evan's room, which had become my hideaway, and shut the door behind me. The room was filled with sunlight reflected off the snow outside, so I closed the curtains in order to feel more sheltered and lay down on the bed. My eyes closed, I took Evan's chain that I wore around my neck, turned it over in my fingers, and held it in my palm, like I did every night to fall asleep. All I wanted was not to think about it for an hour. Just one hour. To pretend it had never happened, that Evan was only away on a mission—because the way things actually were made me feel I was losing my mind. But then, letting myself forget his death would have been egotistical. I didn't deserve it. It was right for me to suffer because it was all my fault Evan was gone. How could I live with the burden? How could I forgive myself, when it had been my lips that had stolen his last breath? How could I wake up morning after morning feeling the pain of his absence? Every night I sought his touch yet found only cold fabric under my fingers. My life had been dyed a single color: in my future I saw only black.

I got up from the bed, went to the bookcase, and carefully took out the ancient volume of Tristan and Iseult. A tear silently slid down my cheek because I knew what I would find between its pages. I tried not to think of the afternoon when that book had kept us company, but my drawer of memories promptly ignored my command, breaking the seal I'd put on it. Evan's laughter filled my head, his voice caressing the words locked away in the book.

They were like the honeysuckle vine,

Which around a hazel tree will twine,

Holding the trunk as in a fist

And climbing until its tendrils twist

Around the top and hold it fast.

Together tree and vine will last.

But then, if anyone should pry

The vine away, they both will die.

My love, we're like that vine and tree;

I'll die without you, you without me.

I could practically feel Evan's forehead resting on mine like he was still there, his dark eyes full of promises. He had been right: just like the honeysuckle and its hazel tree, now that I was parted from him I too felt I was slowly dying. Still, despite everything, like the plants that grew from Tristan and Iseult's tombs, our souls would remain entwined forever. No one would ever be able to separate them.

In those moments, hidden away in that room, we had lived our little fairy tale, with no idea that that cursed day would be the beginning of the end. With no idea that, like Iseult, who died of grief over the loss of her love, I too would grieve for my Tristan forever, letting desperation slowly sap my life.

I opened the leather-bound book, revealing its little secret carefully tucked between the yellowed pages. With a trembling hand, I took the slip of burnt paper. I couldn't hold back any longer and a silent tear slid down my face and wet my hand as I crumpled to my knees. The book, now sprinkled with my tears, fell to the floor and I curled up with Evan's note clasped in my hand. *His last message.*

There was no need for me to reread it—I remembered it word for word. By now it was engraved on my brain. I had read it hundreds of times and yet my eyes insisted on going back over every line, trying to imagine what the message would have sounded like coming from his lips. But the flame had consumed the edges of the paper, so part of his words had disappeared along with him. I ran my thumb over the elegant handwriting, as though with this gesture I could touch his hand,

and imagined him as he wrote it an hour before dying. If only I had read it in time . . .

As I clutched the slip of paper, his words whirled in my head as though he were whispering them in my ear.

You can't separate a body from its heart without killing it.
One more hour, my love.
Just one more hour and I'll return to you.
Yours forever,
Evan

I closed my eyes, my chest wracked with sobs, and imagined Evan there with me, his arms encircling my shoulders in a warm embrace. My heart was trapped in a cage that was growing ever tighter, so tight it couldn't pump oxygen through me any more. I couldn't breathe. I wished everything would fade away so I wouldn't feel the pain any longer. I wished I could shed my skin for a new one, but I knew it would be useless because he was in my bones. Whenever I closed my eyes the scene played over and over endlessly in my head. I wished it would stop. I wished *everything* would stop. And the worst thing of all was that I continued to live, even knowing that something inside me had died forever.

The only emotion as powerful as my anguish over losing Evan was my remorse for having killed him. My guilt ate at me like a woodworm and the pain was a fire that consumed me from within. It hurt. And nothing except death would ever make the hurting stop.

As the tears continued to flow, I ran my hand over my belly and realized there was only one thing keeping me from putting an end to the torture, only one buoy to cling to in the stormy sea that dragged me further and further from shore into deeper and deeper water. When you were adrift it didn't matter where you landed—all that mattered was the promise of a safe haven. And that's what the baby was to me: my safe haven. I raised my head with effort to look out the window and wondered whether one day I would be less fragile.

Once again I rested my hands on my belly. It was all I had left of Evan.

THE SCENT OF NOSTALGIA

Someone gently knocked on the door. I was still curled up on the floor with my head on my knees, my cheeks streaked from the dried tears that had left my skin tight. I looked up, waiting for the pain to ease, then stroked Evan's note one last time, tucked it back between the pages of the book, and stood up.

"Come on in, Gwen," I murmured. My voice was too low for anyone to hear it, but the door opened and a tuft of short hair peeked in. "Oh, Simon, it's you." I tried to compose myself but it was too late; he had already walked into the room and was staring at me, a desolate look of helplessness in his eyes. I was in pieces.

"I came to see how you were."

I rubbed my sides and shrugged. "A bit better," I lied.

His discouraged sigh told me I hadn't been very convincing. "Why don't you come downstairs and join us?" he asked, but I was too depressed to take him up on the offer. The fact that he and Ginevra were always together did nothing but remind me how alone I was. "Staying cooped up in here isn't doing you any good."

"Do you think there's something wrong with me?" I asked.

My question seemed to catch him off guard. His eyes wavered. Maybe he didn't have the answer to that either, or if he did, it couldn't have been anything reassuring. He swallowed and clenched his fists, clearly embarrassed, but then looked me in the eye, this time firmly. "Gemma, in a short amount of time, life gave you an amazing gift and then unexpectedly took it all away from you. You and Evan were so close that when he was torn away from you, a piece of you was torn away too. There's *nothing* wrong with you. You just need time to learn to live with the pain."

Simon had chosen his words carefully and I was grateful for that. He seemed to realize that my only option was to learn to accept the pain, to grin and bear it, because I was certain I would never get over losing Evan. "It'll get better with time. It'll heal, you'll see," he promised, stroking my shoulder.

"You guys keep saying that, but it never happens. It never will," I said softly, overcome by my pain. "It's like there's a knife still lodged in my heart and whenever I move, whenever I *breathe*, the blade tears away another piece of flesh."

Simon half closed his eyes and sighed, clenching his fists even tighter. He knew perfectly well how I was feeling. "I miss him too," he admitted, "but you really need to try to stay strong. Come downstairs . . . please?"

I looked up and the words came out before my brain could process my unexpected wish. "I'd like to go see Peter for a while, if you don't mind."

My request seemed to surprise him. He thought it over for a second and looked at the sky through the half-closed curtains, pensive. "In a few hours it'll be dark," he said, his frown betraying his concern. "It might be dangerous."

"I won't be gone long. I just really need a change of scenery," I insisted.

Simon's face darkened, but he nodded. My request clearly worried him, but at the same time he didn't want to refuse it. "Take your phone with you and if you need anything call me right away."

I didn't know where the impulse had come from, but as soon as the words were out, I realized I really did need to get out of that house and leave the past behind me, just for a couple of hours. Just long enough for me to breathe. I went into the bathroom and rinsed my face. Looking at myself in the mirror, I got ready to put on a new mask before going to Peter's.

I parked the car on the wet driveway that had recently been shoveled clean of snow. A string of unlit Christmas lights trimmed every inch of the front of the house—the echo of a holiday that, like a ghost, had slipped away without my even noticing. I wrapped my heavy sweatshirt around me and rang the bell.

"Gemma!" Mrs. Turner gave me a hug brimming with affection, almost as though she hadn't believed she would ever see me again. "Oh, sweetheart! I've been so worried about you." Tears that she tried to disguise filled her eyes. Maybe coming out of my shell hadn't been such a good idea. As long as the world continued to pity me it would be impossible to distance myself from the pain.

"It's good to see you again, Mrs. Turner. Is Peter home?" I asked, hoping she would give up her intention of consoling me. Actually, I'd known the answer to my question even before knocking on their door because I'd seen Peter's outline in his window. He was working out.

"Oh, of course. Come in, dear. He's up in his room." Exasperated, she pointed at the stairs, down which issued an infernal racket. "He's been in there for two hours with the music turned up full blast. I have no idea how he can stand it!"

"Have you tried telling him to turn it down?"

"The problem is he can't hear me—or maybe he's pretending not to. He hung his old *Keep out* sign on his door." I smiled at the memory of Peter and me making that sign. "But if I remember correctly, you're the one person authorized to ignore it." She winked at me as an invitation to go on up.

"Maybe I shouldn't. We're not little kids any more."

"Don't be silly. I'm sure your privilege is still valid"—she gave me an affectionate smile— "and that he'll be happy to see you. I'll be in the kitchen if you need anything. In case you want something to lure him downstairs, I made an apple pie. I always liked having the two of you in the kitchen."

"I'll try." I bit my bottom lip as Peter's mom walked into the other room and slowly climbed the stairs, gathering my courage. Before I knew it I found myself turning the knob on Peter's door.

My face was so used to tears that the smile that spread over it felt almost foreign as I leaned against the doorframe. The room was just as I remembered it, the walls covered with his drawings of Marvel heroes, the Blue Bombers banner above the lacrosse equipment hanging from a hook, waiting for spring, pencils and markers scattered over a sheet of paper on the desk, his comic book collection proudly lined up in the bookcase, and a pile of clothes on the chair. Peter had his back to me and was throwing punches at the worn punching bag hanging from the ceiling. He wore the blue pants from his lacrosse uniform and the muscles in his bare back flexed with every blow. From the sweat trickling down his still-tanned skin, I could tell he must have been at it for hours. The bag jerked wildly beneath his blows. He seemed to be taking out all his frustrations on it. I was used to seeing Peter work out for both hockey and lacrosse, his true passion. I knew every muscle in his back, having watched him many times, but recently he seemed to have kicked things up a notch.

I smiled and turned off the ear-shattering Iron Maiden music to get his attention. Peter spun toward the stereo and smiled the instant he saw me. I crossed my arms and leaned against the wall. "Trying to punch a hole in that thing?" I joked, gesturing at the still-swaying bag.

Peter pounded his fists together. I felt a void in my chest, remembering Evan and the afternoon in the workout room when I'd unwrapped the tape from his hands and he'd used it to pull me closer. Forcing back the thought, I looked at Peter and said with a grin, "I don't get why you're so pissed off at it. What did it ever do to you?"

Peter came closer, wiping his neck with a towel. His dark curls were dripping with sweat. Stopping in front of me, he looked at me with a sly smile. "Didn't you see the sign?"

"I thought it didn't apply to me," I teased. I ran a finger down his wet chest. "Ew! You're all sweaty!" Peter cocked his head and his broadening smile made me guess his foul intentions. "Don't you dare!" I warned.

He shot forward but I dodged him. Unfortunately, on his second attempt, he managed to grab me by the arms and lift me up. I burst out laughing. "Put me down!" I shrieked, and he obeyed. But his euphoria had filled my heart with memories and, overcome by nostalgia for a time gone by, I couldn't help but throw my arms around his neck and rest my head on his chest to feel the warmth of his presence. I just wanted to feel like I used to when we were children: free from sad thoughts. "Oh, Pet . . ."

He stood there for a second, surprised by my gesture, but then returned the hug and held me against him. He ran his nose through my hair and kissed me lightly on the head. It was so natural being with him. It felt like we were meeting again after having lived in two parallel worlds—and actually it was partly true. I was happy something was left of us, the old us, Gemma and her friend Peter. The boy next door who healed all my wounds without asking for anything in return.

"I've missed this. I've missed you, Gemma."

His embrace grew gentler and suddenly I sensed the heat his body was emanating. His heart thumped against my chest, its rhythm accelerating. I tried to pull back but Peter wouldn't let go and the silence grew deeper, as though we were both holding our breath. My eyes went to his Adam's apple that rose and slowly descended. I looked up slightly, inadvertently lining my mouth up with his. Taking a deep breath, I moved away, shyly trying to look him in the eye.

"Sorry." He swallowed and headed to the stereo. "I was thinking about you and when I saw you in the doorway, it almost didn't seem real. I let myself get carried away."

"No problem," I was quick to reply, sitting down on his bed.

Peter put on a Linkin Park album and lowered the volume so the music was only in the background. He took a sleeveless white undershirt from a dresser drawer, put it on, and leaned his elbow against the window frame.

"I knew you would come sooner or later," he said, undoing the tape around his knuckles.

"You always know everything, don't you?"

Still warm, his arm muscles swelled with his every movement. "Only when it comes to you."

I smiled at him and he winked back. "I needed a breath of fresh air."

"Then I guess my sweaty room wasn't the best choice."

"Actually yeah, I was thinking of something *fresher*," I joked, feigning disgust.

"Oh, sorry! Hold on, let me open the window."

"I was only kidding!" I protested, but he continued to yank on the window, which wouldn't budge. Something suddenly hit me. "Hey!"

Peter had turned around and thrown an old stuffed gorilla at me. It had bounced off my chest, without hurting me. "I was only kidding too, smartass! Didn't you notice it's freezing outside? I'm afraid you'll have to put up with my fragrance: *Eau de Macho.*"

I raised an eyebrow and held back a smile. "Your self-esteem has definitely improved, I see."

He bit the inside of his cheek, like he always used to do. "So has your mood, *I see*."

"Yeah . . . In any case, it doesn't smell bad in here. I like your smell. It's—comforting."

"*Comforting?*" Peter grinned, and two deep dimples formed in his cheeks.

"It's familiar. It smells like you." I smiled as I picked up the little stuffed animal that had fallen to the floor. I stared at the toy for a moment, clasping it to me in a wave of affection. "You still have it." I'd given it to him ten years before, the day he fell out of a tree and broke his leg, and I'd been afraid he was going to die.

Peter took the stuffed animal from me and fell onto his bed. "Only because it reminds me of your face." He tossed it in the air and caught it like he often did with his lacrosse ball.

"Why you—" My jaw dropped and I tore the gorilla out of his hands to use it as a weapon. He grabbed my wrist and his eyes once again got lost in mine, still with that strange mix of desire and frustration. I pulled my wrist free and looked away. Maybe it hadn't been a good idea to visit him.

"We're playing hockey at the Olympic Center in a few days. You coming to the game?" he asked, filling the silence.

"Peter, there's something I need to tell you," I blurted. "It's one of the reasons I came."

He sat up beside me, ran a hand over his face and through his curls, and turned to look at me. "You're pregnant," he said with a smile.

"H-how did you know?" I gasped.

"Come on, Gemma. We're not in New York City. This is a small town, remember?" He shrugged.

"So everybody knows . . ."

For a long moment neither of us opened our mouths. Peter didn't seem upset; in fact, he looked calm. He must have already had enough time to digest the news. How long had he known?

After a long moment of silence, his hand slid across the bed and onto mine, interlacing our fingers on the blue blanket. "How do you feel?" he asked in a concerned tone.

I hesitated, but the warmth of Peter's hand reminded me that with him there was no need to lie. "In pieces." My voice was barely audible, but he squeezed my hand. "Sometimes all I want to do is scream," I admitted. My empty gaze found his, which suddenly sparkled with enthusiasm.

"Not a bad idea."

I cocked my head and stared at him, not understanding. "What do you have in mind?"

Peter winked at me and got up from the bed, his hand still in mine as his face lit up. "Come with me."

"It should be around here somewhere . . ." Peter continued to mumble to himself, studying a tourist map of the Adirondacks as I followed his directions, driving the BMW up a steep road through the woods.

"I still don't understand where you're taking me," I said, curious, as we ascended higher and higher.

"Pull over," he suddenly told me. "This should be the place."

"What place?" I asked, exasperated.

Without answering, Peter got out and double-checked the path that branched off from the road. "This way!" He grabbed my hand and pulled me through the trees.

"You sure this is the right direction?"

He stared at me, smiling with satisfaction. "Come on—you must remember this spot!"

"Remember it? You mean I've been here before?"

He nodded. I looked around, searching for some detail that might jog my memory, but I couldn't recall ever having been there before. Then the woods opened into a clearing and my eyes lit up as I was whisked back to the past. "I forgot all about this place!" I exclaimed, brimming with enthusiasm as I admired the view. Below us, the snowy treetops formed a mantle of white that enveloped Lake Placid. "I still don't get it, though. Why did you bring me here?"

"You said you remember being here before. Do you remember *when?*"

"Of course! We were thirteen," I said. That day we'd hiked to the top of Whiteface Mountain, one of the highest peaks in the Adirondacks, about fifteen minutes outside of Lake Placid.

"We were on a field trip," Peter added, "and while the others were checking out the view with binoculars, you wandered away from the group and I came looking for you."

"We got lost."

Peter nodded. "And ended up here."

"I remember. But why are we here now?"

Peter took a step and stood behind me, his lips on my ear. "Remember how our voices echoed off the mountains together?"

I turned toward him eagerly and he smiled back. His intentions were finally clear. That day many years ago, when he and I were still just kids, we'd screamed into the wind at the top of our lungs, hoping someone in the group would hear us. But fear soon gave way to excitement, and Peter and I had shouted over and over, feeling like we were flying. We'd left the world behind while our voices soared through the air and came back to us again and again, until someone found us and took us back to the group. I had completely forgotten about it.

"You said you wanted to scream. You can do it here. It's just you and me and our mountains," Peter encouraged me, studying my reaction.

I smiled, a little embarrassed by his suggestion. "Peter! We're not thirteen any more."

"Who cares? We're here. You and me, exactly like back then."

For a second I was convinced he was right. Time fell away: Peter and I were still together, just like back then. Only now there was a huge boulder separating us, and it was in my heart. And yet, just for a moment, I wanted to breathe the air of that distant past . . .

"It's going to work, you know," Peter said in response to my skepticism. "Trust me."

I looked down, unsure, and he walked up to the edge of the cliff. Shooting me a glance, he cupped his hands around his mouth and without taking his eyes off me shouted my name as loud as he could. Then he held his hand out to me as his voice echoed through the air. I approached him with hesitant steps. For some reason I was afraid to give in to the need to do it. I was afraid of what my heart might shout to the whole wide world.

"Go ahead, shout out a wish," he said. "It feels amazing!"

I smiled to myself, took a deep breath, and screamed with all the breath I had in my lungs, letting everything out, ridding myself of the pain. Shouting that I wanted to live, that I wanted to die, that I didn't want to suffer any more. Peter's voice joined mine. My eyes filled with tears, because all I could think about was Evan. I squeezed my eyes shut. Desperation continued to hound me, begging me to listen to it, but I flung it off the mountaintop.

Peter went silent, leaving only his echo ringing through the air. My eyes were still closed when I felt his hand grasp mine. I opened them, short of breath, but in my chest was a lightness I had forgotten.

"Well? How do you feel?" He smiled.

"God, what a sensation!" I said. "It was so *liberating*! I felt like I could have taken wing, and everything was so simple. How did you come up with the idea of bringing me here?"

Peter shrugged and sat down on a rock. "I don't know. I figured it would make you feel better. You needed to vent, to let it all out."

I went and sat down next to him, picking up a stone. I was still exhilarated. A strange breeze stirred my hair, almost like a caress. "What was that?" I exclaimed, suddenly uneasy.

"Relax, Gemma. It's just the wind." Peter smiled and I went back to focusing on the lightness that had filled me. I didn't want it to fade.

"You were right," I admitted, casting him a sidelong glance. Under his coat, Peter wore his white sweatshirt with the hood pulled up over his head, exactly like mine. Our warm breath condensed into little clouds. "Remember this?" He mimed smoking, blowing a stream of vapor through his lips. It made me laugh. You couldn't live in the past, but what harm was there, just that once, given that the present hurt so much and the future still frightened me?

I averted my gaze, focusing on my feet. "A lot of years have gone by since that day, you know," I thought aloud, "and a lot has changed, but there's one thing that's remained constant in my life." I turned toward him, searching for the two kids who had screamed into the wind. They were still there, I could feel it. "Knowing you'll always be there for me."

"It's true, I'll always be there for you. It doesn't matter what decisions you make—mine is never going to change."

"There's a secret I'd like you to share with me," I said. He stared at me, curious. "How is it you always know what I need? Please tell me."

"I don't know," he admitted, smiling. "I just do. Maybe it's because we grew up together." He shrugged again, suddenly becoming pensive. "Maybe we're more connected than you're willing to admit."

I shook my head. "If that were true, it should work the other way around too, but I've never been good at guessing what you need."

"Only because having you beside me is enough," he confessed in a faint voice. He took both my hands and his dark eyes bored into mine, so close and penetrating I couldn't escape them. "Gemma . . ." he said softly, and swallowed.

"Peter, I—" Though I wanted to stop him, the words died in my throat when I felt tears sting my eyes, anxious to show the world my pain.

Peter must have noticed, because he rested his forehead on mine and squeezed his eyes shut. A tear ran down my face and he wiped it away with his thumb, which lingered a second too long on my skin. I could tell he also felt we'd never been so close before. Not like that.

Desperation gripped my heart, but I still felt it wasn't wrong to be there. I *needed* Peter. Another tear trembled on my lashes and slid down, coming to rest on my lips. He stared at it, holding his breath, and brushed it away, moving his finger slowly, doing nothing to hide his desire.

I took his hand and moved it from my face. "Please, Pet," I begged. I was afraid I wouldn't be strong enough to pull away from the warmth of his body, to resist the need to feel him holding me in his arms for a moment. It wouldn't have been fair, because in his embrace I would have closed my eyes and imagined it wasn't him. I would have told myself the warmth was coming from Evan, so I could feel him near me once more. I couldn't do that to Peter—make him believe my heart felt something it didn't. There was no one else for me but Evan. I knew Peter's heart beat for me, but mine pulsed to a different rhythm. And if one day the fire inside me went out, nothing would remain but ashes— it would be an arid, sterile place where nothing would ever grow again.

Peter squeezed my hand tighter and I looked him in the eye. "Pet," I forced myself to say. I didn't want a relationship built on lies. I needed a connection bound by the sturdy cords of truth, cords that might hurt at times, but kept a relationship together forever. "What I feel for him is so deep"—my voice trembled and I wasn't sure I would be able to get it out, but another teardrop fell and the knot in my throat loosened—"so deeply rooted inside me that not even death can dissolve it."

His eyes wavered as it sank in. No matter how much it might have hurt him, it had been the right thing to do. Death had taken Evan from me, but I wouldn't let it steal a single atom of our connection.

Peter gulped, his intense gaze darkened by conflicting, unfathomable emotions. "I know you chose someone else," he began, and I could see the words caused him pain, "but that doesn't mean I've stopped loving you." New tears flooded my face. "We have a lifetime of memories together that won't let me." He looked down at his hand stroking mine.

I closed my eyes and turned my head away, totally incapable of finding a reply as pain lacerated my heart like a steel blade. "Evan . . ." I thought I'd said his name only in my mind, but my lips had moved in a whisper that slipped away on the wind.

Peter clenched his fists at his sides and his expression hardened. He rested his hands on my shoulders, forcing me to look him in the eye.

"Gemma, Evan is dead! You realize that, don't you? He's gone!" The cruelty of his words made me wince. "But I'm not. I'm here, and I love you. I've always loved you. Let me be the one to raise the baby."

I tightened my lips as my chin began to quiver and tears streamed down my face, quickly drying in the chilly mountain air. I felt the light touch of his forehead against mine and when I opened my tear-veiled eyes they found his. For a moment it felt like the world had come to a halt around us. Peter raised his chin slightly and his mouth brushed mine.

I turned my head away before it was too late, leaving his lips puckered in midair, and clenched my jaw. "I'm sorry," I whispered. "I can't."

Maybe my Peter was gone; maybe I'd lost him, because the person in front of me was someone else—more daring, more demanding. But I wanted my friend back, I didn't want another boyfriend. I would never replace Evan, would never even try to.

All at once my eyes went wide and a shudder ran down my spine. I panicked. "What was that?" I asked. An ominous, familiar, icy wind had just swept over my bones. Peter frowned, at a loss. "Did you feel it too?" I twisted around, searching for the source of the strange breeze, but knew it was useless. It was coming from my mind. It was happening again.

"Gemma, what is it?" he asked. A second later, he blanched violently and shoved me back, staring at the ground with terror in his eyes. "Watch out! There are snakes everywhere!" he screamed, darting away from me. His hood fell back and I saw that his forehead was dripping with sweat.

I nervously scanned the ground and looked back up at him, bewildered. Nothing was there. There were no snakes. Suddenly I heard him. Evan. My head shot in the direction his voice had come from, but no one was there—only the empty space beyond the edge of the cliff.

"Gemma, no!" Peter's shout pierced the air, but I barely heard it as my body moved toward the other voice.

"Evan," I murmured to myself. He called to me again. *I'm here.* Another step. I followed the comforting sound and looked down over the edge. Shock gripped my heart when I found myself looking into his terrified eyes. *Evan!* He was clinging to a tree trunk that stuck out from the side of the cliff, his body dangling in the void.

I inched toward him as Peter's anxious voice reached me: "Gemma, come back!"

"I have to help him!" I leaned over the cracked tree trunk, hoping it wouldn't give beneath our combined weight, and desperately tried to grab him. "Evan! Take my hand!" A shriek escaped my throat as his dark eyes, full of dismay and terror, met mine.

"Don't let me die . . ."

My eyes filled with tears. I gripped his hand with all my might but I knew I couldn't bear his weight much longer. "I'm not letting go. Hold on tight!" I screamed, pouring into my words all the anguish tormenting my heart. But Evan slipped away and plunged into the void.

"Nooooo!!" Desperation tore my heart in two. I lunged forward to grab him but lost my balance and tumbled over the edge.

7

MURMURS IN THE DARKNESS

"Hang . . . on!" Peter grunted through clenched teeth.

I looked up and felt my arm stinging. Peter had grabbed my wrist firmly as my body dangled over empty space. "Let go! Let me go! I have to go with him!"

"Gemma! What the fuck are you talking about?! I'm not letting you fall! Hold on tight. Gemma, look at me! Look at me!"

His voice was so harsh it brought me out of my trance. I stared at Peter for a long moment before slowly regaining my senses, like a sleepwalker who's just woken up. "Peter . . ." I murmured. All at once I became conscious of the void below me and thrashed my legs, panicking. "Peter! I'm going to fall! Help me, please! Pull me up!"

"I'm trying to!" He grimaced from the effort but couldn't do it. The veins in his arms looked ready to burst. "Shit! I can't! You're too . . . heavy! There's something—"

I felt myself slipping a fraction of an inch at a time. "Don't let go!" He gripped my wrist tighter. It hurt so much I thought it might snap in two. "Peter, don't let go of me, please!" I shrieked, overwhelmed with terror, slipping farther still. Tears streamed down my face as I thought of the baby growing inside me. Living didn't matter to me any more, but I couldn't let death take our baby too—that would be like killing Evan all over again.

"I'm not letting go," Peter snarled, his every muscle tense from the strain. "Take my other hand too!"

He held it out to me, but my attempt to grab it made my body lurch, loosening Peter's grip, which slid from my wrist to my hand. It felt like some dark force was pulling me down, undermining Peter's efforts.

"Hold on, please!"

"We'll get out of this, don't worry. We'll get out," he grunted, but when I looked him in the eye I saw it: a flicker of desperation. Peter was convinced he couldn't do it. I was going to fall. He strained his muscles once more, pulling back with his legs as the sweat continued to trickle down his temples, but my fingers slid even more from his grip.

"Gemma! Hold on tight!"

All at once a gust of wind, a mixture of hot and cold air, hit me, making me shiver. It swept me up into the air like a whirlwind. My brain felt foggy. Was I falling?

A split second later I crashed down onto the ground with a scream. I took a deep breath. No, it wasn't the ground. It was Peter. His hand was still in mine and I looked into his desperate eyes. Panting, he squeezed me against his chest so tightly I couldn't breathe.

He hadn't let me fall.

"Gemma . . ." He cupped my face in his hands. "I thought I wouldn't be able to do it. Are you okay?" I nodded, never taking my eyes from his. "It's over," he whispered, watching as the empty space beyond the cliff's edge darkened in the twilight. "I don't know who helped me pull you up, but it's all over now, thank God. Let's get out of here."

I tried to stand, but it took a minute for my legs to stop shaking. By the time we reached the car darkness had already hidden everything beneath its black shroud.

"Let me drive," Peter said, but I adamantly took my place behind the wheel. It was true my hands were still trembling and the tingle in my back had crept up to my head, but driving relaxed me. Having to focus on the road would take my mind off what had just happened.

"I said I'm fine. I just want to go home."

"Okay, but I don't want you to go alone. Let's go straight to Ginevra's."

"Your house isn't far."

Peter seemed determined not to listen to me. "I don't care. I'm coming with you. I'll walk home from there."

"Peter, are you kidding? That's ridiculous."

"It's not a suggestion, Gemma."

"Whatever," I said, giving in. "But at least let Simon give you a ride." Out of the corner of my eye, I saw Peter relax in his seat and look away from me. Regardless, I knew he was still shaken by what had happened; the tension between us was palpable.

He turned to face me again. "Now would you mind telling me what the hell you were doing back there?!"

"I—I don't know. I thought that—but you didn't see him, did you?" I whispered. I was almost afraid to say it out loud. Had I seen Evan . . . or hadn't I?

"All I saw was a whole bed of snakes that chose the perfect time to come out and attack me. I kept shouting but it was like you couldn't hear me, and I couldn't go after you because those monsters were slithering in from every which way. I was sure some of them even bit me, but I don't feel anything now." He looked down at his shoe, frowning.

"You're terrified of snakes. How on earth did you—"

"Why should I give a damn about snakes?! You're more important. I had to help you."

"Thanks," I said softly.

All at once, Peter jumped. "Whoa, whoa, *whoa*! What are you doing?!" he shouted, squirming in his seat.

I stared at him in bewilderment. "What's wrong? Calm down!"

But he looked terrified. He stared at me with wild eyes, clutching his hair. "What the fuck! Gemma, turn on the lights!" he bellowed. I stared at the road, not understanding. "The headlights! Turn them on, for fuck's sake! You're freaking me out!"

I did as he said and the road lit up as though it were daytime. "There, happy? I don't get why you're so upset."

"You *what*?!" He stared at me in shock.

"I didn't even notice they were off," I explained with a shrug, still confused.

"You didn't even—Oh! You're unbelievable, Gemma! It's pitch dark out. How the hell could you see where you were going?"

"I could see perfectly well," I insisted.

Peter drew a long, uncertain breath. "You sure you're okay?"

His question hung in the air between us. I wasn't sure I knew the answer.

I parked in the driveway. As I stepped out of the car onto the gravel, my knee gave way, but I managed not to let Peter notice. Strange tingles ran over my skin and crept up my back, tickling the nape of my neck. Peter walked me to the front steps of the sprawling house, but when I set my foot on the first step, the ground seemed to give way beneath me and I had to lean on him for support.

Suddenly everything became confused. "Gemma!" Peter's voice was distant, muffled. I sought his face but could barely open my eyes.

There was only a blurred image. I realized Peter was lifting me from the ground. "Shit! You're burning up!"

"Quick, bring her inside!"

"What happened? Here, let me carry her."

Ginevra's voice was jumbled together with Simon's. Clearly concerned, he took me out of Peter's arms. My head spun faster and faster; it was like being on a carousel. Someone felt my forehead.

"She was fine a minute ago. What's happening to her?" Peter sounded bewildered and alarmed. "Why is she shaking like that?"

"She's having another attack."

"Attack? What the hell are you talking about? Why does she have such a high fever?"

"Quick, we need to cover her up. Peter, it would be better if you went home," Simon told him.

"Home? We need to take her to the hospital!"

"*No hospitals.* We'll take care of her." Simon rested me on something cool—the leather couch, I guessed. The words he had chosen for Peter were kind, but his tone had been stern. *Peter* . . . I tried to whisper, but my lips remained sealed, refusing to obey my command. "Now, would you like to explain to me what the hell happened?" Simon demanded.

I tried again to speak but realized it was impossible. Sleep wanted to tear me away and no matter how hard I struggled to resist it my mind faded in and out.

"I wish someone would explain it to *me*! Damn it, this is insane! So we drive up Whiteface Mountain and all of a sudden she goes out of her mind, talking nonsense. It was like she couldn't hear me, like she'd fallen into a trance. I didn't know what to do! There were all those snakes and she kept talking to herself, calling Evan's name. She seemed crazy. Then she leans over the cliff, loses her balance, and falls," Peter said, agitated.

Beside me, Simon was holding his breath. "She had another hallucination. Why the hell did you take her up there?!"

"How was I supposed to know she would try to throw herself off a cliff? We didn't even go all the way to the top. Somebody should have warned me about these attacks of hers, because it sounds like this isn't the first time it's happened, is it?" Neither of them answered. "I just don't get it. I'm strong enough. I'm in shape, and Gemma doesn't weigh that much. All the same, though I managed to grab her in time, it felt like it would've taken the strength of ten guys to hold her, like there was some invisible force dragging her down. Then suddenly she gets light, like someone is below her, pushing her up, and I manage to pull her back over the edge. It must've been all the adrenaline, I guess—I really was desperate." Peter was talking a mile a minute and his voice was fading in and out, as though he were pacing. "We headed back here, but she was fine. She even insisted on driving. Then, all of a sudden, outside the door, she faints and . . . Are you going to tell me what's going on with her or what?" he shouted. "Why am I thinking this has happened to her before? Am I right?"

For a moment, Peter's question received no reply. It was Simon who finally broke the silence, speaking in a low voice as though he knew I could hear every word. "Losing Evan has been rough on her. She still hasn't overcome the trauma."

"Okay," Peter said resolutely, "but the hallucinations and—" A hand touched my forehead. "Jesus, she's burning up!"

More silence. Peter was clearly asking for answers neither of them wanted to give him, but Simon tried to be reassuring. "It's a psychosomatic reaction. Her mind is trying to ease some of the trauma by expressing it through physical symptoms."

"How would you know? Are you a doctor or something?" Peter shot back contemptuously. "How can you be so sure?"

"Peter, calm down," Ginevra interjected. "It was sweet of you to take care of her. Simon and I will take it from here. Trust us, just this once. Gemma needs to rest. You were right: this isn't the first time it's happened, and we know what to do. Let Simon give you a ride home."

Peter was silent. Ginevra had put him in a tough spot. Or maybe she or Simon had influenced his mind to convince him.

"All right, I'll go. The only thing that matters to me is that she's okay. But tell her I'll keep my phone on tonight."

"We will if she wakes up before tomorrow." Something covered my body. "Let's let her rest." Simon's whisper was so soft I barely heard it. Or maybe it was because I was slipping away into the darkness. I heard the door close and let myself go, a fire burning inside my head.

SOUL TERRORS

Emerging from the deep state of unconsciousness into which I had sunk, I slowly began to perceive my body. At first it was just the frenzied beating of my heart. It surrounded me; I was its prisoner. It throbbed in my temples. Each beat shook me but I couldn't react, trapped as I was in the darkness. I squirmed. The surface beneath me was hard, and my warm, humid breath dampened my face as though the room had suddenly shrunk so small it was squashing me. Slowly but surely I regained awareness of the various parts of my body, of the sweat that left my back damp and my forehead beaded.

I tried to take a deep breath, but my throat closed up as if someone had used up all the air. With an effort, I forced my eyes open. To my terror, I found myself in absolute darkness. Where was I? Though I struggled to breathe, I was suffocating. There was no more oxygen. I attempted to move but my limbs felt hemmed in; I instinctively raised my arms and my hands struck a solid surface. Panic flooded me. Numb with shock, I groped around me, seeking a way out, but realized to my horror that my body was confined in a cramped space. I was trapped. The air grew heavier by the second. I gasped, in desperate need of oxygen, but it felt like steel straps were squeezing my chest. Raising my hands above me, I strained to push upward, leveraging with my whole body, knowing even as I fought to escape that it was hopeless. I was sealed in a cement casket.

I had been buried alive.

I pounded the rough surface repeatedly. My skin cracked open and blood oozed from my fists but it didn't matter—I had to get out before it was too late. "Get me out of here!!" I screamed, still pounding, my voice broken with sobs. "Gwen! Why did you bury me?! I'm still alive! Gwen!"

Suddenly I felt a noose tightening around my neck. My hands flew to my throat but there was nothing there. There was simply no more oxygen for me to breathe. Distant voices reached me, muffled by the thick layer of cement, as I struggled to avoid being crushed.

"Gemma! Come on, breathe!" Though Ginevra's voice was far away, I heard the desperation in her words.

"Gwen . . ." I tried to make myself heard through the stone slab, but my strength was abandoning me. "It's too cramped. I can't breathe. My . . . baby. Save my baby," I gasped, my ears plugged and my head on the verge of exploding.

"Come on! Come on! Try to react! Simon! She's stopped breathing!" Ginevra's voice was ever fainter, ever more distorted.

"Hang in there, Gemma! You've got to fight! Air! She needs more air! Quick, open the windows! We need to get her to breathe!"

The earth shook beneath my body, bringing me back to the surface. My eyes shot open and my lungs avidly gulped in the air. Only then did I realize it wasn't the earth moving—it was Ginevra, who wouldn't stop shaking me. I panted, inhaling the oxygen that every fiber of my body craved, then looked around, terrified by the horrific experience I had just undergone. I threw my arms around Ginevra's neck, sobbing. "Oh, Gwen! How did they do it? Why did they seal me up in there?"

"Shh . . ." She stroked my hair and held me close. "Calm down. You're safe now." I pulled back to look her in the eye, but her image was blurry from the tears. "It's all over."

"What happened?" I asked, but she avoided my gaze and exchanged glances with Simon.

"You were delirious," Simon told me, staring at the floor as though he felt powerless.

"I—" My weary voice cracked with anguish. "I . . . I was sealed in a cement casket. I couldn't breathe." Simon and Ginevra stared at me, slowly shaking their heads. "Someone sealed me in a casket," I insisted.

"There was no casket, Gemma."

I stared at Simon in shock, unable to believe him, then looked around. There was no trace of my prison. "But how—"

"You were hallucinating." Ginevra stroked my hair, speaking sweetly to sugarcoat the pill. I looked at my hands, certain I would find them covered with cuts from pounding against the cement, but there wasn't a scratch on them. "Here." Ginevra helped me sit up, but I was still stunned by her words. "You'd better get back to bed. It's the middle of the night and you need to rest." She tucked me in and handed me a notebook with a dark blue cover. On closer look, I saw it was a diary. "I made this for you. I thought it might help if you let out what you're feeling inside. In our language it's called an *epikor*. It means 'messenger' and it's connected to the deepest part of you. Sometimes we only realize what's inside us, *what we are,* when we talk about it with someone. Otherwise the truth remains buried within us, too deep for us to see or understand it. But it's not always easy to get everything out with other people. A diary, on the other hand, is like a part of ourselves where we're free to say it all. You have no idea how much this can help in handling life's challenges."

"I've never had a diary," I said softly, studying the embossing on the cover.

"You can pretend they're letters that—"

"Gwen, what's wrong with me?" She sighed, just as Simon came back into the room. "I can take it. I just want to know what's happening to me. I don't need you guys to protect me from this too."

Simon and Ginevra looked at each other. "We're not sure," she admitted hesitantly. "The poison is powerful. It didn't kill you on the spot, but that doesn't mean it can't still do it."

"Gin!" he reproached her.

"No, Simon, she has a right to know." I nodded, my heart trembling. "It must still be in your bloodstream and your body can't eliminate it. It's putting up a fight, though, which is why you're having hallucinations and running high fevers."

Simon looked at her out of the corner of his eye. Even in the state I was in, I could tell how little he agreed with her theory.

"Sorry, I haven't found any other explanation for all this," she said.

"Let's say you're right." I looked Ginevra in the eye to make sure she told me the truth. "What will happen if the poison gets the better of me?"

"You'll die," she confessed, her face ashen, as though it were more than a mere possibility.

"But that's not going to happen." Simon came a step closer. "Do you feel up to telling us what happened when you were with Peter?"

"Peter!" I'd completely forgotten how I'd gotten home.

"Calm down, don't stress. Peter is fine. He brought you here and then went home."

"I've got to call him!" I searched the nightstand for my phone.

"It's the middle of the night, Gemma. You can talk to him in the morning."

I nodded reluctantly and gathered my thoughts before returning to Simon's question. "I saw Evan. He was—" My voice broke and my sight fogged, his image reappearing before my eyes. "He was falling from the edge of the cliff. I tried to hold him up but couldn't." For a moment I feared my sobs would suffocate me.

"Evan wasn't really there." Ginevra pronounced each word cautiously, her eyes fixed on mine and her hands gripping my shoulders in the attempt to bring me back to my senses.

I shook my head because I didn't want to believe it, but inside I knew it was true. "I know—I mean, I get it. But I *saw* him!" I wanted to convince her I wasn't crazy, but I wasn't entirely sure of it myself. The memory of Evan dangling over the precipice was too vivid for me to think it was just a hallucination. It was real, not a mere projection. Or maybe Simon was right and my mind was too fragile to handle all the pain. "I'm losing my mind. I'm hallucinating, Gwen, it's not normal! Thank God Peter got to me in time." I rested my hands on my belly. "I honestly thought he wasn't going to be able to do it. It was like some dark force was pulling me down. But then I suddenly felt light, as if something was pushing me up." I clearly remembered what I'd felt. And then there had been that gust of wind, hot and cold at the same time. It had been like two conflicting forces whirling around me, waging a battle for my survival . . . as though something were trying to help me. Still, in a world where everyone was out to kill me, the thought that someone might want to save me seemed ridiculous. I could no longer count on anyone except Simon and Ginevra, and I hoped I wouldn't lose them too, seeing how everything around me died.

Ginevra smiled at me, breaking the tension. "He grabbed you despite his fear of snakes."

I smiled back, but then remembered another detail. "Looks like I'm not the only one having hallucinations, because there were no snakes!"

Simon and Ginevra's expressions suddenly darkened with alarm. "Gemma, what are you saying? Are you sure?" Before I could reply Ginevra scanned my every thought.

"Of course I'm sure. Even when I . . . hallucinate"—it was a struggle to say the word out loud, because it was admitting something was wrong with me—"afterwards I never forget anything that happened, not even the weirdest details. And there were no snakes, I'm positive."

"Hold on a second," Simon exclaimed. Ginevra and I instantly looked at him. He stayed silent, his eyes directed at Ginevra, who was listening carefully to his thoughts.

"Um, guys? I'm right here," I said a bit sarcastically, waving my hand. "Would you mind explaining what's going on?"

Simon came over and took me by the shoulders, his eyes boring into mine and his expression clearing. "Gemma!" He shook his head, trying to follow his own train of thought. "It's not the poison. It's happening again! How could we not have realized it? The crises you've had. Your hallucinations. Don't you get it? *A Subterranean is behind all this!*"

I gaped, unsure whether to consider this good news or a death sentence.

"I've already encountered a power like his," Simon continued. "It's powerful because it lets him act without coming out into the open. He gets into his victims' heads and persuades them to kill themselves. He's already doing it."

"Wha— Wait, hold on. I'm not following you."

Simon nervously ran his hand through his hair.

"I can barely believe it, but it makes sense," Ginevra murmured. "We should have realized it sooner. Just the thought of the risk you were running . . . He's feeding off your fears. Think carefully, Gemma: a moment ago you thought someone had buried you alive."

A shiver gripped my back as I recalled the experience. He was right. Simon was right. "That's why I keep reliving Evan's death."

Ginevra nodded. "He focuses on what torments you the most. It happened in New York, remember? That was the first time you saw Evan. It must have been his doing even then."

"And in the hallway . . ." I whispered, putting the pieces together.

"He's toying with your mind." Simon had a new light in his eyes, as if a burden had been lifted from him. Up until he'd realized this, I knew he'd felt he could do nothing about my suffering, and that had made him taciturn and short-tempered. But now the look on his face was determined because he knew how to battle my demons. "He wants to convince you to take your own life, and he almost succeeded. He used your suffering to convince you that you were going insane, but he made one false move: he outed himself to us by trying to stop Peter with the snakes."

"Peter . . ." I murmured.

"The Subterranean tried to use Peter's fear against him to keep him from saving you."

"But Pet managed anyway. He overcame his phobia for me," I said, amazed.

"He was brave." Simon still sounded proud about solving the riddle. "And it's a good thing he was, because the Subterranean definitely wasn't expecting that."

"You think he might actually have killed her that way?" Ginevra asked.

"Sure. What just happened is proof—you saw it for yourself. He made Gemma believe she was suffocating. Her mind was so convinced there was no oxygen that her body reacted accordingly. She definitely would have died if we hadn't shown up and driven off the Executioner."

I gasped. "You mean he was *here*?"

"Yes. Actually, the most dangerous aspect of a Reaper with a power like his, purely mental, is the ability to make himself invisible to anyone, even a Witch." Simon looked steadily at Ginevra. "It would take serious concentration for you just to detect his presence."

"So what do we do?" I asked, looking them in the eye warily.

"For now, you get some rest," Simon said, his voice firm. "You're still weak, and we need you to be strong enough to fight, now more than ever. It's not our fears that enslave us, but how we face them. He'll attack you again and you'll have to resist until we can catch him."

"Then what?"

Simon arched an eyebrow, a new fire ablaze in his eyes. "Then it'll be his turn to be afraid."

The time had come for him to protect me.

THE DARKNESS WITHIN ME

At last, the room is quiet. So quiet I can hear the pen move across this ivory-colored paper, forever staining it with my gloomy thoughts. Simon and Ginevra left so I could rest, both of them relieved they'd figured out why I've been so unwell. Maybe while I was desperate about losing Evan this whole time they were suffering for me.

So that explains it: another Subterranean. Another creature condemned to die just so I can stay alive. It all seems so unfair. How many more will suffer the fate meant for me before they realize my life isn't worth all this? How many others will have to die for me? Simon? Ginevra? Or maybe my baby? No. I'll never let them take him too.

Ginevra and Simon are relieved there's a logical explanation for my hallucinations, that they aren't caused by madness. But it doesn't matter to me. Knowing it does nothing to ease my pain. Quite the opposite, in fact. At least during my visions, I could fool myself into thinking Evan wasn't dead, and for a moment my desperation would subside, leaving room for hope—an emotion that's otherwise banished forever from my heart. But then he died again before my eyes, and each time it left me even more devastated.

The pain is changing me. Sometimes I'm almost afraid because I end up thinking horrible things. Like that time after my mom talked to me I caught myself wishing she would die. How did this happen to me? I told Simon about it and he says it's normal, that it happens to most people, and that the point is to <u>decide</u> not to listen to those thoughts.

I texted Peter to thank him for his help. I heard his voice when I was unconscious. He told Simon he would wait for news of me, but I don't feel like calling him this late at night. I still can't believe that after all these years he told me how he really feels, even though he knows I don't feel the same. There will never be anyone else in my life because my heart has been shattered and, like a broken vase, it's not capable of containing anything any more. I'll keep my Evan safe and warm, and when the baby is born, maybe I'll see Evan in him, a little piece of him to hold onto. I would give my life to see Evan just once more. One last time together so I could say goodbye. But there's nothing I can do to make amends, and that's the worst part. I feel like a piece of glass with cracks running through it that lengthen with every vibration of my heart, every breath, every tear. And no matter how hard I try not to break down, I'm on the verge of breaking into thousands of pieces. I'm a shattered piece of glass.

Sometimes at night I think I feel his touch and I seek his embrace in the darkness. Everyone asks me how I am, but nothing I can say would ever give them the faintest idea. Sealed inside an endless pain, cold and dark, with no way out. In pieces.

Trapped in a room full of memories, a room I can't escape from.

~~Evan. Evan. Evan.~~

He's all there is in my mind and the memory hurts so much that death would be a relief in comparison to what I'm experiencing now, to the thought of what I've lost. <u>It hurts too much.</u> And every beat of my weary heart, every breath, makes me wish everything would just end, because the pain is unbearable.

It's like it's raining inside me. A corrosive, incessant, suffocating rain. It pours down on me with a roar: deafening, deafening, deafening . . . like a shower of nails on my heart of ice.

The cord that connected me to Evan has been slashed and someone has torn up my roots. I move and breathe, but my heart pumps only poison that corrodes me down to my bones. It burns my blood, darkens my mind, devastates my soul and every part of me.

Soon the pain will annihilate me, and then the shadows will do with me as they wish—because at that point I'll be dead.

"How deep do you think it is down there?" Evan's dark irises stared at me, trying to decipher my expression.

My eyes lost themselves in his, so close my heart skipped a beat, two deep wells ready to swallow it up. "Evan," I murmured, barely moving my lips as he leaned over to examine the pool that stretched out endlessly below us. It was like a mother-of-pearl shell that had been carved into the rock and filled with water. He was squatting beside me on the rocky shore and the water's light reflected in his eyes that brimmed with enthusiasm.

"Come with me, Gemma. I want to find out what's down there."

"No! Evan, wait!" I exclaimed, my voice trembling, but he had already stood up and moved to the water's edge. I hesitated, staring at his back, which was crisscrossed with what seemed to be lash marks and burns. As he turned around to encourage me, I saw his hair was longer. It gave him a wild look.

"I'm tired of waiting, Jamie." Evan's eyes filled with bitterness and he dove in. I lunged forward to grab him, but something held me back. I dragged myself to the edge of the pool and watched him sink further and further down until the darkness engulfed him and he disappeared.

"Evan!" I reached out my hand but instantly jerked it back: the water had burned me. When I squatted, a clang and a sharp pain in my ankles made me look down. "What the—" My ankles were shackled in thick iron chains that were making them bleed and squeezing them tighter with every attempt to pull free.

"How deep do you think it is down there?"

I looked up and jade-green eyes smiled at me, inches from my own. Though I couldn't remember ever seeing her before, the mahogany-haired young woman's face seemed familiar.

"Who are you?" I asked warily as she leaned over the surface of the water and peered into the depths. Her eyes were filled with awe, as though it contained some forbidden treasure.

"I'm Anya." She smiled at me. "Isn't it wonderful down there?" Her eyes sparkled so intensely they seemed to be illuminated by an inner light. "Come with me, Gemma! Let's find out where it leads!" she exclaimed, still leaning over the edge of the pool, her face full of promise.

I shook my head, dazed by the power of her voice. "I can't! I can't go with you." I looked down at my ankles, which were still trapped. The clank of the iron chains drew her attention.

She studied them for a long moment and looked at me again. "Why not?"

"I—I don't know."

"Don't fight it, Gemma. Come with us." I stared at her, unsettled. Her words seemed to be hiding a different meaning that eluded me. "It will be easier for you. Everything will end. The pain will stop. You just need to come with us." Her eyes continued to gaze hypnotically into mine as her voice crept inside me like powerful dark fog. "Make up your mind. *He's waiting for you.*"

"Evan . . ." Her words pierced my heart, but a sudden explosion in my head set my brain on fire and kept me from taking her hand. I gritted my teeth from the terrible pain and stepped away from her. My brain felt like it was about to melt from the intense heat. I tried to speak, but my chest was so tight I couldn't utter a sound.

"You have to choose, Gemma."

Maybe it was actually her voice that was burning my brain. It suddenly seemed like the whole world was being sucked into the pool of water as the pain in my head vanished, leaving me short of breath. I stared at the walls of Evan's room, the echo of Anya's voice fading in my mind.

I looked around, staggered by the strange dream, as my body forced itself to breathe steadily again. I touched my forehead. It was damp and my skin was still hot. I must have run a high fever again. Alarmed, I checked the room but knew that even if the Executioner was there I wouldn't be able to sense his presence, much less call Simon or Ginevra to come to my rescue. My only hope was to strengthen my mind's defenses, make an effort to ward off his attacks. It would be difficult, but I had to at least try, and deep in my heart I hoped that understanding what was causing my hallucinations would work to my advantage.

I pushed off the covers, catching the diary as it fell. I had left it on the bed when I nodded off. Before putting it back on the pillow, I stopped to look at its ivory-colored pages and decided Ginevra was right: laying out my pain like that, letting the paper absorb it like ink, would help distance it a bit from my heart, drain it away, even if only for a moment. Maybe seeing the words from a distance would make them less mine and help me breathe.

The touch of my bare foot against the wood floor sent a shiver down my spine. As I walked down the hall, Simon and Ginevra's comforting murmurs coming from behind a closed door momentarily ceased when she sensed my presence but then started up again as soon as she was reassured that my thoughts were calm.

A hot shower would help wash away the remnants of the night, which had left me with a deep feeling of discouragement and uneasiness. When the spa had filled with steam I stepped under the scalding stream of the shower and even my tiniest muscles began to ease. I wished I could stay there forever, enveloped in that sweet coziness that banished every thought and concern, drawing them down the drain with it. I felt so comfortable in the water, as though it were my element. I washed my hair, gently massaging my scalp, and rinsed it, letting the heat slide slowly down my face like a caress. It was soothing to stand under the water, holding my breath. Opening my eyes to take a breath through the spray, I suddenly jumped in terror.

Two jade-green eyes reflected in the glass of the shower stall stared back at me. I lurched back but then realized it was only my reflection— or maybe an image that had persisted from the strange dream I'd had. Gradually my heartbeat slowed and I almost smiled at my overreaction. My mind had dragged that night's bad dream into the real world. Would it never end?

It was then I noticed there was a dent in the stone wall of the shower. I stared at the cracks and the way they branched out, wondering what had caused them. I couldn't resist the impulse to touch them. An image flashed into my mind: Evan's arms resting tensely against the rock, his head bowed and water streaming down his bare back. He looked tormented. *It had been him.* Who knew how I could be so sure, but I was. I'd seen him brutally smash his fist against the wall. I touched it again, missing him desperately, and made myself get out of the shower.

As I turned off the water and opened the door a shooting pain gripped my belly, making me double over and grit my teeth. A scarlet trickle flowed down my leg, contrasting starkly with the white porcelain of the floor like a gruesome threat. Staring at my fingers with alarm, I saw they were stained red, and stifled a scream. My hands trembled and I could think of nothing except the baby.

I made myself take a deep breath. The Executioner. It had to be the Executioner. Terrified, I tried to wash away the blood and discovered it wasn't coming from between my legs. Just then, I heard Simon and Ginevra burst into the hallway. They began to bang insistently on the door.

"Everything's fine," I shouted to them before they could come in. "Everything's fine," I repeated to myself in an attempt to banish the tension. I used a washcloth to stanch the wound on my belly, then dropped it to the floor and buried my face in my hands, still trembling from fright.

Ginevra waited until I had put some clothes on before coming into the room. "Are you okay? What happened?" She studied the room, her eyes lingering on the washcloth on the floor.

"I don't know, it must have been the Subterranean. There was blood everywhere. I guess I managed to ward off his attack this time."

With extreme caution, Ginevra lifted the bottom of my shirt, her expression indecipherable. "No. I see it too. You're still bleeding." I looked down at the fabric. The bloodstain on it was expanding. Ginevra's eyes wavered and filled with terror. "It can't be . . ." The words escaped her in a barely audible gasp as I tried in vain to understand why she was so upset.

"Gwen, what's wrong? It's just a little blood." I grabbed another washcloth and realized as I patted the wound that the blood was coming right from my birthmark. "I must have cut myself with something. My skin has gotten really sensitive lately and— Gwen, are you listening?"

Ginevra forced herself to look me in the eye and helped me stanch the bleeding, all the while staring at me as though seeing me for the first time. I wasn't sure what was frightening her, but there was something in her eyes—a strange edginess that betrayed how upset she was.

"If the sight of blood has this big an effect on you, I'd better go change."

"Right." Ginevra nodded without picking up on my sarcasm. I walked around her, still baffled by her expression.

In the silence of Evan's room, I examined my belly. There was no wound on my skin and the burning sensation had lessened to a mild tingle, but the birthmark I'd had my whole life had turned translucent like a burn mark or a faint, pearly tattoo. Still, compared to all the bizarre events in my life, this was the least of my worries. I couldn't understand Ginevra's reaction. I decided it didn't matter—I was already too busy finding the energy to face my demons. To face the world. To breathe. I didn't have the strength to worry about other people too.

My thoughts shocked me. When had I become so egotistical?

Simon's voice came from behind the door. "Gemma, everything all right?"

"It's nothing, Simon." Ginevra must have let him know I hadn't felt well. "Nothing serious, don't worry."

He peeked around the door, waiting for permission to come in. I smiled at him, trying to ease the tension. "I saw blood on the floor in the spa," he said with a mix of embarrassment and concern.

"It was just a scratch. It's already stopped bleeding. The baby is fine. I think Ginevra's getting a little overanxious."

"She really cares about you. I mean, you know . . . about you and the baby. The three of us are all she has left, and she's already lost so much."

"Her Sisters, you mean."

Simon nodded. "Giving them up was the most difficult thing she'd ever done. It devastated her. You have no idea what she went through. She's very attached to you, so it's no surprise she's worried, especially given your condition."

"Yeah." I stroked my belly as though the gesture might protect the baby growing inside me. "I wonder if we'll manage to get through all this torture. Sometimes I think that even if the Executioner fails, my body will finish the job on its own by giving in to the agony." Utterly discouraged, I sighed and looked into Simon's eyes. "It's really too much. I can't—I can't find peace, day or night."

He pulled me against him and held me tight. I stiffened in surprise but the awkwardness quickly faded, giving way to a deep sense of calm. He ran his hand through my hair. "It'll get better, you'll see." His soft voice lulled me into some parallel world where the pain eased, muffled by a blanket of pure white roses. "Let yourself go, Gemma. You just need to let me help you."

All at once I noticed that the veins in his forearm were turning black, as though absorbing poison, and my heart began to bleed again, pierced by thousands of thorns. I shoved him away. Simon teetered, his arms in midair. "What the hell did you think you were doing?!" I screamed, violent anger surging through me.

"I just wanted to help you," he said, his voice tinged with guilt.

"I don't need your help! I don't need anyone!"

"Gemma, be reasonable. I just wanted to ease some of your pain. I didn't touch your memories. All this negative energy isn't good for the baby."

I glared at him, overcome by venomous rage. "That's not your problem."

"Gemma . . ." Simon reached toward my shoulder, but I knocked his hand away with a strength I hadn't known I had.

"Don't touch me!"

Simon's eyes wavered and he looked stunned by the contempt in my voice.

"Never touch me again," I snapped.

"If that's what you want." Simon sighed, giving in, but something in his eyes—a shadow of sadness and defeat—brought a pang to my heart. Only then did I become fully aware of the tone I had used. I stood there as Simon turned his back on me and left in silence. Little by little, the cloud of poison that had been fogging my mind dissipated and was replaced by feelings of guilt. Why had I treated him so badly?

CHECKMATE

Simon appeared behind me so suddenly it made me jump. "Sorry, I didn't mean to startle you."

"Oh! You were—"

"Yeah," he was quick to reply, confirming my suspicions: he had just returned from a mission. Though I had lived in their world for months, the thought still made me shiver. "It was an elderly person, if that puts you more at ease." He sat down at the kitchen table and invited me to join him with a nod.

"Simon—" My eyes met his.

He clenched his jaw, his face full of resentment. "It's not a problem," he said.

"I don't—I honestly don't know what got into me. I'm so sorry. I'm horrified by how I treated you." I pulled a chair back from the table, gripping the wood tightly.

"Don't worry about it. It doesn't matter."

"You just wanted to help me, and I went and—I was a total bitch."

"It's water under the bridge."

I nodded and, hanging my head in embarrassment, sat down at the table. Ginevra came in, carrying something, but I didn't look at her. "It's just that all this is seriously fraying my nerves. As if that weren't enough, every time I close my eyes I find myself flung into a nightmare. I keep—I keep dreaming about a woman. It's like she's haunting me." I looked up and noticed Ginevra's expression freeze, though she was trying to look unperturbed. "I had them before too, but I've been having them more and more often lately."

"Is she always the same? Do you always dream of the same woman?" Simon asked.

"I can't remember. All I know is I have the feeling I know her."

"Ginevra, what's wrong?" Simon asked. He'd also noticed the worried look on her face.

"Nothing. It's nothing. Just thinking." Simon tightened his lips, perplexed.

"Do you guys think it's possible that I"—I hesitated because it was so hard to voice the suspicion that had weighed on my heart for some time—"that I could have had a premonition of Evan's death?"

"What are you talking about, Gemma?" Ginevra asked.

"I dreamed it before he died. I dreamed of him dying. More than once. That's why I'm so upset about the nightmares haunting me now—I'm afraid they might reflect reality. Maybe it's the price I have to pay for coming back from death."

Simon tried to reassure me. "Relax, Gemma. It was probably caused by your fears. It definitely wasn't a premonition. Hold on." A glimmer of illumination lit up his face. "Maybe that's also his doing. Maybe the Subterranean can enter your dreams, like Faust or like—" He left his sentence unfinished to avoid naming Evan, who had had the same power. "It would make sense. After all, he's already able to get past your mind's defenses when you're awake. Maybe he can do it while you're asleep too."

"You're right!" I exclaimed. Ginevra, on the other hand, didn't seem very convinced. "He probably takes on a woman's guise to hide his real appearance and confuse us," I said.

"It's possible," Simon agreed, deep in thought.

"I think he wanted to convince me to follow her," I added.

"He must have the ability to entrance people. It's a dangerous power that could lead you to surrender to him completely—an almost irresistible attraction."

"It sure is," I mumbled, remembering the sensation that had seemed to creep under my skin.

A metallic click made us turn toward Ginevra. She was polishing some weapons. "In any case, since he likes to play around, I've prepared some little toys just for him." She slid something across the table. It looked like a handgun but with a more complex structure.

"Guns?" I asked, surprised.

"Were you expecting bows and arrows?" Ginevra flashed a half-smile.

"No, seriously. What do you mean to do with *those*?"

"They're not ordinary guns," explained Simon. He seemed to understand what the weapons were, though I guessed he'd never seen them before, given how closely he was examining their details.

Ginevra pushed an iron case lined with black leather toward us. A grim smile hardened her features as we looked at the contents.

"They're perfect. You did an excellent job, *chérie*," Simon told her with a smile.

"Thanks." Ginevra winked at him while I frowned, still puzzled. Did they really mean to face such a dangerous Executioner with handguns?

Exercising extreme caution, Ginevra took out one of the projectiles and showed it to me. It was pointy, like a spearhead, and in the middle of its metal surface was a tiny glass section containing a drop or two of clear liquid.

"Your poison," I murmured.

"My serpent and I had our work cut out for us. I was busy all night making these."

"Think it'll work?" I asked skeptically.

"I don't *think*, I *know* it'll work. With these"—Ginevra loaded the gun with one of the tiny projectiles, the safety making an ominous click—"we're guaranteed a huge advantage. This way Simon can protect himself and I'll be less worried."

I stared at the gun on the table in front of me. Actually, I had to agree with them: it was perfect. Ginevra had created weapons with her poison to battle the Subterranean. "You're amazing!" I said, and sat back in my chair as she and Simon slid the guns into various holsters. She even had a little one strapped around her thigh. She winked at me, making me smile.

"What do we do about school?"

"No school today. Too dangerous."

"Okay, but what do we do? I mean, are we going to hang around here until we nail him? On top of that, if it's so hard to detect his presence, how are we going to catch him?"

"She's right. We need to lure him out into the open, set a trap for him." Simon's eyes lit up, relishing the new challenge.

"But how?"

Simon looked at me and smiled. It was a predatory smile.

"Let's saddle up." Ginevra loaded her gun and cast me a glance. "It's hunting time."

"I'm still not sure this is a good idea," I shouted, trying to be heard over the aggressive roar of the engines that filled the garage with foreboding echoes.

Simon rested his arms on the roof of the Lamborghini. Ginevra was revving the accelerator to warm up the engine. "You sure it'll work?" she asked him.

He nodded. "Trust me, the Subterranean is only waiting for the opportunity to attack Gemma. He's less likely to do it if we're at home."

"Why don't we all take the BMW?" I asked hesitantly.

"We need to split up. I'll go out first but I'll keep my eye on you. Gin, the second the Subterranean turns up, you and Gemma get out of there," Simon ordered. "I'll take care of him."

It warmed my heart to see how concerned they were about each other. Ginevra nodded and Simon slapped the roof of the car with his hand before climbing into his Bugatti Veyron. He pulled out next to us in his blue missile, his eyes locked on his girlfriend's.

The garage door closed behind us. It was too late to turn back now. We were going to hunt down my Executioner. It was dangerous, I realized that, but it was a match I couldn't miss out on.

The bright red traffic light kept our wheels glued to the street. It felt like the starting line of a race whose finish no one could imagine. Impatient, Simon and Ginevra revved their engines without taking their eyes off each other. Fearful, I stared at them in silence, wondering who would win and—most importantly—who would pay the price this time. I wouldn't be able to bear losing either of them.

Suddenly another sports car nudged its way between us and revved its engine challengingly. I leaned forward in my seat to look at the driver. Behind the wheel was a young woman who clearly didn't understand how dangerous it was for her to be doing that. She wore a sexy, skintight, dark-gray racing driver's suit. Her hair was blond and straight, and her big blue eyes stood out beneath thick black lashes. She looked to be around twenty-five but she might have been younger— one of those rich, spoiled, city girls whose daddy had bought her a fancy car. She was probably attracted to Simon's good looks and thought flaunting her car might be a good way to seduce him. We, on the other hand, were about to race toward death—a detail she certainly wouldn't have liked. The red light prolonged the tension as the woman continued to rev her engine.

I smiled to myself, finding the situation amusing. "What a weird-looking car."

"It's Italian," Ginevra replied, checking it out from the corner of her eye. "A Pagani Zonda R. Not too shabby! Central monocoque in carbon-titanium, 750 horsepower, and shifts gears in twenty milliseconds thanks to a magnesium-cased dog-ring gearbox. In a nutshell, a car designed for racing."

"Hey, check it out. Looks like she's got it in for you two," I told her, noticing that the young woman wasn't only trying to provoke Simon, on her left, but also Ginevra, on her right.

Ginevra tapped her fingers on the steering wheel and glanced at her impatiently. "Unless she's looking for trouble, I hope for her sake she stays out of our way. This is not the time."

The light turned green and the wheels of the three cars squealed as we all shot off like missiles amid the protests of nearby pedestrians. Just outside Lake Placid, Simon's car disappeared, pushed by its thousand horsepower, while the woman's dropped back behind us. Maybe she had realized that Simon and Ginevra weren't interested in racing her—or, more likely, she'd detected the threatening look in Ginevra's sharp eyes. I took a deep breath, holding back the panic that threatened to suck me up into its dark vortex. The more Ginevra accelerated, the faster my heart raced, beating in time to the roar of the engine as I wondered when the Reaper Angel would show himself.

In my heightened state of alert, I jumped when I saw the front of the Zonda pull up alongside the Lamborghini's back wheels. "I thought she gave up!" I complained. "Didn't you lose her?" The woman was putting her life in jeopardy by interfering in our plans. Her pearl-white car zoomed along, matching our speed. "What does she think she's doing?"

Ginevra ignored the woman, who instead looked at me with a fake smile that sent a shiver down my spine. The Zonda roared louder and edged toward the Lamborghini, forcing Ginevra to veer away so the cars wouldn't collide.

"What the—what the hell does she want with us?" Ginevra hissed between clenched teeth. She watched the car in her mirror, bitter irritation on her face. "Take a hike, blondie. You could get burned in this game." She accelerated more, but the woman insisted, pulling up alongside us again. "Damn it!" She tightened her lips.

My heart lurched. "Gwen!" I shrieked as a ball of fire burst from the woman's outstretched palm and shattered the window of the Zonda.

"Son of a—" The car swerved dangerously as Ginevra took us out of the trajectory of the fireball. It missed us by a hair.

"What the hell is going on?!" I screamed, panic surging through me.

Simon reappeared from far down the road, spun his car around and positioned himself opposite us.

"It worked." Ginevra's voice betrayed no emotion, her icy gaze locked on the road as a crafty smile spread over her face.

"A woman?!" I asked, trying to keep my voice down. "I thought Subterraneans were all males!"

"You did? Why would you think that?" Ginevra cast me an amused glance. "This will just make it more fun to get rid of her."

"Wha—" I put my hands on my head, more confused than ever. In the rearview mirror I saw Simon's Bugatti tailing the car behind us.

"They must *seriously* want you. I know from experience that the females are as lethal as they are rare." Ginevra continued to drive, keeping her eyes glued to the road. "Extremely lethal." She seemed pleased that the challenge was getting even more exciting and at the same time fully confident about how our deadly game would play out. I, on the other hand, had learned at my own expense not to take anything for granted. Suddenly Ginevra's eyes lit up.

"What is it?" I asked, nervous. I knew that look—I'd seen it on her face lots of times during their clandestine races.

"Simon has decided to make things a little more interesting."

"W-what do you mean 'interesting'? Isn't this interesting enough?"

"It'll be even better without powers." She winked at me, excited by the thought.

"You mean he's not going to attack her with his fireballs?"

"Yes, but the race on our end won't be run using our powers." She shrugged casually as though she were talking about the weather. "We like to let the engines do their own thing—the sound is so much cooler when the cars are under strain."

Despite Ginevra's apparent confidence, my heart thumped wildly and a knot gripped my stomach. I dug my fingers into the leather seat and jumped at every spark emitted by the two cars battling it out behind us. Simon did everything he could to block the Executioner's car so it couldn't reach our Lamborghini, but the woman must have been more skilled than he'd expected, because she was giving him a serious run for his money.

"Is she the woman you see in your dreams?"

Ginevra's question made me start. It hadn't occurred to me that the two might be connected. "I'm not sure. She might be."

"Maybe I was wrong," she muttered to herself.

"Wrong about what?"

Ginevra seemed surprised by my question, as though she hadn't realized she'd spoken out loud. "Nothing. Never mind." Her expression darkened momentarily and then cleared.

"How the hell could you not have sensed her?" Though I wished I could have asked more nicely, what came out of my mouth was an accusation.

"She has the power to shield her mind. I didn't perceive anything strange in her thoughts. I told you, she's going to be a challenge."

The Zonda eluded Simon's attacks and raced toward us at warp speed. "She's going to hit us! She's going to hit us!" I squirmed in my seat, cursing as the blond Angel shot toward us like a bullet toward its target, but before I could catch my breath the car zoomed past us. "Gwen, look out!"

A huge semi full of tree trunks suddenly swerved in front of us, cutting us off. It looked like an out-of-control giant about to crash down on top of us. Ginevra frowned, searching for possible escape routes, then smiled, barely touched the gearshift, and hit the gas. I held my breath and braced for impact as the semi skidded toward us, blocking all the lanes, but the Lamborghini roared louder and flew beneath the wheels of the semi. I stared at Ginevra's smiling face and struggled to control my breathing.

"Relax." Ginevra winked at me. "We've just started playing."

But another doubt gripped my stomach. "Simon!" I unbuckled my seatbelt in a second flat, spun around, and shot to my knees in my seat, terrified he hadn't made it through. Peering through the rear window I saw the semi lying on the road like a sleeping behemoth, enveloped in a cloud of dust. The tree trunks had scattered everywhere. "I don't see him, Gwen!" I shot her a glance and her lips arched in a captivating smile.

Just then, Simon came skidding out across the asphalt to the left of the semi. I collapsed into my seat and allowed myself a sigh of relief. Ginevra let out a laugh. "I told you to relax. It would require more than a truck to take Simon out."

Without losing speed, he pulled up alongside our car and traded glances with Ginevra. I looked around nervously, wondering where the Executioner was, and felt the earth disappear beneath me when a gray

Ferrari identical to Evan's pulled up on our right. I bit down the pain seeing the car caused me and looked up. My heart lurched. Evan was behind the wheel. I threw myself against the window, shouting his name and pounding my fists on the door.

"Gemma, calm down! Gemma!"

"Let me out! Let me out, I have to go to him!" Completely hysterical, I jerked on the door handle again and again.

Gemma . . . His voice burst into my head. Desperate, I burst into tears. All at once my window exploded. Flying shards of glass were everywhere. Evan leaned over and reached toward me. "Take my hand, Gemma! Come with me!"

My seatbelt clicked closed around my waist as Ginevra continued to shout, "Gemma, snap out of it!" Fighting to maintain control of the car with one hand, she shook me hard with the other. "It's her! It's her, toying with you!"

I could barely hear her; her voice reached me in confused fragments. "Come on, Gemma! Take my hand!" Evan urged me, but I was lost halfway, unable to decide which of the two voices to cling to. The Ferrari continued to keep pace with us, despite Ginevra's maneuvers to avoid it. "Come with me, Gemma! Don't listen to her. She just wants to keep you away from me!" I impulsively grabbed the steering wheel.

"Gemma! Gemma, what are you doing? Snap out of it!"

"I have to go to him! Let me go to him! Please, pull over!"

The car swerved, threatening to go out of control. Suddenly, Simon's Bugatti appeared in front of us, aiming at the Ferrari. What was he doing? He risked hurting Evan! "Simon!"

"Your mind! Keep control of your mind, Gemma!" Ginevra screamed.

Little by little, her words penetrated the wall that the Subterranean had built around my mind. I turned to look for Evan but saw in his place only the blond Angel, who shot me a sly smile. The Zonda abruptly slowed and spun around, avoiding impact with Simon's car, which pursued it as Ginevra sped forward in an attempt to get me out of there.

"Gwen, I—" My guilt trapped my voice in my throat.

"It doesn't matter. Everything okay?"

I nodded, still shaken. "How does she do that? How the hell does she do that?!" I couldn't fathom the strength of her power. *I had seen*

Evan. I had been completely convinced it was him, that he had come to save me. How could that woman instill such a sense of security in me that not even Ginevra's words had been enough to stop me?

"You have to focus and force yourself not to let her in."

"But I don't know how to shield my mind!" I wailed.

"Make an effort, Gemma! Now you know she can attack you at any moment, but you can be prepared when she does. Focus and keep her out!" Ginevra gritted her teeth and clutched the wheel. The asphalt burst open as we drove over it, as though we were racing over the mouth of an erupting volcano. "Brace yourself!"

I sank my fingers into the seat, lurching with the car's abrupt movements. Ginevra downshifted and veered off the road, pulling up alongside the Zonda. A bolt of lightning shot out at the Angel's car, but the blond swerved to avoid it, saving all but a lock of her hair from the lightning bolt. "Ugly Witch!" she hissed, her face dark with rage. She cranked the steering wheel, preparing to attack, and shot a fireball at the Lamborghini.

Ginevra nimbly sidestepped the attack, making the back tires skid. The incandescent ball shot between our wheels and crashed into the trees. "Wow! It passed underneath us!" I exclaimed with admiration. Ginevra sent her adversary a challenging smile.

"You've got to give me lessons someday. Where on earth did you learn to drive like this?"

Before she could reply the Zonda rammed our side so hard I lurched in my seat. Ginevra let out a string of curses. "You bitch! You are so dead." She pulled a lever next to the steering wheel, switching off the traction control and putting the car into sport-shift mode. The back of the Lamborghini tilted and the car negotiated a hairpin turn, its tires screeching against the asphalt as the Zonda shot toward us on our right. I gasped, panicking. In the midst of the confusion Ginevra took out her gun, raised her arm in front of my face and fired several shots through my window. The Angel dodged them. Ginevra jammed her foot down on the accelerator, her eyes ablaze, the threatening expression on her face making me shudder.

"Now let's make good use of every last horsepower." Ginevra focused on the road and the car shot forward like a fiery arrow. Through the back window I saw Simon blocking our adversary's way. A long hairpin turn put the two cars' tractions to the test. For a second I thought they had lost control, but then I realized Simon was trying to force the Zonda off the road. Mid-curve, his Bugatti swerved left and rammed the blond's door, making the windows explode in a shower of glass.

The Lamborghini entered a tunnel and the battle disappeared. The ominous echo of our engine was soon joined by the roar of the two other cars. Suddenly Ginevra screamed, losing focus for the first time. I turned toward her and my heart leapt to my throat. She was fluttering her hands over the steering wheel. "What's wrong?!" I cried, trying to grab the wheel as the car barreled out of the tunnel at breakneck speed. Behind me, Simon had overtaken the Zonda.

"The fire! It's burning hot! Don't touch it! Don't touch the wheel!!"

I looked at the steering wheel, bewildered. It was suddenly clear: Ginevra was under attack. "Gwen! Gwen! Listen to me!" I shook her shoulder while trying to keep the car on the road. But it was impossible; Ginevra was hysterically jamming her foot on the accelerator. The Lamborghini plunged off the road and into the trees. "Gwen! You've got to listen to me! It's not happening!" I shouted in an attempt to reassure her. "Everything's fine! There is no fire, you're not burning!" A tree ripped the driver's-side mirror off the car. *We were going to crash.* "Block your mind, damn it!"

My words finally penetrated the shield around her mind. Ginevra regained control of herself and grabbed the wheel. She swerved and skidded to a halt, dodging a tree a second before hitting it full on. I closed my eyes, relief flooding through me.

"I'm sorry," she whispered, letting her head fall back against the headrest. "I had no idea she was so . . ." She shut her eyes, clearly trying to banish the memory of the terrible sensation that had possessed her. Simon and the blond shot by us on the road flanking the woods at an insane speed.

"Breathe," I said, well aware of how the experience had shaken her.

But Ginevra started the engine, the light in her eyes fiercer than ever. "There's no time to breathe." The wheels spun threateningly, raising a cloud of dust, and the car took off through the forest.

At first the other two cars were blurry specks racing ahead in the distance, emitting sparks and swerving wildly, but the Lamborghini quickly caught up to them. We could see a single stream of energy flowing between the Zonda and the Bugatti. I held my breath but then noticed the beam was coming from Simon's palm. The blond Angel was resisting it with equal strength and the air between them trembled with energy. Simon attacked more ferociously, forcing the other car to swerve onto a side road.

Ginevra tried to pull up alongside Simon but braked when the Zonda reappeared on the overpass we'd just gone under. The blond swerved suddenly and the car flew off the bridge and over the low roof of the Bugatti in front of us. "My God! She drives even worse than you do!" I shouted, panic gripping me. The Zonda crashed back onto the road. Its door burst open and snapped off. "Look out!" I bit my lip.

Simon tried to dodge the door but it was too close. Shearing off his passenger side mirror, it continued to skid across the asphalt straight toward us, sparks flying. Ginevra steered around it, fire in her eyes.

As we sped by, the lake bordering the road churned and rose into a crystal wall. Nature itself seemed to be rebelling, a furious witness to the battle between two Angels in the service of Death. I shifted my attention back to the road. Fear pressed me back into my seat and I jammed my foot down on an imaginary brake pedal. Ahead of us, the gates of a railroad crossing were slowly descending.

"Oh my God, Gwen!"

Ignoring my protests, Ginevra shifted into sixth and stepped on the gas. I clapped my hands to my mouth as Simon, glued to the rear of the Zonda, slipped under the gates a split second before they lowered completely. Our way was now blocked but Ginevra continued to accelerate. I clenched my fists on my seat, my entire body stiff with panic and my lips moving quickly in a silent prayer. The Lamborghini was quite low-slung but I wasn't sure it could cross the tracks without smashing into the gates. Ginevra, on the other hand, didn't seem the least bit concerned. It was her against the train in a race we couldn't afford to lose.

We were scant yards from the tracks. "You can do it! You can do it! You can do it!" I urged her on, then held my breath and braced for the worst.

Ginevra's face twisted with rage. Her lips tightened and a curse unbecoming to her normally graceful demeanor escaped her. The car skidded to a dead stop parallel to the tracks. I flinched as the freight train sliced through the air.

"Damn it!" Ginevra pounded on the steering wheel with both hands.

I took a deep breath, my heart still trembling. "Did we lose them?" I asked, my voice unsteady.

"Don't count on it."

The Lamborghini zoomed off the highway and onto the flattened earth alongside the tracks, moving parallel to the train. From time to time, in the gap between one boxcar and the next, I could see the two automobiles chasing one other on the opposite side.

"Shit! The ground drops off up ahead!" My heart stopped beating when I heard Ginevra's snarl, but instead of slowing down she put the car in fourth and sped up.

"What are you doing? Stop!"

Ahead of us, the tracks continued onto a narrow bridge over a gaping ravine that looked like a giant had taken a bite out of the land. There was no way to get to the other side from where we were now.

"Gwen! Stop! Damn it! There's a ravine up ahead! You've got to stop!"

"Brace yourself as hard as you can! This time I can do it!"

"What the—" My body instinctively flattened itself against the seat as the Lamborghini leapt forward, challenging the train. "Oh my God! What are you doing, Gwen? We're going to crash! You can't—you can't mean to jump it?!" Ginevra said nothing, her eyes locked on the ravine ahead of us. The Lamborghini overtook the train. "You can't jump the ravine, Gwen! Tell me you don't mean to jump it!!"

The ground opened up in front of us like a demon opening its jaws, ready to swallow us. "Oh my God! Oh my God! Oh my God!"

Ginevra swerved brusquely and the car careened right, skidding up onto the tracks. The train whistle blasted behind us. I leaned out to look at the empty space below us as shivers ran through my body. Closing my eyes, I leaned back in my seat, gasping for air. "Has anybody ever told you you're utterly insane?"

Ginevra turned to look at me, a complicit smile spreading across her lips. "A few times." She saw something over my shoulder and her expression darkened. The blond Angel must be behind us. Her stubbornness far exceeded our expectations. Simon's continued attacks couldn't stop her, and she barely left him enough time to defend himself against her offensive.

A loud blast shook me out of my thoughts. Another train was rushing toward us along the opposite tracks, sounding its whistle in an ominous warning.

"Damn it!" The Lamborghini slowed just long enough for Ginevra to downshift as the locomotive behind us thundered toward us, then swerved sharply to the left, crashing down onto the ground on the other side of the ravine. The second train zoomed by like a ghost and disappeared behind the first.

All at once there was a huge explosion, followed by a loud screech. The ground shook beneath the Lamborghini's tires. I jumped in my seat in shock: a fireball had struck the train. It was threatening to derail and hit us.

"Christ, Simon. Be careful!" Ginevra's voice sounded worried, but she didn't allow it to affect her driving, simultaneously accelerating and pulling on the chromed handbrake to make the car sideslip. I held on as best I could as the car tilted onto its side, continuing alongside the train at top speed as Ginevra controlled our angle with the steering wheel. "And to think Evan always used to say the drifting brake was useless!" she cried excitedly. I bit my lip to push back the memory of Evan, afraid the Angel might use it to her advantage. "Damn it! The cops are here," Ginevra grumbled.

"Huh? Where?" I couldn't see any cop cars. She must have picked up on the officers' thoughts. We couldn't risk involving innocent people, not to mention what would happen if we drew attention to ourselves.

With incredible agility Ginevra downshifted into third. The tires squealed and the pistons screamed as if they would burst out of the engine. The Lamborghini took off like a missile in front of the police car and crossed the tracks in front of the train a nanosecond before it derailed. The police leapt forward in hot pursuit but the runaway train instantly cut them off. I leaned back in my seat in time to see the cruiser spinning around after being clipped by the iron giant.

"His doughnut's going to go down the wrong pipe." Ginevra smiled at me, easing the tension a little. We turned onto a highway and set off after Simon and the Subterranean.

The roar of our cars was like a war cry that instantly cleared the highway of other drivers. The Zonda tried to pull back and approach us, but Simon blocked it with his Bugatti. Right in front of us, the gate on the back of a long cargo truck broke open, dumping a massive amount of dirt on the road. As soon as the driver realized he was losing his load, he slammed on the brakes and slowed to a stop. He started to get out, but found the Zonda zooming toward him. The man paled and stepped back, leaving the door open. Meanwhile, Simon sped up on the opposite side.

A shriek escaped me. "Gwen!" Simon had spun his car around and was facing the Zonda. The two cars collided head-on. The Angel found

Simon in front of her, his gun aimed straight at her face. Shots rang out as the Bugatti danced backwards across the asphalt, propelled by the Zonda. I squirmed in my seat as Simon pushed out the cracked windshield. Beside me Ginevra flinched. I knew she was seeing through Simon's eyes.

"What's wrong?!" I shouted, panicking.

"She's not in the car."

I leaned out the broken window to see for myself and the ice-cold wind lashed my skin. "Simon!" I screamed, to warn him of the danger.

The blond Angel materialized on the roof of the Bugatti, dressed entirely in gray. Grabbing Simon with one hand, she yanked him out of the car through its shattered windshield. It was easy to see she'd been trained to kill. The two Subterraneans began to fight on the roof as the two cars beneath them continued to move at top speed all on their own. Simon clutched his weapon firmly but she dodged his shots one after the other. Like a small semi-automatic, the transparent compartment in its center contained several poisoned bullets. I wondered if she also had a secret weapon. What if the Màsala had armed her against other Subterraneans? What if she too had a supply of poison capable of killing Simon? Horrified, I put my hands to my mouth. I couldn't let him die too. In a matter of months I had already killed off half the family.

Ginevra slammed on the brakes, making the tires squeal against the asphalt as a warning to Simon. Up ahead, the road curved sharply to one side and ran along the edge of a deep gully. Still gripping the gun, Simon rolled off the roof and leapt to the ground. The Angel also noticed the imminent danger and glanced at our car, flashing an ominous smile at Ginevra. "One down," she mouthed, provocation burning in her eyes as she dove through the windshield of Simon's Bugatti and agilely maneuvered the car away from the gully, allowing her Zonda to sail into the void.

Ginevra raced to pick Simon up. "She took my car. Now she's seriously pissed me off," he growled, his eyes burning with rage. Ready to kill, he leapt onto the roof of the Lamborghini and Ginevra peeled out after the blond Angel, reaching her in moments thanks to Simon's control of the elements. Ahead of us was a double-decker car-carrier trailer filled with identical cars. Simon slapped the top of the Lamborghini twice and Ginevra nodded. They had obviously formulated a plan.

"What's happening?" I asked anxiously. What was she about to do?

Ginevra gripped the steering wheel as the corners of her mouth curved into a sly smile. "We're wrapping up this hunt."

A violent crash drew my attention to the road and my heart leapt to my throat. A dozen vehicles were sliding off the trailer. As though we were a rock in the middle of a stream, the cars rolled past us one by one without hitting us. Meanwhile, the trailer continued as though nothing had happened. Simon must have been controlling the driver's mind so he wouldn't notice anything. Once the carrier was empty, a loading ramp slid down from the upper deck. Sparks flew. Only then, to my horror, did I realize what Simon had in mind. Before I could protest, Ginevra pressed her foot down on the accelerator, pinning me in my seat, raced up the ramp and soared through the air over the trailer. Simon leapt off the Lamborghini onto the roof of his Bugatti, piloted by the blond Subterranean.

I lurched forward violently when we hit the ground. Ginevra laughed as I gaped at her in disbelief. "Was that really necessary?" I asked. "Couldn't Simon simply have materialized on top of his car?"

She laughed again. "But why? We're having so much fun!" she replied, bursting with enthusiasm. Despite everything, I had to admit I was dizzy with excitement. I sank back into my seat, the Lamborghini roaring like a lion as it pulled up behind the Bugatti. Our enemy was zigzagging violently in an attempt to shake Simon off, but he clung tightly to the roof. Determined to put an end to the battle, he drew his gun but the Angel swerved and the weapon flew out of his hands, shattering under our tires.

"Shit! He lost it!" Ginevra fumed.

"But you gave him more than one, right?" I said anxiously, refusing to accept defeat.

"I read Simon's mind. He left the others in the car." The second the words were out of her mouth, Ginevra's eyes widened as she realized the danger Simon was in.

A shiver ran through me. Before we could try to stop him, Simon leaned down over the windshield to find the Angel aiming a gun straight at his forehead. Horror spread over Ginevra's face and she let out a whimper.

I covered my mouth with my hands, blinded by desperation. It couldn't happen again—not to Simon. Time seemed to stop as I stared at the scene, horrified: Simon on the roof, motionless and defenseless, facing the enemy who was about to kill him. Like a mirror, Ginevra's eyes reflected her boyfriend's terror. I could see him silently touching her mind, sending her a final farewell.

I held my breath, frozen in sheer terror, but the Angel vanished unexpectedly, leaving us all stunned. Only a second had gone by since she'd pressed the gun to Simon's forehead, but to me it had felt like an eternity of agony.

Ginevra let out a moan of pure suffering and pulled the car up, her hands shaking. I'd never seen her so upset. Simon grabbed the steering wheel of his own car to avoid going off the road and slipped in through the windshield. The Bugatti slid sideways and skidded to a halt a few yards ahead of us. Ginevra leapt out of the Lamborghini before it stopped, and the two met midway in an embrace that was so desperate, so intense and intimate I had to look away.

I rubbed my arms and realized they were trembling. When I looked back at Simon and Ginevra, they were standing in the middle of the road as though no one else existed. Simon held her close, one hand behind her neck, their foreheads touching. Neither spoke, lost in a silence all their own. Inside me a voice clamored, still terrified by the danger Simon had just faced. I gave them a few more moments and then walked over to them, discovering that my legs were trembling too.

"I would never have let her do it," Ginevra whispered. "Even if it meant making her head explode, I would never have let her. It all happened so fast, that's all. I was afraid that—"

"Simon!" I exclaimed. He extended an arm to welcome me into his embrace. I clung to him, trying to express all my concern and gratitude for how fiercely he'd fought for me and the risks he'd taken to save me. "What happened?" I asked, my voice breaking from the fear of losing another person I cared about.

Simon and Ginevra looked at each other. "She was pointing the gun at me," he explained. "She could have killed me right then and there, and for a second I thought she was going to. Then, enunciating really clearly, she said, 'Checkmate.' She looked me right in the eye, then dropped the gun and disappeared. This whole thing obviously amuses her." Ginevra's face darkened and I could see her losing herself in the intensity of Simon's memory.

"She didn't say anything else?" I insisted, looking at them one after the other.

Simon nodded and stared at me, his face somber, as though resolutely shouldering the full burden of the message intended for me. "'Until the next match.'"

A shudder of foreboding turned my blood to ice. There would be no escape.

BLOOD RED

January 16

I've been staring at this ivory page for fifteen minutes, hoping to find some comfort in my diary. I'm waiting for my thoughts to come unstuck so I can unburden myself, but they seem to be frozen. This morning the risk of losing Simon was a brutal, unexpected blow that threatened to drag me down into the dark pit I've been trying to grope my way out of ever since I lost everything—since I lost Evan.

I'm so tired that sometimes sleep drags me away like a seashell rocked by the small waves at the water's edge. Strangely enough, I only realized after I wrote down today's date that tomorrow is my birthday. Like I care. There are far bigger things on my mind right now. Even though I knew Ginevra was monitoring my every thought when we were at the table, I couldn't keep myself from stealing glances at Simon as he lay stretched out on the living-room couch. This morning made me realize something: there's a very real danger of losing one of them. The image of Ginevra's terrified face in my mind still makes me shudder. They've both been endlessly loyal to me even though there's nothing connecting them to me any more, and—most importantly—in spite of the fact that I don't deserve their protection in the first place. Why are they doing it? They've brought me nothing but happiness while I, on the other hand, have brought them nothing but death and destruction, putting them in danger and jeopardizing their relationship. And yet the bond between us wasn't severed after Evan's death, like I expected—like I feared. Quite the opposite: in spite of everything, they've both kept protecting me, risking their lives day after day to save mine. And for what? How can they consider me worthy of their protection? I wonder when they're going to realize I've taken everything from them . . . and that I'm going to keep on doing it in spite of my best efforts not to.

Evan. Drake. Whose turn will it be when we play the next match? I do nothing but ask myself that, because I'm sure the game will go on until I die and put an end to this war with my own blood. For some unknown reason, someone wants my life. They've decided I need to die and they won't stop until they've taken me. So what sense is there in prolonging this agony, in risking the lives of the people I love most? There will never be peace, not ever. In the end it's bound to happen, even with all Simon and Ginevra's efforts to protect me. But meanwhile there will be more defeats, more victims . . . You can't always dodge a bullet and not expect someone else to get hurt. The anguish I saw in Ginevra's eyes when that Angel pointed the gun at Simon's head gripped my heart, which I thought had died, and threw it into a cold, dark cell. I realized at that moment I couldn't bear to cause Ginevra the same pain that fetters my soul. I wish I could find a way to keep them safe, a way to fight instead of standing passively by as they wage a war that's mine and mine alone. I wish I could turn back time and stop myself from making the mistake that drained the life from me. Instead I have no choice but to stay here and look on. Life gives. Life takes away. But it's partly our fault too. Our decisions, our mistakes, decide what we ultimately end up with. Sometimes I try to imagine what that cursed day would have been like if I'd been able to read Evan's note in time and keep all this torment from beginning in the first place. But no matter how many times I scream his name in my head I'm answered only by silence—a grim, gloomy silence that pierces my heart with its icy thorns, and I can't breathe because it hurts, it hurts too much. I clench my fists but all I grasp is emptiness. Bitter solitude plagues my heart. I keep seeing Evan's face in my mind, and all I want is to

The steady dripping of water woke me and I found myself on a hard stone floor. My side ached and my head throbbed. I tried to get up. It felt like the dampness in the thick-walled room had sunk into my bones. Only a dim light illuminated the cold, dark place.

I went over to its only window, which was protected by thick bars. Looking outside, I found I was incredibly high up. Below me, trees stretched out to infinity like a dark, threatening mantle. In spite of how far above them I was, though, I could tell something was wrong: the trunks were stunted and twisted as though the ground were poisoned. I backed away from the window, feeling a powerful sense of foreboding tingle beneath my skin.

A loud noise captured my attention.

I crossed the room with long strides but tripped over the irregular stone slabs and crashed into something hard. I felt its surface as my eyes struggled to penetrate the darkness. *Wood.* It wasn't a wall, it was a door. I could have cheered, but a voice made my heart stand still. I stared at the door, my eyes glazing over in shock.

Evan . . .

My lips had struggled to say his name aloud, but a furious whirlwind of emotions had struck me, paralyzed me, as my hands trembled against the door. I stood there listening and another voice came through the wood. A woman's. I froze. After a moment, I heard it again. Sensual. Velvety. Hypnotic.

No. It couldn't be true. I desperately searched for the latch and found a small bolt in the middle of the door. I fiddled with it until I managed to open a small view panel, also barred. My body turned to ice: Evan was pressed back against a stone wall and the woman was circling him like a hawk, stroking his bare chest.

"No!" I cried. The woman's eyes darted to mine, razor-sharp fragments of amber that illuminated a pale face framed by a cascade of hair of the same color. Evan didn't seem to have noticed me. He looked drugged or under the effect of some dark spell. The woman kept her eyes trained on me while she continued to stroke Evan's body as though to provoke me. Full of fury, I gripped the bars impotently.

There was something familiar about the woman's features, though I was certain I'd never seen her before. She touched her lips to his neck and made her way up to his chin, her eyes still watching me with feline stealth.

"No! Evan!" I screamed, clenching the bars in my fists as though I could crush them with the strength of my desperation. At the sound of my voice Evan raised his head, but before he could see me the woman shot to the door of my cell at warp speed. I could see annoyance at the interruption in her fierce gaze. Holding my breath, I tried to resist her commanding gaze and deep, hypnotic eyes. They were evil and had the power to subjugate. The woman seemed to probe inside me; suddenly her lips curved into a cunning smile. She moved aside slightly and it was then that I saw the shackles around Evan's wrists that chained him to the stone wall. I covered my mouth with my hands as he writhed, his terrified, helpless eyes staring into mine.

"You're the one who did this to him."

I jumped. The woman was behind me now, inside my cell. She gently pushed the hair from my face but I couldn't take my eyes off Evan. His skin was covered with bruises and cuts from the iron shackles gripping his wrists. His torn jeans were smeared with dirt and blood.

"Why don't you go to him? Can't you see he needs you?"

I whirled around, but the woman had disappeared. An eerie noise crept in through the silence of the cold walls. Fear kept me from turning back toward Evan. It was the low growl of an animal prepared to attack. I peered through the darkness and thought I saw a glint in the darkest corner of the cell. Something was lurking there, watching me. Something sinister and deadly, a creature ready to devour me. I flattened myself against the wall, a jolt of pure terror running through me and, as though it smelled my fear, a dark shape leapt from the shadows with an aggressive snarl, coming at me so fast it took my breath away. Its claws sank into my belly, tearing my flesh.

I shrieked with pain and opened my eyes, slowly recognizing the walls of Evan's room. My hands were still pressed against my belly, I was panting, and my body was covered with sweat.

The red patch on the panther's paw was still vivid in my mind. I forced myself to breathe and slowly lifted my top. My belly was still throbbing, burning as though the panther's claws had actually torn through me. I stared at my birthmark, where the pain seemed to be coming from. I touched it cautiously and it burned my hand. It was incandescent, like a fire was burning inside it. I stared at my trembling fingers. Could the Angel have done this to me?

In the silence of the night, murmured voices gradually became audible, making my blood run cold. I tilted my head, listening, hoping it was just another aftereffect of my nightmare. It came again: the most sinister sound I'd ever heard. Dozens of voices whispering, joining together in a dark, indecipherable prayer. A shudder of apprehension ran through my body, yet part of me felt helplessly drawn to it. I found myself automatically pushing the covers aside and looking out the doorway into the silent darkness. Slowly I crossed the hall, guided by the bloodcurdling sound—an ancestral call from which I couldn't break free. I longed only to reach it, merge with it.

"Treh. Immuaarimet. Lohe. Keh. Kuta Sih. - Treh. Immuaarimet. Lohe. Keh. Kuta Sih."

The sound led me to Ginevra's door. I hesitated, my hand resting on the knob, as though my mind were torn equally between two forces and didn't know which one to give in to. But then the dark chanting overpowered me and I stepped into the room. A dim glow instantly captured my attention—a summons that was irresistible, though it came from behind a door I knew was forbidden. The murmur grew louder, urging me to follow it, and my body moved toward Ginevra's vault. Driven by some arcane power of enchantment, I walked through the forbidden door and found myself in a garden at dusk. Something drew my attention to the center of a giant glass case and I yearned to reach it as the voices flowed through my mind, chanting faster and faster. In a mechanical gesture that felt inexplicably natural, I lifted the cover off the case and the voices melted into a single one that seemed to come from Ginevra's serpent. I stopped to stare at him, hypnotized by the magnetism he emanated, as if he were the most beautiful creature on earth. The animal slowly slithered onto a trunk, his gracefulness rivaled only by Ginevra's. He rose, swaying almost imperceptibly in front of my face in a hypnotic dance, his green eyes locked on mine. I sensed a mysterious energy flow into me through his gaze and I wanted to meld with him. I was at the mercy of a dark spell from which I didn't want to be released, some sort of powerful black magic that made my blood boil. His voice whispered a mysterious message that seemed to come from the depths of the earth.

One of us. There is no escape. It has begun. One of us. There is no escape. It has begun.

"GEMMA!!" A furious vortex sucked me back and hurled me against Ginevra's bedroom wall as the vault door slammed shut. I found myself on the floor, my palms on the ground and my breathing ragged.

"What the hell were you thinking?!" Ginevra shouted as she pulled me to my feet.

"I . . . I don't know," I admitted wretchedly. Suddenly I couldn't remember why I was there. Her presence seemed to have broken the enchantment I'd been under. "I *heard* him."

"What are you talking about?"

"The serpent. He was whispering something."

"You're raving." Ginevra touched my forehead, frightened. "Holy Christ! Your skin is on fire! You're burning up! Come on, let's get you to bed." Absorbed in her own thoughts, she put her arm around my shoulder and led me to my room. She helped me under the covers, looking at my trembling legs. After carefully checking the baby's heartbeat to make sure he was all right, she said, "Now, would you tell me why the fuck you went into the vault?! You have no idea of the danger you put yourself in!"

Simon rushed into the room. He was bare-chested, his perspiration bringing out the swell of his muscles. For a moment his presence left me dazed and I found myself staring at him: a fair-haired avenger Angel with disheveled locks hanging over his forehead. They reminded me so much of Evan's. "What's going on?" He came over, looking anxious as he wiped the sweat off with a gym towel.

"I found Gemma in the Copse, face to face with my serpent."

Simon paled instantly as his brow wrinkled and his eyes shot to mine. "How is that possible? How is she still alive?"

"I don't know," Ginevra replied, her voice grim.

"How the hell did she manage to get inside it in the first place? It has an armored door!" he added.

"That's what I'm wondering too." Ginevra peered at me, her eyes icy.

"I think the door was open," I managed to say before my voice went faint, "but I'm not completely sure. I don't remember very clearly what drove me there. I was awake, but it was like I was sleeping, in the grip of some sort of alien energy that forced me to move. I could sense its evil influence but couldn't resist it. Where were you two?" I asked, turning to Simon because it was hard for me to hold Ginevra's intense gaze.

She was the one who answered. "In the workout room. Where else would we be in the middle of the night? You were sleeping and we had to train. We need to be ready."

"Apparently, we need to watch over her at night too." Simon's tone was caring but left no room for objections.

"Do you guys think it was the Executioner?"

I noticed an unusual flicker of uneasiness in Ginevra's eye. Simon, on the other hand, seemed to have no doubt about it. "She waited until the two of us were distracted and then led you to the serpent so it could kill you. It was another of her tricks. It's a good thing Ginevra got there in time. Still, I wonder why the serpent didn't bite you."

Ginevra had been lost in thought but his last words snapped her out of it. "It really is strange. He's never behaved like that with anyone before," she admitted, frowning. Suddenly she composed herself. "Let's think about it tomorrow. Simon and I will take turns watching over you so you can rest. We can always work out individually with attack simulation scenarios."

Evan had shown them to me only once, but I well remembered how real the simulation scenarios were. The walls took on a new appearance, giving you the impression you were in another place, another dimension. You could be anywhere and with anyone. The guys often used them to work out because they weren't just passive images but solid figures that interacted with them, responding to their actions and decisions, recreating true-to-life situations like frontal attacks. The swimming pool was enchanted too. Ginevra had conceived it out of her innate love of nature. You could experience swimming in a river or a magnificent lake at the foot of a volcano. All you had to do was press a button to choose an illusion. They looked like holograms, but it was actually magic.

"Try to get some rest. It's four in the morning. You can still get in a few hours of sleep."

I sank my head into the pillow and pulled the covers up to my chin as Ginevra's voice faded away, dissolving into the darkness.

THE POWER OF THE MIND

After my sixteenth birthday and getting my license, I always imagined that eighteen would be an even more important milestone—a special day, after which I would feel different. Instead I felt nothing new. Just the opposite, actually. The painful fire that burned in my chest raged higher as soon as I opened my eyes. From the minute I woke up I did nothing but think of Evan, more ardently and more desperately than any day before. I had lost him forever. Nothing else mattered to me, and the fact that everyone kept telling me what a big deal my eighteenth birthday was only reminded me of it. *Because he wouldn't be there with me.*

Frozen in that torment, I jumped when I heard Jeneane's voice behind me: "Can we help the birthday girl celebrate?" she said cheerfully as she, Faith, Brandon, and Jake sat down at our table, their chairs squeaking.

"Sure, but maybe you're confusing me with someone else. I have nothing to celebrate." The words escaped me with a note of bitterness.

"Come on, Gemma!" Brandon exclaimed. "You only turn eighteen once!"

"Hey." Seated next to me, Faith rested her hand on my knee. "It's been months. You have to get over it. You're only eighteen! Why don't you try to move on?" she whispered, noting the sadness that had filled my eyes. Her concern was so sweet I forced myself to hide my anguish and smile at her.

"And what's this about not wanting to celebrate?" Jeneane pulled out a plastic container and put it on the table as Faith smiled beside me. She took off the lid and handed each of us a big chocolate muffin.

"They're huge!" I remarked.

Faith smiled, slightly embarrassed. "We knew you would never come to a party, so we decided to bring the party to you!" she said, sticking a candle into my muffin.

"Guys, you shouldn't have," I said, touched.

Ginevra, on my other side, smiled. "This way you can't refuse."

"And don't try to make a break for it. We've got a rope and we're prepared to tie you to your chair if necessary." Brandon winked at me, leaning over the table to light the candle with his lighter. His remark made me laugh. What on earth would they be doing with a rope at school?

"Faith made the muffins," Jake chimed in, looking at her fondly. Her cheeks turned pink.

"Yeah, well," she began, embarrassed, "it's not an actual birthday cake, but I'm better at making these."

"They're perfect." I smiled at her. "I'm really moved. It was so sweet of you guys to think of this. I figured you wouldn't even remember it was my birthday."

"We couldn't have forgotten even if we'd wanted to." Brandon tilted his chair back, his hands clasped behind his neck. "Peter wouldn't stop yapping about it all week lo—" He flinched. Jeneane must have kicked him under the table. Though I hadn't spent much time with my friends lately, some things hadn't changed.

Jake cleared his throat. "Here he comes now." I smiled and shifted my attention to Peter, who was heading toward our table, his hands tucked into the pockets of his Blue Bombers sweatshirt.

"Here!" Jeneane slid a muffin in his direction. "There's one for you too."

"Hey." Peter nodded in greeting, looking me in the eye.

"This sucks," Brandon grumbled. "I thought he wasn't coming. I wanted his too." He said it under his breath, but it was right during a lull in the conversation, so we all heard him. Jeneane kicked him again.

"Ow! Would you stop kicking me?!"

His expression was so comical none of us could help laughing, but Jeneane, as practical as always, shut them up. "Okay, okay. We don't have much time. She has to make her wish."

It's a wishing well. Make a wish.

"Gemma, come on!" Faith encouraged me, pulling me from my memories. "You need to blow out the candle. Close your eyes and make a wish."

I bit my lip and blew out the flame. I was all out of wishes, except for the one that would never come true—to see Evan one last time.

"Oh yeah!" Brandon held his muffin protectively as though someone might try to take it from him. "Finally we can dig in!" He scooted his chair back, probably afraid Jeneane might kick him again, and laughter rose from the table.

I looked up at Peter, noticing how tender his expression became when he smiled. His birthday text had been the first one I'd found on my phone that morning. It had been sent at 2:13. Since the accident on Whiteface Mountain, we hadn't spoken a word about what had happened, but he continued to shoot Ginevra strange looks. Sometimes I was afraid he might discover something about them and their world.

"You give her the present yet?" Peter asked.

"What present?" I exclaimed. "Really, guys, you didn't need to get me anything."

Jeneane pulled out a thin, elegant, black box. My eyes lit up.

"I told you to wrap it! She's already figured out what it is!" Faith said.

"That was just the reaction I was hoping for, if you want to know," Jeneane said defensively, already able to tell from my face that I loved it.

"You got me a Kindle!?"

"It was Peter's idea," Faith told me with a wink. She looked prettier than ever with her long red ponytail and fair complexion that brought out her green eyes.

When I looked at Peter he smiled and a dimple appeared in his cheek.

"Amazon is so awesome. I should use it more often," Jeneane went on. "It was delivered in two days and filled with books in two minutes flat!"

"There are books on it? Aw, guys . . ."

Though I felt guilty, I couldn't resist the urge to turn it on right away and find out what they had downloaded. I couldn't believe it. There were lots of my favorite titles and authors. Peter knew me all too well; he must have checked Amazon for my wish list. I would wait before reading some of the books, the ones that were bound to make me cry a river, since I already had enough reason to cry. In my friends' defense, they couldn't have known the plots like I did.

I held the eReader up to my nose and sniffed it, like I always did with paper books. Ever since I was little I'd been incredibly drawn to the smell of books. Back then I hadn't yet learned that it was because of the secret allure of ink. "There are so many titles!"

"We absolutely had to cheer you up."

"Thanks, you totally did." I smiled and Jeneane clapped her hands, bouncing in her chair. I glanced at Peter when I saw that *Jane Eyre* was on the list of titles. It hadn't been on my wish list because I'd already read it a million times, but he knew it was my all-time favorite book and had included it anyway so I could always have it with me. He smiled and winked at me.

"This is the one they made a movie out of, that one we saw last summer, right?" Faith asked, pointing at the second-to-last book of a saga I really loved about demon hunters. Actually, I had already read it but must have forgotten to take it off my list.

"Yeah, that's the one."

"Ah, Jace! I'm still in love with him!" Jeneane sighed. Jealous, Brandon pulled her close, making the whole group laugh.

I had also already read the story about Tatiana and Alexander, but I couldn't wait to reread it and continue with the trilogy because the first book was one of my favorites. I'd cried like a baby for hours.

The shrill sound of the bell made us all frown. "Oh, no! So soon?" Faith groaned.

"Why don't we all hang out at my house tonight?" Jake suggested. "My mom'll be visiting her sister and my dad's working down at the station. We could have a *Teen Wolf* marathon."

"One thing at a time, okay?" I replied, a bit overwhelmed by all the attention. And to think that when I'd first proposed watching the series, Jake had flat out refused. He'd ended up getting as hooked as me.

"Are you sure you don't want to celebrate tonight?" Ginevra got up from her chair. "We could do something nice, intimate, just a few friends and your parents."

"I really don't think it's a good idea," I said. "Besides, my parents already called me this morning. They invited us to lunch—me, you, and Simon, that is."

"Well, see you in class then, Gemma!" Faith waved goodbye as she walked off with the rest of the group.

"Sure, and thanks again, guys!" Jake flashed me a smile and Brandon winked at me before leaving the cafeteria.

"Hey, Gemma!" Peter came over to us and walked alongside me. "Think I could stop by your place this afternoon?"

I shot a fleeting glance at Ginevra to see what she thought, and Peter noticed. "It won't take long," he said.

"Okay, why not? You know where to find it."

"Perfect." Unexpectedly he stroked my palm, clasped my hand, and left a light kiss on the corner of my mouth. "Happy birthday," he whispered, never taking his eyes from mine.

Stunned by the gesture, it was only after Peter had walked away that I felt something hot in my palm. I instinctively hid my hand in my pocket, wondering what it was.

"What did he give you?" Ginevra asked, looking at my pocket with curiosity. Nothing escaped her. When I hesitated she instantly raised her hands in understanding. "Okay, okay! It's none of my business."

The classroom filled up quickly as Mr. Wilson, the Spanish teacher, stood with his back to us, writing the topic he was about to explain on the board. I struggled to focus on his voice and did pretty well for the first fifteen minutes or so, but then my eyes began to dart to the clock on the wall in front of me. A tingle spread over my palms, so strong I rubbed them together to make it go away, but it was no use. A moment later, an eerie murmur of voices sent a shiver rushing down my spine and left me with goosebumps.

"What was that noise?" Alarmed, I turned toward Ginevra who was sitting to my right.

"I didn't hear anything," she whispered back, looking around the room. "Relax, Gemma. She's not going to attack you in front of all these people. You're safe here."

I nodded, gripping my pen, and opened my notebook, forcing myself to concentrate on something other than the ghosts haunting me. I distractedly jotted down a few notes but the whispering started up again, whirling more and more frenetically in my mind. Taking a deep breath, I tried to drive it away but only felt more drawn to it. I wanted to listen to the sound. It seemed to promise to take me to a safe place far away, lulling me into a dreamy state where every painful thought faded.

The sound grew more intense, crisper, and I let myself go, losing myself in that chorus of low voices. I longed to be part of it. I sensed something hidden in the voices that offered me the possibility of unequalled powers. Behind the sound lurked darkness; I could feel it summoning me. I couldn't resist the mystical attraction. It suddenly occurred to me that I *already* felt part of it. It had put down roots inside me long ago and had been growing all the while.

Powerful. Ancestral. Dark.

One of us. There is no escape. It has begun. One of us. There is no escape. It has begun . . .

"Gemma . . . Miss Bloom, do you feel all right?"

My eyelids fluttered as I focused on the teacher's face. He was staring at me with concern. Dazed, I glanced around the room, trying to figure out what had happened and why everyone's attention was suddenly directed at me.

My classmates continued to stare at me, whispering to each other.

"Did you hear that?"

"What's up with her?"

"She was babbling like she's crazy or something. "

"Did you see her eyes? They looked really strange. She was staring into space while her hand kept moving all over the paper. Gave me the creeps."

"Yeah, she looked possessed. It's gonna give me nightmares tonight."

"It's gonna give me nightmares *forever!*"

"I wonder what she wrote."

"Poor thing. I feel so sorry for her."

"She hasn't gotten over it yet. And did you hear she's pregnant?"

"Miss Bloom, I asked if you felt all right," the teacher insisted. "Would you like me to call you a doctor?"

"Forget the doctor. Get an exorcist," someone said, covering their words with fake coughs. Everybody laughed. I looked down at my notebook and jumped at the symbol I saw scrawled on the page. There was something familiar about those lines and yet I was sure I'd never seen the drawing before. How had it gotten there? Could I possibly have drawn it *myself?* Even Ginevra was gaping at me. Though she was trying hard not to let it show, she seemed shaken. She was also probably wondering what was wrong with me. Meanwhile, the class continued to gossip.

"They say he ran off because of the baby."

"Yeah, but then they found his car."

"He staged it all just to get away from her, if you ask me."

I closed my eyes, devastated.

"Idiots." Ginevra murmured one curse after another as she reached for my hand under the desk. "I don't know what's keeping me from setting them all on fire." She shut the notebook. "Gemma." She squeezed my hand, encouraging me to look at her as I tried to emerge from my trance. "Mr. Wilson, maybe I should take Gemma home. She hasn't been feeling very well lately."

"That's a good idea." He felt my forehead and jumped. "*Madre de Dios,* she's burning up! Why would she come to school in this condition?! Take her to the nurse's office immediately!"

"She wasn't running a fever this morning. She just needs to go home. My boyfriend is a doctor," she lied. "He'll take care of her. If you'll just give us a permission slip . . ." Ginevra directed the power of her captivating gaze at the teacher who immediately gave in, entranced.

"Yes, of course. I'll fill it out right away."

Embarrassed, I tucked my fists into my sleeves as Ginevra helped me collect my things. I had never felt so awkward and out of place before. I forced myself to ignore the class's whispers as we walked out, followed by their stares.

"Where did you see that symbol?" Ginevra's voice sounded steady but I detected a trace of uneasiness she was trying hard to hide.

"I don't know. I must have dreamed it, I guess. Gwen, what's happening to me?" I pleaded, hoping she had an answer. "What is that symbol? And how did it end up in my notebook?"

Ginevra let out an exasperated sigh, as though she were hiding something from me and it was taking its toll on her. "It's like you get lost in some other dimension where I can't reach you. You sink into a trance state and I can't hear your thoughts because your mind is possessed. Right after that you get a fever. Come on." She squeezed my hand, but her words had accelerated my heart rate. "Let's go home."

Lunch had passed uneventfully, as though we were a normal family. Simon had turned out to be really funny, keeping up with all my dad's bad jokes. My fever had passed minutes after we left school, vanishing as quickly as it had come like it always did after my daytime trances. It was the same with the terrible nightmares of Evan that hunted me down like predators only to evaporate with the morning light.

I ran my fingers over the surface of the bathwater, watching the steam rise from the tub like a ghost. My parents had been less apprehensive than usual, welcoming me so calmly it caught me off guard. But then again, they didn't know my real mood. On days when I didn't stop by to visit they would call, asking Simon and Ginevra for news, and when I talked to them myself I was always careful not to let on too much about my problems. I felt kind of sorry for them because Ginevra had manipulated their minds so they would let me stay with her. But it was necessary. I couldn't destroy my parents' lives with my problems.

For my birthday they'd given me a gift card for a flight to any destination, with no expiration date. I had tried to refuse and managed to convince them I would never use it, especially in my condition, but they had insisted I keep it so that maybe soon I could at least visit my grandparents in Rochester. And so I'd put it away in a drawer along with my desire to celebrate.

The thought brought Peter to mind. I quickly dried my hands on a towel, leaned over the side of the tub, and searched the pocket of my jeans on the floor for his present. I clasped the small object between my fingers and pulled it out, curious. Under the soft spot lighting, the metal object sparkled in my damp hands like a tiny treasure.

A key.

It was very small—barely over an inch long. I turned it over, admiring the two letters interwoven in an intricate design that made it look like an antique. PG. Peter and Gemma. I clutched it tighter, wondering what he meant by it and imagining how much effort it must have taken him to find it. Peter never left anything to chance.

"Ow!" I gasped, suddenly in excruciating pain. My belly felt like it had been torn in two. The key fell from my hand and clattered onto the floor. I gripped the edge of the tub with one hand and clasped my abdomen with the other. It hurt so much I couldn't breathe.

I felt something hotter even than the bathwater on the inside of my thigh and froze, unable to look down, afraid of what I might see. Raising my hand from the tub, I slowly looked at it, petrified with fear. A crimson droplet dripped off my fingers and splashed back into the water with a sound that broke my heart.

Hot tears streamed down my cheeks and the pain that gripped my chest was so intense I thought my tears too must have been the color of blood. My baby. Something had happened to my baby. The water in the tub had slowly gone red, glimmering like a molten ruby. Sobbing, I thrashed my hands in the water, trying to push the blood away from me, but it was no use.

"Gwen! Help me! My baby! Please!! Help my baby! Gweeen!" I shrieked, stabbing pains piercing my belly. This time it was all over. I had killed Evan and now the baby too. The stress I had made him undergo had ended up killing him. "Gweeen!" I was on the verge of collapse, between the tears, my bloodied fingers, and the water that turned redder by the second, taking my baby from me. Taking all I had left of Evan. "Help me, please! Somebody help me!"

In a silent summons, light glinted off a pair of scissors that lay on the edge of the tub. I reached for them. I couldn't take it. I couldn't bear any more pain. It made no sense to deny myself the comfort of death if I had nothing more to live for. I opened the scissors, grabbed one of the blades and clenched my fist tight. The blood already on my fingers mingled with the blood that began to seep from my palm. It didn't matter, because soon I would no longer feel the pain. A murderer doesn't deserve to live . . .

"She's having another hallucination!"

The scissors flew from my hands and smashed against the wall.

"I lost him," my lips murmured, responding to the voice, though my glazed eyes couldn't see past the darkness into which I had fallen. "I lost my baby."

"Gemma, listen to me! She creates fears in your mind. Only with your mind can you destroy her. The fear is real only if you allow it to be. Fight back!"

"I lost my baby . . ."

"Look at me! *Look at me!*" Someone grabbed me by the shoulders and shook me hard. The instant my eyes met Ginevra's she held me tight. "You didn't lose him," she whispered tenderly, stroking my hair. "You didn't lose him."

Clinging to her words, I snapped out of it. I disentangled myself from her embrace and looked around. The water in the tub sparkled crystal-clear, tinged only by a few crimson droplets that had come from my palm.

Ginevra smiled at me and stroked my belly. "He's here. He's still inside you. I can hear him." I smiled, my eyes still full of tears. "His heart is beating like a tiny bird's, but he's strong."

"I thought . . . I thought he . . . I was about to . . . My God . . ." I covered my mouth with both hands and stared at Ginevra.

"It's not your fault." Ginevra pushed a strand of hair out of my face. Behind her, as still as a bronze statue, Simon was scrutinizing the room, his face stern and all his senses on guard. Relieved the baby was safe, I put both hands on my belly and looked around the room too, as though I could have perceived what had eluded both a Subterranean and a Witch.

All at once Simon lunged forward, moving so fast he was a blur, coming to a halt next to the wall and pressing his elbow against it.

Ginevra shot to her feet. The Angel suddenly materialized in Simon's iron grip, her lips curved into a ghoulish grin. I glowered at her. She'd been there all along, making me believe I had lost my baby so I would decide to take my own life. What kind of monster was capable of such evil?

"Fire . . ." Ginevra whispered, covering her arms with her hands. Judging from how pale her face had turned I guessed the Angel was attacking her again. In confirmation of my theory, the room burst into flames around Ginevra, showing me her fears. The fire rose up and blackened the walls as Simon, keeping a firm grip on the Angel, shouted at Ginevra to snap out of it. I covered myself with a bath towel and rushed over to shake her, desperate to tear her out of the darkness of insanity that had engulfed me until seconds ago. Who knew what Ginevra might do with her powers. What if the Angel made her believe Simon was an enemy? I shuddered at the thought. "Gwen! *Wake up!*"

I leapt back. The veins in her arms had swollen and something was coming out of her wrist. *Her serpent.* The animal dropped to the floor and moved toward the two Subterraneans. Simon tightened his grip on the enemy but his eyes wavered as Ginevra's serpent slithered up his ankle. Simon's worst nightmare.

Ginevra perceived the flash of terror that crossed the mind of her beloved and it snapped her out of her trance. Both the fire and the serpent instantly disappeared. "Simon!"

The Angel took advantage of Simon's distraction to escape from his iron grip. With lightning speed Ginevra whipped out two guns. Bullets peppered the stone wall from one end of the room to the other as she pursued our attacker. Simon caught up with the blond Angel at the far end of the room and pinned her against the wall. Ginevra threw him a gun. He caught it and jammed the barrel under the Angel's chin.

"Sorry." Simon raised an eyebrow, his eyes burning with satisfaction. "Your little mind games won't work on me." She froze, her proud gaze fixed on Simon's, clearly prepared to die.

"What are you waiting for, Simon?" Ginevra's insistent tone made it sound like a reproach, and yet he hesitated.

"I can't." Simon's jaw stiffened in frustration. He eased his grip on the gun but kept it trained on the Executioner. "I'm sorry—I can't do it."

"I don't see the problem." Ginevra flashed across the room and took Simon's place, pinning the Angel to the wall. "It won't be the first time for me." She cocked her gun and the metallic click echoed ominously through the silence.

"Wait!" I shouted.

Simon and Ginevra's eyes flew to mine, frowning slightly. I allowed the silence to build, drawing the gaze of our prisoner. "What if we don't kill her?" The Angel's eyes wavered in surprise.

I studied their faces. I could tell Ginevra was thirsting for revenge. Simon, on the other hand, seemed curious about my proposal. "Think about it: her death would just call down others." I looked from Simon to Ginevra. They were both torn, but for opposite reasons. "What if we kept her here?"

"It's a thought." Simon had guessed my plan. "It might work."

The blond Angel raised her chin a notch and Ginevra tightened her grip on the trigger. "Don't move, if you want to save your skin. I still don't know if I like the idea."

"Gwen, I've seen your serpent fuse with your flesh like he's a part of you. If his poison is capable of annihilating a Subterranean, your blood must be poisonous too." I let the sentence hang in the air, giving Ginevra a moment to let it sink in.

She seemed surprised by the implications of what I had said. "Poisonous, yes," she said, the shadow of a shrewd smile on her lips, "but not lethal."

"Think it would be enough to keep her under control for a while?"

A dark glint appeared in Ginevra's eyes and the mask that hid the Witch inside her momentarily slipped, letting her true nature emerge. "Let's find out, shall we?" Ginevra clenched her fist and drew her long fingernail across her palm. A scarlet trickle slid down her fingers. She pressed her hand against the mouth of the blond Angel who struggled in her grip, trying to resist.

"I told you to stay still," she ordered, raising her gun. "I can always change my mind."

The Angel gave in and stood still, staring at Ginevra defiantly until she moved her palm away from her bloodstained lips. The Angel spat, leaving a crimson splatter on the brown floor. "I am not a filthy vampire!"

When Ginevra let her go, the Angel doubled over and crumpled to her knees, weakened by the poison. I stared at the red splotch. The blood seemed to quiver with energy. It was a deep, hypnotic red with fine, golden, metallic-looking strands in it. That must have been the poison.

"What a shame." Ginevra leaned down to look her in the eye, unable to repress an evil grin. "I would have had loads of fun with crosses and wooden stakes." She pinned the Angel's wrists behind her back. "But I'm sure you and I will find other ways to amuse ourselves," she hissed.

I followed them downstairs to a passageway that led down from a trapdoor hidden in the floor of the workout room. "I had no idea this was here. Where'd it come from?" The walls and worn floor brought to my mind the terrible dream I'd had the night before. Torches in sconces that lit up as we neared them cast our shadows on the walls, transforming them into ghoulish silhouettes that looked like they might escape us and move with a will of their own.

"Torches? Seriously?" I whispered to Ginevra as Simon pushed the Angel down the foreboding passageway. "I mean, modern lighting wasn't good enough?"

Simon's lighthearted laugh echoed off the walls. "Don't bother, Gemma. I've already tried. With her it's a lost cause."

Ginevra shrugged, amused. "What can I say? Once in a while I get nostalgic for the old days." A loud noise made me jump. Simon had unbolted a heavy wooden door that looked like it opened into a medieval prison cell. I shot Ginevra another look of silent reproach and she held up her hands. "I wanted to recreate the atmosphere!"

I shook my head as Simon bound the Angel's hands with a chain that he attached to a ring set into the wall over her head, forcing her to keep her arms raised. "You mean to leave me down here?!" asked the Angel. She seemed disoriented from the effect of the poison.

"No. We're just trying it on for size. Then we'll let you go," Ginevra replied with bitter sarcasm. The Angel glared at her, her eyes full of contempt. At this, Ginevra walked up to her and bit her bottom lip.

"Want a little more?" A drop of blood swelled on her sensual mouth. The Angel's attitude changed as she grasped the threat, but Ginevra insisted, placing both hands on the sides of her head and looking her in the eye. "Drink," she commanded in her most entrancing voice. Staring at Ginevra as though she worshipped her, the Angel obeyed and sucked the blood from her lip. Simon smiled to himself and Ginevra winked at him as she left her adversary in a state of torpor.

"Come, Gemma," Simon told me, leaving the room as I stood stock-still beside the Angel, feeling a vague uneasiness. "We have to go." I walked past her, feeling her eyes on me like those of a vulture waiting to devour its prey. I couldn't hold back a shudder.

"Try not to do anything foolish while we're gone." Ginevra glared at her and slammed the door. In the lugubrious silence, the sound reverberated off all the walls like a clap of thunder shaking the sky before a storm. "Good night," Ginevra whispered maliciously, staring at her through the small barred window.

The torches died out behind us and darkness engulfed the cell and what it concealed.

A scream pierced the silence, but we sealed it inside.

SECRETS UNDER LOCK AND KEY

Back in the living room, we heard a knock on the front door and exchanged fleeting glances. "Someone's here," I murmured, like it wasn't obvious already.

"What a genius!" Simon tousled my hair playfully, visibly relaxed from having locked up the danger.

"It's for you." Ginevra looked at me and pulled Simon away by the hand, leaving me alone in the living room.

"Anybody home?" When I opened the door, Peter's fist was poised in midair. His eyes found mine. "Hey!" he lowered his hand and let it hang at his side.

"Pet, this really isn't a good time," I admitted regretfully. I knew him well enough to pick up on the disappointment that flashed across his face.

"All right. I can come back some other day," he said, careful not to look me in the eye.

I sighed. "No, come on in. Simon and Ginevra just went upstairs."

"You sure?" I nodded and a solitary dimple appeared near his smile. "I'd rather stay here in the yard, if you don't mind. Feel like coming outside?"

Tightening my lips, I nodded again and closed the door behind me. As we walked along the path, the only sound was the damp gravel crunching beneath our feet. A breath of wind made me jump. "What was that? Did you feel it too?"

"It was just the wind. You sure you're okay?"

I had to stop seeing ghosts everywhere. The Angel was locked up, so I had nothing to fear. For once, I could relax. "Of course, I'm great." I forced a laugh to banish the tension.

Peter sat on the low stone wall in the garden to the west of the house and I did the same, crossing my legs. "Did you find it?" he asked. I realized he was referring to the present he'd tucked into my palm as though it were to be kept a secret.

I pulled the key out of my pocket and held it up. It was so small it looked fragile. "What does it mean?"

When he saw I had it with me, his face lit up. "What, you didn't figure it out?" He moved his face close to mine and gazed at me. "It's the key to my heart, Gemma. Okay, maybe it's a little silly . . . but I gave it to you so you'd know it'll always belong to you. No matter what." His voice trailed off, but in his eyes I glimpsed a flicker of hope that told me he still harbored the illusion I might change my mind.

I stared at it on my palm. It was so tiny and yet so meaningful to Peter. With that gesture, he had wanted to offer me his whole self, to give me his heart. "I wanted to make it out of silver," he added, interrupting my thoughts, "but I didn't want it to tarnish over time. It's pure titanium, which wasn't easy to find. My dad showed me how to shape the mold. Then I melted the metal and waited for it to cool. It left me with this." He showed me his hand, still marked by a burn.

I brushed my fingers over the scar, speechless. "You *made* it?" I gasped, seeing the key in a new light, as touched as I was amazed.

"You know I've been helping my dad out more often lately. In a few years he's going to hand the smithy over to me." He looked at me to underline the responsibility that would be entrusted to him. Noticing how I was staring at the key, he went on. "I wanted to make it look really old, like our friendship, and to forge it with a material that was strong—like the bond between us." He looked up and into my eyes. "*Indestructible.* Then I decided to interlock your initial and mine to let you know what I was offering you." Peter hung his head and stared at my hands, as though now that he'd explained everything he felt embarrassed. Stroking the scar, he said, "I know it's small and it's not worth much, but I spent a week making it."

I was quick to disagree. "It's priceless." I had loved the key the moment I saw it, and discovering all those things about it filled my heart with emotion. "'What is aught but as 'tis valued?'"

"A line from one of your books, I imagine?"

That got another smile out of me. "Shakespeare. *Troilus and Cressida.* I don't know how to thank you, Peter, really. I'll take good care of it."

"Happy birthday, then." Peter stared at me for a second, his head tilted. Then he smiled, and the dimples in his cheeks made an appearance. "I have to admit I didn't come here only because of your present. There's something I want to ask you, but first you have to swear you won't give me an answer right away."

"Go ahead, Peter. Don't keep me on pins and needles!" I punched his arm affectionately like I always did. It was so nice talking to him. Sometimes it made me feel like I was a little girl again.

"Marry me, Gemma. I can take care of the baby."

A little grin spread over my face. I couldn't hold it back. It was funny, seeing Peter so serious. In my eyes he was still the little boy who used to chase me through the trees, yelling at me for climbing too high.

"Peter, are you actually *proposing*?" I couldn't believe my ears. So that was why he had told me his dad's shop would soon be his—he wanted to prove his commitment. Looking him in the eye, I realized I'd been wrong: Peter wasn't a little boy any more. He had become a man. And he was offering me a future together with him.

"It'll be great, I promise. I won't let anyone make you suffer ever again."

"What about your plans for college?"

"I can always decide to stay here."

"I would never ask you to give up your future for me."

"You wouldn't be asking me to."

"Pet . . . we've already talked about this."

"That's not true. We started talking about it but got interrupted when—actually, I'm not really sure what happened. You fainted and your friends wouldn't let me stay with you. Since then we haven't had a chance to finish the discussion."

"My life is too complicated. You think you know me, but a lot has changed over the last year. *I've* changed. You have no idea how I feel, what I'm going through. It's like I'm falling: I just keep sinking lower and lower—every single day."

"I'll always be there to catch you. I'll help raise you up again, if you'll let me."

"I don't want to drag you down with me." I looked him in the eye.

"Gemma, when are you going to understand I already hit rock bottom when I lost you?!" he asked, suddenly angry. "I don't want to get back up unless you're by my side."

"Don't ask me that, Peter. I can't."

"It's not fair. You can't raise the baby all alone. You can't *reject* me. I don't deserve it!"

For a second the light in his eyes alarmed me. Rarely had I seen him so angry. But then I understood the bitter sorrow he was hiding. I couldn't give him what he was asking for. There was nothing I could do and he had finally realized it.

He ran his hand over his face, looking resigned. "Sorry. I don't know what came over me," he said wearily. "At least promise you'll never leave me. I still want to be part of your life anyway, like it's always been."

"Like it's always been." Hiding a tear, I smiled and leaned over to nudge him with my shoulder. "Otherwise who would be here to lift my spirits?"

Peter wrapped his arm around me and I put my head on his shoulder. When I talked to him, I almost forgot the supernatural pall that hung over my life. For a second, I let go of my apprehension and forgot about Executioners, Witches, serpents . . . It was restful to immerse my mind in clearer, calmer waters and think about college, summer vacation, and plans for the future, though I couldn't see any for myself. Listening to Peter, I even managed a few smiles. But then the sun set, warning us of the lateness of the hour, and the darkness lowered a curtain between us, returning me to Angels under lock and key—and my own ghosts that I couldn't imprison.

"Now? But we have to celebrate our big catch," Ginevra whined, sitting on Simon's lap. She kissed him as though it might convince him to disobey Death's orders.

"We can always celebrate when I get back," he whispered, breathing the words against her lips. She continued to tease him with tiny kisses on his earlobe. He smiled sheepishly because I was right there, but he couldn't help it—he was unavoidably turned on by her.

"Want me to leave the two of you alone?" I paused, my fork halfway to my mouth, and raised an eyebrow.

"Hear that? She'll leave the two of us alone," Ginevra said provocatively.

My jaw dropped at her audacity. "For your information, that was a rhetorical question," I teased.

Simon laughed as Ginevra stuck her tongue out at me. "For all I care you can stay and watch." She winked at me, enjoying my shocked reaction.

"Much as I would love that, ladies, I'll have to take a raincheck."

"Simon!" I gasped.

He spread his arms, grinning. "Just kidding, Gemma. We're in a great mood because we captured the Executioner. I'd rather have a few hours free, but there's going to be a tornado in Nebraska. When I get back we can all celebrate together. And don't get me wrong—I'm not talking about sex, obviously," he was quick to point out, embarrassed.

"Just out of curiosity, I've often read about fallen angels. Is that another way to define Subterraneans?"

Simon stifled a smile and tried to cover his laughter with a coughing fit. "What you read are just stories, the fruit of able writers' imaginations. Actually, Fallen Angels do exist. They're an all-female circle."

Ginevra's lips curved into a seductive smile. "He means us. Witches are the Fallen Angels. I imagined you'd figured that out. Or at least, the first of us was 'the Angel who fell by the hand of God,' though many continue to refer to us all that way. But believe me, it's not the most ridiculous name we've been given. In the past, some called us 'Witches from beyond the water.' Over the centuries they've used more names for us than I can remember. Valkyries, Sirens, Amazons, in stories, legends, myths—that's us. It's always been us. Most of the tales arose from the experiences of those who survived a Reaping, a gaze from an enchantress, a promise from a huntswoman . . . My Sisters use fear, superstition, *temptation*, to get what they want."

"And what do they want?"

"Souls."

"It's a never-ending battle between Witches and Subterraneans," Simon added. "Speaking of which, I'd better go before I leave too many of them at their mercy."

Ginevra pouted and got off his lap. "Aw . . ."

"Address your complaints to your Sisters, not to me," he shot back.

Another question came to my mind. "You said there was going to be a tornado. Does that mean that earthquakes, tsunamis, and things like that are the work of Subterraneans?"

"Not always. Our nature isn't destructive. Subterraneans aren't interested in spreading chaos or destroying the Earth. Just the opposite—it's our duty to preserve it. Though sometimes we use our powers to wipe out entire populations if we're ordered to."

"But most of the time it's our fault," Ginevra added.

"Witches are the ones to cause catastrophes and natural disasters?"

"We control the atmospheric agents and Witches often have fun toying with nature—toying with *you*. Their aim is to destroy not the Earth, but humans, especially when they don't respect it. Sophìa, in particular, has a deep connection with nature, which bends to her will," Ginevra explained.

"And *we* intervene to mitigate the disasters and repair the damage," Simon put in. "We make sure the missing whose time hasn't yet come are found before the Witches can claim their souls; we look for new Subterraneans before they become their prisoners; and we liberate the Souls who need us. That's why our role is so important. We're the cord that binds Eden to the earth. This would never happen, of course, but if there weren't a single Subterranean left to ferry Souls there, all hope would be lost. The Witches would end up ruling the world and all mankind, including future generations, would be their slaves."

"But would all those people die even if it wasn't their fate?"

"Good and evil are two sides of the same coin. Witches can also act on fate's behalf by shuffling the deck however they like. Actions on both sides need to be calibrated to maintain balance in the world. They know what destiny holds in store, who has to die, and whose time hasn't yet come. Humans don't necessarily have to die for Witches to get what they're after. All they need to do is put them in a position where they'll be willing to barter their souls. Fear is the most precious currency."

"What happens to someone who's not ready to cross over?"

"If we don't manage to save them and they're unable to resist the Temptation, they fall into the Witches' hands and compromise their souls. When they die, there will be no Subterranean there waiting for them," Simon explained.

"Did you do those things, Gwen?"

"I couldn't help it. Actually, if you want to know the truth, I enjoyed it," she admitted with a shrewd smile.

"Do you think evil might ever take you over again?"

"Sometimes I think it might, but then I look at Simon and realize that love is the only invincible power there is. If you let love fill you, there's no room left for evil."

After dinner I went upstairs, seeking the comfort of Evan's room. I felt calmer, probably because I knew the source of my episodes was locked up and I could afford to abandon myself to my memories. Though I wasn't sure why, I couldn't stop picturing the house on the lake, with Evan sitting on the shore, smiling and ready to tease me like always. And yet it only took a moment for the image of the two of us to grow distorted, like a reflection in the lake's perfectly still surface when it was rippled by the rain. The memories began to burn in my heart—memories held together by a cord so worn it threatened to snap at any moment; memories that faded, sputtering like a fire that's devoured everything in the dark of night and is eventually reduced to ashes, darkness, and death . . . all that was left to me now.

"Gemma?" Ginevra peeked in as she knocked gently on the door.

I waved her in and she stared at me for a long while as though about to reveal something important. Something *difficult.* "I have something for you," she said, confirming my suspicion. "It's still your birthday." She approached me, reached into her pocket, and pulled out a little silver case that looked like an antique jewelry box.

With a sigh, I quickly looked away. "I don't want anything," I whispered, my voice breaking.

"Gemma." Ginevra came closer and forced me to look her in the eye. "You have to stop suffering." I tried to hold her gaze but quickly lowered my eyes, attempting to swallow the knot in my throat before it suffocated me. "Try to get a grip on yourself."

I looked up into her eyes. "You can't tell a fire to stop burning," I said matter-of-factly, fighting back the tears. What she was asking me to do was impossible.

Ginevra held my gaze. She opened her hand and a tiny golden flame rose from her palm. On an impulse, I brushed my fingers over the fire, but Ginevra moved it closer and made the flames tremble on my palm without burning it. "There's nothing we can't do in our minds. Find the strength inside you, Gemma."

I pulled my hand back without taking my eyes off her and the fire went out. "There are places the mind can't go when the heart has darkened them," I said firmly. "I . . . I feel like a dead tree."

"Not dead. Just bare. When the time comes, the leaves will grow back—you'll see." Ginevra respected my silence and put the case on the desk next to the portrait of Evan and his family in 1720. Then she turned to the door and rested her hand on the knob. "It's not from me. He would have wanted to give it to you. I read it in his mind."

I teetered a little as a tremble warmed my heart and my eyes filled with tears. Ginevra slowly closed the door behind her. I stayed where I was, staring at the case, frightened at the thought of what it might contain. I stroked it as my heart begged me to stop, screaming no, screaming that if I opened it I wouldn't be able to stand the pain. In the end, however, I gave in to the temptation. The silver box opened with a little click. I hesitated, shuddering, and slowly raised the lid.

I blinked and three crystal droplets slid down my face. My lashes wet with tears, I clutched the case in my fingers, unable to take my eyes off the ring inside it. It was small, dainty, with a pearl glowing in the center like a tiny version of the moon. I clasped it against my chest and let the pain wash over me. Overcome, I fell to my knees and clenched my fists against the floor, as though its solid surface could keep me from sinking. The ring pressed into my palm as I squeezed it tight—the ring Evan had vowed to give me when he'd proposed. The one on his mother's finger in the centuries-old family portrait. I closed my eyes and could almost feel Evan's arms around me, the heat of his body fusing with mine as we made love in the secluded place where we'd hidden from the world: on a military tarp in an old hangar, his voice caressing me like a sweet melody, promising never to leave me.

"I'm the one who was supposed to die," I sobbed in a tiny voice. "You promised." I curled up on the floor as though that would be enough to make me disappear. "You promised me, Evan. You promised you would never leave me." I silently waited for his reply but, like all the other times, I heard nothing but the silence of my heart.

The emptiness left by his absence was acid corroding me from the inside, slowly devouring me. Nothing would ever be able to give me back my Evan. The past had swallowed him up forever and iron chains imprisoned me in a limbo from which I could no longer escape, a cold place without light.

Heartbroken, I looked up and saw through the veil of my tears the blue cover of my diary that had fallen under the bed. I stared at it for a second before reaching for it, the ring still clasped to my chest like a little treasure I would never part with. That ring was the most precious gift I could ever have received. Despite the excruciating pain, I still belonged to him.

I went to the window, pushed the curtain aside, and let the air sweetly fill the room as I sought comfort in the night, silent and solitary. Just like me. I leaned back against the wall and slid down to the floor, my knees drawn up to my chest. As I closed my eyes, a breath of air snuck into the room and caressed my hair. I opened the diary and teardrops dripped from my chin, marking the page with my pain. The ink glided across the ivory paper, staining it with the poison distilled from my blood, imprisoning my agony forever on those pages.

January 17

Ginevra is right. It's still my birthday. Everybody keeps telling me I should move on, loosen my desperate grip on the past, and open myself up to what the future has in store for me, but all I keep doing is thinking about what I've lost, what no one can ever give back to me. It's as if my lifeblood has been drained away, leaving me lifeless: an empty shell deprived of its true essence.

Sometimes—but only sometimes—a breath of air brings me his scent and I breathe it in. Then I close my eyes and he's behind me, his hands on my waist, his lips on my neck, the warmth of his body so vivid that the disappointment kills me when I open my eyes and discover he's not there . . . that he never was.

What no one understands is that the comfort of that short-lived moment when the memory of him warms my heart is so intense, so necessary, that I would rather continue this slow death day after day for that brief illusion than awaken to the constant awareness that he's not with me any more, he'll never touch my face again, his lips will never smile against mine again. Evan. His very name threatens to disappear, smeared by a teardrop that's dripped onto the ink. I don't want to forget his laugh. I don't want to forget the feeling of his hand clasped in mine. But his features are beginning to fade and I'm scared—scared of losing the memories too, because they're all that's left to me. Without them, my heart will wither completely. I won't be able to bear it.

I wish I had never wanted Evan to save me, not at this price. It was his love for me that ultimately destroyed him. Evan's death was a mistake for which I and I alone am responsible, and I paid for it with my heart. If only I knew why fate is so set against me, the reason behind my death sentence . . . But no one can ever lift this burden from me.

No, actually. Maybe there's someone who can.

I shot to my feet, my diary falling to the ground. Drying my tears, I crossed the room and peeked into the hall to make sure no one was around. Simon and Ginevra couldn't discover my intentions or they would try to stop me. I tiptoed out, groped my way down the stairs in the dark, and crept across the living room. My hand trembling, I reached for the knob to the door leading downstairs and slowly turned it.

Someone owed me some answers.

An Angel under lock and key.

DANGEROUS TRESPASSES

I shut the door behind me and quickened my pace in the direction of the workout room. My chances of reaching the dungeon without obstacles were slim, but my fears vanished when I heard the sound of lapping water mingled with soft laughter from Simon and Ginevra. They were in the swimming pool enjoying some privacy, temporarily freed from the constant burden of my presence. Now that the Angel could no longer cause me problems, their voices sounded more carefree, as though a load had been lifted from their shoulders. I hurried past before one of them could notice me.

Staring at the trapdoor, I felt unsure about whether to continue, but before my common sense could reassert itself and change my mind, I followed my instinct and crept into the depths of the house. Once the pitch dark had swallowed me up, the reasons that had driven me to break the rules didn't seem so important any more and I considered the thought of going back upstairs. The air smelled so strongly of earth it was almost unbreathable, its dank odor filling my nostrils. Still, my curiosity was overpowering. Though Subterraneans didn't always know the reasons behind an execution order, Simon was almost certain that this one had been in contact with the Màsala, so I had to at least try. Putting one foot in front of the other, I ventured into the darkness, accompanied by the ominous echo of my footfalls in the lugubrious silence. I groped forward, tripping over the rough floor, trying to get my bearings from the memory of the only other time I'd been down there. Had it really been only a few hours earlier? It felt like months.

My fingers recognized a curve. I turned the corner and a faint glow guided me to the heavy door that confined the Subterranean. My heart trembled. I didn't know if it was from fear or the hope of finally learning my destiny. Gripping the door tightly to keep my hands from shaking, I undid the latch. It clicked open with a sinister sound that penetrated my bones. I grabbed a small torch from its sconce on the wall of the passageway. The door opened with a blood-curdling squeal.

"You were reckless to come here alone."

Her voice made me cringe even though I had prepared myself to face her. "I brought you a little light." I hung the torch on the cell wall, trying to appear calm.

The Angel's mocking laughter rang icily off the walls, making me shudder. "I am not afraid of the dark." She tilted her head and flashed me a spine-chilling look. The torch flickered. "But you are."

For a second, the shadows cast by the torch tricked me into thinking her eye sockets were empty. I knew how beautiful and alluring she was, but just then she looked like a monster spawned by the darkness. No—not a monster. An Angel of Death.

I took a deep breath and spoke in a steady voice. "I didn't come here to taunt you, and I don't think you're stupid enough to gamble away your only chance of staying alive—at least for a while. Don't forget, I'm the one who kept Ginevra from killing you." My hands wouldn't stop shaking so I slid them into my sweatshirt pockets, hoping she wouldn't notice. My fingers clutched the silver case as if it could instill courage in me.

"Why did you come, then?" She struggled not to seem weak, but her face betrayed her. "Unless you mean to free me, I suggest you leave. I do not socialize with humans." She looked away, her expression cold yet entrancing.

"You've never been human?"

A glimmer of surprise appeared in her eye. "Long ago, but it is a memory I care not to recall," she replied disdainfully.

I moved closer and she stared at me, her eyes veiled with wickedness. "What's your name?" I asked impulsively. Something about the Angel drew me to her just as strongly as it frightened me. Actually, *she* didn't frighten me—it was the emotion that stirred within me the moment I got close to her, some strange energy I could tell was wrong. Evil. Had I gone there driven by the same longing for revenge I'd seen in Ginevra's eyes? Was it possible that part of me was ready to vent all my rage on this chained creature that now looked so vulnerable?

"Is that what you wish to know from me?" The Angel interrupted my train of thought, bringing me back to the darkness of the cell.

"No, but I felt it was right to know your name before talking to you." It was insane how determined my voice sounded, so free from uncertainty, when actually every fiber of my body was trembling, begging me to get out of that accursed place.

The Angel chuckled. "You were brave to come here, I will grant you that."

"And you were a bitch to make me think I'd lost my baby." The instant the words escaped me I felt satisfied, freed from a burden. It wasn't so difficult to face her with my head held high under these circumstances. I wondered if I would have had the same courage if she hadn't been under the influence of the poison.

To my astonishment, the Angel laughed and her voice echoed off the walls. "Desna."

"What?" I asked, puzzled.

"My name. It is Desdemona, but you may call me Desna."

"Fine. I imagine you already know mine."

"Now that we have introduced ourselves, is there a reason you came here or do you simply have suicidal tendencies?"

I took a deep breath. I wasn't sure I could ask the question—not to someone who could actually give me the answer. I summoned up my courage, though, and asked, "Why?" I had murmured the word, but when I looked up into her eyes my voice began to rise, filling with bitterness. "Why are they so determined to see me die? Is my life so important? How many of you have died already trying to kill me? How many more will die? Are the Màsala willing to pay any price to kill me?" To my horror I noticed I had moved too close to her face, but Desna smiled, not the least bit intimidated by my reaction.

"The point is not why you must die"—she looked me straight in the eye as though giving me a warning—"but why you must not *live*."

I took a step back, stunned by how promptly she'd replied when I'd been so sure she wouldn't answer my question. Still, it wasn't enough. "It doesn't make sense. What did I ever do to deserve such a terrible sentence?"

Desna chuckled. "I cannot give you that information. Not without receiving something in exchange." Her eyebrow raised, lighting up her face. "What you ask of me has a price."

I held my breath. Could it actually be this easy? Would she really give me what I wanted? I was prepared to promise her anything, but what could she possibly want from me? "What can I give you that you don't already have?"

"Free me."

"I might be reckless, but I'm not stupid. The first thing you would do is kill me."

The piercing, crafty look in her eye sent a shiver through me. "I cannot deny it."

A despondent sigh escaped me and I turned my back on her to hide the bitter sorrow on my face. The Angel was of no use to me. I had been wrong to take the risk.

"Perhaps you do not want to free me, but . . ." Unwilling to listen to her any more, I headed for the door, resigned. " . . . would you leave your beloved Evan chained up down here?"

"Gemma!" I flinched at the sound of Evan's voice but squeezed my eyes shut and forced myself not to turn around. I knew the Angel was trying to penetrate my mind again. Weakened from the poison, Desna had less influence over me. I covered my ears with my hands to block out her voice and ran toward the half-closed door.

"Gemma! Free me, please! It's me, Evan!" I turned toward him and a shock ran through my body, freezing me in my tracks. "Free me, quick! Before she gets here!" he pleaded, his eyes locked on mine.

"Evan," I murmured, stunned. It was so wonderful to look into his eyes again. At last I had found him! He wasn't dead! The urgency in his voice made me leap into action. I grabbed the key from where Simon had hidden it and unlocked the shackles, trying to keep my hands steady. I took the cuffs off Evan's wrists and he toppled forward onto me as I braced myself to take his weight, anxious to help him. But the moment he raised his head Desna's evil grin petrified me, releasing me from her spell.

A shiver ran through me. I had set her free. I gasped, but the Angel had already disappeared through the door, swift as a ghost. I fell to my knees, my hands on the floor and my head hung low. Beaten. How could I have been so stupid?

The door creaked open, tearing me from my torment. My head snapped up. Desna was cautiously backing into the room. My eyes bulged: Ginevra's serpent slithered across the floor in pursuit, ready to lunge at her. The door slammed shut, sealing us inside. I pressed myself against the floor, unable to take my eyes off the serpent. He was so hypnotic, so fascinating. My desire to touch him was so powerful it left my throat dry. Was this the seduction used by evil to bend a mortal's will? How could mere humans hope to resist such power?

The Angel's terrified expression shook me out of my thoughts and I saw Ginevra. I shrieked and flattened myself against the wall, a jolt of pure terror running through me: her face radiated evil and her body was levitating inches above the floor. The pure energy she emitted made her hair whirl around her head, and darkness filled her eyes. Like a bolt of lightning she rushed at Desna and slammed her against the wall, doubling her over.

I had never seen Ginevra unleash the Witch inside her. The raw power she gave off inspired both admiration and dread in me. "Where did you think you were going?" Ginevra's eyes filled with brilliant streaks that extended into the whites like rays from a dark sun. The green of her irises came to life, vibrating with golden reflections, and her pupils elongated, like a cat's . . . or a snake's.

She put Desna back in chains, jerking them tighter this time. Her serpent slithered back up to her arm as the Angel cringed in terror against the wall. "I thought my blood would keep you under control, but I can see it wasn't enough." Sensing his adversary's fear, the serpent hissed.

"Gwen!" I shouted before her serpent could bite the Subterranean. She looked so different. I'd never seen that darkness in her eyes before. "You're scaring me! Stop it!"

The animal froze, coiled around Ginevra's upper arm twice, and disappeared beneath her skin as she stared at me sternly, her eyes still filled with liquid emeralds.

"Ugly Witch!" Desna screamed, but before she could say anything else, her captor struck her violently, knocking her against the wall. Ginevra broke open the skin on her palm with her teeth and pressed it to the Angel's mouth. "Maybe you didn't have enough. Did you lure Gemma down here?" Ginevra gritted her teeth and glared at her, seething.

"I did nothing." Desna broke free of Ginevra's grip and spat out the blood. A drop landed on my skin. "But you already knew that, did you not?" She threw her captor a challenging look.

Ginevra turned to look at me. "What the hell were you doing down here?"

"I wanted to see if everything was okay," I replied warily.

"Jesus Christ! What's wrong with you? She's not our *guest*, Gemma, she's our *prisoner*! Get it through your skull! What made you think she would give you the answers you wanted?" she accused me, searching my mind. "She tried to kill you and she won't hesitate to do it again the second she finds the smallest opportunity! Carrying out orders is the only thing that matters to Subterraneans. You should know that by now!"

"But I didn't think—"

"*What* didn't you think? You entered the wolf's den. What were you expecting?"

Suddenly I thought back to when Ginevra had asked me if Desna was the woman I'd dreamed of. Maybe it was true. In my dream I'd also seen Evan and she had taken on his appearance. She wanted me to follow her. *He's waiting for you*, she'd said. But Evan was dead. I couldn't have followed him unless I accepted death by her hand, the hand of the blond Angel who had come to kill me.

"I'm sorry. You're perfectly right, it was thoughtless of me."

"Thoughtless?!" Ginevra closed the distance between us, glaring at me. "I'm trying to protect you, but you're not helping."

I nodded, suddenly aware of the seriousness of my actions. Simon and Ginevra were risking their lives to protect me, and I was putting myself in danger. She was right on all counts. What had I been thinking?

"Come on." She helped me to my feet, her gaze softening. "Let's get out of here."

"Wait! You cannot keep me imprisoned here forever!"

"You're right." The door slammed shut behind us and Ginevra tilted her head, staring through the bars at the chained Angel, a cunning smile on her lips. "It won't be forever, just until I decide to kill you." A gust of wind blew out the torch. Desna's shrieks grew fainter, swallowed up by the passageway, until the trapdoor silenced them.

FRESH AIR

The school bell announced the end of classes and the empty halls were soon flooded with students who couldn't wait to leave the building and start the weekend. Though I didn't share in the general enthusiasm, the collective chatter emanated a contagious energy that in the end managed to make a dent in my shell. I had a strange feeling of freedom. Probably some of my uneasiness had been wiped away along with my fear of another attack by the Angel. Or maybe I just felt relieved that after what seemed like forever, I'd slept through a whole night without bad dreams. On top of that, I had expected to be greeted by a multitude of strange looks and whispers after the disturbing episode of the day before, but it hadn't happened. The students at Lake Placid High had turned out to be unusually supportive and hadn't brought it up. Was it out of pure compassion? Or had Simon had a hand in it by manipulating their memories? It didn't matter to me as long as they left me in peace. It was also the first day Ginevra had decided not to come with me, loosening the strings of her strict surveillance. She'd even given me the afternoon free. After all, with the Angel locked up I had nothing to fear apart from the ghosts haunting my soul.

Earbuds in, I pulled out my SLR camera and took a few shots for the assignment Mr. Madison had given us for photography class. We had to pick a theme—like faces, locations, or animals—and take a series of pictures using different lighting and lenses. I had chosen nature as my subject, so I zoomed in on some hoarfrost that had crystallized on a tree branch and noticed a little white flower growing through the ice right at the foot of the tree. I knelt down to take a few more shots, cranked the volume and lost myself to Sia singing *She Wolf* by David Guetta. I added a blue filter and the effect was amazing:

the picture came out exactly the way I wanted. The little flower looked sad and solitary . . . just like me.

I looked up and noticed Peter waving to get my attention. I pulled out an earbud. "Gemma!" He beckoned me over, waiting for me beneath the twisted branches of a bare maple with the rest of the group.

"Hey, you're all here." I walked over to them, dropped my backpack on the ground that had been cleared of snow, and used it as a stool, sitting down next to Faith.

"Get any interesting shots?" asked Peter, who must have been watching me. I handed him the camera and he carefully studied my photos.

"Oh, shit! The assignment for Mr. Madison!" Jake groaned. "I forgot about it."

"Why do you take that class if you don't like it?" I asked. To me, taking photographs was more of a passion than an obligation, so it was hard to imagine anyone finding it a drag.

"Great question!" Brandon threw something at him and I understood: he must have signed up for it because of Faith. Jake, Peter, and Brandon were the stars of the Blue Bombers. They played hockey in winter and lacrosse in summer. Between practice and games they spent a lot of time together and they definitely confided in each other.

"Hey, this one's great! It looks like a flower from heaven," he said. I looked at the picture and a flashback filled my mind:

"No, Evan. Stop it!"

We'd been crossing the river inside a giant water lily that was blue streaked with silver, and when it closed over our heads, Evan had immediately moved closer to tempt me. I'd been afraid that any show of affection was forbidden in that sacred place, though.

"Come on, no one can see us."

"We can't make out like this, not here."

Ignoring me, he'd pressed his body against mine and kissed my neck, making my head spin. *"I would make love to you right here."*

"Evan!" I had avoided his kisses, pushing him away and laughing. *"You dope!"* I'd bitten my lip, burning with passion.

"Did I say that out loud?" Despite his attempt to cover for what he'd said, his sly smile had betrayed him.

"Gemma. Gemma!" Peter's insistent voice roused me.

"Yeah?"

He handed me my camera. "Here you go."

Evan and I had been in Heaven, but now it all seemed like just a dream. "Oh. Thanks."

"What should we do, guys? I'm bored!" Jeneane complained.

"Update your Facebook status," Brandon teased her. She threw a snowball at him.

Peter rested his arm on the tree, studying the necklace I wore, his expression pained as he searched for his pendant. I raised my arm, pushed back my thick sweatshirt and shook my wrist to show him his present, which dangled from a thin silver chain. He smiled at me, grasping my tacit message, and stared into my eyes as the group's voices became an indistinct murmur in the background.

"Gemma, why don't you come with us?"

"Huh?"

"Yeah, that would be great!" Peter exclaimed, looking hopeful, his gaze locked on mine.

"I don't know what you're talking about."

"What do you mean?! It's all over town!" Jeneane squealed. "There's a Lana del Rey concert at Bandshell Park tomorrow night. Everyone's going."

So that's why no one paid any attention to me at school today. "An outdoor concert? With all the snow?"

"That's why it's called the White Concert," Brandon said. He was sitting with his back against a tree, hands clasped behind his head, chewing gum.

"I don't know . . ." For a second, the invitation was tempting.

"Come on, you *love* Lana del Rey!" Faith insisted. It was true— though we'd already gone to lots of her concerts, since she'd grown up in Lake Placid.

"Well, at least it's not a no," Jeneane said, glancing at Peter. Taking his cue from her, he came over and crouched down in front of me.

"You're. Coming. With. Us," he said, taking advantage of the indecision I'd shown.

"Hey, Pete!" Brandon threw a snowball at him, startling him. "What are you trying to do, hypnotize her? I doubt it'll make her fall in love with you."

"Shut up, dumbass." Jeneane said, giving him a reproachful shove. Something flickered in Brandon's eyes and she ran off with a shriek, but he pinned her to the ground over her protests.

Peter let out a laugh. "Your approach is way more effective, I see. At least Gemma didn't try to escape!"

He threw a snowball at Brandon, starting a snowball fight that spared no one, not even me. When a well-aimed projectile threatened to hit me full on, Peter darted in front of me protectively, but lost his balance. A second later his body was on top of mine, my back against the damp ground. The smile on his lips slowly faded, yet in his eyes the warmth of the bond that had always connected us persisted.

"Sorry I knocked you over," he said, his gaze as tender as his tone.

"That's okay. You did it to pro—Look out!" A snowball flew toward us and Peter leaned closer to me to dodge it. He swallowed slowly, his gaze locked on mine. Silence enveloped us like a dome, shutting us off from the amused cries of the others.

"Will you come to the concert?" he asked, turning serious. "With me?" His eyes lingered on mine for a long moment as I thought it over. After all, what could happen to me now that the Executioner was no longer a problem? Maybe some company would do me good, especially if the whole group was going.

"Maybe." I hid a little smile and Peter raised an eyebrow, dimples appearing in his cheeks. "But now you have to let me go."

"Maybe?" He grabbed my wrists, threatening to keep me there until I'd given him a better answer.

"Okay! All right, I'll go! Happy?" He hadn't given me much choice.

"Hey, you two!" Brandon interrupted us, his wet hair sticking to his face as the others grinned. "Keep that up and you'll melt all the snow, and then we won't be able to play any more. Does that seem fair?"

I shifted on the ground, embarrassed by what the others must think at the sight of Peter and me off on our own, and in that position.

"Shut up, Bran," Peter shot back. "If you behave, one day I might teach you my hypnosis techniques, seeing as how they work better than yours."

"So you're coming with us?" Faith hugged me tight, bursting with enthusiasm. "I'm so happy! We'll all bring blankets and lie down on the lakeshore. I know you won't regret it. We'll have loads of fun!"

"Okay, okay! Don't suffocate her." Peter reclaimed my attention, holding out his hand to help me up.

"Hey, what do you say we get some shooting in?" Jake suggested. He was the police chief's son and had always loved going to the firing range. There were several of them scattered around the village, but his favorite was in a clearing where people practiced for deer hunting. I hated hunting almost as much as Faith did, but shooting at inanimate targets was fun so we did it often, mostly during spring and summer.

"Feel like it?" murmured Peter, who had come much closer as though to protect me. I tightened my lips to confirm his suspicion and he understood at once. "Doesn't seem like a good idea. Besides, we've got the hockey game later on."

"So what? You know we're going to destroy them!" Brandon said confidently.

"You bet we will. But right now Gemma needs a hot shower. Her clothes are damp and this cold weather isn't doing her any good in her condition."

"Oh, of course," the others agreed, instantly solicitous.

Not knowing how to respond to all the attention, I looked at my hand clasped in Peter's. He knew me so well. Ours was a bond that challenged every physical law, because even if all the parameters changed, he was a constant.

"It would be nice if you came to the game too." Peter lowered his voice as he spoke just to me again and stroked the back of my hand with his thumb. His question hung in the air as we looked each other in the eyes. His face was so close I could feel the warmth of his breath. Suddenly, he touched the edge of my mouth with his thumb. "A snowflake," he explained, his face serious. When I raised a skeptical eyebrow, he gave himself away, a dimple appearing in his cheek. "Want me to take you home?" he asked sweetly.

I never used to miss Peter's games and I knew how much they meant to him, but I wasn't sure I wanted to be around so many people. He must have realized that even though I hadn't given him an answer.

"Thanks, but Ginevra left me her car. Besides, I'm having lunch with my parents today."

"Great!" he exclaimed, baffling me. He tried to compose himself. "I mean, it's great that you're spending more time with them. It means you're feeling better, and since they've been so worried—"

"Right."

Of course Peter didn't know the real reason I'd been forced to undergo such strict surveillance. My being away from home wasn't because of my mood but because the Angel of Death had put me in grave danger. Now that she was locked up I could grant myself a little more liberty. Peter probably thought I was distancing myself from Ginevra—and the memory of Evan. The truth was, not a minute went by that I didn't think of him. Still, I felt the need to go out with my old friends, to breathe some normal air. *Human* air. Otherwise I risked going insane.

"Honey, have you thought of where you'd like to fly with the voucher we gave you?"

I raised my fork and filled my mouth with mashed potatoes, trying to avoid answering Mom's question, but she ignored my silence and insisted. "Your father made sure we got one without a destination or an expiration date so you could do whatever you wanted with it. We're good friends with the owner of the travel agency, you know, so you can go to him whenever you like."

"Actually, Mom, I—"

"You could use it to visit your grandparents in Rochester. They're not so young any more, and a change of scenery would do you a lot of good."

"Thanks, Mom, but honestly I—maybe it would be better if you guys used it. It's been years since you and Dad took some time off work."

Dad took my hand. "You don't have to use it now if you don't want to. Josephine, you're pushing her too hard."

"No, it's okay. Please don't fight because of me."

"Your mother is just concerned about you—like I am, for that matter. We know you're going through a hard time. It's been hard for us too, facing so many changes all at once. Your being away from home . . . your pregnancy." Dad ran a hand over his face. "I still don't know how I ended up agreeing to letting you leave. Oh God, you're still my little girl," he said, his tone grief-stricken. I'd never seen him so upset before.

"Dad, of course I'm still your little girl. I always will be."

He squeezed my hand and I returned the gesture. "You'll always be my Squirrelicue. When Ginevra told us you would be staying at their place for a while, my first reaction was to be mad at you, but then when she explained how badly you were doing, we felt like the whole world was crashing down around us and everything else was put on the back burner—including our shock at hearing you were expecting a baby. You must've gone through such awful moments, you poor thing, but now we're happy to see you're starting to get better."

"Thanks, Dad."

"No need to thank me. I'll admit I've always been pretty strict and maybe a bit apprehensive when it comes to you, but believe me, that's just because I love you so much." He looked like he was about to cry. I wondered how long he'd been waiting for me to become strong enough to tell me how he felt. "You'll be a parent soon too and maybe it'll help you understand what I'm trying to tell you."

"It's just— Well, like you said, I went through some awful times. You can't imagine how terrible. And I'm happy I can count on you two. Other parents in your shoes would have been furious. After all, I'm only eighteen and I'm already pregnant and the father is—I only wish you'd found out about it differently. I wish everything had gone differently. Evan—" I swallowed. My mom, behind me, squeezed my shoulders comfortingly. "He disappeared before I could tell him and—and there are so many things I'll never be able to forgive myself for."

"You'll manage, sweetie. Time heals all wounds, I promise."

"Okay, but for now let's change the subject before I start crying again."

"No tears!" My dad flashed one of his encouraging smiles, but not before I caught him turning to quickly wipe his eye. "How about a game of chess, like the good old days?"

"But it's late. Shouldn't you two already be at work?"

"My daughter is more important than any job in the world, especially if she's about to give me a fine grandson."

"Dad!"

My mom slapped his shoulder with her oven mitt. "Leave her alone, Josh! Can't you see you're embarrassing her?"

"Woman, go to the living room and get me the chess set so I can play a game with my daughter," he teased her.

Another slap, this time on the head. "You, *man*, drag your behind out of that chair and get it yourself."

I laughed as Dad massaged the back of his neck, flashing her his most charming smile. "Come here, little dictator!" He tried to grab Mom by the wrist but she slipped out of his grasp.

"No way!" She turned her back on him to hide her smile.

"I love it when she plays hard to get." He waggled his eyebrows and leaned over the table so she wouldn't hear him. "The problem is she figured that out a long time ago."

I smiled, but then made myself turn serious. "Dad, would you mind if I took a rain check on the chess? I'm exhausted."

"That's normal, sweetheart." Mom came over to me. "I was the same way when I was expecting you."

"Really?"

"Of course! Sometimes I would even fall asleep smack dab in the middle of a conversation. It's the baby that's sapping your strength. That's why you need lots of nourishment."

"I hadn't imagined that might be causing it."

"It is, especially toward the end, and my pregnancy lasted almost ten months! Everyone in Lake Placid was talking about it."

"The doctors wanted to induce labor," Dad interjected, "saying you might be in danger, but your mother flat out refused. She said you would be born when you were good and ready. That's where you got your stubbornness from."

Another slap to the head.

"I didn't want to force my baby if she didn't feel ready to come out of her shell yet. And now look—she turned out just fine. In fact, she's always had something special, different from all the rest."

Was my mom right? Could my ability to see Subterraneans possibly be due to that? Maybe during the extra gestation time my body had developed extra senses.

"Don't listen to her," Dad said, grinning. "She just came up with that theory to justify being so obstinate. Your baby's going to come out healthy and intelligent even if he only takes the normal nine months. As for the game, you're right, maybe we should do it another time. I forgot that little Davey is having his birthday party this afternoon."

"Mr. Burns's son? Isn't that Peter's youngest cousin?"

"Oh, right—Peter! How is he?"

"Great. Tomorrow I'm going with him and the others to the White Concert."

"Why, that's wonderful! You have no idea how much that boy cares about you. Lately he's stopped by every day to ask how you are. Only when we told him about the baby did he seem upset. He didn't turn up again for a week, but then everything went back to normal."

"He just needed a little time to let the news sink in. He's a fine young man. It'll do you good to spend time with him again."

"The whole group is going, Mom—Faith, Jeneane, Brandon, and Jake will be there too. Don't start getting any ideas, because for me there will never be anyone but Evan." My reply was so unexpectedly sour it left them wordless and I instantly regretted it. "In any case, tomorrow's Saturday and I don't have anything to do this afternoon. If it's okay with you I'll stop by the diner to give you a hand."

"Are you kidding?" My dad's smile broadened, lighting up his face. "It would be great if you came to spend time with us. Besides, it'll be packed, so an extra set of eyes will come in handy—if you feel up to it."

"Why shouldn't I? I'm pregnant, not sick. I like to feel useful. It'll do me good."

"Then it's agreed," Mom said, "but first Gemma needs to get some rest, otherwise she might fall asleep on one of the tables."

"Like mother, like daughter," Dad said in a singsong voice.

"I don't believe it! Did that *really* happen to you, Mom?"

"Um . . . only a few times," she said, caught off guard and looking embarrassed.

Dad covered his mouth with his hand and yawned. "A few times *a day,* that is."

"It wasn't my fault! Gemma was already a tomboy inside my belly. She drained all my energy. In the beginning I even lost weight!"

"Oh, thanks, Mom." I shot her a look brimming with sarcasm.

"Come on, don't tell me you've forgotten how your father and I always had to go searching the treetops for you when it was lunchtime."

Her words made my heart lurch. The memory of Evan lying on the snow came into my mind, so clear that for a second I felt the earth move under my feet. I had spent one of the most wonderful nights of my entire life skating on the lake that he himself had frozen over before my amazed eyes. We'd stayed there for hours talking, watched over by the starry night. I told him about how my parents had resigned themselves to my rebellious tomboy nature and Evan had seized the chance to tease me yet again, but then he'd surprised me by crafting a magnificent ice sculpture. But after that, the memories became tinged with blood. Back then I'd had no idea it would also be the most terrible night of my life—the last one I would spend with Evan.

"Sweetie, are you okay?" My mom must have noticed the change in my expression because she suddenly looked worried.

"It's nothing, Mom. Like you said, I'm just a little tired."

"Let's go to work, Josh," she said, pulling his arm, "and let Gemma rest. She can join us later."

"See you in a few, Squirrelicue." My dad touched his lips to my forehead and a moment later silence filled the room.

I set my feet on the dark ground with extreme caution. The air was thick and cool, the sky veiled with an ominous gloom. With no idea where I was, I had the terrible feeling I was lost, both physically and emotionally. At times I couldn't even remember who I was or what world I belonged to. The foliage rustled at my feet and all around me the forest became denser. The trees seemed to stretch out infinitely.

Something moved behind me, making me jump.

I spun around and peered at the dark silhouettes of the tree trunks, as still as soldiers in the night. My eyes wandered through the semidarkness but the forest seemed deserted. Still, I couldn't shake the feeling there were a thousand eyes spying on me. Threatening, hostile eyes. Creatures ready to pounce.

I turned back and my heart leapt to my throat. Someone was there in the distance—a figure blocking my path. I instinctively took a step back, but a fierce snarl behind me made me freeze. I fought the instinct to scream. The figure moved further away and something inside me urged me to follow it. However, as in a dream, the closer I got the more unreachable the hooded figure became. It seemed to be moving without touching the ground.

"Wait!" I cried.

The figure stopped. I slowed my pace, stepping forward warily.

"I'm lost. Can you show me the way home?"

Without turning around, the figure turned its head enough that I could see it was a woman. Her jade-green eyes shone like beacons in the night.

"Who . . . who are you?" I took a step forward, unexpectedly drawn to her.

A pleased smile appeared on her lips. "That's not the right question." A shiver ran through me at the sound of her hypnotic voice. I wanted to reply, to ask what she meant, but my brain was imprisoned by the sound. It had trapped me like a dark spell. I stood there, unable to stop her as she turned and moved away as silently as a ghost, disappearing into the night. Shaking myself out of my daze, I tried to follow her but my mind got lost again. I clung to the memory of her voice, following the sound like a path that would lead me back to my own world.

Suddenly the forest thinned and I came out into a clearing full of ruins. Pausing, I looked for the woman among the rubble but there was no sign of her. I wandered among the crumbling stones strewn everywhere until I saw her again. She stood at the mouth of a cave, her face turned toward me as though waiting for me. When she saw me she entered the cave, allowing the darkness to swallow her up.

"Wait!" I hurried to catch up with her. I had to exert myself to scramble over the huge rocks and kept falling. When I finally reached it, the mouth of the cave opened up before me like the gaping jaws of an animal preparing to gobble me up. Two conflicting forces struggled within me: should I go forward or turn back?

Part of my psyche continued to send out warning signals, making me shudder at every breath of air, but there was another, more compelling part that insisted I go on, as though the cave could lead me to fascinating, inaccessible places. Under the control of that arcane instinct, my foot took a step toward the darkness. Where had the woman gone? Where would she take me? The questions yearned to be answered.

I advanced through the darkness, my hands touching the walls, accompanied by the eerie sound of my echoing footsteps. A sudden flickering light showed me the way and I continued, taking care not to trip. From time to time I felt strange carvings in the rock. Fascinated, I ran my fingers along the grooves but couldn't decipher them, as if the markings were in some unknown language.

The path took a sharp turn, revealing the place the light was coming from. I flinched and stepped back when I saw a bare-chested figure crumpled on the ground. A whimper escaped me, and with a growl of exasperation the man stirred, the chains shackled to his wrists and ankles clanging.

"Who's there?!" he shouted, his proud voice devoid of fear.

My heart thudded violently against my ribs. "Evan!" A river of tears spilled from my eyes as I impetuously rushed toward him. "Evan . . ." I buried my face in his bare chest that was covered with slashes and burns.

"Gemma . . ." His arms held me tight, filling me with warmth.

"Evan, I've missed you so m—"

The earth trembled ominously beneath our feet, drowning out my voice. As I clung to Evan, another quake thwarted our embrace and the rock gave way beneath him. A huge dark chasm opened up. I screamed as Evan grabbed the edge of the pit that threatened to swallow him up.

"Hold on, Evan! Please don't fall!"

"Don't let me die, Gemma! Help me!"

Gritting my teeth, I tried to pull him up but the heavy chains around his wrists and ankles dragged him down into the void.

"Gemma!!"

"Evaaaan!!!"

As he fell he stared at me, his eyes filled with terror, until the darkness sucked him in and vanished. I fell backwards, my heart drained of all emotion. A gurgle rose from the crater, steadily increasing in volume. I leaned over the edge, my eyes darting everywhere as they tried to spot whatever was swirling in its depths. The sound grew closer and closer, louder and louder, until I could finally tell what it was: a powerful jet of water surging up from the crater, headed straight toward me. I screamed and pulled back as it hit me with the fury of a hurricane. Though I tried to resist, the current swept me into its very center. It felt like it was corroding my skin. I thrashed around in search of oxygen as the water threatened to drown me.

"Evan!!" I cried, desperately attempting to reach him across the barrier of death. Then the water filled my throat.

"Gemma!"

"Evan—" I coughed as someone shook me gently by the shoulders. I tried to focus, my lungs still screaming for oxygen. The ceiling of the living room brought me to my senses. I was at my parents' house.

"Simon." With a sigh of resignation, I looked him in the eye and leaned back into the couch. "Everything's okay."

The look on his face told me he wasn't convinced. "Another nightmare?" When I nodded he looked at me sympathetically.

I still felt a pit in my stomach from having let Evan fall. I had killed him. Again. "I keep dreaming of losing Evan," I said. "He loves me, he's in danger, but I can't save him and he—he dies right before my eyes and there's nothing I can do. It's like an obsession."

"I'm sorry. It's your feelings of guilt that are giving you the same nightmare over and over. It'll stop when you finally understand it wasn't your fault. He didn't die because of you," he repeated, his tone firm, though he knew I would never believe it. *I* had killed Evan. Nothing and no one could ever free me from my guilt.

I shook my head. "But I was having these nightmares even before Evan died, whenever he left me alone." My face darkened as my lips gave voice to a suspicion that had been buried in my heart for far too long. "Maybe coming back from death has consequences. A price. We played against too powerful an opponent. Maybe no one can really escape death."

Simon smiled at me affectionately. "We're going to keep trying."

"Ow!" I doubled up, grabbing my belly.

"Is it the baby?" Simon quickly asked, concerned.

"No, it's just my"—I looked down at my abdomen—"my skin. It *burns.*"

Simon seemed alarmed but I reassured him. "Don't worry, it's already gone. Anyway, what are you doing here, Simon?" I asked, banishing the lingering memories of the horrible nightmare that had come back to haunt me.

"I came to make sure everything was all right." Simon touched my forehead, worried. "When I got here you were just waking up. You had a massive fever again, but your temperature is already going down."

"Sometimes I think it would have been better if I'd never met Evan. Maybe it's better to be born blind than to go blind once you know what light is."

"Why are you saying that? He wouldn't want—"

"He died because of me. Drake died because of me. You might be next. I'm not worth all this."

"Maybe you don't think so, but the two of them did. And so do I. Otherwise we would never have *chosen* to protect you in the first place. Evan was aware of the risks, and he fought for you right from the start. He didn't care about dying—he just wanted you to live. He chose *you.*"

"What about Drake?"

"He cared a lot about you too."

"I know that, but if the Angel who took on Evan's appearance wasn't the real Drake, then what happened to him?"

"He died. Who knows where, who knows when. We'll never find out what happened." Simon's face suddenly darkened. I could see that not knowing the details about Drake's death pained him. "The only way to get to you was from the inside, and they knew none of us would betray you, so they killed him. Another Subterranean stepped in, passed himself off as Drake, and tricked us all. The very idea is insane. The Màsala must have helped him. They sent Evan away so the impostor could take his place too. None of us could have prevented it. In one fell swoop he would have been able to kill Evan and guarantee you couldn't come back from death, because I could never have managed to bring you back to life all on my own. They would have won on all fronts."

"But something went wrong with his plan too because despite the poison I didn't die."

"No one could have expected that. How do you feel?"

"Like someone who keeps reliving their worst nightmares. I can't take it any more, Simon. I honestly feel like I'm in danger of going insane. I—I'm afraid." It felt like I was on the edge, on the verge of slipping into a pit of madness. "He's there in everything I do, everything I see, everything I hear."

Simon opened his mouth but closed it a second later. He knew I would never agree to the only remedy he had to offer me. I preferred to suffer rather than forget everything. "Shall we go home now?" he asked.

"No thanks. I think I'll take a shower. You go back to Ginevra. I promised my parents I would help them out at the diner later on."

Simon shot me a telling glance. "You sure you're okay?"

"Of course," I said firmly, though the listlessness of my gaze betrayed my true feelings of resignation. "I'm starting to get used to it. It'll all stop soon, you'll see. I might not be able to ward off the attacks of a Subterranean who makes me confront my worst fears, but I can cope with the nightmares—though I don't know how much longer I can battle my guilt. Sometimes it feels like it's slowly killing me." Simon was right: the nightmares were a manifestation of my guilt over Evan's death. That was why I never found peace, not even at night.

"Okay, but call if you need us."

"I will."

His eyes locked on mine, Simon vanished. I took a moment to compose myself. Then I gathered my strength, got up from the couch, went into the bathroom, and locked the door behind me.

SCRATCHES ON THE HEART

I gripped the steering wheel and a solitary tear slid silently down my cheek. It was hard to compose myself with James Blunt's lyrics touching the pain I bore inside. I wiped away the tear with the back of my hand and parked the BMW behind the diner.

Inside it was packed with adults and kids. I noticed Alex, the young woman who waitressed for my parents on the weekends to pay for college expenses. She waved to me, then gave a tiny shrug and shot me a regretful glance to let me know she was too busy serving all those customers to come say hello.

"Here I am!" I leaned over the counter where my mom was staring down at the reservation list. She hadn't noticed me walk in.

"Honey! I thought you'd changed your mind."

"No, I overslept, that's all. Pass me that apron. I'll give you a hand."

"Oh, don't bother. You shouldn't exert yourself. Have a seat somewhere. We've got everything under control."

Just then a little boy raced past me and banged into a table, knocking over a stack of napkins. Alex raised her hands and ran over to pick them up, grumbling.

"It's not a bother. Besides, I'd be bored sitting there while you're all buzzing around like bees. I could wipe down the tables or load the trays—anything."

"All right, then. Here." Mom pulled an apron out of a drawer and tossed it to me. I put my hair up in a high ponytail with the hair tie I always wore around my arm and slipped on the visored dark-red cap that matched the uniforms.

"Alex!" my dad shouted from the kitchen. "Orders up for tables twelve, fifteen, eighteen. C'mon, let's get those hungry kids fed!"

"I'll do it, dear!" Mom called back, seeing that Alex had her hands full: she was holding two little boys at arm's length to keep them from getting into a tussle. "Gemma, watch the register, would you?"

"Sure, go ahead. I'll take care of their wallets." I smiled at her before she disappeared behind the counter. I straightened out the pastries in the case—something I did often, almost automatically. It relaxed me as my mind wandered through its winding, endless corridors. Right at the moment, though, they were too dark to explore and I had decided that for one afternoon I would do everything in my power not to let my parents see the burden that weighed on my heart. And so I focused on details, carefully examining the pralines on the brownies, counting the berries on the pies—anything that might help me forget my sadness.

"Aargh!" Alex leaned against the counter, exasperated. "Those brats are terrible!" I smiled at the funny face she was making. "It's impossible to keep them under control. There are too many of them!"

"Want me to give you a hand?" I said, still smiling.

"Are you kidding? Your dad would kill me. All he's done today is tell me to keep an eye on you and stop you from doing any kind of work you might get it into your head to do."

I gaped, surprised by how openly she'd admitted it, but then closed my mouth and smiled affectionately at Dad's thoughtfulness. And to think he had always been so stern.

"Don't tell him I told you, or he would—"

"He would kill you," I teased, imitating her voice. "Don't worry, your secret is safe with me."

"Hey, little boy! Climb down from there this second! I gotta go." Alex rolled her eyes at me and hurried off, leaving me with a smile on my lips.

A customer motioned me over and ordered three slices of pie and two large orange juices. I glanced at Alex and then at my mom, but they both had their hands full, so after preparing the order and putting it on a tray I decided to serve it myself before someone decided to run and help me. I couldn't stand the idea that they were acting differently because of the baby. I knew it was because they cared, but I wasn't used to being treated like a piece of fragile crystal. I lived with an Executioner and a Witch, and in my new world danger was an everyday thing. But they couldn't have known that.

I slowly picked up the tray, my eyes glued to the glasses, careful not to let the orange juice spill. I felt a little awkward, as though it were my first time, probably because of everyone's apprehension. As I came out from behind the counter, I checked the aisle both ways to make sure there weren't any little kids underfoot. Relieved, I looked up so I could see past my visor, but a hazy figure blocked my path. The sight of its green eyes gave me such a fright that I dropped the tray. The noise of the dishes crashing to the floor stupefied me. I knelt down to pick them up and realized no one was in front of me any longer.

"Gemma! Are you all right?" my mom cried in alarm as she rushed over to help. My hands moved quickly to clean up the mess I'd made, but my mind was still absent, bewitched by the jade-green gaze that had just electrified me.

"What happened? Don't you feel well?"

The voices around me were muffled. Only when it was too late did I realize my mom was feeling my forehead. "My God, you're burning up!" She took my arm, helped me up, and led me away. "Leave it, leave it there. Alex, would you take care of this? I'm calling you a doctor right this second."

"No!" Her offer was like a threat, snapping me out of it. I couldn't let a doctor examine me and put Simon and Ginevra at risk. "Freaking hallucinations," I muttered to myself. "Please, no doctor. I'm already a lot better. It was just a dizzy spell. I probably didn't sleep enough today."

"Then let me take you home."

"You can't leave Dad and Alex all on their own. Don't worry, Mom," I pleaded, hoping she would give in. "It's . . . it's been happening a lot lately. I'll be fine in no time, you'll see."

"Gemma, you're running a *high fever*. You need to go home."

I touched my forehead and showed her the heat was already fading, leaving my skin damp, as usual. "Trust me, I'm already better. I'll call Ginevra and ask her to come get me. Simon has a medical degree, you know that," I said, repeating the lie we often told. Actually, Simon could heal people better than any doctor on earth. It was just that my affliction remained a mystery; not even he could do anything against the effects of Witch poison.

"You're right, you aren't burning up any more. Go ahead and call Ginevra, but remember to get in touch later to let me know how you are or I might go crazy with worry."

I walked away from Mom and slid into a booth, realizing only then that my legs were shaking. Damn hallucinations. I forced back the tears. I felt so frustrated. Weren't the nightmares enough? Were they going to torture me when I was awake now as well?

Many people in my situation would have broken down. Maybe my time had come too. Without Evan to shore up the walls of my sanity, my protective shell was crumbling, leaving me fragile and defenseless on the edge of a dark, fathomless sea that led to madness. Like an anchor, the words carved on the table before me kept me from drifting away from shore on that sea of desperation: *Rise up and gather the brightest stars*. Evan had carved them there, maybe to bring me back to reality when I got lost. Back then, the hardest thing I could imagine was giving in to my longing to talk to him. I stroked the tabletop, remembering that moment, and shook myself out of it to focus on the vision I'd just had.

Those eyes . . . I had the funny feeling I'd seen them somewhere before. Could the hooded woman I'd glimpsed in front of me be from the dream that was haunting me? I couldn't remember. And why did the nightmares make my skin burn the way they did? Was it because of the poison too? Was my body really unable to fight it? Or maybe it was the Executioner—had she escaped and tracked me down? I shuddered at the thought and sent Simon a message, asking him to come get me.

He walked through the door minutes later, cordially saying hello to my parents. After reassuring them, we took the BMW back to the house—the only place I could feel the least bit safe.

My phone vibrated and I took it out of my sweatshirt pocket. There were four missed calls from Faith and Jeneane, plus a message Peter had sent an hour before.

Coming to the game?

"Simon?" I began hesitantly. He looked at me. "Turn back." He frowned, confused. "Do you mind if we stop somewhere first? I don't feel like going home. Not yet, at least."

"Where else do you want to go?"

"Peter's team is playing hockey at the Olympic Arena. It'd be nice to go see some of the game."

Simon ran his hand over the back of his neck, unsure. "It's not up to me to tell you what to do, but I'll come along if you don't mind. That way I won't need to worry."

"Of course, no problem. I'd love to spend some time with you."

"Great."

He parked outside the Olympic Arena. It was early evening and the big display on the side of the building said the game had already begun. A strong wind was blowing and along the façade flags from all over the world fluttered as though cheering on the teams. I ran up the steps, counting them in my mind. *Ten*, as always. I smiled. Once in a while it was nice to relive my old everyday routines. I paused to look at the five Olympic rings above the majestic entrance, savoring the sweet nostalgia.

The roar of the crowds hit us as we entered. The stands were packed. The Saranac Lake High team was our biggest rival and the fans were going crazy. According to the scoreboard, the Blue Bombers were winning 3-1 over the Red Storm and there were only seven minutes left in the game. I looked around and texted Faith.

Where are you?

She replied right away.

Look to your right.

I spotted Faith and Jeneane in the front row, waving to get my attention. As I led Simon through the crowd he held onto the hem of my sweatshirt to avoid losing track of me.

"Gemma! You made it after all!" Faith excitedly threw her arms around my neck just as the crowd cheered. The Red Storm had scored but we were still up by one point.

"What are they doing?! We've only got two minutes left! Come on, Bran! Move your ass and score another point!" Jeneane hollered. I smiled. She had always loved making a lot of noise. "Hey Gemma! You got here just in time. The game's in the bag! Peter scored two of our three points," she said.

When she noticed Simon beside me, her expression changed and she shifted into Barbie-doll mode. "Ooh . . . If I'd known you'd be bringing company I would've called you even more times."

Simon caught her innuendo and chuckled, touching his thumb to his nose sheepishly.

"Why didn't you tell us? We would have saved him a seat," Faith said apologetically.

"I wasn't planning on coming. I decided at the last minute and he tagged along."

"Oh, no problem. We can always squeeze together!" Jeneane was quick to say. "There's room for him in my seat." She batted her big blue eyes at Simon and scooched over to make space for him. The red seats were comfortable, but not big enough for two—not unless she sat in Simon's lap, and I suspected that was exactly her plan. I shot Jeneane a sidelong glance and pulled Simon away, giving him my spot. I couldn't stay standing very long or the people behind us would complain, so I sat down in the space between their seats.

Jeneane tugged on my arm and whispered in my ear, all excited. "Wow! How can you live under the same roof with a guy like *that?!*"

"Jeneane, you might as well stop drooling. He's with Ginevra."

"So what? She's been turning on all the guys at school since day one. Besides, she's not here." She winked at me, hiding who knew what intentions. It seemed that Jeneane felt threatened because Ginevra had stolen her place as queen bee. Was this her way to take revenge? I wasn't sure whether to be more afraid for Jeneane or Simon.

"Lucky for you! I wouldn't want to be in your shoes if Ginevra were here."

Just then the crowd burst into cheers and shot to their feet. The Blue Bombers had won. Jeneane grabbed my hand, pulled me down the stairs, and pressed herself up against the partition separating the stands from the rink, gesticulating to catch the attention of the boys gathered in the center of it. Peter, Brandon, and Jake were ecstatic, banging their hockey sticks together and letting out a battle cry. It was their victory ritual. When we were younger, we girls would make fun of them because it was so crude, but we'd since learned to love it. They skated across the ice to us and Peter triumphantly banged his head against the partition several times. Jake grabbed him and put him in a headlock, cheering for him, and Brandon did the same, because Pet had won the game almost singlehandedly. They pulled off their helmets and raised their sticks in our direction as Faith and Jeneane clapped their hands excitedly.

"It seems they won," Simon remarked next to me.

"Yeah, they rarely lose, though the Red Storm always gives them a real run for their money," I said.

"Gemma, hurry up! They want us to go meet them!" Faith took my arm and pulled me away. I noticed the boys were heading toward the locker room.

"Coming?" I asked Simon.

Jeneane seized her chance and linked arms with him. "Of course he's coming! Where else would he go?"

He nimbly shifted his weight, casually detaching himself from her without being rude, and rested a hand on my shoulder. "Actually, I'd rather wait in the car, if you don't mind." He shot me a telling look and I bit my lip. Simon was a gentleman and would never do anything to offend Jeneane, but he wanted to get her off his back.

"Oh, what a shame!" she whined.

Simon leaned over and put his mouth close to my ear. "Sorry, don't get me wrong, it's just that your girlfriend's got the wrong impression of me."

I smiled. Simon was always such a proud, self-confident guy—a perfect soldier—but he seemed so abashed around Hurricane Jeneane! "Don't worry, she gets that impression of practically every guy she meets. But come anyway. I don't want to make you wait in the car. It'll be quick."

"Okay," he said, giving in.

I took him by the hand and led him along as the crowd was still dispersing. "Jen, we can't go into the guys' locker room! Let's wait for them here," I said, but she probably wasn't listening. She pushed her way into the corridor. Just then Peter came out, pulling on a shirt. He instantly noticed my hand in Simon's and it seemed to bother him.

"Hey, hold the door! I didn't come all the way here for nothing!" Jeneane complained, peeking into the locker room.

"Go on in if you want. Brandon's still in there," Peter said.

"Who said anything about him?"

Jeneane threw the door open wide and I turned away, blushing. The entire team was bare-chested and some of them were only in their shorts. I shook my head as she actually walked into the locker room.

"Jeneane!" I shouted after her, but she ignored me. She was so self-confident. Her attitude never failed to amaze me. She'd dragged Faith with her, her red ponytail swishing through the door just before it closed and they disappeared inside. Faith was probably blushing—she was far shyer than Jeneane, though she would go along with things when encouraged.

Simon let go of my hand. "I'm going to take a walk around. I'll be back soon."

"Okay, but don't go too far. We won't stay very long."

Peter smiled at me. Simon must have redeemed himself in his eyes by giving us some time alone. "You came."

"I wish I could say 'Great game!' but I only showed up at the end. Sorry, it was already late when I read your message."

"The important thing is that you're here now."

"I heard you scored two points. You're still going strong!"

"Yeah, it was tough this time. The Red Storm is really good." Peter rubbed the back of his neck, as though trying to say something difficult. "So tell me, you and that guy have grown pretty close, I guess. He was holding your hand a minute ago."

"He's not 'that guy,' he's Simon! He cares a lot about me and I care about him. Come on, you can't be jealous." I nudged him affectionately and added defensively, "You always used to hold my hand." From the look on his face I could tell that was precisely the point. Peter had always felt something for me and his gestures had always meant something deeper than I'd realized—until recently. "In any case, it's not what you think. I've been through some bad times and Simon and Ginevra were there for me."

"You sure you know what it meant *to him?*"

"Yes: that he couldn't put up with Jeneane one more second!"

He raised an eyebrow and I smiled. I hadn't imagined the conversation could take such a ridiculous turn. Peter had finally confessed he loved me and now he felt threatened, but he knew nothing about Witches and Subterraneans. He couldn't imagine how Simon and Ginevra's love could withstand anything and how the bond between the three of us had strengthened over the recent months.

Brandon came out of the locker room followed by Jeneane, Faith, and Jake. They all looked worried. Brandon said, "Guys, we need to go watch a movie at the Palace. Bob's having problems and the theater might go out of business."

"What do you mean, it might go out of business? The Palace is legendary. It can't go out of business!" I said, alarmed.

"It will unless we find the money," he said. They've already launched a campaign to support the theater and tomorrow there's going to be a parade on Main Street. I found out this is the real reason for the Lana Del Rey concert."

"It's true. They were talking about it in the locker room," Faith said. "Unless the Palace comes up with enough money to switch to digital, it'll be shut down for good."

"The whole team's going there to celebrate and help Bob out," Jake added.

"We have so many memories there!" Jeneane put in. "Guys, we've absolutely got to go! It might be our last chance!"

"What, right now?" I asked hesitantly.

"The next showing's in fifteen minutes."

"I don't know . . ."

"Gemma, you can't say no. It's for a good cause."

"Yeah," Peter said. "Besides, I'm sure you'll love the movie. It's *The Hunger Games: Catching Fire.* They held it over."

"Simon?" I hoped he would back me up, but he shrugged.

"Fine with me, if you feel like it."

He probably wanted me to hang out with my friends a little while longer. After all, if he was there to protect me, he didn't see a problem with it. But going to the movies without Evan? And last time we'd taken Drake too.

"Come on, Gemma! Don't be a buzzkill," Jeneane groused.

"Oh, all right, we'll come too," I said. "I would've gone to see it anyway."

"Awesome!" she exclaimed. I could already see her figuring out a way to sit next to Simon.

"Going to see a movie won't kill me—unless you plan to offer me as a tribute, that is."

"Huh?"

"Maybe I should have waited until after the movie to crack that joke. Never mind."

Jeneane shrugged. I doubted she'd seen the first episode in the series—I'd seen it with Peter. She only went to the movies to drool over the hot guys on the screen. By the end of the second one she would no doubt be in love with Finnick.

"Should we ask Ginevra to meet up with us there?" I whispered to Simon as we headed to our car.

"No. It's best that she stay to watch over the Subterranean. We can't leave her unguarded—it's too dangerous."

"Shouldn't you at least let her know?"

"I already did." I looked at him, puzzled. "We don't use phones. That is, with her I don't need to. If I call her in my mind, she can hear all my thoughts."

"Oh."

Simon laughed and tousled my hair before getting behind the wheel. Faith and Jeneane came with us and Jeneane talked nonstop the whole way there. The guys, on the other hand, took Brandon's jeep.

We parked across from the Palace, a large red-brick building. People were lined up at the door, and on the sides of the marquee a message of support welcomed moviegoers:

Please help save the theater.
Go digital or go dark.

We paid for our tickets and went in. As I suspected, Jeneane swooped toward Simon like a falcon, but Brandon grabbed her by the hips and pulled her close. She laughed and in the end went with the flow and kissed him. I sat next to Simon and Peter took the seat on my other side.

The lights dimmed and music filled the theater.

"Want me to get you more?"

I turned to look at Simon. He was staring at me, seemingly amused by my expression. I froze with a fistful of popcorn halfway to my mouth. In no time at all I had polished off a giant tub. "Yeah, thanks, if you don't mind," I whispered gratefully. Simon got up to buy more, a smile on his lips.

"Psst! Hey, Gemma!" Jeneane leaned over Peter. "Let's switch seats."

"No, Jeneane. Stay there and watch the movie," I admonished her, hiding a smile. She stuck her tongue out at me and Brandon put his arm around her shoulders. That girl was incorrigible!

I looked over at Faith and Jake, further down in our row. Their eyes were trained on the screen, but there was a strong vibe between them and I wasn't so sure they were paying attention to the story. From time to time Jake moved his fingers to stroke Faith's on the armrest.

"Like the movie?" Peter asked, leaning toward me. We were so close our heads were touching.

"The adaptation is pretty faithful to the book, so yeah, I like it. *Hunger Games* is one of my favorite trilogies and I don't like it when they distort a book that's important to me."

"I know." He smiled and tried to take my hand, but Simon came back just then and I took advantage of his arrival by reaching for the popcorn. I couldn't let Peter hold my hand. Not there. He loved me and I understood his attempts to bring me closer to him, but the last time I'd been to the movies my hand had been clasped in Evan's, and my heart still ached too much. I was only there to help Bob. I didn't even care about seeing the movie.

Simon suddenly grabbed my wrist and gripped it tightly. I spun around and my heart leapt to my throat. It wasn't Simon, but a man I'd never seen before. "What do you want? Let go of me!" I hissed. I tried to pull my hand away, but he held it tight, his pleading face close to mine. He looked like a desperate vagrant.

"Help! They're going to get me!"

"Stop it! Cut it out!" I managed to break free and the man suddenly seemed to be suffocating, choking.

"They'll get you too," he gurgled, turning my blood ice-cold. Inside his mouth something moved. A butterfly. Its legs popped out through his lips and it crawled out. It was black. Completely black. The man seemed to be in agony. I reached out, but when I touched him he exploded into hundreds of black butterflies, making me jump in my seat.

"Gemma, everything okay?" The voice brought me back to reality. Simon. I looked around and everything was normal. Only Simon and Peter seemed to have noticed anything. Everyone in the room had just jumped in their seats when the monkey mutts burst into the frame.

"Want me to get you some water?" Peter asked with concern.

"No thanks. Everything's fine. This scene is just creepy, that's all."

While Peter seemed convinced, Simon suspected something had actually happened. "Another hallucination?" he asked.

I nodded and he reached for my hand, sensing my desperate need for comfort, but the second he touched me he jerked his hand back as though he'd been burned. We looked each other in the eye and he clasped my hand in his, ignoring the powerful heat I was emanating.

"What's wrong with me? Why am I seeing these things?"

Simon slid his arm around me and I rested my head on his shoulder, feeling safe. "It'll stop. Sooner or later it'll stop."

We were all heading for our cars, talking about the movie. "Why should Katniss have to choose? I mean, they're both in love with her. She should make the most of it. That's what I would do," Jeneane said.

"Oh yeah?!" In protest, Brandon grabbed her hand and pulled her against him.

"What's wrong with it? Until she makes up her mind she can be with both of them. That happens a lot in the movies!"

I rolled my eyes. "I can't stand love-triangle stories. Who knows why they're so popular these days. The main characters discover 'true love,' they promise each other the moon and swear they'll never part. As soon as there's the slightest problem they grow apart, break up, or—in most cases—someone else shows up and comes between them. It shouldn't be that way."

"Love is an immense emotion. You shouldn't squander it on only one person," Jeneane shot back, convinced.

"True love isn't like that. When you really love someone, it doesn't matter how many people knock on your door. You don't let them in, because there's only one key that opens that lock, and it belongs to the person you love. There's no room for anyone else." Peter's face clouded at my words.

"Well, Jeneane, looks like the door to your heart comes with a skeleton key," Jake joked. Brandon shoved him in her defense, hiding a smile.

"Have I ever told you you're a dumbass?" she said, though she didn't seem offended.

"It depends on the circumstances, though," Faith said, her shy gaze studying Peter, to encourage him, perhaps, or maybe to persuade me.

"The heart knows no circumstances," I said firmly. Evan was dead and yet my heart had never stopped beating for him and him alone.

"I propose an Xbox challenge!" Peter said. "Let's get a pizza at Bazzi's and go to my house. I got the latest Halo!"

"Last time I creamed you, if you'll remember," I teased him.

"Oh-ho! That sounds like a dare!" Jake exclaimed, winking at me.

"Nooo, not another multiplayer game, please? There's no dragging you guys away from them!" Faith groaned, a hint of a smile on her lips. She'd always liked spending evenings at the boys' houses.

"Gemma, why don't you come in the Jeep with us? That way Simon can go pick up his girlfriend."

"Um . . . I wasn't thinking of going. Sorry, Pet." We had almost reached our cars and I really couldn't wait to get home.

"Come on! We still need to celebrate our big win!" Peter said. "Simon, why don't you go get your girlfriend and meet up with us there?"

This time Simon realized I didn't want to go and came to my rescue. "It's late. Maybe another time, but thanks for the invite."

We waved goodbye, got into the BMW, and headed home.

A dizzy spell had made me lie down, but since I didn't feel like holing up in Evan's room I opted for the couch. Meanwhile, worried about the visions I'd told them about, Simon and Ginevra had gone down to the dungeon to check on our captured Subterranean and, I imagined, to give her another dose of poison to make sure she stayed put.

I distractedly stroked Irony as I watched an episode from the fifth season of *The Vampire Diaries*. He seemed to sense I wasn't feeling well. I loved the show and never missed an episode but I was tired of watching TV, so I heeded the grumble in my stomach and went to search the kitchen cabinets for something to curb my hunger. I was devouring a chocolate hazelnut bar when a sinister murmur made me jump.

"Simon?" I stepped cautiously into the living room. "Gwen? That you?"

Another sinister whisper. Finding the living room empty and silent gave me goosebumps. I continued to listen and a moment later the sound returned, this time stronger: it was the ghastly hiss of a chorus, a symphony of barely audible voices whispering together in prayer.

"Who's there? What do you want from me?! Leave me alone!"

A sudden breeze coming from behind me caught me off guard. I spun around and the shadowy figure of a woman cut my breath short. She was right in front of me, yet it was like she wasn't there. I gasped, panic seizing me as the sound grew stronger and more threatening. It exploded in my head as her eyes stared at me from the shadows of the golden hood she wore—two jade-green gems so intense they sent a jolt through my entire body. The mysterious, magnetic energy they emanated paralyzed me. Only then did I recognize her: it was the woman who tormented me in every dream—but now she was right there in front of me, so powerful I was afraid I might be electrocuted if I moved too close. Her lips were motionless and yet the strange murmur continued to gain strength in my head. Her body flowed toward me, her long golden cloak barely touching the floor. Frightened, I backed up but tripped and fell.

All at once Simon was there. He ran to me, crossing through the woman as though she didn't exist. She dissolved in the air like a cloud of smoke.

"Gemma, everything okay?" His voice sounded wary, as though he could tell I felt lost in a place from which I couldn't return. "Christ, you're running another fever. Ginevra!"

"She said I have to go to her." A tremor gripped my body when I realized the distant sound had come from my own lips.

"Who did?" Simon looked confused. He rested his hand on my knees, still pressed to my chest. I finally managed to raise my head.

"The woman with the hood." A tingle arose in the back of my neck and crept through my head. Then the image clouded over and everything went black.

"She's waking up."

I barely heard Ginevra's low whisper. Her voice was flat and strangely distant. I propped myself up on my elbows, slowly realizing I was on the couch in the living room. Had it only been another bad dream?

"What happened?" My voice was almost unrecognizable and my head wouldn't stop burning.

Simon and Ginevra came over. "You fainted." Simon stared at me with an indecipherable expression, like he couldn't understand who—or what—I was. Ginevra, on the other hand, had a waxy pallor, her gaze lost in some distant world.

"What? Why?!"

"No clue. You were raving and then you went unconscious."

"For how long?" I asked, wringing my hands nervously.

"Ten minutes, tops."

"Was there a problem with the Subterranean? Did she find a way to escape?" I asked, looking back and forth between them.

"No. Nothing like that." Simon's voice was devoid of emotion, while Ginevra seemed to have lost the power of speech.

"Then the poison you gave her must be wearing off and she—"

Simon shook his head, discarding the possibility. "She's out of commission. Her mind is lost who knows where. She could never regain enough lucidity to attack you—not right now. Ginevra's blood is a powerful drug."

I gulped, desperately searching for another explanation. All the while Ginevra remained silent, as though afraid to speak to me. "Gwen, what is it? What's that look on your face? I know you. There's something you've figured out and you don't want to tell me." Simon quickly looked toward his girlfriend, but she just pressed her lips together. "It's still the poison, isn't it? Is that why I keep having hallucinations? It's not normal for my temperature to shoot up so high and then drop back to normal a minute later." I waited for an answer, but none came. "If the Angel has nothing to do with it, what's wrong with me? Gwen, answer me, I'm begging you!"

"I honestly don't know what to tell you," she whispered. Her gaze was still distant, unable to meet mine.

"Just tell me the truth. If the poison I ingested is slowly killing me, I want to know. Do—do you think I'm going to die? I need to know."

"No, Gemma. I won't let you die," she announced firmly, as though it were out of the question. For the first time, she looked me in the eye. "That's a promise."

What was happening to me then? I hugged her desperately and she returned the hug just as intensely.

"I won't let you go. You're the only sister left to me. We'll get through this, you'll see." She stroked my hair affectionately as I nodded like a little girl. "One way or another, we'll get through this. No one is going to take you from me."

"What was that sound?" I freed myself from Ginevra's embrace and instinctively rested both hands on my belly.

"I didn't hear anything." Simon looked around, circumspect, before turning back to stare at me strangely.

"It's a boy," I whispered, clasping my fingers over my belly. Ginevra's eyes lit up and met mine.

Simon shrugged. "Sure, it might—"

"No, I know for certain. I *heard* him." My eyes filled with hot tears. "How is it possible for me to hear him?" I asked in disbelief.

"It must be some power the baby possesses. Maybe it lets him communicate with you through his mind. After all, he's inside you." Ginevra's face had regained its color. The revelation had wiped away her apprehension and filled her with enthusiasm.

"I can't believe it. I can hear his mind. He sent me a short, confused sound—a meaningless message. But I heard his voice! I'm not even showing yet but his mind has already developed. How is that possible?"

Simon tried to recover from his astonishment. "It's not a human embryo, we know that for sure now, but there's no way we can know how he's developing inside your body. Maybe he's what's causing the fever and the hallucinations," he added, thinking aloud, though he didn't seem entirely convinced.

Maybe we should take her to a doctor after all, someone we can trust. With our powers, it wouldn't be difficult to make—

"No doctors, please," I exclaimed. They turned to stare at me, shock on their faces. "What's wrong?" I asked.

For a moment, Simon looked at me in silence. "I didn't say anything."

My blood ran cold and my body turned to ice.

"He only *thought* it," Ginevra explained, her expression as shocked as it was bewildered. She had heard the remark in both Simon's mind and mine.

"*You* can hear my thoughts?" Simon was staring at me as though seeing me for the first time.

"I don't know . . . No! Come on, that's insane." I looked from one to the other, feeling more and more like a circus freak. "It's probably because of the baby. Maybe his powers are starting to develop and they're affecting me too." What the hell was happening to me? "Gwen?" Unable to handle their stares any longer, I tried to cling to Ginevra's help, but her face had grown grim and her mind seemed unreachable.

Simon leaned over as though to put his arm around my shoulders, but I pushed him away. "Leave me alone!" Suddenly overcome with anger, I jumped up from the couch and stormed off. I wished I could hide away in some distant place or even disappear if it meant I wouldn't have to feel the weight of their eyes on me. I grabbed the car keys in the foyer before either of them could stop me.

"Where do you think you're going? Gemma, wait!" Ginevra tried to reason with me, but the blood was boiling in my veins, shooting up to my head and clouding my brain.

"Don't try to follow me," I warned them in a low growl. "I need some time alone. Please." The way my voice broke when I uttered the last word forestalled any attempt on their part to change my mind as I shut the door behind me. My hand still on the knob, I squeezed my eyes shut as a wave of anger and frustration shook my body, making it tremble.

From behind the door I heard Simon's voice, tinged with compassion. "Let her go. With the Subterranean locked up she's not in danger."

There was no reply from Ginevra. Or maybe I'd taken myself out of earshot so I wouldn't have to hear her. I started the engine, unsure which way to head. After all, where could I possibly go? Peter's house? The diner? No matter where I went there was no escape from everything that was overwhelming me. There was something wrong with me. It didn't matter what it was or why none of us could figure out the reason behind it. What mattered was that instead of getting better, I was getting worse by the day, sinking further and further into it. I wondered when I would reach the point of no return. It wouldn't be long, I could feel it.

Looking up, I realized my hand had turned off the engine in an automatic gesture. I got out of the car, not surprised by the place my body, on autopilot, had brought me. As I made my way to the edge of the lake I shot a bitter glance at the house that stood in solitude among the leafless, snow-covered trees. Our hideaway. Mine and Evan's. My heart constricted, thinking it would never be that again, that it was all part of the past—a memory that time would eventually consume. It would disappear, like ashes in the wind.

Long icicles dripped from the frost-encrusted branches as the gray winter afternoon gradually waned, making way for the queen of the night: a fiery-red full moon that slowly made its solitary ascent to claim dominion over the heavens. Even the stars seemed to be missing; only two lonely specks shone in the darkening sky.

What would become of my life? I couldn't imagine the sun ever warming me again. It felt like nothing would ever be the same, as if the real Gemma had died along with Evan, leaving behind a useless shell emptied of all feeling.

Moved by a deep desperation, I went back to the car and sank into the seat. I felt defeated. There was nowhere for me to go. I didn't want to go back to Simon and Ginevra's and let them feel sorry for me. My eye fell on a flashlight wedged between the seats. I grabbed it and quickly climbed out of the car before my common sense could force me to reason. Twilight thickened the air and darkened the path leading to the old wooden house. The gate let out an unsettling creak but nothing scared me any more except my own demons. Once inside, the door shut out even the faint evening light. The darkness engulfed me. For a minute I stood there, steadying my breathing, trying to ignore the shapes created by the shadows. I switched on the flashlight and the beam illuminated the fireplace. Moving the flashlight back and forth, I scanned the room and slowly crept across the hardwood floor that creaked beneath my shoes. I wished I had a lighter so I could start a fire but I would just have to make do. I knelt on the red rug in front of the fireplace and a knot formed in my throat as I ran my hand over its soft surface. The most precious memory of my entire life burst into my head.

If my heart could beat, right now it would be out of control. I closed my eyes, abandoning myself to the sweet whisper. I could almost feel the warmth of Evan's breath on my skin.

This has been the most romantic afternoon I've ever spent. I wish it would never end.

It doesn't have to.

I lay down on the rug, curled up, and clasped my knees to my chest. Evan's voice was so loud and clear in my head I almost believed he was really there.

God, you're beautiful. I love you to death, Jamie.

I squeezed my eyes shut and a hot tear slid down my face. I rested my hand on my shoulder as though I had actually just felt the gentle touch of his lips on me. In my heart, Evan was still there at my side, whispering his love into my ear. It was a lie I would never stop telling myself. How could it actually be over? I refused to believe he was gone. I couldn't accept having to live only with his memory.

"Evan . . ." My lips moved, whispering in the darkness as the tears silently slid down my cheeks. "You promised. You promised you would never leave me . . . I can't go on without you. I miss you too much." I bit the sleeve of my sweatshirt and a sob shook me. "*Antar mayy as,"* I murmured in a tiny voice. As I lay there, exhausted from the pain, suffocated by the sobs, sleep slowly pulled me away with it as I imagined Evan's body nestled behind mine, enveloping me in its warmth. Wakefulness slowly gave way to sleep and I felt his body heat, fooling me into believing it was real. I tightened my embrace around myself, pretending it was his, and surrendered to slumber, cradled by the soft whisper of his voice.

The crack of a whip pierced the air, making me cringe. I tried to discover where it had come from, but an eerie whisper filled my head, confusing me. A shout of rage made my heart constrict.

Evan. I had no doubt it was him.

I tried to stand up but something held me back. A heavy chain bound my ankles. Another piercing scream sent a pang through my heart. It was Evan, I was certain of it. He must be around there somewhere, and someone was torturing him. Driven by desperation, I dragged myself across the cold stone floor to the edge of the rock wall that imprisoned me. A whimper rose straight from my heart when my eyes confirmed my terrible suspicion. Evan was at the bottom of what appeared to be a crater, wrists and ankles chained to the wall, his muscles jerking uselessly at every blow inflicted upon him. His head was hanging, and his hair—longer and wilder than I remembered it— covered his face. Standing before him was a woman with a thick mane of copper-colored hair, clad in a brown Amazon-style dress that looked like it was sewn onto her skin. She brandished a heavy, lethal-looking whip, her face lit up in a sadistic sneer.

"Evan . . ." I wanted to scream his name, but all that issued from my mouth was a whisper. The redhead's hand rose into the air and my heart beat faster, as though rebelling against the sight. The whip sliced through the air and cruelly slashed Evan's defenseless body. He gritted his teeth in a howl of rage and glared at the woman. Hot tears streaming down my face, I squeezed my eyes shut so I wouldn't see, tugging fruitlessly on the chains around my ankles. Another cry of pain from Evan pierced my heart like a dagger as an explosion of energy burst from my chest and a primitive howl of frustration gripped me. Like a flash of lightning on the darkest of nights, a figure darted toward me, halting at my side. My furious eyes shot to the woman like the lash of a whip. She studied me with a slight smile of satisfaction. Her full-length golden cloak flowed over a green bodice gown.

"What do you want from Evan?!" The snarl that escaped me was unexpectedly fierce, but the woman said nothing. She just stared at me with that enigmatic look on her face, her jade-green eyes piercing. The longer I looked at her, the more I was convinced I'd seen her somewhere before. "I know you," I whispered, studying her intently. "Who are you?"

She leaned over and gazed at me with an expression that didn't seem quite as hostile. Then she smiled and her voice filled my head. "*I told you, that isn't the right question.*"

Trying to rebel against the power of her gaze, I twisted under the chains binding me. "Why are you holding us prisoner?! Free me and let me go to him!"

The woman's eyes lingered on my shackled ankles. "We aren't the ones keeping you imprisoned. You are. All you need to do is make the right choice and you'll finally be free of all your suffering. Only you can unlock those chains."

Confused, I frowned. Evan screamed again and rage blinded me. "What do you want from him?!" I hissed. "Leave him alone! Let him go! Torture me instead! Take me!"

The anguish of another lash made Evan roar like a caged lion. All at once something inside me exploded. My face transformed into a mask of pure evil as a dark energy crashed down on me like a tidal wave. From my chest emerged an unfamiliar sound like the snarl of a ravenous feline. An electric current streaked through my body and my hair rose over my shoulders as though swept up by some mysterious windstorm. The chains around my ankles burst and crumbled at my feet. The deafening noise snapped me out of my stupor and I instantly regained control of my body.

Disconcerted, I stared at the remains of the chains. My hand moved cautiously to pick up some of the iron scraps. They were still hot. What had happened to me? An unknown force, powerful and dark, had suddenly possessed me. How had I managed to free myself? Slowly, I raised my eyes to the woman. She was watching me, a smile as captivating as it was approving on her face.

The whispering returned with even greater intensity as I looked down at my hands, stunned at what I had just done. "Who am I?" I whispered in dismay amid the chorus of voices chanting inside my head.

The woman's smile broadened with satisfaction. *"That* is the right question."

Bolting upright, I found myself sitting in the pitch dark, my heart threatening to burst through my chest. My lungs gulped in oxygen as my hand trailed over a soft surface. Where was I? The blackest darkness shrouded everything. Slowly, my memories resurfaced and the phantom of my nightmare vanished. I was still at the lake house. I must have fallen asleep. As I groped for the flashlight, a shiver ran through my body.

There was a slow creak. In that grim darkness, a spectral sound arose in the silence like the hissing of a thousand snakes. Another shiver swept over my back as my hand searched desperately for the flashlight. The hiss grew louder and I shuddered, my terrified eyes trying uselessly to penetrate the darkness while the voices murmured their ominous message like a whispered litany, as though I were still caught in the nightmare.

I froze. It was as if the sound had penetrated my head and was controlling my movements. Possessing me. Suddenly I couldn't remember who I was. All I wanted was to listen to those voices, let them fill me, let them complete me. They were everything for me.

Come with us. You cannot stop it. It has begun . . .

My body slowly rose, moved by some dark, irresistible power. A strange burning sensation in my hands gradually rippled up my arms. I couldn't tell what was causing it. The pain intensified, and I clenched my teeth. It was as if something was flaying my fingers, grinding them down to the bone. I didn't care; a new desire had taken over not only my body but also my mind. Every trace of fear had left me, making way for an overwhelming feeling of power. If I wanted to, I could bend the whole world to my will . . .

"What are you doing?"

Ginevra's voice burst into my head, releasing me from the evil that had possessed me. I shook myself free of it as a lacerating pain gripped my hands and shot to my elbows. In the glow of Ginevra's flashlight, I read shock and consternation on her face. I looked down slowly to discover the cause of the pain and was stunned to see blood covering my hands and trickling down my arms.

I saw a flash of resignation cross Ginevra's face, and something died in her eyes. Warily, I turned for the first time to look at the wall illuminated by her flashlight. The world crumbled beneath my feet. "Oh my God."

"What's going on?" Simon appeared in the silence and stopped dead in his tracks in front of the wall where my fingernails had gouged a deep, blood-smeared furrow with intersecting lines to form an arcane symbol. *The same one I had sketched at school.*

"Fuck," he swore, but I wasn't listening to him.

"They're coming," I said in a faint voice, my gaze fixed on the macabre scarlet symbol that grew distorted as the blood dripped down the wall. It looked like a V with scratches traversing it, enclosed by a misshapen crescent moon. *A panther's claw marks*, I thought instinctively.

Clenching her fists, Ginevra turned to face Simon. "We have a problem."

THE POWER OF DARKNESS

The noise of a thunderstorm howled through the room and the doors and windows banged open and shut with a deafening clatter. All at once silence fell. From the semidarkness rose a vaguely familiar voice. "Is that what you call your Sisters now? A *problem?*"

A shiver made my blood run cold. *The Witches.*

"Anya." Ginevra dropped her flashlight. It fell to the parquet floor, casting a single cone of golden light across it. Conflicting emotions battled for control inside me as I watched her face. Caught between bitterness and dismay, Ginevra's gaze was fixed on the darkness.

Three women emerged from the shadows and walked toward us in black leather jumpsuits. The image of three panthers crossed my mind. The woman in the middle had long ebony hair with silver tips and eyes that glittered like two sapphires in the night. Another gazed at me arrogantly, her honey-colored eyes ablaze and her long hair an indefinable shade somewhere between blond and auburn. The one Ginevra had called Anya had riveting eyes the color of jade-green diamonds. She wore her long, chestnut-brown hair in braids that hung over her breasts, with a crown of finer braids crisscrossing her forehead. Of the three, her gaze seemed the least hostile.

Simon stepped protectively in front of Ginevra, his face twisted into a threatening expression as he glowered at them.

"No!" Ginevra cried, terrified by the thought of a conflict between Simon and the three Witches. They emanated such power I could feel it under my skin; they could have disintegrated Simon in a split second.

Instead, a contemptuous smile escaped the middle Witch, who I imagined was their leader. It was the smile of a black wolf gripping its prey in its jaws. "Brave of you, minion of Death, but never fear—we aren't here for Ginevra." The Witch kept her piercing, crystal-blue eyes riveted on me, making my heart shudder. "We're here to claim what belongs to us."

I frowned in bewilderment and a friendly smile spread across Anya's lips. She winked at me.

"No!" More than a protest, Ginevra's shout was a cry of desperation.

The woman with the black hair let out a bitter, scornful laugh, her eyes glittering like a million fragments of lapis lazuli. "No? Haven't you noticed the signs? Five hundred years have passed, but the memory should still be vivid in your mind. We are united by an ancient calling. Our lives are bound together in time."

The Witch's voice reverberated inside me, clouding my mind. What was she trying to say?

"It's not going to happen. I won't let it!" Ginevra said defiantly.

The Witch smiled again, but this time an evil light glinted in her eyes as she stared at Ginevra with a challenging air, as though irritated by her words. "You would not dare oppose us again. We will show no leniency this time. I would tell you how many centuries we have waited for her, but I suspect you already know. We have already lost one Sister. It will not happen again."

The Witch shot me a fiery look and instantly a stabbing pain in my belly doubled me over.

"Gemma!" Ginevra and Simon both rushed to help me. I raised my head to look at the Witch, wondering what her intentions were. She smiled at me, a bewitching smile.

"It burns, does it not?" The pain eased at the sound of her voice and I struggled to my feet, trying not to look weak. The Witch pointed a finger at my belly and I instinctively covered it to protect the baby. What did she want with my son?

"Why do you not raise your shirt?" Her question, spoken with a seductive smile, took me by surprise. I turned to Ginevra, who looked aghast. The Witch spoke again. "It is the serpent inside her. He is already forming."

A tremor in my heart gave me all the answers as she continued to fix her eyes on me as though I belonged to her. Her voice began to whirl in my head and my mind traveled to another place as I lost myself in her words. What was she insinuating? Could it be that—

You are correct, Naiad. You and your Dakor will be one. You cannot prevent it. The strange voice filled my head. I was certain it wasn't my own. Suddenly everything, no matter how dark and frightening, made sense.

I was one of them.

I was a Witch.

"Now I see . . . The nightmares. The premonitions. The terrible sensations—"

"No, Gemma! Snap out of it!" Ginevra shook me by the shoulders. "Listen to me. You've got to resist them!" She glared at the Witch. "She'll never choose to join you!"

The Witch laughed at Ginevra's brazenness. "She will when the time comes. She cannot elude the call of power. It has begun. You cannot stop it."

"It can't be her—it's impossible! You're making a mistake. Only four hundred and ninety-seven years have passed. There are still three left to go!" Ginevra sounded on the verge of desperation.

"Evil is inside her and the poison awakened it. That is how we detected her presence. It happened months ago. Its scent awakened her senses and we perceived her, though it was not yet time. When she later ingested it, her inner nature began to rebel. Direct contact with the right dose of poison will complete the process, and it will be irreversible. She belongs to us." The Witch shot me a piercing look. "The task of all the Subterraneans sent to kill you was not to make you *meet* your fate—it was to *prevent* it. You must choose. Do not deny what you truly are. One serpent bite will bind you to us forever."

"I'll never allow it!" Ginevra screamed.

The Witch replied calmly, "Never is such a long time, dost thou not agree? And we are so good at waiting." She threw me a look full of promise. "Remember that dreams hide many secrets . . ."

"Go to hell, all of you!" Ginevra growled contemptuously, but the Witches simply smiled at her.

"Count on it." The power of three evil gazes penetrated my bones before vanishing into the darkness, leaving my mind adrift in unknown realms. A flashback filled my head. I had dreamed of them—that was why their faces were so familiar. I had also seen Evan in those same dreams.

And if *they* really existed . . .

No one knows what happens to a Subterranean's soul. Everyone assumes it winds up in Hell . . . in Hell . . . in Hell. Evan's words surged among my thoughts, engulfing me like a river in flood.

Hell. Evan had spoken to me about it one summer day. Why hadn't it occurred to me before? If Eden existed—and I had seen it with my own eyes—its opposite also had to exist.

What if he was there?

Something stirred inside me. Buried by months of suffering beneath a thick crust of pain, a new emotion emerged from the dark abyss of my heart. Hope.

If there was even a remote possibility Evan was in that place, I had to go there and find him.

EVAN

THE WOLF AND ITS PREY

For centuries I had served Death as its dutiful soldier, yet I'd never known its bitter taste. Not even when it came to me under false pretenses, offering me refuge in the comforting thought that it might free me from the torment of life if the inauspicious star that guided our love ever took my Gemma from me. Back then I'd fooled myself, thinking death might quench the fire that consumed me every time I thought of her. To my dismay, I discovered that nothing would ever relieve my suffering. It was just a lie, an illusion my mind had created to keep desperation from driving me insane. Now I knew that Death— faithful ally of the blackest shadows—had locked my heart up in its darkest dungeon and taken everything from me.

I didn't care how hard or how long my body was tortured. I couldn't feel the pain any more. I couldn't feel the burning sensation eating at my wrists, trapped in poisoned shackles. I couldn't feel the lashes of the whip. I couldn't feel the hunger. I couldn't feel the consuming fire when their accursed serpents sank their fangs into me. Their accursed Dakor. I couldn't feel anything any more. Or maybe it was that the pain didn't matter to me because a far more intense, more unbearable agony devoured me from the inside every time I thought of her, my Jamie, my sun. Without her, I discovered the darkness of the shadows. I lost the heart I had rediscovered after centuries. It had been torn from me in a vile deception of fate. Not a second went by that I didn't think of her, wavering between reason and madness in the desperate awareness that I had left her alone in a world where Death had already drawn its bowstring and trained its black arrow on her. The thought of not being able to protect her any more drove me mad. Just as much as the knowledge that I would never see her again. Like a poisoned woodworm, the thought bored into my mind relentlessly, even during the moments following the serpent bites when my mind was lost to me.

How would Gemma survive without my protection? How would I be able to live without her, consumed by such torment for all eternity?

Would Simon and Ginevra continue to protect her or had they already left her to her fate? After Drake's betrayal, I could be sure of nothing.

Flashes of a tortured existence alternated with moments of total bewilderment when I couldn't even remember who I was. I would try to fight, to get up, but my strength was gone and I would collapse, at the mercy of the dark spell that kept me trapped in that place, forcing me to lose myself in the darkest corners of the bitter-cold rooms of my heart. And yet, like a star in the blackest sky, a glimmer of light continued to bring me back, whispering a single name, and for one instant my heart would delude itself into believing it had begun to beat again.

Subdued laughter reached me in the darkness.

I could barely make out the murmur of voices, but after so many serpent bites I couldn't even count them, my mind was probably refusing to return to that godforsaken place.

"He's really good-looking even with all those scars, don't you think?"

More stifled laughs, followed by the menacing crack of a whip that pierced the air. A tingle crept up my legs; my body automatically cringed at the blood-chilling sound.

"Silence!" shouted a hostile, poisonous voice I'd learned to recognize: Devina, the cruelest, most capricious of the harpies keeping me prisoner.

"What's the big deal? Calm down. If you ask me, all you want is— Oh! The empress is coming." The voices fell silent.

"What is happening here?"

"I was just teaching these two vixens a lesson."

"Oh, listen to her! All hail the queen of the vipers! Why don't you drink some chamomile, Dev?"

"Enough! Suri, Nausyka, why are you not on patrol? And you, Devina, should not use that tone with your Sisters."

"We just got back. The hunt went well. It's just that when we saw this prisoner, we wondered why he hasn't given in yet. Maybe Devina isn't the right one to deal with him."

"That does not concern you. There are other matters that require my presence. Devina will take my place while I attend to the Reaping. Obey her every command."

"It will be done, my lady," the two Witches chorused.

"And you, Devina, make sure the prisoner is always under your control. You may torture him if you wish, but keep your distance from him."

"Why?!" Devina's voice reached me loud and clear. I wasn't sure if she'd raised her voice out of irritation or if my mind was beginning to emerge from the abyss. "None of the Sisters has claimed him! He's just a slave, like all the others!"

"He doesn't belong to you!"

It was another voice that had replied scornfully to Devina's protest. I recognized it at once. *Anya.* Courageous and kind—the only one in that madhouse.

"Who does he belong to, then?" Devina sounded beside herself with anger. "That half-Witch who doesn't even know we're keeping him here?"

"*Do not try to seduce him,* Devina. You had your chance with him centuries ago. It is too late now. That is an order, and it is to be obeyed," Sophia thundered, adding something I couldn't understand in the ancient language of the Witches. It was the only tongue Subterraneans didn't know.

Devina whined with frustration as soon as their empress was gone.

"What do we do with these?" Nausyka asked, more cautiously this time, probably intimidated by Devina's expression that I imagined was brimming with hatred.

"Are you two still here? What else do you want?"

"Sophia said we had to report to you. This week's hunt for Subterraneans went better than we had hoped. We captured seventeen more of them. They're already in their places, but these three aren't entirely convinced yet." There was a loud metallic clang, followed by grunts. "They refuse to bend to our will."

"Lock them in the dungeon," Devina said, her tone still bitter from the insult. She couldn't stand having to take orders from someone else—she preferred to issue them herself. "Make sure your Dakor keep them company. I'm sure it won't take them long to decide which side they're on. Now go. I'm getting a headache."

The room fell silent and I thought they'd finally left me alone. Then a murmur, distant, more confused, filled my head.

What was that? Did you feel it too?

It was just the wind. You sure you're okay?

I couldn't tell where it was coming from, but a new emotion suddenly stirred violently within me, as if my heart had started beating again.

Of course, I'm great!

A shudder electrified me. Gemma! Her voice, so full of life, pulled me out of the dark abyss I was often forced to wander in, lost, thanks to the effects of the poison. Unlike all the other times, though, this time I hadn't imagined it. I had actually heard her voice, so clear it made its way into my heart. As if she were right there next to me.

The lash of a whip brought me back to Hell. I gritted my teeth, steeling myself against the pain as my body reawakened.

"Welcome back, my little Angel."

A mocking grin welcomed me as I awoke. I jerked on the chains that gripped my wrists and ankles, ignoring the burning sensation caused by the poison that coated them.

"It took you a while. I didn't think you were going to recover this time. But maybe it's my fault. I'm afraid I overdid it with the doses of poison—but you make me so *angry*."

"You damned Witch!" I snarled, but mine was just the frustrated roar of a defenseless caged lion. If I had been able to free myself I would have torn her to shreds.

"Don't get so excited, Spartan, it'll only turn me on. I've always liked renegades. I didn't know how to get your attention any more, but I see my strategy woke you up this time."

You made *it?*

It's not worth much, but I spent a week making it.

It's priceless.

"Gemma . . ." I murmured, devastated. Her voice rang through the grotto and echoed off the rough walls like a boomerang that mercilessly returned to split my chest open.

"Don't you think it's cruel of her? Here you are being tortured because of her while she's living it up with her little childhood friend. *Peter*," she spat. "Unless I'm mistaken, that's his name."

The air shimmered before my eyes, blinded by frustration, thickening until it took on the appearance of two hazy figures.

I rebelled against my chains with a growl of dismay as Peter and Gemma's faces appeared, floating like ghosts. They were sitting next to each other and their closeness made me burn inside. Gemma was distractedly stroking Peter's hand, clutching something like it was a treasure. *Go ahead, Peter. Don't keep me on pins and needles!* She punched his shoulder and let out a carefree laugh.

"Turns out she's not doing so bad without you, don't you think?" Devina's lips twisted into an evil grin as I shot her a fiery glare.

"I don't believe you! Your tricks won't work on me!"

"No tricks. What you see has really happened. She really is with Peter. After you died she let herself be consoled by running into his arms."

"Gemma . . ." A jolt of pain traversed my heart. "That's impossible. She would never do that," I said, though I was actually trying to convince myself, not her. Gemma couldn't have forgotten me so quickly.

"Of course she could. She's already replaced you"—she came closer and stared at the shadowy figure—"with *him*. Humans are so weak, so vulnerable, they don't know what true love is. They've started a life together."

Marry me, Gemma. I'll take care of the baby. Gemma smiled slightly and my heart shattered.

"A baby? Gemma's expecting a baby?" I whispered, my mind lost in those words. It suddenly seemed I'd never known any Hell worse than the torture tearing me apart at that moment.

"It's yours." Devina smiled. "But someone else will raise it."

Blind fury pervaded me. Screaming until my voice was hoarse, I tried to wrench myself free from my chains. I'd never felt a more excruciating pain in my entire existence.

"Don't you think it's the right thing to do? Don't you want the best for her and the baby? You have nothing to offer her any more. It's selfish of you to hope she won't rebuild a life for herself without you. After all, why shouldn't she?" The Witch let out a treacherous laugh and moved closer until her lips touched my ear. "Believe me, what you see is the reality. No tricks. I let their spirits reach us so you could see with your own two eyes what's going on with your beloved Gemma. You need to give up and let her go. Forget her and move on—with me." Her hand slid down my bare chest. "Why serve Death when you can serve *me?*"

I whipped my head up and shot her a defiant glare. "Didn't your mistress tell you to keep your hands to yourself?"

The determination in my voice punctured Devina's fantasies. She'd clearly believed she had subjugated me. At the crack of her whip, the image of Gemma and Peter faded and died.

"She is not my *mistress*. The Empress is a *Sister*, just like the rest of us. I don't necessarily have to do what she tells me." She sneered at me. "We're not in Heaven, little Angel, and obedience isn't one of our strengths." She stroked my chest again, moving her hand all the way down to my belt. "There are other highly appreciated qualities around here that might please you, if you let yourself go." She moved her lips closer, breathing on mine.

When I jerked my face away, she bit her lip and offered it to me to drink her blood. Her hand slid slowly between my legs and came up my inner thigh. A crimson droplet made its way down her lip. I stared at it, attracted against my will by its power. It swelled and fell, landing on my bare foot. I followed it with my eyes but the Witch promptly drew my attention back to her lip. She was so close I could smell her blood.

"Go on, taste me. You'll regain a bit of strength. Just imagine it's ambrosia."

I swallowed, attracted to the magic of what she was offering me, but forced myself to spit my refusal in her face. "Your blood is only poison. It's nothing compared to the nectar of the Gods. Deal with it."

"Do you realize how many Subterraneans would kill for a single drop of this?" she whispered on my mouth. "In large doses, the pure blood of a Witch can dull your senses. Given in tiny doses, though, it can take an Angel to a paradise he's never known before. No substance is more intoxicating and gratifying. It's the most potent of drugs, the sweetest of spells. Not even man, despite all his efforts, has ever concocted anything with a similar effect. It can take you to distant, mysterious places where your body can soar, experience the thrill of the purest pleasure . . . and I'm offering it to you. All you need to do is swallow the slightest bit to surrender to your instinct for passion. To know *love*." She pressed her lips to mine.

For a second her blood left me dazed, but I yanked on the chains to break free from her grip and spat out the scarlet liquid. "You don't know what love is. What you're offering is worthless to me. You'll never bend me to your will. And for your information, the pleasure promised by a Witch like you is nothing compared to that of a Subterranean who lives only to love you. But you'll never know what that's like, because you're impervious to love. You'll never have what you want from me. You'll have to kill me—if you can."

Devina smiled and a sharp pain filled my head, making me shriek. My skull felt like it was about to explode. "Don't tempt me, Son of Eve. This tough attitude of yours won't help you. In fact, you should have realized by now I like it. Hard, determined, dangerous, and sexy. I might decide to keep you here forever. I could make you my personal manservant."

I spat a drop of blood-tinged saliva at her feet as I held her gaze. "I'll never be anything of yours."

"Don't be so sure. You struggle so hard to reject me and in the meantime you're already becoming my champion. In the last fight you were so brutal. It was so exciting to watch!"

"Every head I rip off, I imagine it's yours," I growled.

She laughed. My insolence amused her. "You have extraordinary strength. Taking on the Circle and beating them all like that without a single drop of our lymph? Imagine what you could do with my blood in your body."

"I'm not so sure you'd want to find out." I shot her another defiant look.

Each Witch had her champion for the battles in the Opalion. They called it "the Circle" because some of the Witches would gather in a deadly circle to seal off the field, from which only one of the combatants would emerge alive. They tore to shreds the souls of those who lost or any challengers who got too close to them. Though the floor inside the Circle was continually changing shape and size, their sinister symbol was always at its center, interwoven with that of the Subterraneans, like an ancient threat testifying to their power and the submission of our race. The Opalion consisted of different contests in which we faced off using weapons or even our bare hands, depending on the difficulty, and the Witches would hold a celebration for the games. Since I'd been there, I'd battled every kind of Soul found in Hell, and one after the other I had defeated them all. Still, that didn't make me Devina's personal champion—I would only become that if I battled with her blood in my body. But I would never give in to her.

The Witch slid her finger down my neck but I continued to stare straight ahead, the anger seething in me making me squeeze my eyes shut. "There was a time when you couldn't resist me." Her voice was once again a murmur. "I still remember our first encounters, and I would wager you haven't forgotten them either. You were so frightened and confused. Maybe I should have been more insistent back then when you couldn't take your eyes off me."

"You're wrong. I never wanted you."

"Are you so sure? Maybe I should start all over again to see what happens." Devina slowly drew closer and touched her lips to my temple. At the contact, her serpent stirred beneath her skin and slithered around her neck excitedly.

When I opened my eyes, the grotto had disappeared. We were in an orchard and she was facing me, clad in a full-length lace gown, leaning against a tree with a seductive expression.

"Why do you run from me?" My heart leapt in my chest: I could feel it, alive and pulsing as though I were still a mortal Soul. I had been the one to say those words. Confused, I tried to move toward her, but I'd lost control over my body. I wasn't myself any more—I was the me from my past. Devina had taken me back to 1720, to one of the dreams in which she'd visited me ever since I was a boy, the ones where she had power over me.

No! I had to oppose her! If I gave in to her in the past, the present as I knew it would be in jeopardy.

"It's you who keep running away," Devina said, pulling me toward her.

I tried to resist but my body moved on its own, without my consent. I watched my hands place themselves on the tree trunk on either side of Devina's head, imprisoning her, and I felt the desire to possess her growing in me. I stroked her neck with my fingers and my youthful will wavered. Thoughts from the past began to cloud my thinking and suddenly I was no longer sure who I was. Was Devina actually capable of crushing my will like that? Of imprisoning me in the past so she could have me in the future?

No. I couldn't let it happen.

I summoned the most precious image stored in my heart and showed it to him, to the Evan William James of that distant past. I couldn't let him succumb to Devina. He had to resist, just as he'd done then, so that one day he would meet Gemma.

Your heat burns my skin when you're near me.

Gemma's voice filled our minds and the young Evan hesitated. He pulled away from Devina, confused, his heart racing from the vision that had come from he knew not where, the vision I had transferred from my heart to his. Gemma's eyes had dazzled him for a single moment. He didn't know how, but he'd recognized them because his memories were connected to mine.

But Devina came back with a vengeance. "Don't run away, my lord. Stay here with me. You will be mine and I will be forever yours. I can show you worlds you do not yet know."

She pulled the young me against her and I felt desire rise within him. I struggled to emerge, to bring him back to his senses, but Devina's power was strong. She wanted me to accept the new reality she was trying to create, determined to seduce the young Evan and, in so doing, defeat Gemma so she could claim me for her own.

I would never have met Gemma. I would lose all memory of her, all I had left. With a surge of desperate defiance, energy filled me and my mind cleared. My sight sharpened and I found myself in the young man's body. I grabbed Devina's wrists and pinned them against the tree, a look of determination in my eye. I wasn't going to allow her to take my memories from me too.

I was myself now, in control.

I want to be with you and no one else.

The memory of Gemma filled the mind of the two Evans, coexisting in that ancient dream. I could feel his heart beating faster from the emotion. He didn't know Gemma but somehow he knew he belonged to her. I pulled back and let him experience the memory so it would be branded on his mind forever: Gemma and me in the old aircraft hangar, making love, her beneath me, stretched out on a military tarp, her bare skin touching mine, flooding me with emotions, and her big dark eyes fixed on me, making me her prisoner. Yes, I was hers and hers alone. It didn't matter how Devina schemed, how long she tortured me or tried to keep me away from Gemma. *She was mine, all mine. Forever mine.*

"Jamie . . ." The young me uttered her name, amazed by the love that had exploded in his chest for a girl who was still unknown to him.

Devina cracked her whip, bringing me back to the present. I looked her straight in the eye and smiled. Once again, I had won. "Well? Did you find what you were looking for, rummaging around in my head?" I asked her contemptuously. She grunted and clenched the whip in her fist. "Sorry, *milady*. You can't control me. Not in the past, not now . . . not ever. No one can dominate me."

She placed her hand beside my head, her amber irises expanding over the whites like tentacles and her pupils gradually lengthening as rage overwhelmed her. I had never seen her so furious before. "I can control everything!" she thundered, smashing her palm against the rock in frustration. The whole grotto trembled.

I stared at her steadily, flaunting my calm. "That's not true. You can't control *me*."

Her golden pupils quivered with anger and I laughed, satisfied. "That remains to be seen!" she hissed.

"Did you really believe manipulating dreams in my past would be enough to subjugate me? Don't forget—I'm good at that game."

Devina had used my power to enter others' dreams to delve inside me and bring me back to that memory. To ward her off I'd done something she could never have imagined: I had planted the seed of the memory of Gemma in the young Evan, effectively changing my past. I smiled in wonder: I actually had a memory now of waking up and telling my mother about Gemma and how I had dreamed of her. It pierced my heart to know that as of that moment Gemma had become a part of my past—but never again would she be part of my future.

"You've managed to resist me, but you won't always be able to. Your mind is strong and resistant to persuasion but sooner or later you'll give in. We have all the time in the world. I will be your *Amisha*." The whip sliced through the air and violently slashed my bare chest. The sound was bone-chilling. The pain made me clench my teeth, but my eyes didn't leave Devina's for a second.

"Screw you, you ugly bitch."

The blaze of irritation that darkened her face twisted my lips into a grin as I ignored the pain burning every last inch of my body. All at once her gaze lit up with evil, as though she'd found the key to dominating me. I flinched when her serpent materialized from her belly. It sinuously wound its way down her leg and slithered gracefully over to me. I moved as far away as the chains would allow.

"It seems that while the wolf was out hunting it fell in love with its prey. Rather amusing, don't you think? Dangerous, mostly. It's a shame you'll be the one to pay the consequences, because there's something you still don't know about your betrothed." I grunted to drown out her venomous voice. "You should have killed her when you had the chance, because soon your roles will be reversed and you'll no longer be playing the wolf." I looked up at her, furious, and my sudden interest made her smile again. "She belongs to us. She already bears our mark."

A shudder wracked my body. It felt like she'd plunged an icy hand into my chest and squeezed my heart until it bled.

"Every time she came near you, some obscure power gripped your heart, didn't it? You couldn't resist her, and your desire for her clouded your mind. Her *eyes* made you her prisoner . . . That power comes from us."

The serpent shot toward me, threatening to drag me back into the darkness. My body recoiled. "Relax, Spartan. The poison can't kill you here—you've hit rock bottom. Where else would you want to go?"

The rage inside me burst free in a ferocious howl, my fiery glare challenging the Witch's. "You'd better hope I never break free, because you have no idea what I would do to you."

"I can't kill you." Her face twisted into a mask of pure evil, the gold of her eyes glowing until it turned to fire. "But I can always try."

I pulled back further, but the serpent attacked with lightning speed, sinking its fangs into my flesh. A groan escaped me and flames consumed me. The Witch's face blurred before my eyes.

"Sweet dreams, little Angel."

GEMMA

BETWEEN DREAMS AND REALITY

There was complete silence on the ride home. None of us had dared speak once the Witches had disappeared, not even Ginevra, though she had read every thought of mine—I could see that from her shocked expression.

The last piece of the puzzle had finally fallen into place. While my daytime torment was thanks to the Subterranean we were holding captive, at night it had been the Witches torturing me. I'd finally discovered the reason behind everything: I was destined to become a Witch. The thought should have terrified me, but instead the only thing I could think about was Evan and the possibility he was still alive. I would think about everything else later. It was only when we got home that the tension sought escape through my lips, as though the kitchen light had forever banished the darkness and awakened us all from a strange nightmare.

"Gwen?" I shot her a piercing look that demanded her full attention.

"I know what you're about to ask. Forget it." Her answer was as sharp as her crystal-green eyes. It was unexpectedly hurtful. I took in the pain and just as unexpectedly felt it burst inside me, ruled by a savage force. A *dark* force.

"What's happening, ladies? We're all in shock. I don't think it's the time for us to be fighting among ourselves." Simon's face was wan, showing he hadn't yet recovered from the experience we'd just had. He didn't realize what conclusion I had come to either.

"It's an insane idea!" Ginevra railed at me, ignoring him. Her growing anger was intertwined with frustration, like a vine creeping around a tree, hard to eradicate.

Dreams hide many secrets. The Witch's voice continued to whirl through my head, confirming the terrible truth that part of me must have always known.

"I . . . I still can't believe it. *My nightmares.* They kept haunting me and they were *real*, weren't they? I dreamed of them. I've always dreamed of them! They were torturing him," I murmured, trying to follow the stream of thoughts flowing through my head. It was a reverse journey in which everything took shape, finally acquiring meaning.

"The nightmares were nothing but their attempts to turn you toward evil."

I looked at Ginevra, my eyes fiery, and the determination on my face made her cringe. "But that's not all, is it? *You knew.*" I wanted to shout into her face all the pain inside me, but all that came from my lips was a feeble sound. My doubts and fears had given way to certainty. Like a star exploding in the night, the future I'd been unable to see, blinded as I was by a dark cloud of pain, suddenly sparkled with a thousand colors. The sun had begun to shine again.

The thought that Evan was out there somewhere, still alive, banished the fear of what I was becoming. I would bring him back, even if it meant sacrificing everything, if I could just see him again one last time. In the blink of an eye, the warmth that flooded my heart melted away all the tension I'd accumulated. A river of tears filled my eyes, blurring their faces.

"He's still alive." I blinked and the tears streaked my cheeks. "You saw how much I was suffering. You kept telling me to move on, and all the while you knew he was still alive."

"Gemma, I—"

"Don't—don't try to play the part of the protector with me. You already know what I want." I'd tried to keep my voice from trembling, but in the end anger had gotten the better of me.

"Forget it. I won't let you do it."

A stream of energy flowed from my eyes to hers and everything else fell away. A wave of power that felt superhuman began to mount inside me. It lifted me from the ground as my hair lifted and fluttered in the air at the mercy of a wind that blew only inside me. Suddenly I was aware of every cell in my body, the whirlwind of emotions rushing through me, but I couldn't contain or control them. All I could do was let them explode.

"Gemma . . ." Concern edged Simon's voice as I noticed that several objects around the kitchen had risen into the air, moved by the dark energy possessing me.

"You don't have the right to decide about my life!" I enunciated each word as a snarl rattled in my chest and burst forth like a demon

from hell. My body trembled at the realization that the sound had come from my own lips. The objects suspended in the air burst into a thousand fragments of glass, wood, and porcelain. Simon ducked as every window in the kitchen exploded in a hostile warning. My fiery glare was still locked on Ginevra. She stared back at me in shock, defeat mixed with resignation in her eyes.

"She's out of control," Simon whispered nervously.

Gemma, don't let it possess you. Ginevra's voice rang out clear and persuasive, but her lips hadn't moved. I could read her mind.

You should have told me! I growled mentally. My vehemence caused a short circuit and made all the lights go off.

"Damn it, would you two calm down?!" Simon shouted, but not even the deepest darkness could break the visual contact between Ginevra and me. I could see so clearly it might as well have been daytime. "Get a grip, Gemma."

I looked at Simon and my feet settled to the floor as the dark energy drained from me. Looking at their helpless faces, a tremendous urge to run away made me turn to go, but Simon moved like lightning and pinned me against the wall. He observed me, relief on his face, as I realized to my horror what had just happened and how I had demolished the room.

"Why don't you both try to relax? We can talk about this later when we're all calm," Simon suggested, but our thoughts were still engaged in a fierce battle.

"Evil is already inside me! I can feel it growing day by day and there's nothing I can do to stop it," I said.

"You can fight it!" Ginevra answered severely.

"Why should I, when it can give me back what I love most in the world?!" My voice softened, weakened by tears. "Why should I renounce what I am when what I am is what can give me back my *life*? You don't understand, Gwen. I *have to* go, with or without you. *I can't back down.*"

Ginevra grabbed her hair in frustration as she nervously paced the room. "You're the one who doesn't understand. What you're asking me to do is *impossible*. I can't! I can't go back there. It's forbidden to me. I swore an *oath*. If I went back they would kill Simon without thinking twice and I can't let that happen."

"I would never ask you to risk all that. I'll go alone."

"Out of the question," she promptly replied.

"I'm going alone. If I have to search all of Hell to find him, I'm bringing Evan back."

"He can't come back. *No one* can come back from death."

"I did." My determined eyes met hers. "Evan brought me back and I'm going to do the same for him."

"You don't know what you're talking about. That place is cursed! It's full of dark magic and terrifying creatures!"

"I don't care."

"I can't let you go."

"What would you do if it were Simon?"

Ginevra was torn. Her eyes wavered.

"I only have two choices, Gwen: go and save him, or stay and die with him." I wasn't afraid of death any more. This new hope had clarified everything, illuminated a passageway inside me. I had to cling to it with all my strength until my very last breath. It didn't matter what I had to do—I was going to bring him back. The thought of never returning didn't frighten me, not if I could see Evan again one last time. That was all that mattered.

"Gemma."

I noticed Simon's hand resting on my shoulder only after he said my name. Having realized the nature of the connection between Ginevra and me, he hadn't dared come between us. "We can't know for sure he's even there."

I looked at him and shook my head. It was obvious Ginevra had kept him in the dark too. I shot her a challenging look. "We can't know that? Is that so, *Gwen?*"

She hesitated, overcome by guilt. Simon looked at her as though seeing her for the first time. "You knew?" he whispered, bewilderment and a touch of contempt in his voice. "You knew all along? Ginevra, how could you keep quiet about something so important?!"

"I couldn't break my oath! The price is your *life.*"

"You knew Evan was still alive and you did *nothing*?!" Simon clapped his hands to his head in disbelief. "Sweet Jesus, Evan is still alive and you knew it?! How could you?!"

"You think I didn't suffer from keeping you in the dark? I had to choose! It was a burden I've been carrying for months all alone, Simon." Ginevra took him by the shoulders and forced him to look at her. "I couldn't risk putting you in danger. What did you expect me to do, go get him? *You don't know them.* You have no idea what they're capable of! They let us go once—they won't do it a second time."

Simon pulled out of her grip. "You should have talked to me!" he growled, his voice hoarse with frustration.

"Come on, Simon. Don't tell me it never crossed your mind."

Despite Ginevra's attempt to calm him, his anger grew. "I'm a Subterranean, like all the other servants of Death, but none of us knows what death looks like. We can't hope for forgiveness like mortals can, and none of us know where the road your poison takes us on ends up. But it seems you do."

Ginevra had no answer. She hung her head and he intensified his attack. For a second I saw them for what they were: a Subterranean and a Witch, mortal enemies since the dawn of time. "I've always respected your wish not to talk about your Sisters or your world, but damn it— you should have told me about this! We could have come up with a solution together, for Christ's sake!"

"There is no solution, Simon! Not one that doesn't lead to your death."

"We're talking about Evan!" Simon exploded, looking her straight in the eye, almost as if he wasn't sure she was understanding him. "You should have told me!"

"I couldn't! Subterraneans can't learn that our venom is a door leading straight to Hell. If Gemma hadn't had those dreams, no one would ever have suspected it. I had to consider Gemma's wellbeing, and the baby's. I was sure that if she knew she would go there to get him, despite her condition. I had to protect them. I had to protect *you,* and I knew you would never let me."

Simon ran his hand over his face in frustration and turned to me, at a loss. "I'm sorry, Gemma, I didn't know anything about it. And she's right: I would never have let her."

Ginevra didn't seem willing to discuss it any longer, but I was prepared to do anything to convince her. She picked up on my thoughts. "If you went down there I wouldn't be able to help you, and I can't—*can't*—let you go there alone. Try to realize once and for all we're talking about Hell! You have no idea what dangers you would be up against!"

"Oh, you *bet* you're going to help her!" Simon's stern voice cracked in the air like a whip. "Whatever Gemma has in mind, we'll talk it over and deal with it together like a real team, because that's what we are,

Ginevra: a team. A family. Get it through your head: this isn't all about you!"

"Have you both lost your minds? Am I the only one left with any common sense? This is insane, Simon! Gemma wouldn't survive a single hour down there."

"She's one of them. Your Sisters would never hurt her. If Evan really is their prisoner, I'm going to help Gemma find him, with or without you."

"But how? No one except a Witch can take her there."

"I'm sure Gemma can summon them. Their connection is strong and the process has already begun. Either you help her or Gemma can take things into her own hands: the choice is yours."

Faced with this concrete threat, Ginevra went deathly pale. "Well, let's hear it. What do you have in mind?"

"You know perfectly well what I have in mind," I said, giving her a hard stare, "and I'm going to do it with or without your help. They're already there—I can feel it. They've awakened the evil inside me."

"They can try to persuade you but they can't take you by force. It's up to you to decide."

"Then I don't see the problem."

Simon studied my face, trying to understand my intentions. Grateful to him for supporting me even without knowing what I wanted to do, I sighed and answered all in one breath: "The Witches want something from me and I want something from them. I'm willing to grant their wish if it means getting Evan back. We'll make a deal. I'll agree to become one of them. My life in exchange for Evan's."

Simon gasped, shocked by my plan. He was probably wondering whether Ginevra hadn't been right after all in trying to stop me.

"There! You hear that?! It's insane!" Ginevra burst out. "Why can't you two realize that?"

"They're going to take me anyway! It's what I am."

"That's not true—otherwise they would have taken you already. As I said, whether you become one of them or not is your decision."

"Has there ever been a chosen one who didn't become a Witch?"

Her silence gave me the answer. Witches waited five hundred years for the arrival of a new Sister. I was sure nothing would stop them until they had convinced me to accept evil.

"Gemma, everyone has an evil side hidden inside them. Some ignore it, others repress it, but no one is completely without it. It's a part of human nature and has been since original sin. And life on earth was begun so you could choose which side to listen to. According to an ancient Indian legend, there's a battle going on inside us between two wolves. One is evil, self-centered, full of envy and guilt; the other is good, full of joy, love, hope, truth . . . faith. Only one will emerge victorious in the end." Ginevra looked me in the eye. "The one you decide to feed."

An icy silence descended on the room. I didn't want to give in to evil, but I had no choice.

"There's always a choice," Ginevra replied, having read my mind.

I was quick to disagree. "I can't choose to live without Evan. I just can't."

"Gemma," Ginevra lowered her voice to a protective whisper, "the seed of evil is inside you. Don't let it grow."

I sighed and looked into her eyes. "It's already sprouting."

"You must conquer your emotions if you don't want to be suffocated by them. Think it over carefully, Gemma. Saving Evan won't bring you two together again. The Witches will separate you."

"I don't care. It's my fault Evan died. It's up to me to bring him back, even if that means sacrificing everything." I tried to keep my voice steady but failed.

"Don't think I don't realize what you're hoping, Gemma. Once the transformation takes place, you won't be able to turn back."

"You did."

Simon and Ginevra exchanged glances. "It's different. I had centuries to fight the evil inside me. Only my love for Simon managed to overcome it."

"Exactly. Love is the only invincible power—you said so yourself! My connection with Evan is powerful," I told her. I tried to convince her, but not even I was sure of what I was saying. I'd seen how powerfully they could possess me and I suspected I would never be able to defeat the Witches, but it didn't matter to me. I was willing to do anything in order to see Evan again, in order to bring him back.

"That won't be enough, Gemma."

"Are you sure?" Simon, who had been staying out of the conversation, tried to persuade Ginevra. "Maybe Gemma is right. She can't just repress evil." My eyes shot to his expectantly. "She has to let it emerge and then fight it. That's the only way she can eradicate it from her heart. Otherwise it will fester inside her forever."

"Whose side are you on?!" Ginevra asked, incredulous. "She can't give them the opportunity to possess her!"

"But she has to face them! You didn't repress your nature—you faced it and defeated it. There's no other way for Gemma to beat the Witches except by letting evil take root in her too, to then rid herself of it. They'll never stop hounding her—you saw for yourself how zealously they're anticipating her surrender. She can't defeat evil if she keeps repressing it. The Witches will torment her for all eternity. She needs to let it explode if she wants to gain control of it." Simon looked at me, full of hope. "Each of us has Heaven and Hell inside us."

"Quoting Oscar Wilde won't help convince her," I warned him, "but I agree. He also said: 'The only way to get rid of temptation is to yield to it.' Gwen, it was my fate to find you guys. Some strange power summoned me to you the first time I came to this house. It was you—I know that now. My connection to you is what drew me here. It also explains the burst of light I saw in the sky. I sensed your energy, the energy that united us. It was inevitable."

"Well, you can't summon them to offer yourself up. It would be a pointless sacrifice. They would seal the deal with deception—that's their specialty. And once transformed, not even you would let Evan go free. The only way to bring him back is to go down there and get him. They would never just hand him over to you. A promise given by Sophia within her realm, on the other hand, is an indissoluble oath." Ginevra sighed, devastated. "If only you could bring him back before making a pact . . ."

"Then help me! You know Hell, you know the Witches. If you're on my side I can save him without being transformed!"

"I'll always be on your side. That's why I can't let you go. Once you're inside the Castle, they'll never let you leave until they've gotten what they want. No one who's ever been there has returned to tell the tale—no one who isn't a Witch, that is."

"But I *am* a Witch," I reminded her.

"Not yet, you aren't. And going down there would be a fool's errand. It's *forbidden*."

"I don't care. They won't hurt me."

"Yes they will, if you refuse to surrender yourself to them."

"If there's even a remote chance of finding Evan, I won't give up until I feel my heart stop beating."

Then Ginevra said something that touched my heart: "I don't want to lose the only Sister left to me." She hung her head, her voice breaking with emotion and her eyes brimming with tears.

"That's not going to happen. I have too much to come back for. I'll find a way."

"But—" She looked up and for the first time I saw a hint of surrender in her green eyes. "Think of the baby. The last few months have been very hard on you. One more trauma and you might lose him."

I smiled reassuringly at her so she would see how confident I was in my decision. "I'm sure he would die sooner if I stayed because he can feel my pain. I was on the verge of collapse, Gwen. Now I know Evan is alive, that there's hope! Believe me, nothing frightens me more than living another day without him. I'll be careful. Besides, the baby is so strong—half his blood is Evan's. That will protect him."

Nodding, Ginevra exchanged glances with Simon and my heart leapt as she finally gave in. "All right, Simon, I'll do as you ask. Gemma, I can't go with you, but I can explain everything you need to know. Just remember: you'll be alone and you'll have to endure a long, difficult journey before you reach Evan."

I nodded, not the least bit swayed by her attempts to talk me out of it. "I'm not afraid. I'm ready." I pulled out a chair and sat down, ready to receive her instructions.

REVELATIONS

"Man is so self-centered he's only ever wondered about his own nature. No one has ever really been interested in knowing what might have inspired God to create the human race in the first place." Ginevra rested her hands on the table, gathering her thoughts. Before beginning, she'd made little braids in my hair, telling me how Witches loved them because they were like snakes coiled around themselves, just like the Dakor encircling their arms.

"You're right, people always talk about mankind, about the reasons for life on Earth, but never about God, about *His* reasons or His wishes. What I do know is that He created us out of love, right?"

Ginevra smiled and began to pace the room. "God deemed it necessary to create woman for man. Do you think He didn't feel the same need as well? Before even creating man, He made a being that was immortal, like Himself—a being to love and be loved by. But something went wrong. He created the perfect woman for Himself and gave her great abilities, a power almost equal to His own. He called her Sophìa, which means 'wisdom.' Sophìa's grace and beauty exceeded His expectations, but so did her thirst for knowledge. Since power derives from knowledge, little by little Sophìa became insatiable. She wanted absolute power. She wanted to know all of God's secrets and couldn't stand being inferior to Him. One day she tried to usurp His powers and His kingdom. Grief-stricken by her betrayal, God imprisoned her in a cage made of Diamantea, the celestial essence, hoping her spirit would be purified and she would repent of her sins. She was fascinated by the cage's splendor, but when she touched it the diamond turned black and God suspected her soul was already too dark for redemption.

"And so He passed His sentence and banished her to a distant place that He named Hell. To console Himself, God created man, and when man asked for a woman, He was unable to refuse. Nevertheless, God's heart feared the worst, so He took a precaution: having discovered that knowledge might lead man and woman to thirst for power, He left them in the dark about everything. That way they would be free to live solely on their reciprocal love, which they did . . . until Sophìa decided she wanted those creatures for herself.

"When she learned of their existence, partly from boredom, partly from her longing for omnipotence, Sophìa decided she wanted to rule over mankind, so she sent a serpent to tempt Eve and make her crave knowledge. The serpent said to Eve,

> 'The river water blinds your soul
> Let power be your children's goal
> For rulers they are bound to be
> By eating of the sacred Tree

"Sophìa hoped Adam and Eve and the children they had had would be damned to Hell like she was. That way she could rule over them. They would be her creatures. *Her slaves.* Sophìa began to see her world no longer as a punishment but as a wonderful opportunity. Those people would be her first subjects, and after them there would be many more.

"But Sophìa had sinned of her own volition, while man had been driven to evil by her treachery. And so, heartbroken about this new betrayal, God took all His rage out on Sophìa and the serpent that had done her bidding: from that moment on, they were to be a single being, and their souls, poisoned by evil, would be connected for life.

"But man wasn't free of guilt either, nor did he deserve the purity of Eden. However, since God loved His creatures and didn't want to deliver them to Sophìa, He gave them another chance, leaving them in a world halfway between Heaven, where evil didn't exist, and Hell, the kingdom of darkness. It was a world where man would neither be forced to serve Sophìa nor to love God, a world where he would be free to *choose* which side to be on—God's or Sophìa's. Eden would be the reward for those who loved God of their own free will. He granted men a mortal existence, giving them a set amount of time to redeem themselves."

"Incredible." I had listened to Ginevra, breathless with fascination. Great hatred could only have originated from great love. "He gave us free will to let us make a choice, but He also gave us a limited time to do it. So Earth is a sort of Purgatory."

"Exactly."

"Then theoretically Sophìa would be Satan."

"That's one of the names she's been given over the centuries, like Lilith and Hades. You know her better as Lucifer, which actually means 'light bearer,' or Satan, meaning 'she who opposes.' Only we call her by her real name: Sophìa. But it doesn't matter what you call her. She's evil incarnate. She's the devil. Her power is almost limitless and her heart is cold and ruthless. No one knows her better than I do. She even betrayed God, her Creator and only love, so He set his hopes on mankind, hoping they might experience the dream He hadn't been able to."

"Pure love," Simon explained, taking the words out of my mouth.

"But if she was God's wife, doesn't that mean she's a goddess?"

Ginevra shook her head, a poorly concealed smile on her lips. "*Empress.* She prefers to be called that, since she rules over her empire. There's only one God. A God can't be created."

"So what about the other Witches?"

"When she saw her plan had failed, she managed to wrest a promise from God by begging Him not to leave her all alone. And so, every five hundred years, a new Witch awakens on Earth to serve her. Sophìa wanted God's creatures, but He granted her only one every five hundred years—a female, who would also have the power to choose. Every mortal Soul the Witches seduce increases their power. They're getting stronger and stronger. Their abilities have improved over the centuries. Or maybe it's because mankind is forgetting where it came from."

"So those who believe in God have a better chance of not being corrupted by evil? Is that what you're telling me?"

Ginevra couldn't hold back a smile. "Believing in God isn't enough to save someone. Even Witches believe in him. As I said, it doesn't matter what you call the two parts: God, Witches, darkness, light, damnation, salvation. What counts is not losing sight of what they represent: good and evil. Every action, even the smallest, entails a decision that leans to one side or the other, though at times we don't realize it or we simply pretend not to notice. But inside, you know when something is right or wrong. You can tell from how the action makes you feel. It's a never-ending battle. Those who renounce evil and prove they're worthy of God's love can return to His kingdom. But don't think it's just a question of not committing this or that crime. Every mortal Soul has a moment in life when they find themselves facing a decision that will mark their fate. Everyone is eventually tempted by evil, some more often than others. The Witches often win Souls over gradually, luring them one step at a time along the path that leads to Hell. Other times it's a single major decision. What makes the difference is how a person behaves when they're tempted, the *choice* they make when the path of evil lies before them. A mortal might never have committed a sin, but they might sell their soul to the devil in exchange for what they desire most."

"If the Witches have so much power, what's keeping them from taking over the world?"

"What makes you think they aren't already doing it? Man will bring his own world to an end. He's already destroying it by choosing to comply with evil, driven by his lust for knowledge and power. By thinking only of himself and ignoring the consequences his decisions will have on those to come."

"Okay, but why haven't they taken it over already?"

"Because of the few humans who choose to renounce evil. There are always some who decide to follow the path of God, Yahweh, Jehovah, Elohim . . . whatever name they give Him. What difference does His name actually make? All that matters is that they follow the laws, choosing good over evil, love over hatred, hope over resignation. Believing means hoping—hoping there's something after death and it doesn't all end. Behaving accordingly in order to deserve Redemption. Resisting temptation. Their faith is what's keeping the world from falling to pieces. If someone doesn't hope a better place exists, they'll be unlikely to try to deserve it. Witches can't force Souls to follow them, just as God can't force them to love Him. That's why men have a conscience, the spokesman of the soul, though they often choose to ignore it."

"What would happen if everyone stopped believing in a reward?"

"Then there would be no hope for the world and even Earth would follow Hell's rules. It's already happening."

"But why do the Witches want men so badly? For what purpose, after all these centuries?"

"To make them their slaves."

A powerful shudder crept through me. I tried to control it but couldn't keep a tremble out of my voice. "Slaves?"

"The Witches don't want to rule the Earth because it's a place where there is and always will be free will. It's neutral territory, halfway between Heaven and Hell. No, they want to lead Souls into their empire, Hell. Only then can they become Sophìa's slaves, like she always wanted. That's why when the Witches discovered that Eve's banished children had been ordered to take redeemed Souls to Heaven, the Witches began to hunt them down. But I think you already know that part of the story."

"Right. Tell me more about the Witches instead."

"Their powers are almost limitless. They can read minds and nature bends to their will, but the most powerful weapon at their disposal is seduction. Subterraneans are capable of resisting it because they're warriors by nature, but for mortals it's very difficult."

I thought of the day Ginevra had shown up at school and how no one could take their eyes off her, how they'd all hung on her every word. She cast me a reproachful glance and continued. "Once a mortal's soul has been corrupted, Sophìa comes into possession of it when he dies. In Hell, the souls of the Damned are no longer free, the way they would be in Heaven. Witches promise eternal life, but it's a lie—only God can offer such a gift. Actually, all Sophìa wants is to prove that God's creation isn't worthy of His love—that it's easy to buy him off. Some humans even follow her spontaneously."

"How is that possible?"

"There are more humans than you would believe who will sell their souls just to see their dreams come true. They don't realize that in most cases they could do it all on their own if they only made the effort. But many choose the easy way: they invoke the Witches, surrender to them in exchange for their worthless promises, and end up in Hell, where they're nothing more than playthings. Mere puppets the Witches use for their amusement. Slaves—or, if you prefer, *zombies*—as soon as they completely lose their humanity."

"But they go on living."

"If you consider that a life. At first they still have a trace of humanity in them, but it fades with time. However, they maintain a glimmer of awareness that keeps them from forgetting what they were and what they gave up. It's the worst kind of torture, believe me, a condition that leads to madness. It would be easier if they were empty shells, but instead they're forced to exist while retaining the memory of what they once were. They're conscious of what they've become but can't fight it. And that's what they miss more than anything else: free will. Those beings no longer belong to themselves—they're slaves to fear, to hunger, to Hell. They're slaves to Sophìa."

"And they live like that forever?" I asked, almost afraid to hear the answer.

"No. Their souls are corrupt and therefore perishable. Theirs is an empty, ephemeral existence that the Witches can put an end to whenever they like."

"What happens then?"

"They disintegrate. They turn to dust and rejoin the earth."

"Maybe it's a form of liberation, then."

"Maybe, but not even that is their choice. Their instinct forces them to fight for their survival. But listen, this is important: the Damned aren't all the same. As I said, occasionally during a moment of temptation, a mortal who otherwise lives a good life isn't strong enough to battle evil and sacrifices Redemption to see his dreams come true. These are individuals whose will isn't strong enough to resist the Witches' coercion. Some people call them corrupt. But Hell is full of far more dangerous creatures: murderers, maniacs, thieves, lechers— beings you could never imagine meeting. From all epochs, from all eras."

A shiver penetrated my bones.

"Some of them band together in small communities. Others—the ones who have completely lost their humanity—wander aimlessly in search of other Souls to ease their unquenchable thirst for blood. Hell is full of hidden dangers, treacherous Souls, ferocious beasts. There are no rules there, except one: survival. It's chaos."

I gulped. I had suddenly felt a shiver beneath my skin and discovered my hands were trembling under the table. I clutched my knees and forced myself not to give in to fear. Whatever obstacle arose, I would overcome it, led by the new light I carried inside. Nothing and no one would keep me from reaching Evan. Now that Ginevra had begun to tell me about Hell, though, I needed to ask a question that had been weighing on my heart. I couldn't bear the burden any more. "What do Witches do to Subterraneans?" I asked, my voice trembling.

Ginevra broke off the silent conversation she'd begun with Simon, to which I wasn't invited, and looked at me, her face wary. Her expression suggested she'd been dreading the moment I would find the courage to ask her that. Simon ran his hand over his face and through his hair. Maybe he was thinking the same thing.

"They keep many of them in the Castle," Ginevra said, trying unsuccessfully to keep her voice from wavering.

"But . . . for what purpose?" I didn't take my eyes from hers for a second. I had the strong impression she was doing everything she could to hide something. I didn't know if she was doing it for my sake or Simon's.

"For their amusement. The Witches gain strength from the Subterraneans' power and they often have fun using it against them. They keep some as slaves and choose others to do battle for them or take part in their games. They have an army of Subterraneans ready to satisfy their every whim. Unlike other Souls, Subterraneans are immortal, so they're stronger. But most often they're chosen to pleasure them," she said cautiously. A shudder ran through me. "It doesn't matter if their heart belongs to someone else. If the Witches want to be with a Subterranean—or even two or three at the same time—they're forced to obey, since they're the Witches' property. Everything in Hell is their property."

"Some Subterraneans might not think that was so bad," Simon joked, trying to coax the frozen expression off my face. He only succeeded in earning a glare from Ginevra.

"None of it is pleasant when you're being forced. And bear in mind that becoming a Witch's sex slave isn't the worst thing that can happen to a Subterranean. In fact, that only happens to the weakest, the ones who let themselves be ruled. Since Subterraneans are immortal, they can 'decide' whether to give in to a Witch's seduction. They keep the rebellious ones locked up in the dungeons and torture them until they bend to their will."

"My God. Evan . . ." I groaned. The thought of Evan being the Witches' slave had seemed unbearable at first, but now it felt like it might drive me insane.

"Don't worry. I don't think he's given in to evil," Simon added, trying to reassure me.

What actually scared me most was the thought of his being tortured. "No, you're right. I saw him," I said, lost in the memory that had suddenly returned to my mind. "I dreamed they were torturing him, but now I know it was actually happening. I have visions, you know."

"Those are your powers starting to manifest," Ginevra said in an attempt to calm me.

"Did it happen to you too?"

"At times, but my transformation happened differently."

"What do you mean?"

"I mean I had already chosen. Maybe this is all partly my fault. I should have prepared you sooner, but I ignored the signs. I was the last Sister to reawaken, but it hasn't been five hundred years yet, so I kept hoping I was wrong, that you weren't really one of us. That first time you met Evan in the woods marked your fate. The closeness with a Subterranean and then with a Witch kindled the nature buried in your soul. Later, the poison you came into contact with when we killed Faustian triggered something inside you. They sensed you. They heard the call of the Sister destined to awaken and the process began sooner than expected—which is exactly what the Màsala wanted to prevent."

"I was having prophetic dreams. They were warnings. I kept seeing Evan's death. It happened that night by the campfire too, remember? The Witches were already inside my head. When Evan entered my dreams they couldn't approach, but whenever he was gone they would find a way in." I suddenly remembered the nightmares I'd had whenever he was away on a mission. "If only I'd suspected he was in danger . . . my God." I buried my face in my hands, mortified.

Ginevra hugged me. "Hey, it's all right. There's no way you could have known. You had already perceived the essence of evil. Smelling the poison awakened your powers, but ingesting it when you kissed Evan sped up the process. That must be why the nightmares became more frequent. The serpent is forming inside you and that's what's causing your high fevers. Whenever the Witches make contact, that part of you reawakens. It's the Bond. When we discovered there was a Subterranean behind your hallucinations, we imagined that was also the cause of your nightmares—at least that's what I hoped. I hoped it with everything I had. Instead you were under two attacks: the Executioner's by day and the Witches' by night."

It was true. At times I'd even been able to feel the difference on my skin, like hot and cold—two obscure forces battling for my soul. The fever would always come after a nightmare or a premonition, but never after one of Desdemona's attacks. "But then I started having the visions even during the day."

"Right. The more you lost hope, the more power the Witches had over you."

I nodded in confirmation. Dropping my head into my hands, I tried to stifle the pain tearing me apart. I couldn't banish the mental image of Evan chained to the wall, bare-chested, his torn jeans streaked with blood as a Witch tried to seduce him only to whip him when he rejected her.

"Don't worry, Gemma. No matter how much they torture him, Subterraneans can't die in Hell, unlike mortal Souls. The only way a Subterranean can truly die is if he fails to eat of the Tree while he's on earth. In that case his soul is lost forever to oblivion."

"You mean they're going to torture him for all eternity?" I cried. Ginevra's attempt to comfort me had had the opposite effect.

Simon came to my rescue, a determined look on his face. "No. We're going to get him out of there, Gemma."

"First of all, I'll teach you how to block your mind," Ginevra said. "It's essential that they not discover your plan to renounce them once you've saved Evan. They have to believe in your sacrifice: your soul in exchange for Evan's. They can't suspect any kind of trick or you won't make it out alive." I nodded. My heart was beating like crazy. I didn't know if it was because of Ginevra's solemn tone or my impatience to see Evan again. "Renouncing evil will be very difficult once it's possessed you. Everything you've been—everything you've believed in—will disappear. The Gemma you've always known will cease to exist. Only your love for Evan will keep you from giving in."

Terror seized my heart. "Do you really think I'll come out of it?"

"I said it would be difficult—not impossible."

Simon rested his hand on my shoulder. "Ginevra and I hadn't known each other very long, but our love was still strong enough to break her bond with the Witches. The feeling you and Evan share was already powerful, and it's had time to grow and strengthen. I'm sure it'll be enough to prevent evil from subjugating you. You can do it. I've always suspected your love for Evan exceeded human boundaries. You have a supernatural soul—that's why you couldn't forget him. Losing him almost drove you insane because your relationship isn't a human one." I nodded, comforted by Simon's words. He smiled at me confidently. "And don't forget you're carrying his child. That's not a negligible detail. Your love for him will bring you back."

I covered my belly with both hands. I would never let anyone take my baby from me. He and Evan were my whole life. I nodded again. My heart trembled from the fierce battle being waged inside it between yearning and fear. The fear that I wasn't as strong as Ginevra, that I wouldn't be able to cast off the evil taking root inside me. That it would grow until it made me its prisoner. Would I be able to eradicate it once I had allowed it to smother me? Once I'd allowed it to *annihilate* me? Would I actually manage to emerge from the darkness?

There was one thing I was certain of: I wasn't going to let fear keep me from trying. I would bury it, crawl over it, choke it, but nothing was going to keep me from seeing Evan again. I would brave Hell and risk my life to bring him back. Even if it meant not coming back with him.

TIME PRESERVES ALL SECRETS

I moved slowly, trailing my hand over every object in Ginevra's room as though part of me knew for certain I would never see them again. I wasn't sure how much time had gone by since she'd asked me to wait for her there, but I was bursting with impatience. Until yesterday, the sun's rays had offered no warmth. Everything had lost its appeal. But now my heart had begun to beat again. The world was filled with colors once more because Evan, my Evan, was still alive, and I would soon be with him. For the first time we would all be together: he, I, and our baby.

After discussing it all night long, Simon and Ginevra had convinced me to lie down for a few hours. I was so anxious to see Evan, though, that I hadn't shut my eyes for a minute.

My hand stroked the covers of the books stacked on Ginevra's desk as if that touch were enough to reveal their secrets. The scarlet spine of a particular volume sparked my curiosity. I picked it up and a shiver ran down my spine, almost as if the book had given me an electric shock. I slid my fingers down the blood-red cover, slowly following the impressions of the strange symbols embossed on the leather, as I struggled between the almost irresistible urge to leaf through it and the awareness that I should put it back. As though it had a will of its own, my hand ignored the voice of reason and opened the book, revealing the secrets hidden in its ivory pages.

7 December, 1516

Tonight I dreamed of her again. It is the same woman, I am certain of it, as her image still consumes me now that I am awake.

A shudder ran through me and I flinched. I checked the cover, suddenly unsure whether I'd been the one to write those words, but it was Ginevra's diary. Both fascinated and frightened by the discovery, I let my eyes return impatiently to the page.

I hear voices in my head yet fear to tell a soul, as I know it would be the end of me. I would be burned, like the others. Their screams awakened me at dawn. They burned seven more and I knew one of them well. She was not a witch.

I couldn't stop the tremor that invaded my body. I knew I should stop reading but I couldn't. My eyes flew over the lines, grasping snippets here and there, while my mind, hungry for information, tried to memorize as many details as possible. All at once my hand paused on a page that was a slightly different color, dotted with dark splotches. I knew well what had caused those marks: they were tears.

12 January, 1517

This morning they took her away. Father sought to stop them and was arrested. God protect her, poor little soul. They will kill her. I know they will kill her, just as they killed all the others. Why have they not taken me? My heart is certainly more impure than Jana's. How I wish I were a real witch so I could annihilate them all. My sister is innocent. Her only fault is her love-stricken soul. It was not the Devil that led her out into the night, a captive of her tormented slumber. May my brother be damned for seeing her. I would kill him with my own hands for shouting out and waking the whole village, letting them all see the poor thing fainted away in the underbrush. The Devil had not possessed her—it was her love for Cédric that troubled her in her dreams. If only I had noticed her in time, I would never have let her go outside and her life would be spared. Instead they will torture her, and all that will remain of her body is ash . . .

"My God . . ." I swallowed, deeply shaken by Ginevra's thoughts, preserved on those pages for centuries. Appalled by the cruelty of men, I read on. As I turned the pages, I gradually sensed a new strength resonating between the lines. The words conveyed an energy that hadn't been there before, as if something in Ginevra had profoundly changed.

3 November, 1517

I feel invincible, as though the energy of a star had flowed into me, giving me new life. At first I was no longer sure who I was. Everything around me was unfamiliar, which frightened me somewhat, yet it no longer matters. I feel like a queen on a throne. I can do whatever I wish. I can punish whomever I wish. My dear Anya brought me this diary again that it might help me rediscover myself, yet rereading it has been like reading the accounts of a stranger, full of thoughts that belong to another. I know not the Ginevra Nesea Seraina Moser hidden in those pages, yet I feel alive as never before.

Last night I killed him. I killed the man who was once my brother and I claimed his soul, then left him at the mercy of the Insane to fend for himself. It was not difficult to win him over. Besides, no one deserved his fate more than he. I have no memory of his affection, as if we'd never met. Reading of the abominations he forced upon me and my poor sister convinced me it was his rightful place.

The diary slid from my hands and I stared into space, my mind trapped in those memories as if they were my own. My hands shook. I couldn't believe Ginevra was capable of committing such an atrocity. Had she really killed her own brother?

Fear crept into my heart like a woodworm, devouring every certainty. Would I become like that too? Would I really no longer be able to feel affection for my family? My friends? Evan? How could I forget the love that filled my heart for our baby? I couldn't believe evil might annihilate me completely. I would never allow it. I would fight with all my strength to emerge from the darkness and find the light. Ginevra had done it. There were too many things I wasn't willing to give up. I would never let anyone take those things from me, much less myself. Maybe there was a secret hidden somewhere in the pages of that diary that had allowed Ginevra to free herself from evil.

I picked it up from the floor and thumbed through it until my eyes found what they were looking for.

17 May, 1632

Today, for the first time, I hesitated.
I spared a Subterranean. That has never happened before. I must return to him and remedy the error before anyone learns of it. My

head is so full of thoughts! Something new is growing inside me. My human side is struggling to re-emerge.

I am beginning to recall fragments of my past. I carefully checked this diary, yet the images I continue to recall are not contained in any of its pages. They are only in my head. Memories I had buried are unexpectedly surfacing, disorienting me. My mother's smile, steam rising from the bowls as we supped together . . . Jana's cheerful laughter.

I can sense it: not long hence I will find myself again.

3 June, 1632

I could not bring myself to do it. He was ready to succumb to me and yet I did not take him. I set his soul free, though he would have offered it to me willingly. It was unlike the other times. There is something in him, something I cannot elude. I seduced him yet wished for him to be free, wished for him to desire me of his own accord. And now I feel it is he who is holding me prisoner. I made love to him. I made love <u>with</u> him. It was as though our bodies became one.

When he asked to see me again I felt something deep in my heart. A quiver. Never before have I desired one of them. Not like this. What the devil is happening to me? I cannot have such feelings for a Son of Eve. I should have killed that soldier, seduced him and torn out his soul to prevent him from becoming a Subterranean. Only then could I have made him mine. Sophìa will punish me even for hesitating. I cannot risk losing her trust in me. Devina would enjoy that. She lies in wait for one false move so she can take my place.

<u>I must come to my senses.</u>

27 June, 1632

I no longer know who I am. I no longer know what is happening to me. Maintaining control over my thoughts is becoming more and more difficult, as I do nothing but think of him: General Adrian Simeone Dahlberg. I have been unable to get him out of my mind and my body burns anew at the thought of his hands on me. Thanks to us Witches, his Swedish troops have occupied Munich. The war is spreading and the Reaping has been more productive than we hoped. Souls spontaneously offer themselves to us on the battlefield, either so their lives will be spared or to ensure victory. The other night Simeone was slain in battle and instead of carrying his soul to Sophia, I took it to safety. I hid him in a cave in the mountains. Though I know not yet how to have him eat of the Tree, he will be safe there, at least until my thoughts betray me. If anyone discovers him, I will die.

What is happening to me? Something is changing within me, something important, and I know not whether to repress this feeling or nurture it, for I fear the direction in which it is guiding me.

I feel I have betrayed my Sisters. Why did I not claim his soul when the opportunity presented itself? What is different about him? I continue to return to him as though compelled. Why have I allowed him to make love to me again and yet again? Perhaps there is another question I should ask myself instead: why did I make love to him? And most importantly, why was it so passionate, so overwhelming?

Adrian Simeone Dahlberg. There is no way to forget him.

20 January, 1721

The time when I must make a decision draws near, I can feel it. Many years have passed, yet the question still consumes me: how will I be able to eradicate such an important part of me to make room for another—indispensable to me now, a thousand times sweeter? I can no longer keep our secret now that Simeone and I have hidden another Subterranean, Evan. How am I to decide between myself and

"Gemma, what are—"

I snapped the diary shut and looked up to see Ginevra staring at me from the doorway, visibly shocked. "Did you really kill your brother?" I asked before I could stop myself, almost accusingly. I fixed my eyes on her, hoping she would say it wasn't true.

Ginevra hesitated, glancing at the diary, and then seemed to study me. "How did you know that?" she asked cautiously.

I blinked nervously and looked at the diary I'd read without permission, still in my hand. "I'm sorry, Gwen. I knew I shouldn't, but I couldn't resist."

Ginevra strode across the room and snatched the book from my hands. To my surprise, she opened it and held it out in front of my nose. I peered at it, puzzled, and instantly realized the reason for her astonishment. My eyes were immediately drawn to the page, but I couldn't read a single thing on it. It was a jumble of strange symbols.

"How were you able to read what's written there?" she repeated, carefully enunciating every word.

I paled. Not even I knew the answer. "I—I don't know. I have no idea. All I know is—"

"—is that you can," Ginevra finished for me. I couldn't utter a word; my mind seemed suddenly drained. "It's the Witches' ancient secret code," she continued. "To anyone else's eyes it's nothing but an incomprehensible jumble of symbols. For centuries mankind tried to decipher the rare fragments they came across, but without success. Some tried to transcribe a few imprecise snippets, but not even those could be deciphered. Not a trace of this written code survives today— the few examples they had in the past were destroyed. Your powers are getting stronger, Gemma. Your mind is beginning to accept the transformation, granting them access to your body."

Deep in my heart I'd always harbored the suspicion I was a little odd compared to the few girls I was friends with. No, not odd. *Different.* Only now did I understand the reason: the strange power that had started to awaken in me . . . a power that gripped me. *The power of darkness.*

Repressing my fear, I looked up at Ginevra. "Then it's true? You really did kill your brother?" I swallowed, my eyes on hers as I waited for her answer.

She gave it to me without hesitating. "I wasn't myself—I wasn't aware of what I was doing—but yes. I killed him without pity after I'd shown him what a *real* Witch was and what we were capable of. Because that's what Witches do. They have no scruples or human emotions except for the ones that bond them to each other. They're driven solely by the evil that lives within them. That's why I'm begging you to reconsider. Agreeing to become one of them means eradicating every trace of love from your heart."

"Only until you find something that can make it germinate again," I said, resolute.

"It's not easy to free yourself. I should know—I've been there myself. Witches are the essence of evil. They led Eve astray so she would betray her Adam. And who do you think convinced Judas to betray Christ? *I killed my own brother.* Only when my former self began to resurface did I understand the devastation I'd wreaked, but by then it was too late. That's why I started to consider leaving my Sisters and giving up that life when I discovered I loved Simon. It took almost a century for that to happen. But in doing so I betrayed Sophia and was sentenced to death."

"How did you m—"

"It's a long story. I'll tell you another time. Right now we need to focus on you."

I saw the pain in her eyes and nodded. "I read about your sister. Your real sister, I mean. I'm so sorry. What they did to her was terrible."

"You have no idea what my little Jana had to endure. In the early 1500s there was mass hysteria over Witches. Many innocent women were accused of serving the devil and killed." Ginevra looked down, devastated by the memory. "My sister did nothing wrong," she said, her voice trembling. "My brother betrayed her innocence by accusing her of witchcraft. The same brother who abused her for years sent her to her death. He might as well have personally lit the fire beneath her stake. Back then all it took was a single accuser for someone to be found guilty."

"They burned her at the stake?" I was horrified.

"Not before they'd subjected her to unbearable torture and humiliation. When they took her away, she was stripped naked. They even shaved her head to look for the devil's mark on her."

My hand automatically covered my belly where the devil's mark had been left on me. From time to time the scar burned; it was my serpent, trying to come out.

Ginevra smiled, amused by my thoughts. "Humans couldn't even recognize the sign of a real Witch. Often a common birthmark or some other mark on the skin, together with another person's testimony, was enough to have someone sentenced to death. My sister, for example, had a mole on her inner thigh. They imprisoned and tortured her to force her into confessing. She suffered the 'witches' chair,' a diabolical chair of red-hot iron on which she was forced to sit completely naked. Her fingernails were torn out along with the little hair left on her head, and in the end they burned her at the stake to grant her 'the salvation of purifying fire.' Such bullshit!"

"Did it ever happen that a real Witch was accused?"

"Only one time. That time gave rise to the first witch-hunt. It happened in 1017, an infamous year in the history of our Sisters. It was a Subterranean, driven by his thirst for revenge, who began the hysteria that killed thousands of people over the course of the following centuries. His name was Gareth. Legend has it the Màsala sent him to kill a girl before she transformed—just like what happened to you—but the Angel took advantage of people's inherent wickedness and amused himself by killing her in front of everyone. He had her burned in the public square after accusing her of serving the devil and showing them her distinguishing mark. From that time on, humans became hell-bent on exterminating women with suspicious marks."

"How horrible!" I couldn't believe a Subterranean could outdo a Witch in terms of cruelty.

"As I said, he was looking for revenge. It seems that when they were both still human they were married and she was unfaithful to him. Maybe that was why he stripped her naked and humiliated her like that before burning her. But the real hysteria broke out centuries later. In spite of the Subterranean's actions, the Màsala didn't punish him, since he'd done his duty, but he was relieved of all assignments and forced to hide in Eden to escape Sophìa's wrath.

"Five hundred years later Gareth began to thirst for revenge again. He was afraid his wife's spirit might return in the body of another woman, so he returned to Earth on his own and incited men to resume the hunt. Eventually it reached the village in Switzerland where I lived. After all those centuries of isolation with no purpose, with only his tormenting thoughts for company, Gareth had lost his mind. He wanted to find the next chosen one before she transformed so he could kill her like he'd killed his wife, with purifying fire. Word traveled quickly and panic spread. But this time Sophìa found him in time and killed him. She couldn't let it happen again.

"Meanwhile the hunt had taken on a life of its own, costing thousands of people their lives and—to Sophìa's delight—turning Soul after Soul to evil. As you see, I lived in times that were far more difficult and brutal than yours. Unlike you, I hadn't had any contact with the poison before my transformation, but the evil around me was enough to awaken what lurked inside me. You have no idea of the atrocities that were committed in my village. Evil spawns evil. When you've undergone more than your heart can bear, there's not much room left for love and you end up allowing yourself to be subjugated. That's why I was happy to transform. Back then all I wanted was revenge—revenge for my sister, revenge against the world. Jana wasn't a Witch and yet she was slain for being one. The day they killed her everything that was human in my heart vanished along with her, destroyed by my hatred for those heartless men. No one deserved to live more than Jana. She was so sweet and helpful to everyone. I had the opportunity to exact justice. All I had to do was make a decision: to hate mankind. It was a decision I'd already made in my heart. At that time, though, I couldn't have imagined to what lengths I would go. Hatred fed off me and I off it, day after day. I wasn't myself any more. I lost control over my mind. I didn't realize it until I met Simon. Back then he had such a funny, pompous name!" Ginevra smiled. "He reawakened the part of me that had been trapped deep in my heart for centuries, buried under evil—my humanity. It took some time, but fortunately in the end I realized life wasn't worth living without love and I made a different choice—the right one." She gazed at me as I silently absorbed every detail of the new world that awaited me. "And don't worry, you will too."

I nodded to convince myself and took a last look at the pages of her diary, noticing a symbol that appeared more frequently than the others. It piqued my curiosity. Ginevra read the question in my mind. "That's the symbol of the Subterraneans," she explained.

I ran my fingers over the strange, twisted X, fascinated by its lines, elegant yet foreboding. As I put the diary down, I wondered why the pages showed no signs of aging. "How have you kept it so well preserved over the centuries?" I asked, still trying to regain my self-possession. It seemed like the words had always been there.

"I put a spell on it so it would withstand the effects of time. It was my sweet Sister Anya who brought it back to me to remind me of who I was. That's why I gave you one when I guessed what was happening to you—though I was still hoping I was wrong about it." She disappeared into her walk-in closet, re-entering the room a moment later with an old trunk, her eyes locked on mine.

"What's in there?"

A new and tender smile lit up her eyes.

SURVIVAL LESSONS

"Gwen, what's inside it?" I repeated. Ginevra seemed lost in another world, gazing at the old trunk as though it contained a rare treasure. She set it on the bed and waved her hand over its ancient lock, which opened by magic.

She gently raised its lid and I leaned over, wondering what secrets it contained, then looked at her in surprise. She smiled. "In here you'll find everything you need."

I looked at her, mystified, then studied the objects carefully tucked away inside the trunk. "A dress? Why would I need a dress?"

Ginevra lifted the threadbare gown out and held it in her hands like the most precious of objects. "This isn't just any dress. It's mine. It's the dress I wore when I escaped from Hell. Witches are very particular about their outfits. They often dye their hair too: pink with black streaks; violet with purple streaks; black and red; navy blue and powder blue—sometimes even three or four colors together. Mortal women spend time painting their nails; Witches pay the same attention to their hair color. They have a different outfit for each particular event or time of day: hunts, ceremonies, games, the Opalion. Most of them are made of some kind of leather, even the weirdest kinds, but they're all very sexy. This, on the other hand, was my first normal dress—a sort of first step toward my new life together with Simon. It's also what I'd been wearing when I transformed. When I was still with my Sisters but had begun to remember my past, I liked to put it on from time to time. My mother made it for me for my twenty-fourth birthday. I was engaged at the time, but then Jana was killed, I transformed, and everything changed. Sorry, it's a bit threadbare; it was prettier before. When I was expelled from Hell and deprived of my powers, it got a little worn."

"Do I really have to wear it? Can't I go dressed like this?" I asked, horrified by the thought of walking around in a dress from the sixteenth century.

"Sure you can, but they'll kill you right away. You need to go as unnoticed as possible. Modern clothing will give you away—it will let the Damned know you've just arrived, a lost Soul whose last remaining shreds of life are there to be sucked clean. You need to blend in, Gemma, and not attract attention. In this old dress, at first glance you'll look like you've been there for centuries. As long as you keep your distance from the other Souls, that is. The longer a Soul has been in Hell, the more the others fear it because it's managed to survive. On top of that, the Damned don't like old flesh."

"But if this dress means so much to you, can't you use magic to make me a new one?"

"This one already has the odor of Hell on it. It'll help cover up your own scent a little, in case they get near you. New Souls are already a delicacy, but you're still *alive*, Gemma. You have no idea what that means. You're fresh meat, and the blood flowing through your veins will be irresistible to them. Oh God—" Ginevra ran a hand over her face, looking horrified. "This is crazy. It's a suicide mission! Why did I agree to help you?!"

"Gwen, listen to me: I don't care how dangerous it is! You'll never talk me out of it, not now that I'm so close to finding Evan."

"But it's insane! They'll smell you and hunt you down!"

"I don't care."

"Hell is a madhouse full of deadly traps and ferocious animals. Even if you manage to go unnoticed among the Damned, you'll never be able to hide from the Molock if you encounter any."

"Molock? Who—"

"They're creatures spawned from Hell. Half man, half beast. Extremely dangerous, bloodthirsty creatures. They'll smell your blood from miles away. And they aren't the only terrifying creatures down there, believe me! Think about this very carefully, Gemma. Once you're in Hell, there will be no turning back. Are you absolutely sure you want to do this? Even if you save Evan, once you transform, that will be your world."

"I'm not going to let Evan pay the price. Everything that happened was my fault."

Ginevra was silenced as much by the determination in my thoughts as in my eyes. "All right, then." She sighed, placed her hand on my belly, and closed her eyes.

"What are you doing?"

"Casting a spell on the baby. Until it's broken, he'll remain in a deep sleep. This way he won't be able to sense your emotions. If you're afraid, he won't know it. If you're anxious, he'll sleep peacefully. This way your pregnancy won't be an extra concern for you when you enter the Copse. Whatever happens, my magic will protect him. But listen carefully, Gemma: not even my spell will be able to save him if you get yourself killed." I nodded, grateful for the unexpected gift. It would be unbearable if he were hurt. I would never let that happen.

"Prepare yourself, because you're going to feel like you're inside your worst nightmare ever. Forget all those fairy tales you've heard about monsters. Everything you're going to encounter will be far worse."

"Well, after all, it *is* Hell. It's not like I can expect songbirds and rainbows."

"No, Gemma. You mustn't have *any* expectations; they will inevitably fall far short of the truth. Remember: never be fooled by appearances and never let your guard down. Here, take this."

I looked at the small, dark instrument in her hands. It appeared to be a sort of whistle, made of a strange alloy—black stone or metal, I couldn't tell—with a deep groove all around it. "What is it?" I asked.

"It's called a Phœbus. If you need help, use it and help will come. But be careful because it's risky. It's better to forget you even have it. Only use it if your life is in imminent danger. Do you understand, Gemma? Only use it if you really need to escape, and fast. Otherwise you risk drawing too much attention to yourself."

I took it and studied it for a few seconds. Ginevra handed me a small leather shoulder bag. "Put it in this satchel. We'll fill it with everything you need: food, water, and—most importantly—this."

My eyes were drawn to the strange amulet Ginevra was holding up, a stone coiled around itself like a serpent. I had the feeling I'd seen it somewhere before. "What's it for?"

"It's a key. You'll need it in order to come back. If you've already transformed you won't need it for yourself, but you'll still need it to let Evan through. There's no other way he can leave Hell. The portal only opens for Witches or those who have a key. Otherwise all the Subterraneans would try to escape." Ginevra gripped the amulet, concerned. "Come to think of it, you'd better wear it around your neck. It'll be safer there. You can't risk losing it. Listen to me carefully, Gemma: this is your ticket home. Lose it and both of you are done for." She had me put the amulet on, then looked down, her gaze unfocused. "I keep hoping you'll find a way to get out of there without sacrificing yourself to evil."

"Don't worry, Gwen. I won't let the Witches get the better of me. Even if I agree to transform, my love for Evan will prevent evil from possessing me. I won't leave him once I find him again—not if it depends on me. The only thing in life we can control is ourselves."

"I wish I were as confident as you."

I smiled. To me her words were comical. "Since the moment I met you, that's all I've thought about *you*."

"Don't be ridiculous, Gemma. You have a strength few people have. You've grown so much since we first met and your courage and determination have grown with you." Hearing this from Ginevra of all people sent a shiver of emotion through me. "Speaking of courage, you'll need this too."

Another shiver—more hostile and foreboding this time—replaced the first one. "A dagger? What will I do with that?"

"Defend yourself, if necessary."

I took it from her and examined its leather sheath. It looked so small . . . yet I'd learned that power and strength didn't depend on size. I slid it out for just a second. Its blade was black, of the same material as the whistle, while its grip was spiraled like a snake.

"Tie it to your arm or your calf, if you prefer, so it stays hidden under your dress."

"My arm. I'd rather it be around my arm," I was quick to say, praying I wouldn't need to use it.

"Aim for this spot here." Ginevra rested two fingers just below my ear where the blood pulsed through my carotid artery. "It's a small blade, but if you slip it in right there, your enemy will dissolve in a matter of seconds. Speaking of which, I advise you not to breathe in the ashes—they're toxic. Naturally that doesn't go for Molock or other Hell-born creatures. There's only one way to kill them, and that's with a direct blow to the maseolum, in the center of the chest. It's like an elongated root or a beating heart. I doubt you would even be able to get that close to one of them without it devouring you."

"What will happen if I don't stab one of the Damned in just the right spot?"

"You can wound him wherever you like—chop off a leg, an arm— but he'll recompose unless you lop his head off. Or decide to make a fire and eat him."

"Huh?"

"Don't worry—just kidding. Only the Lucid cook the Damned before eating them, and you definitely aren't one of them," she joked.

"What do you mean?"

"That you're already out of your mind, naturally. With the exception of Lucid Souls, everyone else prefers raw meat."

I pressed the back of my hand to my mouth, fighting a wave of nausea. "What are Lucid Souls? And what do you mean 'everyone else'? Is there a difference?"

"I told you, there are many dangerous creatures in Hell. There are lots of sins, and even more kinds of sinners. I couldn't name them all even if I wanted to. The enormous variety of transgressions leads to the formation of new species of Damned Souls. As if that weren't enough, many of them mutate and evolve over time. Quickly, if they have to. Usually, Souls tend to band together according to their natures. It's a sort of selection process based on 'species' or, if you prefer, on how serious the wrongs they committed during their lifetimes were. But each species has various subspecies. It's been that way since time immemorial. It's a nightmarish jungle teeming with danger. A damned place."

"Yeah—okay, okay, I get it. Keep going," I said, recognizing her millionth attempt to talk me out of it.

"All I'm saying is you shouldn't expect to find the souls of the Damned safely behind bars enduring whatever form of torture corresponds to their sins—you can run into them at any moment. In fact, it's bound to happen. They aren't immortal spirits or even dead bodies. They need to eat, but even more important, they need to avoid ending up as someone else's meal. That's their punishment: the constant struggle for survival. Some sinners have additional punishments as well. Egotists, for example, are forced to offer themselves to others as food, suffering the terrible torture of seeing parts of their bodies removed and devoured. The Damned often hunt them down, but the slyest Souls keep one hidden for times when food is scarce. Then there are the Lechers, who in life succumbed to the pleasures of the flesh. They're forced to offer their own flesh in exchange for pleasure."

"That's disgusting," I gasped, horrified by her words.

"That's Hell." The look on Ginevra's face was one of utter revulsion.

"Hold on a second. Egotists? They go to Hell too? Who hasn't been egotistical at least once in their life?"

"You're right, but that isn't the point. It's how far they were willing to go and what they were prepared to sacrifice in their own interests. What counts isn't so much the crime itself as the motivation that drove the Soul to commit it. Take Murderers, for instance. Murderers of the highest order don't need to be persuaded to take someone's life—they have death in their blood already and kill of their own free will. When they die, all the Witches have to do is collect their souls. They're the most dangerous ones, and the most ruthless among them are often chosen for the Circle. However, many other Souls are in Hell because they took a life not of their own free will but by allowing themselves to be seduced by the Witches. They're Murderers too, but that's not all they are. Souls are classified according to the intention that drove them to act. Someone who takes another person's life to save his own will be punished as an Egotist. The same thing goes for many other species. A person who runs away, for example, causing someone else's death as a result, is classified as a Coward. According to this system of classification, a group of Souls condemned to the same punishment may have committed completely different crimes. What counts is how they chose to behave when they were tempted. If someone is egotistical, sooner or later that will lead them to make a decision that hurts others. The Witches wait for this moment. They know which strings to pluck to bring evil out in people."

"So a sin isn't defined by the act itself, but by the emotion that motivates you to commit it, like tarnish on the soul."

"Exactly. It's emotions that rule over all else. Witches leverage them to turn a Soul to evil. They feed off people's weaknesses—wrath, pride, envy, avarice; also guilt, shame, and so on. The human soul can nurture an endless range of dark emotions, and the Witches understand their every nuance. They're enchantresses and weavers of illusion."

"Practically an infinite classification."

"More or less. It's Sophìa who sorts through the Souls from the Reaping. No pastime could be more gratifying to her. I've been there many times while she was doing it. I learned that there are three overarching Echelons. Those who have evil in their blood to begin with belong to the first one, the 'Great Echelon.' She considers them purebreds, Souls who don't need the influence of evil to do wrong. All the groups include purebreds. They're the most ferocious, most feared of all. Souls who give in to evil under the Witches' influence fall into the second Echelon. You can find every species in the first and second Echelons. In the third you'll find only the souls of the Corrupt—the ones who sold themselves to the Witches in exchange for personal gain. Even though most of them didn't commit other evil acts during their mortal lives, in Hell they have to fight for survival just like everyone else.

"As I said before, some species tend to seek each other out. There's a secret shared by the Damned: 'Better to know the color of the soul than the shape of the body.' It doesn't matter what action someone might take—what counts is the intention driving that action. By focusing directly on that, Souls know exactly what to expect from those around them. They often gather in villages, while others prefer to remain hidden, far from their enemies. Then there are the Insane— those who've lost every trace of their humanity. They wander aimlessly in search of food, guided entirely by their instincts."

"Wait, back up. There are villages?"

"Lots of them. Usually they're made up of the Sane, shrewd Souls who still possess a glimmer of reason and attempt to preserve some semblance of civilization. Every Soul—regardless of species or Echelon—is in imminent danger of being overtaken by madness and losing what's left of his humanity. Basically, Souls can either maintain their sanity . . . or go insane. Some of them are in between. Generally, the Souls who during their lifetimes weren't completely consecrated to evil, those who committed lesser crimes, tend to have a better chance of keeping their sanity. Consequently, the Sane, for the most part, fall into the Corrupt category. But listen carefully to what I'm about to tell you: whether they're murderers or people who succumbed to evil as a means of achieving their goals, they all need to eat in order to survive—and there are no candy bars in Hell, if you get what I mean. You can't trust anyone."

I nodded, disconcerted.

"If they're unable to kill others, Souls are forced to do things to survive like feed off themselves. Eating parts of their own bodies causes them atrocious suffering, and when those parts grow back it's unimaginably painful. When they first arrive in Hell, all Souls are still partly human, though deprived of free will, but the more they feed on others, the more they lose their humanity. They gradually turn into the Insane. Zombies, Gemma, slaves to themselves and the evil that led them to that Godforsaken realm in the first place.

"In spite of all this, there *is* another species of Sane Souls that's purer: the Lucid. They're Souls that haven't let themselves be taken over by demonic influences. They aren't immune to evil, of course, but they struggle every day not only with the other Damned but also with themselves, because they refuse to succumb to evil. Their will is stronger. They grow vegetables, hunt game, but most of them don't last long. That's why there are so few of them."

A ray of hope touched my heart. "They're like humans, then."

"In a certain sense. There may also be Souls from the second Echelon among the Lucid, but for the most part they fall into the Corrupt category. As I told you, few of them last long."

"How can I find them?"

"Don't get your hopes up. Hell isn't a place to go looking for solidarity. No one trusts anyone—the Lucid even less than the others. Generally, they're solitary Souls who live in hiding. Even if you ran into one you certainly couldn't consider yourself lucky. In the end they're just like all the other Damned: ready and willing to kill."

What Ginevra said next caught my attention: "Subterraneans are the least dangerous because they don't need to eat. On Earth they served Death because of the curse on them, but in Hell they have no connection to evil. They preserve their identities, though many of them choose to suppress them in order to serve the Witches. They aren't wicked, but Witches' blood is such a powerful drug it reduces them to puppets at the mercy of their desires. The more Witch blood they consume, the harder it is for them to go without it and the deeper they sink into slavery. Some Subterraneans take refuge in the villages."

My heart leapt. "You mean Evan might be in one of them?"

"No, Gemma. With rare exceptions, they're ones the Witches have already tired of. They claim so many of them that a single escaped slave doesn't raise much interest. Don't delude yourself, Gemma. I doubt they would let Evan go that easily. I'm almost positive he's being kept inside the Castle under strict surveillance—maybe by Devina herself. They weren't born yesterday: they want you, and Evan is their bargaining chip. He's not just another Subterranean, he's the key to getting you. The other Executioners are used as slaves at the Castle, tortured and drugged so they'll satisfy the Witches' every whim, including sexually, and most Subterraneans are willing to do anything in order to have their blood. The poison stupefies them, but a few drops of Witches' blood sends them into ecstasies when ingested in proximity to the power the Sisters emanate. It's a rare commodity and many Subterraneans feel fortunate to serve them if it means they can suck a little of it like filthy vampires."

"Evan would never give in to them," I said, trying hard to convince myself. "You're right, chances are he's at the Castle. I saw it in one of my nightmares. You just need to explain how to get there."

"If all goes well, you should reach the Castle after a couple hours of walking. You probably won't even need food. All you have to do is follow the river downstream. It leads to the moat around the Castle. But be careful—it may not be that simple. Hell changes constantly. It's a crazy place, and if I know the Witches, any one of them might try to stand in your way."

"But why? I don't understand."

"That's because you don't know Devina. You need to watch out for her. She's eccentric and unpredictable. When I was one of them she harbored a deep hatred for me."

"How is that possible? Aren't all the Sisters connected by a powerful bond?"

"Evil corrodes all bonds, even the strongest ones. Also, envy is a difficult beast to tame. Devina is especially evil. She was the first Witch. That made her extra close to Sophia and less so to the others. She's blinded by jealousy. Evil is inside us, Gemma, but not all Witches know how to handle it. She wanted to be the Empress's favorite and claim special rights, but Sophia had a weakness for me that drove Devina crazy. Sophia waited a thousand years for me to arrive, since the Witch who was supposed to awaken before me was killed before she transformed. It was the first time in the history of the Sisterhood that something like that had happened. I filled a void, which made me special in Sophia's eyes. I was her Specter, which is like a second-in-command. That was why Devina enjoyed screwing things up for me. She was the one who exposed my betrayal. I'm sure she took my place once I left, and I have no doubt that if you transform she'll hate you too, no matter what you do, because you'll fill the void I left behind. The Bond is a gift God granted Sophia after her exile, and it's the most powerful thing in the universe, second only to true love. Yet Devina is different from all the other Witches in history. The Bond doesn't seem to have the same effect on her. She can't control her deceitfulness even when it comes to Sophia. She's completely blinded by her own hunger for omnipotence, kind of like Sophia was towards God. Even though the Bond among Sisters is strong, the most powerful connections of all—which can't be eradicated from the heart of any Witch—are the ones with Sophìa and our own Dakor, since they're born of our essence. At the other end of the spectrum, there are Witches like Anya. She was the best of my Sisters."

"Anya. The name sounds familiar."

"I'm not surprised. I'm sure she's the Witch who visited you in your dreams."

"She must have been the one who called you Gwen," I said, remembering her words the first time I'd called her by that name.

Ginevra nodded. "There are days when I still miss her. She was a trusted friend and a loyal Sister. In any case, you don't have to worry. No matter how many obstacles you encounter, the Castle will show itself to you. Whatever happens, just keep following the river. As I said, Hell is an unstable place. It's crazy; it defies all logic. You might think you've reached the Castle only to see it vanish before your eyes. The landscape changes so suddenly it'll make you feel like you've lost your mind. As you make your way through the forest, the paths may become shorter or longer, but they'll inevitably lead you to her, to Sophìa, the High Empress."

"The devil," I corrected her.

Ginevra smiled. "Exactly. The important thing is never to lose sight of the river. I'm sure Sophìa is waiting for you."

I nodded and she bit her lip. "Once you and Evan are out of the Castle, you'll need to retrace your steps along the river until you reach the summit of Mount Nhubii. It stands above the tallest waterfall. Many call it Hell's Crown because its jagged peaks rise into the sky in a ring, like a barrier protecting what's hidden within it. You'll only have your own strength to rely on. Evan's powers will already be sapped since he hasn't eaten of the Tree for so long."

"Can't I take food with me for him?"

"No, Gemma, you can't. Ambrosia can't leave Eden. Simon will take care of that once you've both returned."

"You didn't say 'if.' That's comforting."

"Now you need to focus. There's a level area on the summit. There you'll find a circle of standing rocks with another circle inside it. We call it the Dánava. It's a passageway between dimensions. Long ago men on Earth, enchanted by the Witches who were toying with them, built a crude imitation of it, but obviously it never worked. What remains today is what humans call Stonehenge. Mankind has never learned what its true purpose was. In any case, you and Evan need to reach the center of the Dánava. Then it will be time for you to use the key, the Dreide. Don't worry, it will show you the way."

I nodded, overwhelmed by all the information. "Okay. River. Mountain. Key. I can do it."

"Whenever we make a decision it's a sort of bet between ourselves and the world. Winning and losing are two sides of the same coin. When it's tossed into the air, it's not only chance that decides whether it turns up heads or tails—the result also depends on the hand that flips it and on how hard it's flipped."

"I'm all in."

"I realize that. That's why I know you'll come back to me. You *have to*, Gemma. I'm counting on you. *Come back to me.* I don't want to lose you and the baby."

I hugged her. Ginevra snapped the hair tie that had fallen from my upper arm to my forearm. "*This* should have made me realize it."

"What does that have to do with anything? I've always worn it, even when I was a little girl."

"Exactly. I bet it makes you feel secure and you miss it when it's not on you. Every Witch wears her Dakor around her arm. That's the point of contact where the serpents prefer to merge with us. They say that when God cast the serpent into Hell for corrupting Eve, it bit Sophìa's wrist, crept inside her and took her soul. From that point on she was bound to her serpent for life. If you kill a Dakor, his Witch dies too. You've always worn a hair tie where your deepest essence says your Dakor should be. Though you didn't know it, your soul instinctively felt its absence. Like nostalgia."

"How can you be nostalgic for something you've never known?"

"Because your Dakor is inside you."

I wasn't sure whether the idea fascinated or frightened me. I'd seen Ginevra's serpent merge with her after coiling around her forearm. The thought that it would happen to me too was mind-boggling.

"I wish I could help you more."

"You've already done so much, Gwen. Now you just have to tell me where the entrance to Hell is."

Ginevra sighed as though she'd deliberately saved that detail for last, still hoping to change my mind, then gave in to the inevitable. "There's only one way in: the gateway that remained open when God banished his wife: Hell's Mouth, in the Yucatán."

"In the Yucatán? We have to go to Mexico?"

"Men have always searched for a passageway to the underworld. The Maya came close. There was a time long ago when some Witches had fun toying with men by showing themselves to certain tribes and revealing secrets unknown to the world, for the sheer joy of being worshipped as goddesses. They would grant men's wishes in exchange for their souls. The people didn't realize they were making a pact with the devil, just like people today who are drawn in by their empty promises. Sex, money, power—in exchange for what? A gratifying yet fleeting existence on Earth only to become slaves to their own hunger and that of others. Many sacrificed other Souls in addition to their own, so women and children were thrown alive into cenotes as offerings to the 'goddesses.'"

"How horrible!"

"Beliefs make the world go round. They're mankind's most dangerous weapon. Many of those peoples' prophecies and dogmas derived from the Witches, or at least from their interpretation of the Witches' promises. They took advantage of the people's ignorance, threatening to destroy the world. So the Maya built an important ceremonial complex named—and not by chance—Chichen Itzá. It literally means 'at the mouth of the well of the water enchantresses.' It was called that because they were on the other side of the well. Even today, there are winding tunnels and hidden passageways leading to underground temples beneath the complex. There, in the throne room, the Witches would show themselves to the Mayans to amuse themselves. Later, the Temple of Kukulkan was built in the center of the ruins, atop an earlier temple. It's a pyramid with stairs going up all four sides. During the spring and fall equinoxes, at sunrise and sunset—when the Witches would show themselves—the edges of the steps cast a snake-shaped shadow that appears to slither along the northern stairway. The pyramid was designed this way as a sign of respect for the Witches and to honor their Dakor. For the Maya, the universe was divided into three parts: the underworld, the earth and the heavens. For centuries they tried to find a way into the other worlds, searching for passageways in the cenotes and building temples over them. But no one ever discovered the location of the only way into Hell: a cenote hidden in the earth that no one has ever seen."

"Ready, ladies?" Totally fascinated by Ginevra's explanation, I hadn't noticed Simon standing in the doorway.

"Impatient, actually. 'Ready' is a big word. I don't think I ever will be."

Simon smiled, but only to ease the tension. "I'll wait for you downstairs."

"You don't need to come with us," Ginevra was quick to say.

"Why shouldn't I? This is as important to me as it is to you two," he said.

"It would be a lot wiser for you to stay here and keep watch on the Subterranean."

"I can go with you and come back to check on her whenever I want."

"We can't risk it, Simon!" Ginevra seemed anxious to do everything she could to keep Simon away from the Witches. To protect him, just like I would have done with Evan. She opened a drawer and took something out. "Here. You might need this."

Simon stared at the syringe she had handed him and smiled teasingly.

"Hey, watch it, I'm reading your mind. Don't try to have fun all alone. It wouldn't work anyway."

"I'm sure it wouldn't, *chérie*. It wouldn't be the same without you." Simon looked seductively into his girlfriend's eyes and stifled a smile as I wondered what was going on between them. Actually, I wasn't sure I really wanted to know. It was a good thing my mindreading powers weren't fully developed yet, since the erotic charge their bodies emitted was already enough to unsettle me. They looked like they were constantly on the verge of pouncing on each other.

"Um, guys? I'm right here!" I warned before the fire in their eyes could set the room ablaze.

"Agreed, then." Simon's eyes were locked on Ginevra's. "I'll wait for you here." It probably eased his mind to know that Ginevra would be far from Desdemona, since she was just as great a danger to her as the Witches were to him. He hugged me and I could feel his tensed muscles and his disheveled blond hair tickling my skin. "Come back soon."

I nodded as my heart began to race, though I didn't know if it was from excitement or fear. Probably both—that's what Evan would often say.

"Now what? How does it work?" I asked Ginevra, not knowing how she might use her powers to take us to Yucatán. The two of them exchanged an amused glance as I waited for an answer. "Well? Do we teleport ourselves there?"

23

FLASHBACK

"The airport?! We're at the airport?"

Ginevra hid a grin. "Were you expecting something more biblical? Your body hasn't transformed yet. You can't use teleportation."

"Great! Right when my transformation could come in handy. But nooo—my powers have to manifest only as premonitions, terrifying nightmares, and sinister apparitions."

"Calm down and enjoy your humanity while you still can."

I sighed and got out of the car as Ginevra handed me a backpack containing the satchel with my supplies and her dress that I would put on once we reached Yucatán. If I'd known we'd be flying somewhere on a plane, I would have brought along the flight voucher my parents had given me, though I strongly doubted Ginevra would have let me use it.

The wind howled outside as Ginevra and I waited patiently in the check-in line. On the other side of the large windows was a row of planes lined up on the tarmac like soldiers at the mercy of the storm. I couldn't believe I would soon see Evan again. Tears threatened to suffocate me at the thought, though they were sweeter than the bitter pain that had been slowly sucking the life out of me until just days before. "If this keeps up, I'm afraid they'll cancel all the flights," I said, worried, staring out at the storm that raged with growing intensity.

"Don't worry, it won't stop us. Look, there's our plane." Ginevra pointed at a large Boeing outside with mobile stairs being pushed up to it. They had just sprayed something on its wings, and Ginevra explained that it was a de-icing procedure.

All at once I noticed something unusual. Outside, right on the runway, men I hadn't seen a second ago had suddenly appeared, seemingly out of nowhere. They were scattered everywhere. One of them near the window turned toward me, almost as though I'd called to him, and his piercing gray eyes probed my soul.

He was a Subterranean.

"What do you th—Gwen!" I shouted suddenly.

In an instant the waiting area filled with screams. A plane in the process of landing had lost control and was racing toward us at top speed. Someone screamed that it was a terrorist attack and panic exploded in the terminal. Ginevra grabbed my hand and pulled me out of the way of the horde of hysterical people as the plane crashed through the parked aircrafts, mowing them down like soldiers felled by the enemy.

"Gwen!" I shouted again as the mob crushed me. A paralyzing pain burst in my temples as the crowd shoved me every which way, leaving me breathless. The shrill noise of a thousand voices poured into my head and I felt as helpless as a mollusk being dragged away by the current in a river full of fish.

"Don't let go of my hand, Gemma!" Ginevra called. But the pain made me double over and clap my hands over my ears in an attempt to block out the noise piercing my temples. Even the deafening crash of shattered glass when all the windows throughout the airport exploded couldn't block it out. I thought I was going insane.

"It's your powers, Gemma! You're hearing their minds," Ginevra explained, fighting her way into my thoughts. "Look at me. Isolate my voice. Cling to the sound of my voice and shut everything else out." Her instructions slowly helped me breathe again and I managed to look up at her. She gave me a sideways hug.

"What happened?" In shock, I watched the crowd scatter in all directions.

"I'm sorry, their panic triggered it. Fear is the strongest summons for a Witch because mortals are willing to do anything when they fear for their lives—even sell their souls. I'll teach you to block your mind, but right now we have to get out of here. The planes are all damaged. It was the Màsala, I'm sure of it. Come with me." She grabbed my hand and pulled me through the mass of people heading in the opposite direction. A policeman came toward us and barred our way. It seemed no one was allowed to leave the airport, but Ginevra didn't look the least bit intimidated.

"We need a plane. *Now*," she said to him.

"Follow me." With just one glance from her, the policemen blocking the exits stepped out of our way and escorted us onto the tarmac.

Like a bird huddled in the cold, a private jet hid in a corner, its wings covered with snow. A man came toward us, bracing himself against the wind. I thought he meant to stop us, since the storm had gotten worse, but Ginevra squeezed my hand reassuringly and walked up to him. Obeying the power of her eyes, he gestured for us to climb aboard and took his place in the cockpit.

I buried my face in my hands. "What the hell is going on?" I was terrified. It had all happened so fast I was still reeling.

"I thought at least this part of the journey would be easy, but I guess not. They tried to stop us and I'm sure they'll try again."

I leaned back in my seat, staring out at the lines racing by on the runway. The jet nosed up and took off. "Are they dead? All those people on that plane, are they dead?" I asked, begging for her to say no. Amid the general chaos I hadn't had the courage to look at what had happened after impact. Not to mention that I'd been the one who'd made all the windows in the airport explode. And then the Subterraneans! There were dozens of them. I'd seen them on the runway a moment before the plane crashed.

"I don't want to lie to you. Help arrived in time for some of them, but many didn't make it. Hey—" Ginevra moved my hands away from my face and looked me in the eye. "It wasn't your fault."

"How can you say that? It was! Come on, Gwen, everything keeps happening because of me. Sometimes I think it would be better if I were dead." My words trailed off. "It's just—I don't want to die before seeing Evan again," I admitted wearily.

"Don't talk like that, Gemma. Don't give up now that you're so close to finding him. The Màsala might try to get in our way, but they can't stop us. Those people's fates were already written."

I nodded, but before I could reply a sudden drop in altitude made me swallow my words. Clinging to my seat, I looked at Ginevra, but the pilot quickly reassured us by saying that the bad weather would be causing a little turbulence, that was all.

"Try to get some rest now," Ginevra suggested with concern. "It'll take us at least eight hours to get to Yucatán. The bad weather will soon be behind us and the flight will be smoother. Take advantage of it to sleep for a while. You'll need all your strength for what you'll be facing."

I nodded as my eyelids closed obediently.

From time to time my active mind unsettled my body and I woke with a start, wondering where I was, but Ginevra smiled at me from her seat and I returned to oblivion, wandering between wakefulness and slumber.

"Simon!" Ginevra's alarmed voice abruptly woke me. I had no idea how much time had passed since I'd dozed off.

"What's wrong!?" I bolted upright, trying to overcome my grogginess.

Ginevra looked at me gravely. "Desdemona. She managed to break free before he entered her cell. The effect of my blood must have partially worn off, allowing her to regain some strength, but not enough to disappear. She waited for Simon to arrive, surprised him from behind, and escaped."

"What happened to the syringe with your blood? Simon didn't manage to administer it to her in time?"

"No, she caught him off guard. She was faster and injected it into Simon."

A moan escaped me. "Don't worry, he'll be fine." Ginevra smiled mischievously. "It's no big deal. Simon is accustomed to the power of my blood. Intimate relations between a Subterranean and a Witch can be rather . . . unorthodox."

"Okay, spare me the details."

"If you insist. Anyway, if I'm not around he'll just have a nice long sleep."

"So you can hear him even from this far away?"

"Our bond is very strong."

"And how do you plan to—Gwen!" I grabbed hold of my seat just in time as the plane shuddered violently. An entire flock of large birds had just crashed into us.

Ginevra disappeared suddenly and was back in a fraction of a second. "Damn it!" she exclaimed, then grumbled something in a language I didn't understand. I was sure she was swearing. "They're giving us a run for our money. The pilot's gone."

"Gone?!" I jumped to my feet. "What do you mean *gone*?"

"I mean dead, Gemma. And unless you know how to fly an airplane, I'll have to take over the controls."

"Unless someone stops you."

I cringed, my blood running cold at the sound of the familiar voice. My eyes bulged as the blond Angel materialized behind Ginevra. "Gwen, look out!"

Desdemona hurled a fireball and I ducked, but Ginevra dodged it and cast a lightning bolt that smashed through one of the windows. The wind howled through the gaping hole it left in the side of the jet and we quickly lost altitude. Panic threatened to overwhelm me as Desna and Ginevra battled furiously between the seats. The Subterranean shot another fireball at Ginevra but she generated a shield around her body. Though the fire didn't burn her, the impetus pushed her farther and farther back toward the hole.

I let out a wail of terror when I saw treetops through the windows. On the verge of hysteria, I had a sudden thought. Clinging to whatever I could, I grappled my way to Ginevra's backpack and rummaged through it with trembling hands while behind me raged a ferocious battle in which I would be the victor's prize. Finally my hand closed around cold metal and my index finger quickly found the trigger. Before the Angel could stop me, I raised the gun, took aim and fired. Desdemona's back jerked. Ginevra gaped at me over her shoulder as the gun with the poisoned ammunition slid from my hands. A spasm gripped the Angel. Ginevra pivoted and with one finger pushed her through the hole in the side of the plane. "Bye-bye, blondie. It's a real shame I'm not in Hell any more. It would have been fun to play with you."

Desna dematerialized and vanished before hitting the ground. Ginevra rushed to me and swept me up in a hug. I was still shaking. "You saved me! You were fantastic, Gemma."

"Okay, but now would be a great time to repay the favor—in case you forgot, we're about to crash!"

Ginevra smiled. "Don't worry. We're not going to crash." She leaned out through the hole and the massive air current hit her, whipping her hair back.

"Hey! You planning on jumping without me?"

Slowly, the howling of the wind calmed and the plane seemed to go silent, as though we were a UFO in descent. Ginevra was using the power of the earth below us to cushion our landing. A few minutes later, almost delicately, what remained of the jet floated to the ground before my amazed eyes.

"We're there." Ginevra smiled at me affably, helping me climb out through the hole in the fuselage.

Still stunned, I looked around. My surroundings triggered a flashback, shocking me.

"I've been here before."

A LEAP INTO THE VOID

"How—how can I possibly be *positive* I've been here before?" It was unbelievable that the place could seem so familiar. "It's not just a funny feeling or déjà vu—I have a perfectly vivid memory of it."

We were in a clearing surrounded by dense jungle. The trees looked like they had withdrawn in reverential fear of the huge, ancient, stone blocks strewn around the open space, survivors of what once must have been a majestic temple. It now lay on the ground in ruins, the trees watching over it like guardians of a bygone empire. In the distance, peeking over the treetops, I caught a hazy glimpse of the main temple of Chichen Itzá.

"The Witches were the ones who led you here. They tried to win you over in your sleep, the only time I couldn't protect you from them," Ginevra explained.

"You mean I could have delivered myself to them even during my nightmares? How is that possible?"

"Come with me." She led me past the timeworn blocks that looked like sleeping giants. It felt like I could hear them breathing. "It doesn't matter if it's real life or only images created in your mind—what counts is your will. If you had *chosen* to go with them, you would have already delivered yourself to them. You would have already transformed. In dreams they can reach your unconscious, your deepest self, the part of you that makes decisions. Every one of their apparitions was nothing more than their attempt to turn you to evil, to convince you to join them, to conquer your soul."

"That's why they showed me Evan," I murmured. "They were hoping I would follow them. There was a pool of water, I remember now. Hell's Mouth." My eyes shot to Ginevra's as I connected all the dots.

"The Witches are trying to seduce your mind, but your mind is also a weapon you can use to fight back. They showed you what you most desired, but your will was so strong it resisted their attempts to persuade you."

"I was in chains," I suddenly remembered, "but why didn't I follow Evan to the other side of the well? I don't understand . . . I would do anything to be with him again—I'm sure I would."

"Because part of you knew the consequences of that decision and they can't force you, they can't deprive you of your free will. It was your unconscious that put you in chains. They couldn't just take you by force—it had to be your decision to follow them. But don't forget that loyalty and virtue aren't part of their ethical code. Once you're in Hell, you won't be in one of your nightmares any more. No one will be able to wake you up. You've decided to venture into the wolf's den at your own risk and peril. The Witches will play dirty and try everything they can to make you give in so they can keep you with them."

"They can't take from me anything I haven't already lost."

"As they see it, you belong to them, Gemma. Don't forget that. And they're not going to give up until evil has possessed you."

"But I might find a way out, escape together with Evan. What will happen if I don't give in to them? If I refuse?"

Ginevra looked at the ground and then fixed me with a piercing look. "You'll die."

"How is that a choice, then? Isn't it supposed to be my decision?"

"They'll never accept a flat-out refusal. Then again, a Sister has never denied the call. They have the power to get into your head, to make you promises no human can resist. If you oppose them they can decide to drive you insane. So no, they can't force you, but they would rather see you die than accept defeat. In any case, if you decided not to succumb to them, Simon and I would be there to protect you and the baby until death."

I gave Ginevra a sidelong glance and raised an eyebrow. "Mine or yours?"

"This isn't the time for wisecracks. I'm not sure you honestly realize what you're going up against, Gemma."

I smiled, ignoring Ginevra's tension. "Though you can read my mind I think you're the one who doesn't realize something: for the first time in a long time, I feel alive again. I'm not afraid, Gwen. Not any more. For months I lived in terror of everything, every day, every breath, but now I'm finally hopeful again, and nothing and no one can keep me from finding Evan. I've listened to everything you've told me, memorized every scrap of information. I know what I'm doing—and I can't wait to begin."

"Good, because we're almost there." Ginevra stopped before a high wall built of blocks of stone, which puzzled me, since the temple stood quite a distance from where we were. The dense jungle lined the clearing like a theater curtain concealing ancient secrets. "We need to go up there."

I raised my head to follow Ginevra's eyes and could barely make out an opening high up in the rock. I opened my mouth to speak, but a violent gust of air tore the words from my mouth and swept me up off the ground. I only realized what had happened when I was on my feet again: Ginevra had hurled me all the way up to the opening.

My head spinning, I looked down. Ginevra was just a distant speck. "Would you mind warning me next time?" I shouted to her from the edge of the opening in the wall.

Ginevra made an incredible leap and landed beside me with feline grace. "I thought I did," she replied with a dazzling smile. I turned around to peer into the darkness of the cave. It seemed to summon me in a whisper that was hostile yet seductive. "Didn't you say there was only one way into Hell's Mouth? This doesn't look like the temple in Chichen Itzá. That seemed pretty far away."

"Weren't you supposed to not be afraid of anything? All I said was that the temple was built *over* Hell's Mouth—not that we would reach it from there. Too many tourists. No one knows about this path. We'll reach the entrance through an underground passage. Now follow me. We've got a long way to go."

"Not to nag, but doesn't 'underground' mean we should be going down? Why are we so high up?" I stiffened at a sound as ominous as the groan of a mountain on the verge of collapsing. "What was that?" In the darkness of the cave, my alarmed voice rang out behind Ginevra, who was strangely silent. The ground shook beneath our feet. "Gwen, something's moving down there."

"Everything's under control. Try to relax." She came to a halt. I quickly caught up to her and focused on her face, which was shrouded in darkness. Her lips were moving quickly, her hands suspended in the air, palms down.

"This would be easier if you explained what's happening," I whispered as an unknown instinct warned me not to move. The ground shook harder. "Gwen?" I wasn't sure whether the tremor in my voice was caused by the quaking ground or my fear of what was moving beneath it.

"Would you shut up for a minute? I'm asking the terrestrial powers that guard the entrance for permission to go in."

"Right! Great! Now everything is clear! Let me know when they ans—"

All at once the earth cracked open beneath my feet as though angered by my sarcasm, swallowing up the rest of my sentence. I let out a shriek and clung to the edge before the darkness could devour me. Ginevra grabbed my arm and pulled me up. "Seriously? What is it with you today? All you had to do was take one step back."

"An occasional heads-up would be nice."

"Oh, sorry, I figured you would notice the earth gaping open beneath our feet."

"Forgive me for not having eagle eyes. I can't see a thing in here!"

Ginevra laughed at my sudden awkwardness. "You're right, my bad. Sometimes I'm so convinced you're my Sister that I forget you haven't transformed yet. It sure would come in handy if you could learn to control your powers."

"But how? My body hasn't transformed yet. It only happened to me once—I could see so well that Peter freaked out, thinking I was driving in the pitch dark. But no, sorry, I can't control them yet."

"No problem. I'll make a little light for you."

That wouldn't be bad. Before I could say the thought out loud, a shimmering sphere of light flickered to life and floated around us.

"My God . . . What place is this?"

"A place where it's not very wise to say that name."

I couldn't believe my eyes: an intricate, crumbling, stone stairway wound around the walls in a downward spiral that grew narrower as it descended. The bottom was hidden in darkness.

"Why didn't you think of that sooner? And would you mind telling the glowy thingy to stop circling around me? It's making me dizzy."

Ginevra laughed and took me by the hand. "Come on. We'd better start down."

"Is that a will-o'-the-wisp?" I asked, fascinated by the waves that flowed across its spherical surface. "I've seen Evan make spheres of light, but this looks different."

"Don't touch it unless you want to end up roasted," Ginevra warned, cutting short my attempt to take a closer look at it. "It's a sphere of pure energy. It can carbonize you in a split second." Her laugh rang crisply against the close walls, which smelled of mildew.

"What's so funny?"

"You should see your hair," she teased as I tried hard to match her pace.

"What's wrong with my hair?" The instant I raised my hands to my head, my fingers were zapped by static electricity.

Ginevra continued to make fun of me. "Told you not to get too close."

"Maybe you didn't tell me soon enough."

"Maybe . . ."

A shudder crept down my back and I couldn't smile along with her. The walls grew more humid with every step downward and—contrary to what I had feared—the air grew colder. A blood-chilling rumble warned us the earth was moving. I looked up in time to see the rock sealing shut above us.

"Gwen, what's happening? It's closing! The ground is closing up above us!"

"I know. Stay calm. Everything is under control. Breathe."

"But we're trapped underground! How will—"

"Gemma, *relax*! You're about to walk into the mouth of Hell and you're worried about a cramped space? Take a deep breath and don't look up. Focus on the descent."

I did as she said, but my heart was still pounding and I had the nagging doubt I wouldn't be strong enough.

"Of course you are. Don't let panic overwhelm you or you'll lose control over it. Fear is like a lion in an arena: unless you tame it, it'll kill you in two seconds flat. Keep that in mind."

"You know I'm claustrophobic. Besides, couldn't we just go down the same way we went up the wall? I mean, why don't you make me do another one of those super jumps?"

"I can't. Your body needs to adjust itself to the changing oxygen levels gradually, otherwise you risk suffocating down here."

"Well, that's really annoying. We'll never get there. This hole is endless! Where does it end up, at the center of the earth? Professor Lidenbrock would be ecstatic!"

"Jules Verne had an incredible imagination, but this isn't *Journey to the Center of the Earth*. Try to relax, Gemma. I can understand your impatience, but I can use the time to explain a few more things about Hell."

"What else is there to know?" I asked, still exasperated but resigned.

"I don't think I've told you about Devil's Stramonium yet."

"I'm almost positive you haven't. A name like that is hard to forget."

"It's a plant that grows only in the infernal realms, though you might have already seen some in my vault."

"What am I supposed to do with it?" I asked, puzzled.

"You can use it to protect yourself. It grows in thick tangles like thorn bushes. Its flowers are black, graceful, and dangerous. Its pretty appearance masks its true nature. Just like with Witches."

"Lethally beautiful, basically."

"Irresistible and deadly. Devil's Stramonium once existed on Earth too—Witches planted it there—and they say the flower was so beautiful it destroyed humans' free will. It could even capture their souls. But the Earth had to remain neutral territory for God and Sophìa, so legend has it that because it was so attractive and so dangerous to humans, the flower was separated from the plant.

"To render its magic less powerful, its essence was divided into two different species: the one humans know as the black bat flower took on the appearance of its blossom—elegant, majestic, and black. Many still call it 'the devil's flower.' Datura Stramonium, on the other hand, retained some of its poisonous properties, as well as the shape of the plant from which the blossom grows. It causes hallucinations and even death in large enough doses, but it's no longer a gateway to Hell, although many continue to call it Witches' Weed.

"In compensation, Sophìa was allowed to grow Devil's Stramonium in Hell, where no flower had ever grown before. Witches worship nature in all its forms, but the poison of their souls had made the land barren, preventing plants from sprouting. It was one of their curses: to hopelessly yearn for Eden, where nature flourishes. There are still vast, arid areas in Hell, like the Stone Forest, where not even the Damned dare hide.

"Even so, trees began to grow in Hell after that, though their trunks were deformed by the poison they absorbed from the soil. Various other plants of different shapes and properties grew too, all of them irresistible and dangerous, but none of them as powerful as Devil's Stramonium. Our Dakor crave its seeds, but in order to eat them they need to inject the flower with their venom, which spreads through the stalks down to the roots, making the plant extremely poisonous. Sophìa is particularly fond of them. She has many of them growing in one wing of the Castle. It's a vast garden planted in the interior courtyard where you'll find the Well of Souls, Sophia's greatest joy. Anyway, the plant can help cover your scent. On top of that, the Damned are afraid of it because even brief contact with it sears their skin and cooks their flesh."

"How revolting."

"Wait until you see it. Some of the Damned lure less clever prey into a patch of the plants so they won't have to eat them completely raw."

"When I get back from Hell I could write a screenplay. I bet Joss Whedon could make an awesome movie out of it."

"Who?"

"The director of *Buffy the Vam*—Never mind. What else do I need to know?"

"Not much. I've explained everything I can. The rest, I'm afraid, you'll have to find out for yourself. Oh, one more thing—watch out for the raptors."

"Raptors? Like, birds?"

"Giant, ferocious ones. The trees should offer you shelter if you come across one, but don't be fooled if it doesn't seem to notice you. Once it sets its sights on you, it'll stalk you and attack when you least expect it."

"Nasty birds. Seek shelter under trees. Check. Next tip?"

"Try not to die."

Meanwhile, we'd reached the end of the staircase, a narrow, funnel-shaped vortex that led into an enclosed circular space that forked in two different directions.

"This place gives me the creeps." In the distance, I could hear the faint dripping of water. "Abandon all hope, ye who enter here . . ." I said under my breath, staring at the gloomy walls that seemed to want to imprison us.

"We're still on Earth, Gemma. Wait till you're actually in Hell."

"Should I expect the ground to crack open under my feet, fire and brimstone and all?"

"Not at all. Hell is a place you'll feel irremediably drawn to—but don't trust its appearance and remember everything I've told you. This way."

I followed Ginevra into the cavern on the left, which was darker and more cramped than its twin. The sphere of light quickly lit up what was hidden there.

"Whoa!" I exclaimed, looking around. Stalactites and stalagmites reached out toward one another, creating a magical display of colors the instant the light touched them. Fascinated, I went up to a wall. Arcane symbols covered the rock like an ancient parchment. "I've seen these markings before, but I can't—What does it say?"

Ginevra smiled at my curiosity without slowing her pace. I hated it when she did that. "I heard you, you know." Her voice reached me from around a curve, echoing through the tunnel.

"It's about time you taught me to block off my thoughts."

"But every now and then you come up with a good idea."

"Very funny. Come on, teach me so I can finally keep you out of my mind when I feel like it. No offense."

Ginevra looked back at me, pouting. "Am I really that bad?"

"Only once in a while." This time it was my turn to grin.

"Shut up!" She slapped my arm, smiling again. "Otherwise I'll leave you here in the dark."

"You would never do that. I know how much you care about me deep down," I teased.

"Don't put me to the test. If you started counting instead of babbling, we would make much better use of our time."

"I'm not babbling! Or am I? It's just that, I mean—I have so many things inside my head I could scream."

"Don't you dare. Instead, do what I told you."

"You mean count? Why should I count?"

"So you'll shut up, for starters, since you need to use your mind to do it." Ginevra chuckled.

"But you would hear me anyway."

"Okay, it's time to really focus. I'm not kidding. You're inside your mind now. Imagine erasing all your thoughts. Count slowly. Numbers will take the place of words. Imagine your brain is a blackboard. It's dark and shiny and the numbers are written down in white one by one as they appear in your mind. It's hard at first, I know, but it'll be easy once you've learned how to do it."

I tried to pay attention to Ginevra's voice as I followed her instructions, but I wasn't sure I could.

"Now picture the blackboard inside an empty room that's completely white. Imagine the walls—solid, all around you. Impenetrable walls. There's a door, see it? Focus on it, shut it, and lock it. Good. Now you can fill the room with whatever you want.

Everything else will stay outside. No one can go in until you unlock the door and allow them access to your thoughts."

"How am I doing?" I asked shyly. I hadn't closed my eyes but was concentrating so hard I couldn't even see where I was walking.

"Either the Witches have possessed you again or you're successfully keeping me out, Sister." I smiled at her, hiding my enthusiasm. I hadn't thought it would be so easy. "Okay, but now let me in. I taught you so you could keep the other Witches out, not me."

Forget it, I told her in my mind. *You have no idea how long I've been waiting for this moment.*

"Hey, I heard that!" *Damn it, she still hasn't learned to block off her thoughts.*

"What makes you think I didn't let you hear that on purpose?" Suddenly I realized there was something different about her voice. "Wait a second, Gwen. I heard that too. I just read your mind."

Ginevra's lips tightened, then relaxed into a warm smile. "That's not surprising. We're near the source. Don't forget that we're Sisters and our mental connection is going to get stronger and stronger. When you reach Hell, your spirit will struggle to emerge. Your body may be affected."

"Like when I run a high fever?"

"I imagine so. Your mental powers will get sharper—the Witches may even sense them—but your body still isn't ready because it hasn't transformed." Ginevra heard the note of discouragement in my mind and squeezed my hand. I realized I would be facing a daunting challenge, pitting myself against God only knew how many and what kinds of dangers. I hoped my body wouldn't fail me; that would make everything even more difficult. I raised my hand to my neck and clasped my chain to build my courage. Before setting out, I'd put Evan's ring back in its little silver case. Now, carefully concealed beneath the thick fabric of my sweatshirt, I wore my butterfly pendant with the diamond from Heaven, interlaced with Evan's dog tag and the serpent-shaped amulet, the symbol of what I would soon become—three realms that were inseparable now.

"We're there."

Ginevra's voice made me look up and my frown vanished as my eyes were dazzled by our enchanting surroundings.

THE MOUTH OF HELL

"Oh. My. God."

"Haven't I already said it would be best to use a different exclamation?"

I wanted to reply but couldn't find the words. I had imagined Hell's Mouth as an ominous black hole that would try to gobble me up. Instead, the cavern had led us to a grotto hidden in the heart of the rock, dominated by a pool of water that reflected the myriad hues of a diamond. No longer necessary, the shining sphere had disappeared, allowing the cenote to sparkle with its own light. Golden shafts danced beneath its surface, creating a network of iridescent reflections as though the water was run through with strands of light. I couldn't believe such an amazingly ethereal place could contain the only entrance to the Underworld.

"This is it." I suddenly remembered seeing it before. It was unquestionably the focal point of my dreams. "This is where they always tried to bring me." A shudder ran down my spine. I had been dreaming of that place for a long time, even when Evan was still alive. "So all I had to do was cross through this and they would have made me their prisoner?"

"Not their prisoner—their loyal ally."

"What difference would it have made, if they'd taken Evan away from me?"

"You're here now," she reminded me, "and unless you save him you'll be forced to sacrifice yourself to them in vain."

"It's a price I'm willing to pay to see him again. We've already talked about this, Gwen. Tell me what I have to do."

"Be patient." Ginevra slid the backpack off her shoulders and pulled out my things. "Meanwhile, get ready. We can't overlook a single detail."

For practice, I tried to block my mind as I took off my jeans and put on Ginevra's old dress. She didn't even seem to notice that my thoughts had gone silent. My Sister suddenly looked lost, sitting on a rock across the grotto from me, her sad face reflected in the surface of the cenote. I put on the long green cloak, its hood falling heavily against my back, then slung over my shoulder the satchel containing food, water, and the strange whistle Ginevra had given me. I approached her, giving myself a few seconds to watch her from afar. It was clear from her expression how difficult it was for her to go along with my plan. She must have cared about me a great deal, judging from how upset she seemed to be.

"Gwen?" She slowly turned to look at me. "Would you mind?" I held out the sheathed dagger so she could help me put it on.

Ginevra took it and fastened both its buckles around my forearm. "I hope with all my heart you won't need it."

"Don't worry, Gwen. Everything is going to go fine. Soon we'll be a family again and no one will be able to separate us. I'm not going to give up everything over something I can learn to control."

Ginevra forced a nod and clasped me in a warm embrace. "I only wish I could help you more." A solitary tear slid down her cheek. I'd never seen her cry before.

"I know." I stroked her face, sensing in that tiny crystalline droplet the intrinsic energy that united us. I had never seen Ginevra so vulnerable and her pain tugged on my heartstrings. "Just wish me luck."

"The goddess of luck is blindfolded. If you don't guide her she won't find you."

"I'll do my best."

"Make sure you come back in one piece. You're the only Sister I have left. I don't want to lose you."

"That won't happen. I promise."

Ginevra smiled as another tear spilled over. "While you're at it, bring back that hardheaded boyfriend of yours. I miss making fun of him."

My heart skipped a beat, telling me the time had come to go get him. I knelt at the edge of the cenote, gazing at it with reverential respect as though it could return my look. Then I stood up and clenched my fists at my sides. "I'm ready."

I took a deep breath and Ginevra's powerful energy slowly lifted my body inches above the ground. Closing my eyes, I felt the energy surge through me from my toes to the tips of my hair that blew around my face as I levitated over the surface of the water. Sensing an arcane force stirring beneath me, I opened my eyes and saw the cenote churning, moved by a dark power.

From the water's edge, Ginevra watched, powerless, as the whirlpool forming beneath me roared, grasping at me with invisible hands that pulled me down toward the abyss.

I raised my eyes just in time to glimpse a man standing at the mouth of the cave, his face covered by the hood of a sweatshirt. "Look out!" I shouted. A fireball raced toward Ginevra while a second one headed in my direction. "GWEN!!" My eyes bulged as I felt its heat searing my skin, but a wall of water shot up in front of me, protecting me. I struggled to catch sight of Ginevra on the shore battling the dark Angel who had appeared out of nowhere in the Màsala's final attempt to keep me from reaching the Witches.

A second wall of water crashed down onto the Executioner. He staggered, fell to the ground, and dissolved instantly.

"Go!"

For the last time I looked into Ginevra's eyes in a silent farewell, then the abyss consumed me, pulling me into its depths. The sharp pain of a thousand needles pierced my skin, making me shriek. It felt like the water was burning me.

"It's the poison!" Ginevra's distant voice reached me as my senses grew weaker.

"*It burns,*" I whispered, unsure whether she could hear me.

"The water's tainted! It's filled with poison! Hang in there, Gemma! It'll be over soon."

I jerked my head out of the ferocious whirlpool that was swallowing me up and tried to breathe, but my lungs filled with water as I caught one last glimpse of Ginevra huddled on the shore.

What came to me first was a feeling of lightness, as though my body were suddenly weightless. I opened my eyes a crack, and a stinging sensation burned them like salt, reminding me where I was: in Hell.

My lungs screamed for air. I thrashed my legs, but it only made me rotate in the water. I had no clue which way the surface was; I seemed to be going down rather than up. The whirlpool in the cenote had sucked me down and dumped me into the depths of a river. The heart of the Earth had ejected me directly into Hell. My foot touched something and my arms automatically reacted, striving for a way out in the opposite direction. My face emerged from the water. I coughed and sputtered, then filled my lungs with air, but the current was strong and soon pulled me back under. Losing hope, I searched for something to cling to as my skin burned from the poison. I had to find a way out of there or my head might explode. Suddenly the sound of the water grew louder, deafening me. A horrible suspicion gripped me but before I could even look around my head struck something solid, leaving me dazed. A moment later, as the water swiftly pulled me away, my vision blurred, I glimpsed the rock I had hit. I struggled against the current but felt consciousness abandoning me. I surrendered and plunged down an unfathomable void.

I shook my head dizzily. It felt like a swarm of bees was buzzing in my brain. The low rumble of a waterfall came from the distance but it was hard to figure out where, exactly. When I finally managed to open my eyes it felt as though the bees I'd heard in my head had attacked me all at once with their poisonous stingers. Doubling over from a pain that was so strong I could barely breathe, I curled up, expecting to pass out.

Instead, the burning feeling eased gradually until it throbbed only at my temples. I rested my palms on the dark sand and attempted to stand. My whole body ached as though a train had run me over. Only when I got to my knees did I see the waterfall in the distance and remember that the current must have swept me over its edge.

I checked to make sure nothing was broken and put my hands on my belly where my baby was sleeping under Ginevra's protective spell. There was no cut on my head and my clothes were dry again. I had no idea how long it had been since Ginevra and I had said goodbye. The sky was dark and a sinister twilight threatened to fade into the gloomiest of nights.

"Well," I mumbled to myself, "no flames or lakes of fire. Seems like a pretty good start." I was happy that that part of the stories about Hell wasn't true. I looked around. Despite Ginevra's warnings, it didn't seem like such a hostile place. Quite the opposite. There was a strange tingle under my skin as though Hell's dark magnetic power were reaching its tentacles out toward me. What scared me the most, actually, was that, deep down, I felt I belonged there.

A giant prehistoric-looking creature flew across the sky and my heart leapt to my throat. I wasn't sure whether to be frightened or fascinated. Suddenly the ground trembled beneath my palms, tearing me from my thoughts. At first it was only my fingers, but soon my whole body began to vibrate and a deafening noise filled the air—the sound of a stampede of wild horses.

I shot to my feet, my heart thumping to the rhythm of the approaching hooves. I had to find shelter fast. Instinct led me toward the forest that skirted the river and, panicking, I hid in a patch of prickly bushes that scratched my skin. The noise grew louder and louder, shaking the air as I held my breath and hoped they wouldn't see me. I squeezed my eyes shut as they crossed in front of me, their hooves pounding against the ground. They looked like men riding horses.

Slowly I began to breathe again, relieved they hadn't discovered me. Not far away, though, one of them stopped in his tracks and my heart went still with terror.

"My God." I instinctively backed up, my eyes wide. They weren't men on horseback. They were man and beast fused into a single monstrous creature. Beings like centaurs, but half buffalo instead of horse, their faces distorted by sharp teeth and murderous expressions.

Blood. The spine-chilling whisper crept into my head. It didn't sound like a word uttered in a human language but I understood it all the same. My senses must have sharpened. Uncontrollable terror made my stomach clench but my eyes were so paralyzed at the sight of the infernal creature I couldn't move a muscle.

"Blood!" This time the shout pierced the air, snapping me out of my trance, as the one who seemed to be their leader gestured for the others to follow him. I backed up and fled. I felt that I'd never run so fast in my life, but their hoof beats came closer and closer. I could feel them shaking the ground as their ghoulish roars rang out. Ginevra was right, they had smelled my blood. The creatures had to be Molock. I'd hoped never to come across them and instead they'd tracked me down before I even had a chance to take in my surroundings. What hope could I ever have against these Hell-born monsters?

Evan . . . Had my attempt to save him failed already? I doubled over as a stabbing pain lacerated my abdomen, then hid behind a tree to catch my breath, squeezing my eyes shut in desperation. There was no way for me to defend myself. I was about to die in that cursed forest. The thunder of the approaching hooves spurred me on, and I began to run again, holding my belly.

Suddenly the ground swallowed me up. For a few moments all I heard was crackling and rustling. When everything stopped, I realized the earth had given way beneath my feet and I'd fallen into a ravine choked with strange-looking spiny bushes. I could hear the Molock drawing near. Curling myself up in the brambles, I waited for the end.

When they were directly over my head, the thundering hooves abruptly went silent. Trying to control my breathing to avoid giving myself away, I raised my eyes. The Molock had stopped at the edge of the ravine and were uttering hoarse noises in a language that this time was incomprehensible to me. Something warm dribbled onto my cheek, maybe blood or drool, and a moan of disgust escaped me. I stiffened when I saw that my reaction had drawn the attention of the leader, who turned to look in my direction.

For some reason he couldn't see me, but I had a clear view of him. His enormous mouth took up most of his face. Large upper and lower fangs protruded from his lips like a saber-toothed tiger. His nose was completely flat, almost absent, and his nostrils were two slits that ran along his cheekbones. His demonic eyes were dark and bloodshot. He didn't have actual hair, but the fur that covered his body spread from his back up to his head and chin. His powerful limbs were totally covered with long fur in colors ranging from black to brown to reddish. His skin was black as a buffalo's. On his skull, small horns formed a spiky crown. His chest was a frightening mass of muscles that looked powerful enough to kill someone with a simple squeeze. The only hairless section of his body, it was covered with scar-like furrows that met in the center. He had no navel and instead of nipples I saw a single tiny hole in the center of his chest that opened and closed. That must have been the maseolum, the weak spot Ginevra had told me about. But there was no way I could ever have gotten close enough to try to attack him without being devoured in the process. I had never imagined—not even in my wildest dreams—that such horrifying creatures could exist.

To my amazement, the beasts began slowly to turn away and leave, snorting with dissatisfaction and grunting something incomprehensible. A familiar smell filled the air, though I couldn't put my finger on what it was. It was so powerful it almost made me dizzy. I held my breath without moving until their hoof beats faded into the distance. Only then, all my strength drained, did I pass out, blotting out my surroundings.

When I opened my eyes, I was relieved to discover I hadn't been dragged off in the jaws of some wild animal. I found myself inside the thorn bush, exactly where I'd lost consciousness. Even the sky was unchanged. I had no idea how much time had passed, but night still hadn't replaced the ghastly twilight. Instinctively I raised my hand to the bodice of my old dress, afraid I might have lost Ginevra's amulet, but it was still there. Suddenly thirsty, I pulled the canteen out of my satchel and took a gulp of water. Only when I looked up through the branches of the bush I was hidden in did I see it.

A village.

THE JAWS OF SILENCE

Before going out into the open, I pricked my ears, listening for even the slightest movement, but everything was shrouded in spectral silence. I brushed off my dress, hoping I hadn't ruined it, and set off down the path that led to the village, repeatedly looking over my shoulder.

I didn't know what kinds of creatures inhabited it. Maybe the souls of the Damned there had kept their humanity. At first glance it looked abandoned, but I still advanced cautiously and slowly, moving between the tiny stone houses, their roofs, doors, and window frames made of finely woven branches. The silence was deafening. I swallowed, scrutinizing every corner. A well sat at the point where the roads intersected at the center of the village while just beyond that a wooden swing hung perfectly still, abandoned, just like every other thing in that bone-chilling ghost town watched over by eternal twilight.

I passed the houses one by one, looking for a sign of life, but the doors and windows were all boarded up and there was no trace of anyone. I convinced myself it was a good thing, though deep down I harbored the hope I would find Souls that weren't completely evil.

Behind me an ominous hiss sliced the air, making me jump. I spun around but saw nothing. With horror, I discovered that the swing had begun to slowly move back and forth with a foreboding squeak, though there wasn't even a breath of wind. Goosebumps rose on my arms and my eyes darted around, searching for whoever had pushed it, but there was no one in sight.

Further along the street a house caught my attention. Unlike the others, its windows weren't boarded up. I walked up to it, peered inside to make sure it was actually abandoned, and gripped the door handle, then warily opened the door and closed it behind me. I rested my back against the wood and slid down to the cold floor. Only then, in the total silence, did I realize how hard my heart was pounding. Taking a deep breath, I rested my head on my knees. Maybe I could hide there until it was daytime. The twilight in Hell was more foreboding than any dusk I'd ever seen and shrouded everything in a ghoulish gloom.

A squeal made me start. My head shot up and I held my breath. Cautiously I rose to my feet, trying hard not to make a sound, but the dry wood of the door betrayed my presence by emitting a sinister creak.

Another squeal, this one louder. I checked the house's only other room, which must once have been a bedroom, but it was deserted. It contained only a crude mattress and a crib. I went back to the front door. All the furniture was made of finely interwoven twigs and branches. It looked solid, though worn by centuries of use. Four chairs and a table stood in the center of the room while a bookcase covered an entire wall. In it were a few stone objects, others of wood that looked hand-carved, and some books. I touched one. It was bound in some sort of animal skin and something was scrawled on the pages in black ink as though with a quill pen. I sniffed it and gagged. *Demon blood,* I thought, but instantly banished the idea. I turned around and noticed the giant fireplace that took up almost the entire wall opposite the bookcase.

It looked like a comfortable hideaway. Who knew why whoever had lived there had abandoned it. And yet . . . I rested my hand on the table and something dampened my fingers—a viscous liquid. My body went ice-cold, gripped by the terrible presentiment that it was blood. A strange sound from the bedroom made me return to the doorway. I peeked into the room and saw the cradle rocking gently. Repressing a shudder of fright, I took a step forward as my mind screamed at me to run. A strange prickle warned me to stay away from the cradle but I couldn't stop myself. A baby girl turned her round face to look at me, moving her little hands. I covered my mouth, shocked. Could someone actually have abandoned her there? She couldn't have been more than a year old.

Without thinking twice, I picked her up and cradled her tenderly. My eyes closed, I snuggled my head against hers. How could a babe in arms have ended up in that accursed place? What sin could possibly have stained such a tiny creature? Still holding the baby, I turned around and my heart leapt to my throat. Another child, this one around four years old, was standing there, perfectly still, staring at me through the gloom. I tried to steady my breathing but my instinct returned to warn me not to get near him. He must have been her brother and, given that there were four chairs in the other room, the children probably weren't alone.

"Don't worry, I don't want to hurt you. Wh-what's your name?" I forced myself to ask in a comforting tone, but the little boy continued to stare at me without speaking. "Do you understand what I'm saying?" He nodded but remained silent. "Where are your parents?"

His answer came only after a long pause. "They're dead," the little boy told me, his voice emotionless, his eyes glued to mine.

Dead.

It was so horrible that two little creatures had ended up all alone in that infernal place. "Did you see who did it? Who killed them?" I asked.

I soon regretted my question. He raised his arm and pointed his finger at the baby just as I noticed the terrifying noise she was making. She was *sniffing me.* Shocked, I held her out at arm's length and my heart lurched when I saw that her eyes had turned completely black. I let out a scream and tossed the baby toward her brother, but the creature landed on the floor on all fours and scuttled toward me, her eyes locked on mine.

She did it. She was the one who had killed her parents.

The two children watched me intently as, horrified, I tried to back up into the other room, but tripped and wound up on the floor. When I looked up they were gone. I peered around, searching for them in the gloom, still petrified by the memory of those eyes.

Getting hurriedly to my feet, I took refuge behind the table, but the little boy surprised me from behind. I spun around. His eyes were completely black now too. He smiled faintly, baring teeth that were narrow and came to a point, like a shark's.

"Do you want to play?" His voice came out in a dark, hair-raising snarl. It wasn't a sound made by a little boy, but by a demon.

I threw a chair at him and made a break for the door, but he was there waiting for me. Frantically looking for another way out, I noticed a door I hadn't seen before and threw it open. Inside a cramped closet, a tall man in his thirties wearing medieval-looking clothing gaped at me with bloodshot eyes. "Eat thy fill, but prithee, kill me not!" I stared at him in horror as he offered me his arm, which already had chunks of flesh bitten out of it.

I slammed the door shut and the baby scuttled over to me at a frightening speed. I let out a shriek and scrambled up the bookcase to escape her, but she crawled up after me, grabbed my leg and bit me. *She wanted to eat me alive!* The burning sensation was as immediate as it was intense. With a howl, I grabbed a heavy book and struck the baby with all my might, trying to make her release her grip, but her teeth were sunk deep into my flesh. When she finally let go, she twisted her head all the way around, leaving me in shock. I suddenly remembered the dagger. My hand shot to my forearm and I whipped it out. The blade plunged into the baby's neck with a sickening gurgle. She let out an inhuman screech. Black liquid filled her eye sockets and oozed from her nose and mouth, suffocating her. Seconds later, her body exploded in a cloud of grayish dust. I began to spasm and cough uncontrollably, my trembling hand still brandishing the dagger. I remembered Ginevra's warning about the toxicity of the ashes of the Damned, so I instantly held my breath and scrambled down from the bookcase.

The second I turned my back to the wall I saw him. Everything had happened so fast, I had forgotten about the boy. We stared at each other across the kitchen table, my eyes locked on his. He backed up and I took a step in the opposite direction. I'd seen how fast he could move but now he was slow, looking almost frightened. Without breaking eye contact, I stepped past the table and we moved in a circle. When his back was against the wall, he turned around, rested his hands and feet against it and began to crawl up it like a spider.

I was next to the front door. Opening it, I rushed outside and continued to advance cautiously through the village. It still looked deserted, but sinister hissing noises that sounded like the whistle of arrows suggested the opposite. They were all lurking in the semidarkness, moving so quickly they were only a blur. As I walked forward I held the dagger well in sight. Blood still dripped from its blade and I hoped it would frighten them off. Once I'd passed the last of the houses, I sprinted as fast as I could, leaving the horrifying village behind me.

Now I knew it: I was in Hell.

HIDING PLACE

Once I was a good distance away, I stopped to catch my breath and leaned against a tree, exhausted. Among a nearby cluster of rocks I saw the mouth of a small cave that might offer shelter. I gathered what was left of my energy and crawled inside it. Only then, far from everyone, did the tears stream from my eyes.

What had I done? A baby! I had killed a baby. I looked at my hands. They were shaking. I covered my face with them, sobs wracking my chest. The long skirt of Ginevra's dress was splattered with my blood, its odor so pungent I could smell it. I grabbed the canteen and rinsed some of it off my wounded calf, hoping no creatures would smell it. Not even the stinging pain in my leg bothered me as much as the guilt I felt over what I had just done. When Ginevra had given me the dagger I'd hoped I would never need to use it—but I had used it, and to kill an infant. What kind of horrible mother would I be? I felt like a monster. I was alone, devastated, and incredibly frightened. What would become of me? I felt farther and farther away from Evan, and the terrible fear that I might never see him again assaulted me.

Wiping my eyes, I tried to be brave, making myself remember that my current fear was nothing in comparison to how much I'd suffered at the thought of having lost Evan forever. Now that I knew he was alive—wherever he was—I was determined to cling with all my strength to the hope of finding him and never let it go. I was going to fight, and nothing would keep me from seeing him again.

I left my hiding place just as something darkened the sky, like a black cloud crossing in front of the sun. The leaves on the trees around me began to tremble.

"What the hell . . ."

The words died in my throat as the sky filled with extraordinary creatures that had human bodies but long feathered wings that were blacker than night. An entire swarm of Angels of darkness. No—not Angels. Demons. Terrified, I sought shelter under the trees and watched them soar across the sky. The instant the last of them was out of sight, I hurried off in the opposite direction, ignoring my exhaustion.

I walked for what felt like an eternity, trying to find my way back to the river that I'd distanced myself from in my flight from the Molock. By then it was clear that night was never going to arrive to dispel the twilight, nor could I hope for day to break. The sky seemed to be stuck at dusk. Even the moon and stars refused to cast their light on those accursed lands.

Though I'd walked a long way, I still hadn't reached the river. Without its precious guidance I was lost, with no idea of which way to go. The Castle could have been anywhere. Besides, with each step I was growing more convinced someone was following me. I had the terrible feeling I was being watched, as though the forest had a thousand eyes trained on me. I couldn't see anyone in the vicinity but I couldn't be sure, and I had the impression something was lurking in the bushes.

Ginevra was right—it was a mad, dangerous place. All my certainties began to fade. What if it really was a suicide mission? What if I never managed to reach Evan? I would be responsible for my baby's death.

I couldn't give up and accept that possibility. It didn't matter what became of me, I had no intention of losing either of them.

Something warm trickled down my calf. I raised my skirt to check and was horrified to see that my wound had reopened and blood was dripping to the ground, leaving a trail that led straight to me. *Forgive me, Gwen.* I tore off a strip of the hem of her beloved dress and bound the wound to stop the bleeding. I couldn't afford to leave any trace of myself or it would be the end of me. Little water remained in the canteen, and soon my food supply would run out too. What would I do then? I absolutely had to find the river as quickly as possible unless I wanted to end up as someone's next meal.

The forest looked endless. The trees grew denser, then opened up into clearings only to become dense again, but there was no sign of the river. If only I could utilize the power growing inside me—but I couldn't, though I felt its dark, constant presence hidden in a corner of my mind.

I tripped and fell to my hands and knees. Though my mind warned me to get up immediately, all my strength was gone and my body refused to continue the desperate search. I tried over and over but couldn't get to my feet. Desperation took hold of me: I had no idea where the river was hidden, Evan was the Witches' prisoner, and I was still convinced I would never reach him. Exhausted, I crumpled to the ground. Clenching my fists, I tried one last time, but my brain shut down, carrying me off to an unknown place. To safety.

In the dream, a chorus of voices was mixed with inhuman grunts. Slowly, my eyes made out a grim landscape with trees grayed by the approaching darkness. I didn't know where I was, but a hair-raising snort suddenly brought everything back. I wasn't in a dream. I shot to my feet, wondering how long I'd been lying on the ground. Frightened, I looked around. Then I heard it again.

It was distant, I was sure of it, but for some reason I heard it clearly. My senses had sharpened. I crept to a large rock not far away and the grunts grew louder. My instincts begged me to run away, but the instant my eyes fell on the macabre source of those sounds I was paralyzed: a herd of Molock were fighting over pieces of what once had been a man, snapping the bones apart and devouring the flesh. And he wasn't their only prey. There were others inside the circle of beasts. Some were still alive, kicking and trying to free themselves. Though I knew they weren't actually men—just other Damned Souls who in all likelihood would try to kill me if given half a chance—the sight still made me shudder.

A shooting pain throbbed in my temples and made me double over. I leaned against the rock as a groan escaped me. Raising my head with an effort, I cursed myself as the Molock scanned the area. Taking a few steps back, I kept my eyes locked on the monsters as they sniffed the air with their cheekbone nostrils, trying to pinpoint me, but the pain in my forehead made me stagger and collapse against a tree. Just then someone rushed past. I shook my head and the pain lessened and slipped away like a ghost. Another figure darted by, but this time I recognized one of the Molock's captives. My presence must have distracted the beasts, allowing a few of the Souls to escape. A shuffling of hooves forced me to take off at a run, my heart pounding almost hard enough to burst through my chest.

Suddenly a Soul grabbed my arm. Desperate, I pulled back with a strength I hadn't known I had, broke free, and ran away. Rather than wanting to help me escape, he no doubt wanted to insure himself a food supply in case he managed to escape the Molock. Just as the forest grew denser, the last handful of Souls overtook me and then—

All at once they were gone.

In front of me the trees opened into a round clearing. I came to a halt. The others had all vanished into thin air. I had nowhere to hide and the Molock were about to catch up with me. I still had no idea how I'd managed to elude them the first time but I wouldn't be so lucky a second time, not with the bleeding wound on my leg that even I could still smell.

The ground trembled beneath the Molock's hooves, announcing their imminent arrival. I shook myself out of my daze and started running again. Suddenly something grabbed my ankle and I crashed to the ground. I looked behind me to see what it was and froze. A woman had appeared from a trapdoor in the ground and was gripping my leg with inhuman strength, staring at me with a haunting expression. I tried to kick her away but she grabbed me with her other hand and began to drag me underground.

"Let go!" I screamed desperately. "Let me go!"

"Shh! They're coming. You have to hide!"

At the sound of her voice I stopped struggling and turned back toward her. Her face was gaunt and her deep-set eyes had dark bags under them. It looked like she hadn't eaten in weeks. Her complexion was waxy and her copper-colored hair was cropped close to her head. Was she honestly offering to help me?

"Hide in here, quick!" I searched the woman's face, trying to decide which was worse—the creatures hunting me down or her. "Quickly, there's no time! Do you want those monsters to eat you alive?"

The Molock's ever-closer hoof beats convinced me. I let the woman pull me down beside her and the trapdoor closed over our heads.

"What is this place?" I asked, looking around at what seemed to be a room carved into the rock.

The woman held a finger to her lips for me to be silent but when I heard hoof beats immediately overhead I couldn't hold back a whimper. I scrambled back from the trapdoor and the woman smiled.

"Don't worry, they won't find you here. They're too stupid. They've never discovered our hiding places."

"You mean this is—"

"My home."

I ran my fingers over the strange mineral that illuminated the room. Its glow was dim but bright enough for me to make out my surroundings. At first glance it looked like a normal dwelling: a table with one chair, an unlit fireplace with a pot hanging over it and, in the back, a niche in the rock made up as a bed. "In this hellhole, if you're clever you stay in hiding as much as you can. You must be new around here. There's something unusual about your smell," the woman continued.

She had quite a human appearance, but I wasn't sure I could trust her. Was it possible she was a Subterranean? Ginevra had said they were the only ones who weren't wicked, and I still hoped to find someone to ease my overwhelming discouragement and solitude. Suddenly I remembered: the woman had mentioned there were other hiding places. So that was why the Damned who had escaped the Molock had vanished before my eyes—they must have hidden in other underground caves.

"Thank you. You probably saved my life, at least for the time being. My name is Gemma. Yours?"

Her reply came after a moment of silence that sent a shiver down my spine: "Xandra." I wasn't sure, but in the dim light a strange glint seemed to appear in her eye as she tried to hide a smile. She pushed back a curtain attached to the wall. I thought I glimpsed someone hidden behind it, but she merely took something from inside the cubbyhole.

A sudden sound made us both jump. "By all Hell's devils!" Xandra rushed to the trapdoor and barred it with wooden planks, cursing in some unknown language. I heard a low growl that made me shudder with terror in the dark room.

"What's happening?!" I cried, panicking.

Another clatter of hoof beats rattled the trapdoor. "They tracked you down!" she shouted, trying to be heard over the war cries of the Molock gathered overhead. "They must have followed your scent. Quick, open that jar next to the basin!"

"What for?"

"Just open it!"

I grabbed the large clay jar and pulled off the lid, my hands trembling. A familiar smell filled my nostrils, leaving me dazed. Hearing the urgency in Xandra's voice, I slid my hand into the jar as the Molock stomped on the trapdoor more violently. Finally my fingertips touched a tangled clump inside it.

"Quickly, rub it on yourself! It'll cover your scent!" I pulled my hand out and in the dim light saw some familiar-looking black petals and leaves. "What are you waiting for?! We don't have time! Hurry, or they won't go away!"

A massive blow from a hoof smashed open a hole over Xandra's head, compelling me to do as she said. I scrubbed the plant against my skin and my temples began to throb again. The pain doubled me over. I raised my eyes to the woman and saw her face fill with an emotion I wasn't expecting: astonishment.

Her thoughts filled my mind. *What in Hell is happening? Why isn't the Devil's Stramonium burning her?!*

"What? This is Stramonium?!"

Her eyes bulged and from her lips came a gasp. *"Witch!"* The Molock pawed the ground over our heads, trying to widen the hole they had smashed in, but she continued to stare at me, petrified.

"You wanted to kill me," I whispered in shock. My hopes that the woman might be a Subterranean vanished. "You thought this stuff would burn me! I heard you!"

Finally it dawned on me how I'd managed to escape the Molock the first time: the plants around me in the ravine were Devil's Stramonium. Ginevra had told me it might protect me since the Damned were afraid of it. Xandra, however, couldn't have known I was a Witch. Thinking I was a Soul like her, she'd told me to rub it on my skin not to save me but so it would cook my flesh. I shoved the plant into the satchel slung over my shoulder and smashed the jar to the ground at her feet, glaring at her in disgust as the Molock raged above us. Xandra stared at the remains of the jar and then looked up at me. On her gaunt face, an unnerving smile appeared beneath her hunger-darkened eyes.

"I too must eat," she whispered, sending an eerie shiver down my spine. More pounding on the trap door made me back up. The Molock were on the verge of knocking it in.

"You said *they* would eat me!" The catch in my voice betrayed my disappointment. I shouldn't have trusted her. After all, what could I have expected?

"I said they would eat you *alive*. Xandra doesn't like her meat raw. You should thank me!" She smiled again, but disappeared a second later as a giant beast dropped down onto her, crushing her. The Molock had gotten in.

I screamed and flung myself through a partially hidden door in the wall, trying not to look at Xandra's body being torn apart. As I ran, I plugged my ears to avoid hearing their grunts and the crunch of bones. At the end of a short tunnel I came out into a circular chamber illuminated by the same glowing rocks I'd seen in Xandra's hideaway. Tunnels and doorways led out of the chamber. It looked like an entire village dug into the rock, an intricate system of caves in which the Damned hid while remaining in contact with each other.

The doors along the tunnels must be entrances to other dwellings, which meant that sooner or later someone was bound to notice me. I had to find a place to hide, and fast, though by that time I'd realized there was nowhere I could feel safe down there. Ginevra was right: mine was a mad endeavor, a suicide mission. Hell was too dangerous. That was why I'd seen her cry for the first time: she was saying goodbye.

My legs trembling, I forced back the tears and ventured into the darkest tunnel, away from the dwellings.

HEAVEN AND HELL

I walked for hours, resting only to take tiny sips of water. Even my supply of dried meat was almost gone. I couldn't tell if I'd been there for hours or days. My hope of seeing Evan again was steadily fading. Would this tunnel become my tomb? I didn't want to give up but was beginning to think there was no choice.

Every so often the tunnel branched out, forcing me to choose a new path. At first it felt like I was going in circles but then I realized I hadn't seen any doors lately and concluded that the underground village was behind me at last.

Small animals occasionally scurried past my ankles, making me squirm, though I soon learned to recognize their noises and keep them at bay. As I turned into one of the galleries, a swarm of what I thought were bats attacked me, making me shriek, but on closer inspection I realized they were just butterflies—huge black butterflies. Soon I ended up in a cave full of chrysalises at least as big as me. I stood there staring at them, petrified, then ran off.

After a long time spent groping through the pitch dark, my sight suddenly sharpened inexplicably, allowing me to see just enough to gain my bearings. From time to time my skin felt feverishly hot—it was my nature rebelling as it recognized where I was—but my temperature soon returned to normal.

In the distance a barely perceptible glimmer illuminated the darkness in which I was lost. At first it was so dim that for a second I thought it was just my imagination, like a mirage in the desert. I hurried toward it but when I got close I also heard a crescendo of grunts.

The light was coming from above. It had to be an exit—the first one I'd seen in hours. I couldn't pass up the opportunity. Even though the noises made me think I might be throwing myself into the jaws of some horrible creature, I went toward it.

Just as I was nearing the exit, a bitter laugh escaped me at the sight of some Souls coming out of one of the tunnels behind me. I still had a chance—with a little luck I might reach the opening before they could turn me into their next meal.

I quickened my pace. When I reached the opening, I grabbed hold of a crack in the wall and climbed up with a strength I didn't know I had. I could already smell fresher air that cleansed my nostrils of the earthy stench that impregnated the walls underground. Making a final effort, I hoisted myself up, but one of the Damned beneath me grabbed hold of my calf. I let out a shriek that was like an explosion in the cramped space.

The Soul let go. Looking down, I saw his face crack and shatter like porcelain. I stared at him in astonishment as his head exploded in a cloud of dust. *He had covered his ears.* Could my shriek have been what had carbonized him? I touched my forehead. It was burning. Maybe Ginevra was right and my powers really were starting to emerge.

When I wedged my foot into the uppermost crack, the rock gave way beneath my weight and I fell back. I could hear footsteps approaching. Someone was coming. I struggled to shake the cloud from my mind as a ghoulish smile loomed over me, but I didn't have the strength and darkness washed over me.

Through the blackness I was submerged in came the murmur of soft, vaguely cheerful voices and for a second I deluded myself that the nightmare was finally over. I clung to those sounds as I slowly came to, a sharp pain lacerating my head. I rubbed the nape of my neck, the spot where the pain radiated from, and found that my hair was dry and matted. Then I remembered. I must have hit my head when I fell from the rock wall. Ignoring the pain, I tried to get up from the old wooden bench on which I lay. The room was packed with all sorts of people. Whoever had found me must have carried me to some kind of tavern where everyone seemed to be having a good time.

It took me no more than a moment to figure out where I'd ended up. Where I was could only be one specific, terrifying place, and the creatures that surrounded me could only be one species of Damned.

Lechers. The air was heavy with the smell of sex.

At first sight the place might have been mistaken for a "normal" house of ill repute except that no one was acting normally. Everywhere I turned, people were indulging in every aspect of carnal pleasure:

between the tables, on the benches, against the walls. A woman straddling a man stared at me steadily as she whispered something in her lover's ear, giving me the creeps. I noticed that the glasses were filled with a reddish liquid that definitely wasn't wine. Terrified, I looked around for a way out and noticed to my horror that the skirt of my dress was raised. I quickly covered myself, painfully aware that whoever had taken me there had done so for a specific reason. I had to escape. I hoped it wasn't too late, that they hadn't abused me while I was unconscious.

"Awake at last." I jumped at the clear sound of a male voice and focused on a young face. His eyes, black and hypnotic, instantly sent a shiver through me as they gazed at me. His lips curved into a smile.

I instinctively pulled my knees to my chest and scurried away over the long bench. Touching my neck, I felt the medallion. It gave me an instant sense of security. "Don't come near me," I warned the young man, looking him in the eye.

His long, raven-black hair was tied into a low ponytail with a leather thong. "Come now, don't get worked up. I don't mean to harm you or"—he looked around and grinned—"whatever it is you think I have in mind."

Though his expression wasn't hostile, I couldn't trust anyone any more. "Who are you? What is this place? Was it you who brought me here?"

Another grin. The guy's cocky expression made me think he was laughing at me. I was frightened and couldn't hide it.

"You ask a lot of questions for a girl who just banged her head." He put his feet up on the table, tilted his chair back, and clasped his hands behind his head, a cunning smile on his lips. His eyes were glued to mine. "Ahrec. Jigol's. No."

"What's that, a riddle?" I said acidly.

His laughter rang out. "Just answering your questions, Peachskin." His eyes unabashedly studied my neckline. "My name is Ahrec, this is Jigol's tavern, and no, I'm not the one who brought you here."

"Don't call me that again." I looked at him warily. "My name is Gemma. Who's Jigen? And if it wasn't you, who brought me to this place?"

"*Jigol* is that fellow over there." He jerked his head toward a massive, broad-shouldered man who was bald and dressed entirely in buffalo pelts. "And that's the answer to both questions."

I gulped when I saw the burly man slide his hand between the thighs of a woman sitting on the bar with her legs spread wide. She really seemed to be enjoying his attentions. Ahrec followed my eyes. "Ugly fellow, isn't he? Don't worry, I kept my eye on you the whole time. No one laid a hand on you." I swallowed again and my eyes darted to Ahrec's, grateful he had answered my thoughts and relieved my most horrifying fear.

"I think he wanted you all to himself. Luckily I showed up in time." He winked at me, broadening his sly smile.

"What do you mean?" I cocked my head and shot him a piercing look, suddenly frightened by his expression.

"I claimed you for myself." My eyes widened in shock as my hand moved toward my arm. "I have to admit it wasn't easy. I had to fight to get you. I'm sure you'll thank me later." I clutched the hilt of my dagger. "Whoa, whoa, whoa! You're dangerous, it would seem," he joked, but my eyes didn't leave his for a second. "Don't worry. I was only kidding!"

I continued to stare at him warily.

"Truth is, Jigol was just waiting for you to come to. He's not too fond of passive lovers, you see."

"What?!" My uneasiness was beginning to verge on despair. Was that nasty-looking guy actually just waiting for me to be awake before raping me?

"Drink a bit of this." Ahrec offered me a tankard of the strange red liquid they were all drinking. Still distraught, I refused, so he tilted his head back and took a long drink. "That's a pity." He wiped his mouth with the back of his hand as a scarlet trickle ran down one corner of his lips. "It would help you relax." He stared at me as though wanting to worm his way inside me, probe me for answers to questions I couldn't even imagine.

"What is that stuff?" I asked, nodding at the cup with a hint of disgust. I had the feeling I wasn't going to like the answer one bit. The liquid was thick and scarlet with golden streaks, and my instincts told me it wasn't cherry juice.

"It may not be the nectar of the gods, but this 'stuff' can definitely take you to paradise." Ahrec shrugged and finished it in a single gulp. "It's forbidden around here—rare goods—but it would seem Jigol has connections. That's one reason his tavern is always full."

The more Ahrec talked, the clearer it became to me what the red liquid was. Ginevra had talked to me about her "little games" with

Simon, and I'd already seen those golden streaks when we captured the Executioner.

It was Witch's blood. My heart skipped a beat at the thought that they might use it on Evan. What effect would it have on him? Would he really succumb to them? Was it powerful enough to break down his defenses like some dark spell? Or did the Witches use it to dull his senses, like we'd done with Desdemona?

"Welcome back, princess." A huge hand gripped my shoulder. I whipped around and a shiver of terror raced down my back when I looked into Jigol's hard, hungry eyes. "It was about time. I was getting tired of waiting."

I tried to break free but he held me tighter and slid his other hand down my bodice. Frozen in terror, I sought Ahrec's gaze. He sat there without moving, seemingly caught off guard, but there was a determined look in his eyes that darted furiously between me and Jigol. I shot him a pleading look, though there was no reason to hope for his help. Even if he tried, Ahrec wouldn't have a chance against him in a fight; he was toned but lean, whereas Jigol was built like an ogre.

"Hey, don't be like that." Jigol tried to pin me down as he began to rub his body against mine. His tongue slid down my neck as I squirmed with disgust. "Relax, we're in my kingdom now. There are no Flesh Fiends allowed in here. We can have some fun. I bet nobody offered you a bit of my elixir yet. I'll have to chop off some heads for their lack of hospitality."

Out of the corner of my eye I saw his hand grab a tankard full of it. I sealed my lips tight, but Jigol pressed the tankard against my mouth, forcing it open. "It's magic," he insisted. "You wanna stay in this living hell or let me take you to paradise?" He grabbed my bodice, ready to yank my dress off, and the medallion popped out.

Suddenly an inhuman howl silenced the room. I immediately spat out the blood and turned around. The shriek had come from Jigol. He was clutching his arm that was now missing a hand. I let out a scream when I realized his fingers were still clawing at my shoulder. With horror, I shrugged off the hand.

I looked up and Ahrec grinned at me cockily. "Don't worry. He'll grow a new one." With a single, flowing movement, Ahrec had snatched the dagger from me and chopped off Jigol's hand. He'd done it so quickly I hadn't even noticed he'd moved toward us.

Jigol continued to moan, clutching his arm. "Get them!" he bellowed, his voice even hoarser from the pain.

Ahrec grabbed my arm and yanked me toward the door. "We'd best be leaving, and fast." He clasped my hand firmly in his, without giving me the chance to object, and led me across the room. Some of the Damned rushed to stop us and he fought them off by hurling tables at them, lifting them with one hand and making them seem as light as papier-mâché.

Once we neared the door, however, a group of men blocked our way, putting an end to our escape. Before I knew it, Ahrec had grabbed me by the waist, hoisted me onto a counter, nimbly leapt up beside me and with a firm kick smashed in the wooden planks of a boarded-up window. He took me by the hand and a moment later the twilight air cooled my face.

I ran after him as he headed toward the forest. He was going so fast I could barely keep up with him. Suddenly something moved in the darkness. I tensed, but Ahrec started to laugh.

I squinted and a gasp escaped me. "My God!"

A man with long black hair and the body of a Greek God was taking a woman against a tree while two other women contended for his mouth in anxious anticipation.

"He's a Flesh Fiend," Ahrec explained. I wanted to look away but couldn't. "The ladies, on the other hand, are Nymphs. During their lifetimes they were slaves to sex."

"You're kidding, right?" Ahrec laughed again. "Nymphs? I thought Nymphs were some sort of—I don't know—*fairies!*"

"They are. Fairies who lure unwitting victims to do their sexual bidding, like it or not. Even the Witches are called Nymphs sometimes, because of their powers of seduction and their unbridled lust. Where do you think the word 'nymphomaniac' comes from? Those Nymphs want nothing more than to copulate with him, at all costs. I recommend you not watch. It won't be a pretty sight."

"Watch? What do you take me for—some kind of creepy voyeur?"

"Do as you please. I only said it to spare you the shock of seeing him feed on them."

I teetered and slowed my pace, bewildered. "What do you mean, he's going to feed on them?"

"Exactly what you think."

"But they're together, they're all over him, and—"

"And he's going to rip their heads off and eat them. Eat them alive. Devour them. I'll draw you a picture if you like. I have all the time in the world."

"But that's insane! You mean one minute she has his tongue in her mouth and the next he'll be gobbling hers up like it's no big deal?"

"I would have described the scene differently, but I'll admit you do have a lively imagination," Ahrec joked.

A shudder crept down my spine. "It's horrifying. Can't we warn them?"

"No need. They already know."

"Why are they still there, then?! Why don't they run away?" I stared at the three women. Another of them was pressed against the tree now. The man was taking her vigorously, making her shriek with pleasure.

"They can't help it. I told you, they're slaves to their own lust."

I blinked and turned toward Ahrec, forcing myself to take my eyes off the spectacle that would soon be tinged red.

"Don't look at me. It's the price Lechers have to pay—male and female alike. They're slaves to sex and here they're forced to pay for it with their lives. They can't help it. For the most part they only dally yet often they can't stop, and once they've sated their appetites they meet with a gruesome end. Just like these ladies. Lucky for them they didn't encounter a female Flesh Fiend."

"Why? What's the difference?"

"The females are also called Praying Mantises. People say they can give you the most phenomenal sex you'll ever experience, yet during coitus they bite your head off in chunks. They don't have the brute force of male Flesh Fiends, so their victims experience a slow, agonizing death—along with rapturous pleasure. So it's not such a terrible end after all."

"God, how revolting!"

Ahrec shrugged. "There are Flesh Fiends lurking everywhere around these parts, yet Jigol's tavern is a safe haven. Those three women were probably headed there and didn't make it."

"Wait." Instinct made me stop before we made our way into the trees. "Why did you do it?"

His face didn't look hostile, but his black eyes flashed like a wolf's that's tracked down the hiding place of its prey.

"Did you rescue me so *you* could be the one to devour me or . . . who knows what else?" I asked defiantly.

His laughter rang out crisply through the cool air, like the first time I'd heard it. "You think I rescued you from Jigol so I could devour you or . . . *who knows what else?*"

"Shouldn't I think that? It wouldn't be the first time it's happened to me down here. Besides, why should I trust you?"

Ahrec came closer. Having him so near made me stiffen. "For at least two reasons." I arched an eyebrow, waiting for his explanation. "The first is that I just saved you from Jigol. You can always go back to his tavern if you'd rather discover the paradise he promised you." This time he was the one to arch an eyebrow. The shadow of a smile appeared on his lips.

"And what would the second reason be?" I asked suspiciously.

Ahrec cupped my chin in his hand and turned my head in a surprisingly gentle gesture. "The second would be those fellows over there." I jumped at the sight of a horde of men in the distance advancing inexorably in our direction. Ahrec took my hand again and I was forced to look him in the eye. "I don't believe you have much choice."

I sighed in frustration. He was right. I didn't want to trust him, but what alternative was there? I let him lead me into the forest and away from the men following us. I would just have to be careful never to let my guard down.

"Why were you there?" We had walked for a long time in silence, seeking the shelter of the forest to shake our pursuers.

"Beg pardon?" Ahrec must have grown so used to my silence that my question took him by surprise. Or maybe he just wanted to stall or avoid answering.

"What were you doing there, in the tavern? Are you one of them?"

Another mocking laugh. Ahrec was starting to get on my nerves. "Are you asking me if I'm a Lecher? Deep down, who isn't a bit lustful?"

I instinctively backed away from him. Ahrec looked around to make sure we were alone. "Don't worry, I'll give you all the time you need." He came closer, his eyes slightly wild. "However, sooner or later you'll have to show me your gratitude for saving you. Don't tell me you wouldn't enjoy it too."

My panic was so overwhelming I couldn't move a muscle. Ahrec was inches from me, his eyes not leaving mine for a second. Then his lips spread into a smile and he burst out laughing as I stood there blinking. "Come on! You didn't really believe me about my 'reward,' did you?"

"It's not funny." As I stomped past him I punched his shoulder, but hidden under his sweater were rock-hard muscles. My wrist hurt, but I didn't let it show. I didn't know whether I should be afraid of Ahrec or feel safe. Every ounce of me hoped it was the latter.

"Come on now, don't pout," he shouted after me as I stormed away. "Hasn't anyone ever told you what fun it is to tease you?"

Something contracted inside me but I was careful to hide how upset I was. "Yes, actually. Someone used to tell me that all the time."

Evan.

A quiver in my heart reminded me what was at stake. "Who are you and why did you save me?" I insisted. "The truth this time."

Ahrec caught up with me and clasped his hands behind his neck without slowing his pace. "I saw you slung over Jigol's shoulder and followed him. At first I had no intention of saving you—I was simply curious. Don't know what came over me. Challenging Jigol wasn't wise of me, yet I couldn't help it."

"You seemed at home back there. How did you know about Jigol and his tavern if you're not one of them?"

"When you're in a place like this for a long time you learn to know your enemies. It's not easy to survive unless you watch your back."

I jumped over a strange stone that protruded from the ground in my path. Only then did I notice that all around us were hundreds of small skulls dangling from spiny tree trunks. I froze in terror.

"*Antirrhinum Skull.*"

"Huh?"

"That's their scientific name. They're just flowers." Ahrec laughed, enjoying my expression.

"So you're a botany expert, are you?" I asked with sarcasm, given that it was the only language he seemed to understand.

"I'm an expert on skulls—at least enough to know that those aren't skulls."

"But how do you know their name?"

"It's better if you don't ask." Ahrec winked at me and I sighed, deciding to drop it. All his answers did was prompt more questions in me, while I should have been focusing only on what really interested me.

"Who are you?" I tried again, but Ahrec continued to tease me.

"You do like to repeat yourself! I'm the fellow who saved your life, isn't that enough?"

"Are you a Subterranean?" I asked point-blank.

Ahrec let out a long whistle. "My, you are direct."

"I didn't ask you what color underwear you have on."

"Who says I have any on?" He grinned at me mockingly as I rolled my eyes at his insolence.

"Are you or aren't you?" I insisted. I couldn't trust him unless I knew what kind of Soul he was.

"You're asking if I'm a Subterranean?" Ahrec looked at me out of the corner of his eye. Once again, I suspected he was considering how to answer. He must have survived thanks to his shrewdness in addition to his incredible strength. "You know a lot for someone who's still a mortal."

"How do you know I'm a mortal?" I shot back warily.

He smiled, not taking me seriously. "Anyone could tell that. I'd wager they could even smell your scent underground. You're rare goods around here. And by rare I mean *unique*."

"Is that why you want me with you?"

Ahrec chuckled. "Again?! Look, I've already told you I'm not after your blood or your body—though I'm not saying I wouldn't like it if you were to have second thoughts."

"Hey! You dodged my question again. Are you or are you not an Angel?"

"We're all *Demons* here, Peachskin." He paused before going on. "Perhaps there was a time when I used to be one; however, in this accursed place it doesn't matter which race you're from. All that matters is which races you have to steer clear of to avoid being—Look out!"

There was a sputter and a hiss. Ahrec grabbed me and shoved me against something before I realized what was going on. I tried to breathe but he was squeezing my chest. When he eased his grip I looked around, frightened. I was backed against a tree and he was in front of me, his arms still wrapped around me. "This would be a fine time for you to have those second thoughts." He arched an eyebrow as an amused grin appeared on his lips. I glared at him and shoved him away.

He moved aside and seemed uncomfortable, but only for a second. "You should be more careful. One false step and—*poof*." He gestured with one hand and I noticed his palm was burned.

"You're hurt!" I pulled away from the tree trunk, which prickled like a million needles. I noticed it was covered with tiny thorns. They must have been poisoned and he'd leaned his palms against them to protect me—from what, I still didn't understand.

Without replying, Ahrec started walking again and I followed him. Soon another sputter caught my attention, but this time I saw where it was coming from and stopped to watch it. A column of steam burst from the ground, pulverizing a big black butterfly flying over it. They were geysers. Poisonous geysers hidden in the black earth. Dazed and suddenly breathless, I looked at Ahrec, who simply shrugged.

He had saved me. Again. "Who are you?" I insisted.

Ahrec looked me in the eye, this time serious. "I'm just someone who's trying to survive, like everyone else." He pulled out my dagger and I stiffened. Holding it by the blade, he handed it to me, still looking into my eyes. "You can trust me." I glanced at the hilt and then at him. "Otherwise why would I give this back to you? You might even kill me with it. I know you've used it before—I smell cursed blood on it. Take it if it makes you feel more at ease."

It was then that I spotted something beneath his left sleeve and my heart filled with hope. Slowly, without taking my eyes off Ahrec's, I took the weapon and slid it back into its sheath, then swiftly snatched his wrist and bared his arm. The mark of the Children of Eve appeared before my eyes like a promise. I was right: Ahrec was a Subterranean.

"My! Don't you think you're moving a bit too fast? Want to see me naked already, do you?" Ahrec pulled his arm back, away from my scrutiny. "If you want me to strip, you could have simply said so."

"Sorry. I have to admit you seemed *human*, or at least different from the others I've run into so far. I had to do it."

Ahrec whistled. "Two points in my favor, then. I'll take that as a compliment."

"Why is your tattoo so distorted?" I asked, hoping he wouldn't be offended.

Ahrec's face darkened and he paused in stubborn silence. Just when I thought he wasn't going to answer, he admitted: "They captured me and disfigured it."

I had other questions, but I was clearly making him uncomfortable. Besides, all things considered, it wasn't important. Ahrec was a Subterranean—that was all that mattered to me. He might really be able to help me after all.

"Think you could help me find the river?"

Ahrec shrugged obligingly. "I have no other commitments."

My heart leapt with hope. "Really?! I mean—thank you! It's very important for me to get there."

"Come on, calm down. There's no saying I won't change my mind about that reward." He winked and smiled at me mockingly while inwardly I chastised myself for revealing all my enthusiasm.

"I'm not going to give you that kind of reward," I assured him, serious again.

"Really? I have a little of Jigol's elixir, if it'll help you unwind a bit." I glared at him and he shrugged. "A pity. You don't know what you're missing."

"Are you going to help me or aren't you?" I insisted.

"Very well, I'll help you find the river. However, first we'd better stop for a while. I haven't eaten in days."

"I hope that's not a threat," I warned.

Ahrec's laughter rang through the trees. "You're beautiful *and* witty." I shot him a glance and he moved his face close to mine, lowering his voice. "In case it wasn't clear, that was a compliment."

I blinked, his nearness making me uncomfortable. He took a couple steps back with an ill-concealed smile on his lips.

"Want to eat?"

With one hand I rummaged through the satchel slung over my shoulder and found myself considering his offer. As though he'd read my mind, Ahrec smiled at me and disappeared into the shrubbery.

Suddenly I felt alone in the darkness, lost without him, as if Ahrec had been with me from the first second. I'd almost convinced myself that I'd grown used to the agonizing screams that broke the silence from time to time, but without him at my side they frightened me again. I rubbed my arms, looking around warily, and thought I saw a shadow moving among the trees.

"Ahrec," I called, a terrible presentiment taking hold of me. "Ahrec . . . someone's here."

In front of me a shrub stirred, sending an eerie shiver up my spine, but before I could give in to panic, Ahrec reappeared, still in the shadows, carrying an animal he'd caught. There was something strange about him, something sinister. I backed up and a stifled cry escaped me. His eyes were ravenous and in the darkness his pupils had dilated, turning blacker than night, as though he were there to kill me. "I th-think there's something in the trees," I warned him as he approached.

He whipped his head to the side in an unnatural movement. A second later, he emerged from the shadows of the trees and the dim light illuminated his face.

"For a moment I thought—" Realizing his face was normal, I let out the breath I'd been holding. Fear had clouded my thinking to the point of making Ahrec look like a monster to my eyes.

He peered around, clearly alarmed someone might be out there. Then he came and showed me what he had caught. It looked a bit like a fox but was the size of a rabbit.

"How did you—"

Ahrec wiped his mouth with the back of his hand and tossed the animal at my feet. "It's better if you don't know."

"I don't eat raw meat," I warned him, trying not to retch.

"You're always jumping to conclusions. Actually that wasn't what I had in mind." He sat down cross-legged and in seconds a flame flickered up between his palms.

"How did—" I stammered, puzzled.

"How do you think the cavemen did it?" He showed me the sticks he was holding. "It's something so rudimentary, I didn't expect it would amaze you."

"Another point in your favor." I crouched down to take in some of its warmth as Ahrec fed the flames with kindling until it had grown into a small fire.

I watched the flames dance in the twilight. Their heat seemed to ignite all the emotions I held within, and they exploded inside me as I sat, my face immobile, my gaze trapped in the dazzling lights that danced in the air. Finding Evan, the hope that held my heart prisoner, seemed farther and farther away.

I closed my eyes and imagined Evan beside me. Every fear disappeared when I was with him. Right now I felt in danger of losing him forever. Searching Hell for him was a desperate endeavor. I was risking everything just to chase after that glimmer of hope. Despite all the hardships, fears, and uncertainties, though, I would never give up. I stroked my belly, thinking of my baby—a part of Evan growing inside me, protected by Ginevra's magic, in case his half-Angelic blood wasn't enough to keep him safe.

Thinking of my baby brought to mind the baby girl I'd killed, and I struggled not to sink into depression. Suddenly I couldn't remember why I'd done it. Had I honestly not had any way to escape? Had I really been forced to do it, or had it been my evil nature taking control of me? Would evil really annihilate who I was without leaving me any alternative? Would I lose the capacity to choose? Or, even worse, would it happen without my realizing it?

"Was it hard?" Ahrec's voice was muffled and distant to my ears, but it was a lifeline I could cling to and pull myself out of the pyre of guilt in which I was burning. I raised my eyes and found his waiting for me. I'd been so absorbed in my thoughts I hadn't realized he was studying me. "It must have been hard for you," he continued, his direct gaze telling me he didn't need confirmation.

"You were right," I found myself whispering. The words had slipped out without my permission.

"About what?" Ahrec's tone was cautious but comforting.

"About the dagger. When you said I'd used it. I've been forced to do horrible things since I got here." Ahrec nodded understandingly. "I even—" I struggled to admit it out loud. "I killed a baby." I paused for so long I thought I wouldn't go on, but then I said, "It was terrible and I can't forgive myself."

Ahrec chucked a stone into the fire, stared at it a moment, and turned to look at me. "You shouldn't feel guilty about it. This place isn't your world."

For some reason, hearing the truth from someone else startled me. Maybe deep down I *had* been forced to do it.

"Your rules don't apply here," he added, the tension on his face slowly easing. "You must have ended up in the Forge of the Antichrist, the village of the Unholy. There are no other babies down here. You were right to defend yourself—they would have killed you otherwise. Many are fooled by their appearance, yet those Souls aren't really little children. They're the Damned who didn't receive purification, the Divine Blessing, on Earth. It doesn't matter what rite it's done through—every religion has its own way to consecrate one's life to

God. Also the souls of those who lost faith in God and never found it again, like atheists. No belief in Heaven, no interest in going there."

"You mean even innocent children who don't know anything about life yet end up in Hell just because someone else didn't purify them? That's ridiculous."

"It would be ridiculous, if it happened that way. Not receiving purification isn't enough for a Soul to end up in Hell. Don't forget, a personal decision is always involved. Mortals have free will, and only a freely made choice can damn them forever. Many unbelievers or unpurified people are pure in spirit and at the moment of temptation make the right choice, so their souls are saved. The Unholy, on the other hand, are the souls of the unpurified or atheists who during their lifetimes chose to live in evil. While they're here, they slowly experience what we call the Dwindling: they grow younger and younger until they ultimately look like infants. Though no one knows why, a few keep their adult appearance—perhaps because they've retained a bit of their humanity. However, most of them get littler and littler until they cease to exist. They aren't babies. The younger and smaller they are, the more skillful and dangerous they are. Despite their appearance, they're strong, fast, and deadly. You're lucky you're still alive. They're a ferocious race because they've never known the divine touch. With a few exceptions, of course. I still don't know how you managed to escape from them alive." Ahrec looked at my amulet and I instinctively raised my hand to my chest to cover it.

I nodded, silently thanking him for convincing me I wasn't a monster.

The flames crackled and lit up our faces. From time to time I would take a piece of meat I had cooked over the fire and put it in my mouth. The flavor wasn't the best, but I needed nourishment.

"There's something I have to confess," I blurted. He remained silent, waiting for me to go on. Up until then, I hadn't wanted to take the funny feeling I'd been having too seriously, but I felt safe with Ahrec, so it was easier to face my fears. I peered around at the darkness. "Ever since I got here I've had the feeling someone was following me."

To my surprise, Ahrec stiffened. His eyes scanned the shadows under the trees.

"Once in a while it's like I can see eyes hiding in the darkness—an animal's eyes, like it's stalking me. Who knows, maybe it's just my imagination. Sometimes it feels like this place is making me lose my mind," I admitted. Ahrec tried to hide his uneasiness behind a forced smile, but his face was rigid. "But basically, if there really was something out there, it would've already had lots of chances to attack me, wouldn't it?" I smiled, but the eerie silence that suddenly surrounded us made a shiver crawl beneath my skin.

"No doubt." Ahrec continued to smile, though he still seemed to be forcing it. "It must be your imagination. Why don't you get some rest now?"

Instinct made me peer into the darkness again. No one was there—the forest was silent—but the presentiment was strong and I felt vulnerable. My predator was hiding out there, waiting for the right moment to attack. Something was hunting me down, I was sure of it.

"I'll stand guard while you sleep. It's a long walk to the river and you'll need your strength to make it there."

I lay down on the ground, using my satchel as a pillow. There was something hypnotic in Ahrec's dark gaze. "Don't worry, I'll watch over you." Suddenly I felt incredibly tired and all the strength drained from my body.

"Now sleep, Peachskin."

His words lulled me like a dark spell, persuasive and comforting, until the coils of darkness enveloped me completely.

POISON AND BLOOD

When I gradually began to awaken, I had no idea how long I'd been asleep. Time didn't seem to count in that place. I felt something tickling my skin and slowly returned to my surroundings as the fire crackled and the flames danced in the half-light, casting sinister shadows on the ground. Squinting, I made out a figure doubled over on itself. No—crouched over something it held in its hands. The figure seemed to be contemplating whatever it was with a mix of desperation and satisfaction, as if it were his own still-beating heart. The palpable intensity of his gaze made me tremble . . . or maybe it was something else causing that feeling in me.

Suddenly I felt naked and vulnerable. Something was missing. My hand flew to my neck and a shudder turned the blood in my veins to ice. The medallion was gone. "Ahrec—"

He spun around in surprise, but his face was . . . *different*. I scrambled backwards with a shriek of fear, but he didn't move. His eyes followed me ravenously, as black as those of an animal poised to kill. My medallion was clutched in his hands.

I stared at him in terror. It was as though Ahrec was gone, as though every trace of humanity had vanished from his eyes. I stealthily reached for the dagger, but Ahrec must have guessed my intentions because he vanished in the blink of an eye. I scanned the darkness, afraid he might attack me from behind.

"Looking for this?"

I raised my eyes. Overhead, perched on an incredibly high branch, Ahrec stared down at me, his shoulders leaning against the trunk. He slid the blade of my dagger over his tongue, licking off some blood that still looked fresh. Ahrec had tricked me. He was a monster like all the others. And this time I had no way out.

"You told me you were a Subterranean," I cried, my voice cracking with horror.

Ahrec shoved the blade of the dagger into the tree. "I lied," he said in a low growl that didn't sound like his voice. "You shouldn't give your trust so easily. After all, we *are* in Hell." He leapt down and moved closer. "Besides, you wanted so badly for it to be true. Why not let you believe it? I certainly couldn't have told you I was an Unholy Soul."

"You're a—" His words wrenched a groan from my chest.

"Of a sort, actually. I received a holy blessing yet later I stopped believing and lived only by my own rules." The reddish glow of the fire made his face even more threatening as he inched closer. "They didn't know what to do with me, so they damned me as one of them. It's just that I'm stuck at this age. Though I've no idea why, I've never undergone the Dwindling."

"It can't be. I saw your tattoo."

"What, this?" Ahrec bared his arm, smiling. "It's not hard to brand your own skin."

"You did that to yourself? Why?"

"Survival. Subterranean Souls are the only ones who can't die here. No one is daft enough to challenge them—no one except me, naturally. I had to capture more than one of them to finally get the tattoo right. Took me years to perfect it." His eyes were those of a monster, like they'd been when he'd returned with the food. I should have realized it then: Subterraneans don't eat. What a fool I'd been.

"Y-you tricked me. But if all you wanted was the medallion, why didn't you kill me right away?"

Ahrec continued to creep forward. "I wasn't quite sure what you were. First I had to understand what risks I was running. You're human, yet you wear a Witch's trinket around your neck. I was a bit confused by that. Then I thought that perhaps if you trusted me enough to lower your guard—"

"Give it back! That medallion doesn't belong you!"

"Yes it does. You have no idea what it means to have been damned to this place for centuries. Every. Day. Every. Minute. *This*"—he held up the amulet, which he was clenching so tightly his hand had begun to bleed—"is my ticket to freedom. No one is taking it from me. Taking it from you proved easier than I thought. Can you believe I was actually going to keep my word? Before stealing it from you I truly was going to take you to the river, yet when you said you were being followed I realized I had to act quickly." He took another step forward and I scooted myself backwards across the ground. He was so close I could see his teeth. They were incredibly sharp and deadly.

"Do you mean to kill me?" I asked, my voice trembling. Shivers spread over my entire body when Ahrec didn't answer. He just stared at me.

"They're pro—" Sudden terror flashed across his face as something lunged from the darkness and landed heavily on him, knocking him brutally to the ground. I saw it was a large feline. I tried to move away, shrieking with horror as the beast sank its fangs into him. When Ahrec's body stopped twitching, the creature turned its head and looked me in the eye. I cringed, terrified it would tear me to pieces, but instead it continued to stare at me, perfectly still, as though trying to tell me something. I blinked, unable to focus on anything else.

Suddenly all my fear left me. A single thought filled my head: the animal was magnificent. I felt a strange desire to move closer and merge with it. It had fur darker than night and green eyes that emanated a glow that was somehow familiar. Could this be the animal that had been following me? Where else could I have ever looked into a black panther's eyes before?

Acting on an irresistible impulse, I leaned toward it, holding its gaze, but the panther leapt gracefully over the fire and disappeared into the darkness. I crumpled to the ground, speechless, still unable to believe it hadn't slain me too.

A gurgle distracted me from the thought. *Ahrec.* I went to him, trying to avoid looking at the gaping wound in his chest, the deep slash in his neck, and the blood that gushed from it. He wasn't dead yet. He reached out his arm, slid his hand over the ground and touched mine. When I opened my palm he rested my amulet on it.

"Ahrec . . ." I murmured, my voice trembling. His eyes were once again the eyes of the trustworthy young man I'd known, and seeing him like that tugged at my heartstrings.

"I . . . just . . . wanted . . . to be free," he said with effort. A tear streaked my face. I took his hand in mine and he squeezed it tightly. "Take care of yourself . . . Peachskin." He smiled at me affectionately and vanished.

I stared at the cloud of dust into which he had dissolved and new tears slid silently down my cheeks. I had held them back for too long and suddenly I couldn't contain them any longer. I wept because deep down Ahrec hadn't really wanted to kill me. I wept because I had lost even the tiniest hope of finding the river.

Once again, I was alone and vulnerable, trapped in a world without Evan. A world without light. He was out there somewhere, but I hadn't managed to find him.

I had failed—I had no choice but to accept it.

When the ground had absorbed every last tear, I opened my eyes, utterly exhausted. It felt like there was nothing worth fighting for any more. I might as well wait right there until someone came and put an end to my suffering. Even the fire had died out, depriving me of its warmth.

My unfocused gaze lingered on a shape that stood out against the twilit sky, a darker patch against the dreariness, but I was too depressed to pay attention to my flights of fancy. There was nothing out there beyond the hills, nothing I could cling to to help me recover my courage and determination. Just images projected by my mind that, like me, had been beaten down by disappointment.

Blurred by my tears, the shape split in two, then fused into one again. I blinked. The dim light had to be playing a cruel joke on me. And yet . . . I pushed myself up on my palms, electrified. It was still there. *The Castle.*

It wasn't a mirage. It was really there, beyond the hills. Like a giant, it rose into the sky and towered over everything, staring at me as though to guide me to it. The blood began to pulse strongly through my veins again and my heart pounded so hard I felt it would burst from my chest. The joy that flooded me almost knocked me over. Evan was there and I still had a chance to save him. The Castle was far away, but *it was there.* I had found it. And after everything I'd faced already, those last miles wouldn't be enough to stop me. I would conquer the two hills that protected it like soldiers guarding a fortress. I would brave the forest and the dangers lurking there. I would walk for days on end, climb the Castle walls if need be, but in the end I would reach it. Nothing else mattered any more.

Without realizing it, I had already started walking. My feet were moving on their own, my eyes riveted on my destination, fearing it might fade away. I felt as if I were flying. Suddenly every dismal thought vanished. Soon I would see Evan and nothing would ever separate us again. I still had the feeling that hidden eyes were following my every movement from the forest, but I didn't even care about that. I was prepared to face and kill anything that dared attack me.

I felt invincible.

The forest was swarming with creatures—I could hear every little sound—but they all shied away from me, as though they too sensed the energy I was emanating.

Something glinted on the ground. I looked down. At the foot of the tree Ahrec had climbed lay my dagger. How strange—I remembered his leaving it lodged in the trunk high up on the tree. Had he made it fall just for me? I looked around warily before picking up the weapon and sheathing it. My eyes instantly returned to the Castle in the distance. It was so imposing it even challenged the sky. Not even the thick treetops could cover its majesty. A flock of ravens soared overhead, but instead of being afraid I watched them, fascinated, until they disappeared beyond the trees.

I couldn't believe I would soon see Evan again. For a long time my heart had faltered, like an old clock on the verge of dying. But now, with my renewed hope, it threatened to burst through my chest.

From the corner of my eye I saw something move in the semidarkness. A shiver ran down my spine but I did my best to ignore it and continued walking. Another movement—quicker this time. I tried to follow it with my eyes but saw only the gloom of dusk. A low, hair-raising growl filled the air but I couldn't tell where it was coming from. I instinctively rested my hand on the hilt of my dagger, my eyes scanning the gloom, but the sound seemed to surround me, coming from several directions at once. All at once, dark shadows crept out into the open, their hackles raised and their throaty growls growing louder.

Wolves. An entire pack of wolves prepared to lunge at me. The blade sang as I drew it from its sheath. I wasn't afraid. I stood there waiting, challenging them with my eyes. Nothing would come between me and Evan.

I gulped as the pack surrounded me. The largest wolf snarled louder than the rest and drew ever closer. I prepared myself to face it, but it leapt onto my chest and knocked me to the ground as the rest of the pack looked on. I struggled, but the wolf was too strong. It aimed its massive, powerful fangs directly at my throat as a scream escaped me.

Suddenly the animal pricked its ears and backed away, whining faintly. I narrowed my eyes, trying to understand what had just happened and what could have caused the wolf to retreat. What creature could be terrifying enough to frighten that wolf?

It was still right there in front of me, only now it regarded me with a completely different attitude. Its eyes studied me with curiosity. I propped myself up on my palms and the wolf bowed its head in what seemed to be a show of respect. I cocked my head, baffled, trying to understand its behavior as I slowly rose to my feet.

The wolf withdrew to rejoin the pack and a howl pierced the night. Their frightened, uncertain eyes didn't leave mine. I realized their instincts were telling them something that their sense of smell couldn't fathom: my body smelled of human blood, but there was a Witch buried inside me. I cautiously stepped forward and the wolves moved back as if in some dark dance until they disappeared into the forest. It seemed impossible they could be afraid of me. Could it have been something else that frightened them? I looked around. I didn't see anyone, and yet I had the impression there was someone else out there, hiding.

I sheathed the dagger and continued walking, marveling at how brave I'd been when facing the wolves. I hadn't been afraid at all, as though inside me lay the certainty I would be able to subdue them. The feeling of power was perceptible beneath my skin. Had that been enough to drive them away? Had they actually sensed it too?

I noticed suddenly that all the trees in the forest were bare, and stopped in my tracks. Hundreds of thick branches all around me were twisted like bodies paralyzed by terror. Abruptly, the rooftops of a village that had been hidden behind two tall hills appeared in the near distance. An irrepressible shudder ran through me. I knew it was better to steer clear of villages—the very thought of going through another one terrified me—but I had no choice.

I looked beyond the hills and the village. The Castle was getting closer. It seemed to stare at me, as though to encourage me—or frighten me away. I swallowed and my heart sent a message to my brain, ordering it to banish my fear. A moment later, my legs moved toward the village.

TRAPPED

People scurried in every direction, staring at their feet, their faces covered by long hoods. For a long time I'd remained hidden behind a cart, observing them, waiting for the right moment to go out, but it seemed the coming and going would never lessen, so I raised the hood of my green cloak and blended into the crowd. Being so close to so many Damned Souls made my heart race. Maybe it was just my nerves, but they seemed to be casting me grave looks as though they sensed something different about me. Something wrong. I continued along the street, anxious to leave the village behind and reach the Castle and Evan. But no matter how hard I tried to keep a low profile, I gradually realized an empty space had opened up around me as though the people, afraid of me, were keeping their distance. I walked on, as frightened as a rabbit in a wolf's den, their murmurs haunting me.

"What is she?"

"Can't you smell that she's human? It can't be!"

The sudden, ominous blast of a horn pierced the air, making me shiver. The next thing I knew chaos broke out all around me. What the hell was going on?

Then I saw them. A shudder ran all the way from my legs to my neck: a swarm of dark Angels was flying toward the village. I froze in terror and looked around for a place to hide but a woman in the crowd suddenly stopped and fixed her gaze on me. The whole world seemed to grind to a halt around us as the fire in her eyes burned into mine.

"Stop!" she thundered without taking her eyes off me. "The Indavas have never attacked us before." She raised her hand in my direction and everyone stopped to listen to her. Panic gripped me. "'Tis *she* who brought them here! Let us deliver her to them!"

The silent crowd seemed confused, unsure of what the best course of action would be.

"Ofelia is right!" a man's deep, powerful voice shouted. "They'll kill us one by one until they've taken her! Let's feed her to them!"

The crowd cheered in unison and charged in my direction. I backed up, terrified, but the men were on top of me before I had time to react. I struggled to break free, but their grip was too tight.

"Quickly! They're coming!" someone said anxiously. Despite my attempts to escape they shoved me against a post, knocking the breath out of me.

"Let me go!" I screamed in dismay, but none of them paid any attention. Someone pulled my hands behind my back and a rope was wound around my wrists and then my ankles. I felt like Andromeda, chained up with no Perseus to save me.

"Set me free! Please! I just wanted to cross through the village!" I looked overhead: the Indavas, as the villagers had called them, were getting closer and closer. "Let me go and I'll lead them away from here!" I tried to convince them in a steady voice, but there wasn't a shadow of hesitation in their eyes. Instead, they stared at me as though I were some strange monster.

A man came over, reached out toward my medallion, and exchanged glances with his friend. "'Tis true, 'tis the Dreide she wears. But why did she not fight back?" I tried to squirm away from his hand as someone let out a sudden scream of terror.

The man jumped and pulled back his hand. "They're coming!" Screams filled the square again as the crowd scattered in every direction.

"Let me go!" I shouted, trying to pull free of the ropes. "Don't leave me here, you cowards!" But no one listened to me and in seconds the only sound was the echo of my desperation. The streets had gone silent. They had all run off to hide, leaving me bound to a post as their sacrifice.

A living, pulsing dark cloud appeared overhead. Seconds later, the swarm of dark Angels had obscured the sky, covering the twilight with their mighty, bat-like wings. A shudder ran through my body as the creatures plunged down to attack the village.

No—not the village. To attack *me*. I tugged against the ropes over and over in an attempt to free myself but soon realized it was no use. I began to sob, not with tears of terror—there wasn't a trace of fear in me—but of desperation. I would never see Evan again or hold my baby in my arms.

One of the Angels swooped toward me. It wasn't until it was very close that I could make out its features. A single word filled my mind:

vampire. It was a vampire with a reptile's face, a long serpentine tail, razor-sharp claws, and a beak lined with teeth. A strange horn stuck out of its head, occasionally emitting an unearthly bioluminescent glow. I wanted to close my eyes to avoid the sight, but instead I tilted my head and held my breath as the Angel of darkness wrapped itself around me. I felt its strong body squeezing me, forcing the air out of my lungs. I moaned from the pain and tried to break free but the creature's long tail was coiled around my body, crushing me as it prepared to sink its vampire fangs into my flesh. I screamed with all the breath I had left, and the monster slashed my cheek with its beak.

Unexpectedly, something hurled the demon away from me. I stared at it in shock, its body crumpled on a rooftop, its tail still twitching. A spark shot out of its body. The fire quickly spread and in the blink of an eye the whole house was engulfed in flames. I looked up with a mix of terror, relief, and confusion as two jade-green eyes bored into mine.

Anya.

My heart leapt as a group of Witches on winged steeds chased off the Indavas, shooting thunderbolts and lightning that briefly lit up the sky. Meanwhile, the fire slowly destroyed the village, consuming the houses one after the other. The Souls ran into the street, screaming in terror and fleeing in every direction.

My head was throbbing frantically, trapped in a tangle of emotions. It was over. The Witches had saved me from the Indavas and they would finally take me to Evan. In exchange, they would demand my surrender, but it didn't matter. I didn't care about sacrificing myself to them as long as I could finally reach the Castle. It was my last hope for Evan to be set free.

Once the village was rid of the horrible Indavas, Anya flew her steed toward me, but a bolt of lightning sliced the air between us and the animal reared in the air.

Anya's gaze turned furious. I followed it and found myself looking into Devina's fierce, icy eyes. I would have recognized them from among a thousand others. The amber of her irises seemed to have caught fire.

"No one is to go near her."

Her voice rang out like an order—hard and implacable—while she studied my face with interest. I did my best to block her from my mind, but I could feel her tentacles unfurling in my brain, trying to bring down my defenses. I held on, though; I couldn't let her discover my plan, not now that I was so close to Evan, and after a long moment of silent struggle, she cracked her whip in frustration and gave up.

Devina pulled on the reins of her strange armored steed and turned to leave, followed by the other Witches. Only Anya didn't move, her face filled with resentment. I looked over their shoulders and was almost overcome with desperation: the Castle had vanished, as though it had been only a mirage.

"Wait!" At the sound of my voice, Devina stopped without turning her steed around, granting me only a sidelong glance. "Take me with you!" I cried, my back still pressed against the post. I tried to sound confident, but my voice betrayed my desperation. "I have a message for your Empress."

Devina's only response was mocking laughter. "What do you take me for, your carrier pigeon?" She looked at me, tilting her head, and her smile twisted into a mask of pure evil. "I'm afraid you'll have to find her on your own"—she raised an eyebrow, her expression challenging—"at your own risk and peril."

"Devina! You can't leave her here!" Anya said reproachfully, shooting her a defiant look, but Devina wasn't the least perturbed.

"Anya is right," said a third Sister with big eyes and straight raven-black hair. "Sophia won't be happy when she learns about this."

"Then don't tell her," Devina said to silence her, a hint of derision in her voice.

Anya spurred her steed and rode over in front of Devina, lowering her voice. "Have you gone mad? What are you thinking?"

The two Sisters silently challenged each other for a long moment. I wished I could read their minds but was afraid that if I tried to Devina might be able to penetrate mine.

"Sophia left *me* in charge." Devina's voice was as sharp as her gaze. "You've already helped her enough. We do as *I* say now." She cocked her head and cast me an icy look that sent an involuntary shiver through me. "Leave her there and wish her good luck." She spurred her steed and took flight.

Anya gave me a look full of regret. It was clear she wanted to help me but couldn't go against Devina's orders, since Sophia had left her in charge. Suddenly the pressure on my wrists eased. I looked at Anya, both confused and surprised. She smiled back.

The well, Gemma. I jumped when her voice filled my head. Once Devina was gone, I'd lowered my defenses and Anya had managed to reach my mind. *There's a tunnel beneath the well. It connects to the river. Follow the river and it will lead you to the Castle. Don't give up, Gemma. You're almost there.*

As I shook the ropes off my wrists I smiled and looked into her eyes with my own tear-filled ones, trying to express my gratitude. Anya returned my look, then spurred her steed and rose into the air, joining her Sisters.

I watched her figure grow smaller until every trace of it was swallowed up by the twilight. Then I untied the ropes from my ankles and went over to the well, which wasn't far away. I peered down into it, struggling with fear and uncertainty, but there was no time to hesitate. I felt I could trust Anya. I grabbed hold of the wooden bucket and lowered myself into its depths until darkness engulfed me.

At the bottom I rested one foot on the ground, shuddering. I was standing in an icy pool of water. A stinging sensation crept up my legs but the water was so cold that the discomfort soon vanished. After one last glance up, I took a deep breath and made my way into the tunnel. It was narrow and less dark than I'd expected, though it was possible I was seeing clearly only because my encounter with the Witches had reawakened some of my powers. A strange smell that reminded me vaguely of something I couldn't identify pervaded the air.

After a while, overcome with thirst, I leaned over to examine the water that reached my ankles. I wasn't sure I wanted to drink it, but I was so parched my tongue felt like it had crushed glass on it. I scooped some water into my hands and squinted as I raised it to my lips. It took only a second to finally recognize the familiar smell.

Poison.

The water must have contained only a small amount because my skin wasn't burning like it had when I'd fallen into the river. An idea occurred to me: I leaned over again, took the canteen out of the satchel, and filled it as full as I could. If nothing else, it could at least serve as a makeshift weapon, though I hoped I wouldn't have to use it.

I lifted the bottom of my skirt to wash away the dried blood between my calf and ankle. When the water touched the wound I gritted my teeth and bit my lip to keep from screaming, but the pain disappeared as quickly as it had come. I checked my leg to make sure it was clean and my eyes bulged with surprise: the wound inflicted by the Unholy Soul was gone. Had the poison actually had a healing effect on me? I couldn't believe it.

I stroked my cheek where the gash was still throbbing and poured some poisoned water over it, squeezing my eyes shut against the pain. It only lasted a second and the wound vanished beneath my fingertips. I straightened up, shook my head in surprise, and started walking again.

A short while later, something brushed against my ankle. I jumped, but saw it was only a small animal, which scurried off. It probably thought I was too big to tackle. As the hours wore on I came across a few other animals, but none of them were any larger or braver than the first. They inevitably ignored me and crawled away, so I stopped jumping at every strange grunt and squeak and continued to make my way down the narrow tunnel, trying to focus solely on the sound of the water dripping steadily from the walls.

Another sound, however, gave me chills. I wasn't sure if it was real or just my imagination, but I had the impression someone was whispering in my ear. The sound paralyzed me and I looked around in alarm. The water continued to drip with an eerie sound, but there was no one else in the passageway, I was sure of it. All at once something touched my arm. A shiver spread from the spot I'd been touched through my whole body like an electric current, making me shriek.

"Who's there?" I shouted, but the only reply was my own echo coming back to haunt me. I swallowed, listening as silence returned to the tunnel, and another whisper touched my ear. I spun around and saw it: a partially visible face peering at me, inches away. My heart banged against my ribs and I flattened myself against the wall. I should have fled, but I couldn't take my eyes off the strange being. The face moved closer to mine and I let it study me. There was no telling what it was—an ethereal creature that looked like it was made of water, or air that had changed consistency and crafted itself into a human semblance. It didn't look at all hostile. The way it flowed through the air with soft, graceful movements fascinated me. Before I realized it I'd raised my hand, drawn by my desire to feel the curious creature's consistency beneath my fingertips.

"Don't touch it!" I whirled around and caught my breath at the sight of the hooded figure before me. I knew that voice. "Shh . . ." Slowly, she pulled back her hood and raised a finger to her lips.

"Gwen!" My heart did a somersault when my eyes met hers. Though I longed to rush to her and hug her, the ethereal creature swirled around me, recapturing my attention. I was entranced by its enchanting movements. The almost irresistible urge to touch it came over me again, blocking everything else out.

"Stop, Gemma!" Ginevra insisted.

"Why? I just want a closer look. " My voice sounded muffled and distant even to me—it was like being under a spell.

"Don't touch it. It's a Pariah. Look at me, Gemma. Focus only on me."

Ginevra's presence was enough for me to listen to her and ignore the overpowering attraction the creature was exercising on me. I flattened myself against the wall, eluding the strange, wraithlike creature. "What's a Pariah?" I asked, tearing my eyes away from the creature with an effort.

"They're the souls of those whose sin in life was being so vain they sacrificed everything else. *Don't let it touch you*," she warned as the creature circled me again. It seemed to be performing a graceful, hypnotic dance. "The proud, the egocentric, narcissists, those in love only with themselves, those who see nothing but themselves are ostracized here, condemned to virtual invisibility."

"What would happen if I touched it?"

"Your essence would flow into it and your body would dissolve. That's how Pariahs feed. They need others to survive, although the effect wears off fast and they need to feed again. They can't take you by force, no matter how much they would like to or how hungry they are—they can only try to draw your attention. They're masters at the art of enchantment. It's a gift granted them in memory of their previous lives. If you stare at one for too long you won't be able to look away. Because of its hypnotic powers you'll ultimately fuse with it. They're capable of bonding any Soul to them."

"But it's so pretty . . ."

"Gemma!"

"What do I do?!" I cried, frightened of the translucent creature for the first time.

"I can only warn you and guide you. I'm a projection of your mind. I've been trying to establish a connection with you ever since you got here, but this is the first time I've achieved it. Your powers are getting stronger."

The Pariah came closer, blocking my way.

Ginevra stared at a spot deep inside the tunnel and her eyes widened in fear. "There are others. Run, Gemma! Quick! They're coming. I can't help you! You have to get out of here. They can't leave the tunnels."

I automatically darted forward, dodging the Pariah, and rushed down the tunnel. Ginevra had disappeared, but her voice still filled my head: *Run, Gemma! Get out of there!* The Pariah moved swiftly, as though one with the water. I knew it was behind me because I could hear its eerie whisper in my ear.

To the right! Turn right! Ginevra ordered, guiding me into a broader tunnel that suddenly forked into two smaller ones. From the end of one of them came a pale glow, but my enthusiasm disappeared when I approached it and found it was a dead end. An opening at the end of the other tunnel led outside toward the river, but boulders blocked it. I tried to crawl around them, but it was useless. I was trapped with my back to the wall, and the Pariahs were quickly approaching. I felt like a rabbit in a wolf's den.

Then I remembered the Devil's Stramonium. I searched the satchel for the plant I'd saved, but my hands were shaking too hard. When I finally had it in my fingers, a ghastly whisper echoed through the tunnel, making me start, and the plant slipped from my fingers and disappeared into the water lapping at my feet. I felt for it frantically, but was too panicked to find it.

"Gwen!" I pleaded. "Come back! Damn it!"

I looked over my shoulder to see where the Pariahs were and rushed off in the opposite direction. All at once, a light caught my attention. There was another tunnel! I took it and raced breathlessly toward the twilight as a strange roaring noise grew ever louder, echoing off the dripping tunnel walls around me. I was almost there—I could see the exit. Sprinting the last few yards, I readied myself to jump—and came to a screeching halt before I could plunge into the void. The sound of the waterfall below hit me full on.

I'd almost ended up being washed over it, and it was higher than any waterfall I'd ever seen. Feeling like I'd been punched in the face, I wheeled around, frantic. I was too high up to jump. Taking a deep breath, I realized I had no choice but to go back the way I'd come. A whisper filled the tunnel and brushed my ear. I repressed a shiver and forced myself to continue the desperate search for a way out, but the farther I went the smaller the passageway became until I was ultimately forced to get down on all fours. I felt as if I was living a nightmare. The air grew thicker and danker and my lungs cried out for oxygen.

One of the Pariahs touched my ankle. I pulled it away instantly with a scream that echoed through the cramped space, desperate and grim.

The whispers returned in unison, warning me of their arrival en masse. Suddenly it felt like all the air was gone. I coughed. My legs were heavier and it took tremendous effort to drag them across the damp ground.

There's an exit! I jumped when I heard Ginevra's sharp voice in my head, realizing only then that I was on the verge of passing out. *Come on, Gemma! Hang in there. You're almost there!*

I gritted my teeth in a final effort and a dim light reached me from the end of the passageway. I crawled forward, staring at it, afraid it would vanish. I'd learned by that time that nothing could be taken for granted in that accursed place. When I finally made it to the opening, I dragged myself out on my knees, exhausted, and avidly gulped down the air of twilight.

Get up, Gemma! Get out of there! The urgency in Ginevra's voice made me look behind me. The Pariahs had slipped out of the tunnel and flowed over to me. I looked at them in fear as they surrounded me.

"You said they couldn't come outside!" I shouted at Ginevra.

It used to be that way! They must have evolved! she said, panic in her voice. *Run, Gemma! Run away! Now!* Her voice faded, carried away by the wind until it vanished.

I got up and began running through the forest, but the Pariahs followed me like ghosts, whispering in my ears in an unknown language. I could sense their longing to possess me. They must not have eaten for months, because they clearly had no intention of letting me go.

"Gwen!" I cried out for Ginevra's help, afraid I couldn't hold out much longer, but she was nowhere to be found. Our connection had been broken. I squeezed my eyes shut in an effort to contact her.

Suddenly the threatening growl of a big cat sliced through the air and filled the forest. I opened my eyes and froze. The black panther stood in front of me. We stared at each other for a long moment. I lifted my eyes and my heart shot to my throat. Behind the panther, beyond a thick patch of trees, surrounded by a forest of black stone, stood the Castle, challenging the sky. How absurd it was that I would die there, only a few steps from it.

The panther moved toward me and I stepped back, but a spine-chilling whisper touched my ears. The Pariahs were closing in. I found myself between a rock and a hard place, unsure which fate would be worse—dying by their hand or being devoured by the feline.

All at once, to my amazement, the panther bowed its head without taking its eyes off mine, just like the wolves had done. I stared at it, mystified, and saw something familiar in its green eyes. I felt I'd seen them before, but the idea was too ludicrous to be true. Was it possible that—

I pushed the thought out of my mind and moved toward it warily. The panther didn't move. Instead, its eyes lingered on mine as though to convey a message—an urgent one. I stepped around it and proceeded toward the Castle with long strides, urged on by the murmurs coming from behind me. I couldn't believe it was actually there. A vast, black castle. Foreboding. Magnificent. And dangerous.

A threatening growl made me spin around. My heart skipped a beat when I saw the panther had disappeared. In its place was a hooded figure, its back turned to me. I stared in shock as a wave of energy burst from the figure's palms, disintegrating the Pariahs.

We were the only ones left in the grim surroundings. The figure turned to look at me, its face concealed by the hood.

Do not resist me. The voice was sensual and hypnotic in my head as I struggled to block it. *Let me in.*

A shiver ran through me as the figure quickly covered the distance separating us. Unable to move a muscle, I braced for impact but instead it stopped in front of me and lowered its hood. Two jade-green eyes smiled at me. A strange warmth filled my head and suddenly I could no longer feel my legs.

"Gemma!"

I felt her arms around my body as consciousness left me. Yet there, comforted by Anya's voice, for the first time I felt safe. I closed my eyes and let the shadows carry me away.

"Was it you who brought her here?"

A voice forced its way into the darkness I drifted in. It sounded muffled and distant, from another dimension. I was confused, with no idea where I was.

"She got here on her own," another voice said defiantly.

"Certainly not without your help."

The hostility that oozed from those words penetrated the dark cloud fogging my mind and I recognized the voice. Devina.

"Sophìa told me to protect her!"

Anya.

I tried to force my body to react, but my mind seemed unable to find a way to communicate with my muscles.

"The Empress won't be pleased when I tell her how you tried to get in her way; how you left her in danger, at the mercy of the Damned. Do you have any idea what she had to endure?! You may be Sophia's Specter, but that doesn't give you the right to disobey her orders."

The crack of a whip pierced the air: Devina's threatening response to Anya's scornful accusations. I felt my body grow heavier, as though I was slowly regaining my senses.

After a pause, Devina's voice came again, her tone dramatically different. "Oh, good." She gave a light laugh as I struggled to emerge. "The Spartan is coming to."

Something in those words sent a shock through me. I struggled with all my might until the veil separating me from them began to dissolve. My eyelids fluttered. When I finally managed to keep them open I found myself in a giant chamber full of cushions, draperies, and tapestries that adorned the walls with mystical elegance. I blinked, trying to focus. The ceiling was so high that looking up at it made me dizzy. With an effort, I pushed myself up onto my elbows and discovered I was lying on a pile of black cushions that felt like silk to the touch.

A soft creak made me turn and notice a door. It was ajar. I got up and took a step toward it but froze when I spotted two panthers guarding it on the other side. One of them had faint leopard spots on its black fur.

"Keep your hands off him, Dev."

I started, surprised to hear the voices again. So it hadn't been just a dream, I really had heard them. I tried to follow the sound and found myself facing another massive wooden door, closed this time. I leaned against it so I could hear better.

"Don't you think you're taking this protective role a bit too seriously? You're a Witch, not her nanny."

"She's one of us, whether you like the idea or not."

I gripped the handle, hoping the room would stop spinning, and found that the door wasn't locked.

"Do you honestly think I care?" Devina's voice was suddenly more sensual, dropping an octave. "After all, he and I have spent a lot of time together lately. Enough for me to claim him."

I opened the door a crack as the silence was broken by another, more familiar sound. I couldn't be sure I hadn't just imagined it, though, because at that moment a shooting pain gripped my temples. I squeezed the door handle, waiting for the pain to ease, then looked around for Devina and recognized her copper-colored locks.

She was standing beside a bare-chested man, clearly trying to seduce him. There must have been someone else with them but the image continued to blur before my eyes. I felt dazed like never before and couldn't make any of them out clearly. On top of that, my head was pounding excruciatingly from the effort of blocking off my mind. I couldn't risk letting Devina discover me.

The man growled at her. That growl, the sound of a ferocious animal trapped in a cage, echoed through the dark rooms of my mind and shook the part of me that was still at the mercy of the shadows. I summoned my courage and opened the door a little more.

The blurred image split into two and then grew clear . . . and I saw him. "Don't touch me, bitch." A tremor rocked my heart when I heard his voice.

Evan.

I wanted to shout but could only do so in my mind. My low groan, however, drew their attention. My eyes instantly locked onto his as a single tear made its way down my cheek.

"Gemma?" His lips whispered my name, his eyes filling with astonishment. I stood frozen, overwhelmed with emotion, afraid it was only a dream. "GEMMA!" Evan's desperate shout thundered off the walls and trembled in my heart as he struggled to break free from the chains that bound him to the rock.

"EVAN!!" The barrier holding back my emotions burst and I flew to him, tears flooding my eyes. The two panthers instantly leapt out in front of me, blocking me, but an uncontrollable wave of dark energy washed over me, hurling the beasts out of my path. My body collided with Evan's. He threw his arms around me and held me tight.

"Evan!" I rested my forehead on his, my tearful eyes prisoners of his loving gaze. Everything else faded into obscurity.

"Jamie . . ." He sank his hand into my hair, clasped the nape of my neck, and pressed his lips against mine in a desperate kiss. A kiss that tasted of salt and blood. A kiss that tasted of pain and infinite love. Of us.

"You're here." Hot tears continued to slide down my cheeks as every part of me trembled, once again wrapped in his embrace. "You're here. It's really you . . ." My voice broke with emotion. I thought I had lost him, but there he was with me.

"You have to get out of here." His eyes bored into mine, desperate. "It's dangerous," he whispered onto my lips, cupping my face in his hands as I shook my head between them.

"No. I'm not going anywhere without you."

Evan stroked my bottom lip with his thumb and closed his eyes. "Gemma, you've got—"

"Enough." Our eyes darted to the side in unison at the sound of Devina's icy voice. "I have had quite enough."

"Wait, NO!"

Devina ignored Anya's shout and hurled a thunderbolt at me. My eyes widened and I couldn't move. With a savage howl Evan ripped the chains out of the wall and shielded me with his body, taking the blow on his bare back. His scream shook the room.

"Evan!"

He clung to me, his muscles jerking from the pain. "You recovered quickly this time," Devina told him mockingly. Evan turned and fixed his eyes on hers, maintaining an icy calm.

"Devina, stop it!" Anya shouted. Her Sister ignored her, her face transformed into a mask of evil. Evan gritted his teeth and crumpled to his knees as a new attack from Devina tore a shriek from him.

"Evan!" I threw myself onto him, but I could see his suffering was excruciating. He seemed to be burning up from the inside.

"I said stop it. Now!" Anya shouted.

"I don't take orders," Devina replied icily. "Much less from you."

"Stop it, please!" I begged her, my eyes filled with tears as Evan tensed his muscles, though he defiantly held Devina's gaze. "That's enough! What are you doing to him?!" I was on the brink of despair.

"If you really must know, I created a force field inside him," she replied with a sly smile. "I can make it expand until he explodes." Evan howled again, wracked with pain.

"You're killing him! Stop it!" I pleaded, distraught.

Devina laughed. "He can't die any more than he has, not if he's already here. But I can inflict a great deal of pain on him." Vindictiveness flickered in her eyes. "Of course, if I did it to you . . ."

"Don't. Touch. Her," Evan growled, his silvery eyes aflame with rage.

Unexpectedly, Anya stepped protectively in front of us and Evan crumpled forward, exhausted.

"Evan!" I tried to hold him up, clasping him in my arms, and he squeezed my hand.

"You've had enough fun," Anya told Devina firmly.

Devina shot her an icy glare. "Get out of the way. This is none of your affair," she warned.

"I don't take orders from you either—not when they go against Sophia's. The *Empress* ordered me to protect her, and that's what I'm doing."

They stared at each other, nose to nose, in a tacit challenge.

"She may have given you instructions but while she's gone I'm the one giving orders. *I'm* her Specter. Where the hell are the Drusas?!" she called without taking her eyes off Anya.

Two panthers padded over and stopped at Devina's feet, their heads bowed. From what I had gathered, Drusas were guards. Each of the Sisters had her own role to play. There was no internal hierarchy—except when Devina was around.

"Safria! Nerea! Throw them into the dungeons," Devina ordered. Her face twisted into a grin. "Separate them, naturally. If one of them speaks on the way there, punish the other one."

The panthers bowed their heads submissively. A second later their bodies lengthened, taking on a human appearance. The two Witches looked like Amazons. They wore dark-brown leather shorts and vests of reddish-brown fur and were barefoot, with only a strip of brown leather running from their big toes to their ankles. From there it wound its way up their legs like a serpent. One of them had yellowish eyes like the Dakor coiled around her wrist and long blond hair spotted at the tips like leopard's fur. The other had dark skin, blue eyes, and thick, curly, artfully braided hair. Her Dakor was wrapped around her thigh. Each wore a small braid across her forehead like a diadem or a symbol.

A hostile energy crept up my legs and suddenly I found myself standing, Evan beside me, as an invisible force pushed us to move against our will. I looked back at Anya and she stared at me, an expression of regret on her face, until we went through the door and she disappeared from view.

The two Witches escorted us through the Castle in single file, our hands behind our backs. Evan's wrists still bore what was left of the chains that had imprisoned him. Their occasional clank comforted me, reminding me he was still behind me though I couldn't see him. The thought that he was there with me was all that counted. Suddenly everything had regained meaning. It didn't matter if I stayed there forever as long as he was alive.

We made our way down a hallway that seemed endless, its walls made of some kind of polished black stone I'd never seen before. The entire fortress seemed to have been carved out of a massive black diamond. Black silk drapes covered its broad windows and crystal sconces illuminated the rooms. The black floor had a strange glow to it that almost made it look like it was lined with silk. Even the butterflies I saw fluttering near the ceiling at times were black. They seemed frightened, as though they also wanted to escape.

Outside, we found ourselves in an inner courtyard enclosed by various wings of the Castle, joined together by tall, ominous-looking towers. The courtyard looked like a battlefield: lots of Witches wearing Amazon outfits were facing each other in open combat; it must have been where they trained. One of them turned toward me, her expression still fiery from battle. She moved like a panther in her black outfit, but her incredible blue eyes stood out like bright stars and her long white hair was tipped with a dazzling cascade of black diamonds.

Nausyka. The name filled my head. I didn't know where it had come from, but I was sure it was what the Witch was called. A black panther leapt at her with a roar and the two Witches resumed their fight.

Some of them used magic, transforming in midair and turning the forces of nature to their advantage, while others engaged in hand-to-hand combat, moving in a dark dance like graceful felines battling over their next meal. I found it spellbinding. At first I was appalled by how ferociously they were fighting, but then I stared at them, fascinated, until we were taken into another wing of the Castle.

We entered a vast hall full of silk cushions and draperies. It must have been some sort of temple of pleasure: hordes of Witches were entertaining themselves with their lovers. The males must once have been Subterraneans, but now they were mere playthings in the Witches' hands, helplessly addicted to their mistresses' blood. I thought I glimpsed a familiar face among them, but what they were doing forced me to look away in embarrassment.

Leaving the pit of perdition behind, we walked down another long hallway. Just as I was wondering if they would lock us up in one of the black crystal towers I'd seen from the courtyard, we started down a flight of stairs that seemed to descend infinitely into an even darker and more ominous Hell.

The passageway was so narrow I could feel Evan's warmth right behind me. Neither of us dared speak out of fear for the other's safety, but I could hear his breathing and that was enough for me. The farther down we went, the less light there was. Finally we reached a long hallway full of cells. I jumped when a prisoner slammed against the bars and reached out to grab me, his face gaunt and his eyes darkened with hunger. Evan rushed at him in my defense, pushing past one of the Witches. His body touched mine for a second, filling me with warmth, but the Drusas shoved us forward toward an isolated wing of the dungeon at the end of which were two thick wooden cell doors similar to the one Ginevra had imprisoned Desdemona behind.

"We're there," one of the two Witches said, her tone flat.

"Evan!" I broke free from the Witch's grip and ran toward him. His arms held me tight. As though he'd never left me, our bodies enmeshed like two perfectly fitting halves of some mechanism. I couldn't bear for them to separate us again, but the Drusa yanked me away by the shoulders.

"Let her go!" Evan tried to fight, but could do nothing against the Witches' dark powers.

"Why don't you take a nap, little Angel?"

"No!" I screamed as the Dakor coiled around the Witch's arm sank his fangs into Evan's flesh. "Evan!"

The Witch shoved him into one of the cells and slammed the door shut. I screamed his name in desperation, squirming in the Witch's clutches, but she pushed me into the cell next to his, freed my wrists, and closed the door. I slammed my body against the wooden door, pounding it with my fists, cursing at the two Witches.

Before walking away, one of the Sisters bowed her head slightly. "I'm sorry." She looked at me, her eyes full of remorse. "Devina's orders." From her expression I could tell there wasn't anything she could do about it.

I leaned against the door, my forehead pressed to the hard wood, and felt the tears sting my eyes. "Evan . . ." The cell was dark and cold and not a sound came from the adjacent one. I rested my shoulders against the door and slid down to the floor, burying my head on my knees. The cell seemed so familiar to me—it felt like I'd already been locked up there. Then I remembered: it had happened in a premonitory dream the Witches had induced. Overcome, I sobbed harder, my tears choking me. They had foreseen everything—how could I fight against their power? My ridiculous plan had no chance of working. Evan and I would never find a way to escape from the fortress together. There was only one thing I could do: sacrifice myself so they would set him free and hope I could resist the evil that would attempt to annihilate me. For a long time my one wish had been to see Evan again, even if it was only one last time, and now I had to keep my word. A tear wet my lips, bitter as poison. I'd found Evan, but fate would part us again, because I would have to swear my loyalty to the Witches. I had no choice. Suddenly the thought of escaping with Evan seemed absurd. We were children of two different worlds: good and evil. I belonged to the Witches and no one could change that. But I would find a way to bear it. Anything, to save Evan. Anything, to know he was alive, somewhere in the world, even if he was far from me.

Wracked with sobs, I huddled on the stone floor. Slowly but surely my exhaustion won out and I slid into sleep.

When I opened my eyes, I realized I was shivering from the cold. "Gemma!"

A tremor shook my heart at the sound of his voice. "Evan!" I bolted awake and searched for him in the darkness.

"Over here!"

I turned toward his voice. In the wall separating us was a narrow floor-to-ceiling gap with thick iron bars through which I could see Evan's eyes. I rushed to him. "Evan!" I clasped my hands over his fists that were gripping the iron bars and stroked his wrists, still prisoners of the chains. It broke my heart to see him like that, his knuckles bloodied and blood encrusted on his face.

Evan unclenched his fists and touched his palms to mine as our eyes—silent messengers—bridged the painful distance between us. "I waited for you to wake up." He reached out and stroked my cheek, his eyes on mine, as though afraid I might disappear. "You're so beautiful." I was filthy, my hands worn and my dress ripped, but he didn't care. There was pain in his whisper. The pain of nostalgia.

I rested my forehead against the bars and he did the same. I couldn't believe he was actually there, that it wasn't just another dream. So close and yet so infinitely far away. I stared at his lips. Feeling the warmth of his breath so near made me quiver, though I knew I couldn't bridge the distance between us. As though shaken by the same desire, he stroked my bottom lip with his thumb. I closed my eyes, emotion trembling through me.

"You need to drink something."

I slowly opened my eyes. His voice still seemed like a figment of my imagination, but the instant my eyes met his caring gaze, the tears threatened to overwhelm me again. After everything I'd been through, I couldn't believe Evan was finally there.

He slid his hands through the bars, cupped them, and concentrated. I waited silently, wondering what he was doing, looking back and forth between his face and his hands. A small bubble of water slowly surfaced on his palms. "It's not much, but drink it."

I moved my lips to his hands, pressed them together on his palm in a light kiss, and tilted my head so he could caress my cheek. "I felt like I was dying without you," I confessed, my eyes closed as I remembered the desperation that still lived in my heart.

"I serve Death, but I had never truly known what death was until the day I lost you. I never stopped hoping I would see you again, even for a second," he said softly. "But you shouldn't have come here. Sooner or later I would have found my way back to you. This place is too dangerous for you."

"I don't care. How could I leave you here after what I did to you?"

"It wasn't your fault," he said, trying to convince me, but my remorse over his death was inconsolable.

"You took the poison from *my lips*. I should have realized it was you. And instead I—I killed you. The day you died I died too."

"You didn't kill me," he whispered, moving his hand to stroke my cheek. "I'm here with you now. No one can separate us ever again."

My eyes shot to his, stricken. How could I bear to tell him that we would soon have to part? Fate had been against us from the beginning and now it had won. Like the sun and the moon that pursued each other eternally without success, Evan and I weren't destined to be together, and I had to accept that.

"Evan, I—"

A sudden clang drew our attention. In the semidarkness, the door to my cell creaked and opened, admitting a hooded figure. I cringed, but Evan squeezed my hand tighter. As she approached me, the woman raised a finger to her lips and uncovered her face.

"Anya! What are you doing here?" I exclaimed in surprise.

"Shh," she said, keeping her voice low. "We don't have much time. Move away from the bars."

Still kneeling opposite each other, Evan and I exchanged wary looks. Then I nodded. "We can trust her," I reassured him, but every trace of doubt had already vanished from his face.

"I know." Evan looked at Anya for a few seconds. "She's been a good friend to me. At least she didn't torture me when she was on guard duty."

Anya gave him a little nod of recognition as he and I moved away from each other. The bars bent before our eyes, creating an opening wide enough for Evan to squeeze through. His shackles broke apart and clattered onto the stone floor. Evan rubbed his wrists in surprise and looked into my eyes. His lips instantly found mine as he held me tight, his hands wandering desperately through my hair.

"You have two hours."

We stopped, suddenly remembering Anya was still there. She raised her hood but paused by the door, her back to us. "Then I'll have to put things back the way they were. I'm sorry. I wish there were more I could do."

"Wait!" I said. Anya looked over her shoulder at me. "It was you," I said, voicing the certainty that had taken root in my mind. "In the forest. It was you all along. You followed me. I could sense you."

The Panther has dwelled forever in each of our spirits. The thought filled my mind. It was spoken in my own voice, confusing me momentarily as to its origin. Anya gave a little nod, confirming my suspicion.

"Then it was you who killed Ahrec. But why? He wasn't going to hurt me." I let the sentence hang in the silence and waited for her reply. That was what Ahrec had been trying to tell me: *They're protecting you.*

Her emotionless voice broke the silence of the cell. "The Dreide wouldn't have given him his freedom. He could never have left this place. No one goes back. If he had crossed through the gates his body would have disintegrated, but he didn't realize that. I read his mind: he was struggling with himself," she explained. "His human part was fighting not to harm you, but the other part was ready to attack. He was on the verge of losing control and I couldn't let him do that. I watched over you from the start, though Devina constantly tried to prevent me from doing it. Watch out for her," she warned. She turned to go, but Evan stopped her again.

"Thank you," he said. Anya paused, waiting. "For taking care of her," Evan finished.

She nodded and reached for the door, but something seemed to be holding her there. "How is Gwen?" she asked after a long silence.

Gwen. Anya was the only one of her Sisters that called Ginevra by that name. "She told me about you," I said. Anya smiled beneath her hood. "I could tell she cared a lot about you. That's what made me trust you."

"I've never stopped thinking about her," she said, a hint of bitterness in her voice. "But I'm happy about the choice she made. I wasn't as brave."

"You mean—"

"His name was Alexey, but our lives were destined to part."

"I'm sorry," I whispered, dismayed.

"Don't be." Poised on the threshold, Anya turned to look me in the eye. "I'm the one who should have fought for him. But that was long ago." I gulped, wondering if her words were meant as a warning for me.

"I'll return in two hours. Meanwhile, I'll make sure no one disturbs you." She cast me a last glance and closed the cell door, leaving us on the floor clinging to each other.

My eyes lingered on the door as I tried to understand what she'd been attempting to tell me. Was there possibly a way out of my predestined fate? How could I save Evan if I refused to succumb to them?

"What are you thinking about?" Evan's low voice made me start. He tenderly brushed my hair from my shoulder. "Judging from the look on your face, it can't be pleasant."

I took his hand and clasped it in mine, not wanting him to think I wasn't happy he was there with me. "Evan—" I looked into his eyes and he frowned, puzzled.

"Why are you staring at me as if this is the last time you're going to be with me?" I turned away and his hand gently slid into my hair, reclaiming my attention. "We're together now." He rested his forehead against my temple and a light kiss caressed my skin. I closed my eyes, unable to explain to Evan what I was going to do. "Gemma?"

"I'm one of them," I blurted. His hand froze on my neck. "I . . . I'm a Witch. I belong to them."

A tear slid silently down my cheek and Evan slowly brushed it away. "You're mine," he said, contradicting me. "You belong only to me."

I shook my head in his hand. "I'm going to have to swear an oath of loyalty to them. My blood is already infected. All that's left for the transformation to be complete is for me to agree."

"Why on earth would you?" he asked sharply.

I raised my eyes to his. "I won't leave you here to be tortured by Devina."

Evan clenched his jaw, instantly understanding my intentions. "You're not going to agree to join them to save me," he said sternly. It almost sounded like an order. He grabbed my face in both hands and his eyes hardened, inches from mine. "I'll never let you do it, Gemma."

In spite of his words, I knew I had no choice.

"If we ever leave this place—whether it's in a day or a lifetime— we're leaving it together. I'm not going without you." My eyes brimmed with tears. I blinked and another teardrop silently descended. "We'll stay here together until we find some way out," he reassured me.

I was quick to protest. "They'll torture you to convince me to join them!" My voice broke from the pain I bore inside.

"Who cares?!" He gripped my shoulders, demanding the eye contact I was trying to deny him. "My only hell has been being away from you. If I can't have you I'll find my way back here."

"I can't, Evan. I can't allow them to torture you. They're already inside me. My nature has already awakened."

His eyes wavered as the truth dawned on him. "So that's why you were able to see me and sense my presence."

I nodded, despondent. "I can't stop it."

He stroked my palm with his thumb like he'd always done, then interlaced his fingers with mine, lowering his voice to a whisper. "Yes you can. We'll stop it together." He looked steadily into my eyes, sealing his vow.

I smiled and held back the tears. Would I be able to fight the part of me that would try to annihilate me? At Evan's side, I felt I could challenge the world.

"They told me, but I thought it was just another one of their tricks," he said. "It must be terrible for you. I can't imagine what you've gone through."

"Can you believe that when I found out, seeing you again was the only thing I could think about? I considered it a fair price to pay."

Evan tenderly stroked my cheek and his face filled with pain. "The very thing that allowed us to meet is the same thing that's threatening to divide us now," he whispered, devastated. He touched my lip with his thumb and gazed into my eyes.

"No one will ever separate us." I squeezed my eyes shut, trying to convince myself. "Now that I've found you again I'll never let you go. Even if they take me, they'll never be able to remove you from my heart. I'll stay by your side. I can fight it."

"If you become a Witch you'll only want to kill me, Gemma. Evil will take you over and you won't even realize it."

"No."

"You won't be able to resist!"

"I'll find a way. Everyone has a dark side, but most people manage to overcome it."

"The people you're talking about don't have the devil's venom in their bodies, Gemma. You can't let them transform you. At that point the evil will be unstoppable."

"Ginevra did it!"

"But after how long? I'm not leaving you in those harpies' clutches for centuries."

"Meeting Simon changed her. I already have you. The love that unites the two of us will save me from them—save me from myself. We each have our own demons to fight. I just need to find the way to face mine so you can be safe. They'll never separate us."

"I won't let you do it," he whispered against my lips, resting his forehead on mine.

"There's nothing you can do to stop me." Another tear slid from my eye and Evan wiped it from my lip. I raised a hand and touched his chest, which was black and blue. "What did they do to you?" My finger followed the deep scars on his shoulders and torso. His jeans were torn and his skin caked with dried blood. It was unbearable. "I'm so sorry," I murmured, but Evan rubbed his forehead against mine and sought my gaze.

"Physical torture I can bear. The real torment was in my heart," he said softly, closing his eyes, a prisoner of the memories. "I suffered the tortures of Hell knowing you were far away without my protection. I'm never going to leave you again."

"Simon and Ginevra risked a lot to protect me."

"And they have my eternal gratitude for that, but I'm going to take care of you from now on." His hand slid down my side, slowly, and his thumb brushed my belly. He looked into my eyes. "Take care of you both."

I stared at him for a long moment, astonished. *He knew.* Evan knew about the baby. "How did—" I began.

He put a hand behind my neck, sank his face into my hair, and drew a deep breath. "Then it's true." His voice told me what was in his heart.

"Does it scare you?" I asked.

Evan stroked my belly with extreme tenderness. "A tiny creature is growing inside you, testimony to the love that binds us. How could that scare me? It's extraordinary. This baby has a part of you and a part of me, and in order to be happy it needs both of us." His voice grew serious. "I'm not going to let you make such a huge sacrifice."

I wanted to nod, but I knew his words wouldn't be enough to release me from my fate. Evan had protected me long enough. The time had come for me to save him. My eyes traced the scars that the poison had burned into his skin. Some were recent. I almost burst into tears at the thought of what he'd endured. It was never going to happen again, I would make sure of that.

Without speaking, I took off his dog tag and put it around his neck, looking him in the eye. "This is where it belongs," I whispered, touching the metal. My fingers lingered on his skin, stroked his chest, and slowly rose to his shoulders. I had longed to have him beside me so many times that my heart ached merely from touching him and reminding myself he was actually there.

I ran my fingers down a scar on his shoulder, then touched my lips to it and sealed them in a tiny kiss. Evan's muscles tightened—whether from pain or emotion, I didn't know. My mouth moved over his skin, alighting on his chest, his abdomen . . . on each and every mark, as though my kisses could erase them. Brimming with desire, our eyes exchanged silent promises. Evan's hands slid down my back, making me tremble. I could happily have died right then, cuddled in his embrace.

As though Evan had heard my thought, he swept the hair from my shoulder and gently touched his lips to my neck, as though asking for my consent. I felt their warmth on my skin, their every movement, as he kissed me tenderly. I closed my eyes and felt his hand slide the dress off my shoulder, baring my skin so his lips could explore it. "My God, have I missed you . . ."

The soft whisper against my skin made me moan. I caressed his abdomen and let him kiss me. Moving of their own free will, my hands slid down and undid the button of his jeans. In the silent cell, Evan breathed deeply, trembling with emotion. Resting a hand on the floor, he gently pushed me back, his mouth lingering on my breast. I closed my eyes and felt his warm hands on me, sliding under my skirt.

A wave of emotion washed over me when he pressed his body against mine. Yearning to erase the distance between us, I could have ripped off the scant fabric of the underwear separating us, the heat of his hard body setting me aflame where our bodies touched. I felt feverish, on the verge of catching fire beneath him.

"I never want to be away from you again. Promise you won't leave me," he whispered against my lips, at once determined and desperate as he laced his fingers with mine. "*Samvicaranam. Samyodhanam.* Stay together. Fight together." He rested his forehead on mine. My heart raced, anxious for me to seal the vow, convinced the evil within me would never be able to penetrate me deeply enough to eradicate my love for him.

"My heart belongs to you forever," I murmured, and suddenly I was certain of it: not even the transformation could end my love for him. That was all I could promise.

Evan closed his eyes, brushed his cheek against mine, and was inside me. I quivered, tingles of pleasure flooding my body. I sank my fingers into his shoulder as he moved inside me, setting me aflame until I lost my mind. His warm chest brushed against my breasts, making me shudder with ecstasy. I clung to him, fusing my body to his, skin on skin. His heat was so familiar . . . I yearned to merge with him, disappear inside him so we would be joined forever. The heat of passion flooded my head, bringing me to the verge of delirium. I gazed at his chest, his arms, trying to memorize every contour, every flexed muscle. The Subterranean tattoo stood out on his forearm, creating a sweet nostalgia in me, imprinting on my mind the ardor of his body, the strength of his arms as he held me, the quiver his hands left behind when they touched me. I'd missed him so much . . .

"I love you, Jamie."

I stared at the soft curve of Evan's lips as they uttered my name, then felt their warmth on my mouth. He took my hand, rested it next to my head and clasped it as though wanting to fuse it forever with his own as he plunged deeper and deeper into me, generating a surge of pleasure with each thrust.

A new heat inundated my body as Evan climaxed inside me, waves of passion surging through every fiber of my being. I quivered as my contracted muscles relaxed. Evan rested his forehead on mine, smiling at me as I lost myself in his gray eyes, longing for a world where no one was after us, a world where we would never have to part.

But no such world existed.

The twilight filtered in through the small barred window that opened to the outside, barely illuminating Evan's features. He was still lying on top of me, his head propped on his palm, his eyes gazing into mine. I couldn't remember ever being so happy and so frightened at the same time. Frightened of what I would be confronting. My heart had already known the pain of separation and couldn't bear it again. Part of me feared I wouldn't be able to banish the evil that would try to separate me from him. Yet I had no choice. I only hoped I would be strong enough to face my demons.

Evan brushed his fingertip over my skin, drawing imaginary lines on my tummy. His face was relaxed, his lips hinting at a smile. I wished I could read his mind, reach wherever it was that he was wandering. Given the look on his face, I presumed it was someplace nice.

"I can't believe it's happening," he said softly before I could ask him. "A baby, Gemma. Before meeting you, I wasn't even sure life made any sense. Then you arrived, and now . . . a baby! It's amazing." I smiled. "How do you think it's possible? I mean, I never thought, never had the faintest idea my life could be so full with—with so many things. But—a baby?" His rambling made me laugh. He was so happy and surprised he couldn't even express his emotions. He ran a hand over his head. "God . . . I never even dared hope something so big might happen to *me*."

"Why shouldn't it have?" I asked, smiling.

"I didn't know I was physically capable. After all, I'm not human."

"You're capable of taking a life with a single touch of your hand. It's not so far-fetched that you could create a life too."

Evan smiled and cast me a strange glance. "Speaking of taking lives, who the hell is *Ahrec*?"

At the sight of the new expression on his face, I couldn't help but smile. "Some guy who helped me escape from a seedy bar full of Lechers, that's all. Your age, more or less."

Evan blinked, looking confused. "What was he doing there? What did he want from you? Down here, nobody gives anyone something for nothing."

I raised an eyebrow, deciding to keep him on pins and needles a little longer. "I'm not sure, but all things considered, he wasn't as bad as the other Souls I ran into." He narrowed his eyes. "You're jealous," I teased, playing with a stray lock of his hair. It was so long and wild it fell down over his silvery eyes, giving him a dangerous look.

He grabbed my wrist and pinned me to the floor, fire in his gaze. "If I hadn't heard he was already dead, I would have tracked him down and killed him."

I looked into his eyes and fell captive to them. He was so handsome, I could have stared at him forever. He was propped up over me, holding my wrists against the floor. From that position his hair fell forward and in the twilight his eyes seemed sharper, inaccessible. No— not inaccessible. *He was mine.* The dog tag dangled between us. I had the urge to grab it and pull him against me; I couldn't stand even that small distance between us. I wanted to fuse with him and not let anyone separate us.

His eyes rested on my lips and my heart leapt to my throat at the unexpressed desire I read there. As though he sensed my heart rate accelerating, Evan leaned down and his mouth found mine with new passion, as though he could never get enough.

He released his grip on my wrists and his hands slid into mine, over my head. I opened my fingers and let him clasp them, interlacing them with his own. He didn't need to be afraid I wasn't his, because I would be forever. His and his alone.

"I can come back later if this is a bad time."

Startled, we looked toward the window from where the male voice had come. I scrambled to pull my dress over me and then propped myself up on my elbows because I couldn't see his face clearly—or more likely because I couldn't believe it was actually who I thought it was. Evan burst out laughing and walked over to the bars to grip his forearm.

"Hey, sunshine, you just going to lie there or are you coming over to say hi?"

My heart raced when it heard the voice again. "Drake?" I gasped, approaching the window cautiously as though he were a ghost.

"At your service, baby doll." He winked at me, a smile lighting up his face. "Need a hand?"

"Drake!" I exclaimed, so excited I risked dropping my dress. Luckily, he noticed in time and turned back to look at Evan.

"It's good to see you again, bro, though I would have chosen a different place—and a better time."

"What are you doing here?" I blushed at the question. Like it wasn't obvious.

Drake cocked his head and checked out the cell. "I could ask you two the same question. This is a pretty weird place to hook up—unless you have *freaky* tastes."

I flushed, trying not to think of the possibility that he'd seen me half-naked. I would definitely have remembered it as one of the most embarrassing moments in my life.

Evan clapped his hand over their locked fists, still smiling. "Good to see you again, bro."

"Okay, we'd better save the thanks for later. We haven't got all day."

"Thanks for what?" I asked, still stunned by his unexpected appearance.

"I'm breaking you out of here—unless you've got any objections, that is."

Evan pulled me in close, his arms around my waist, in a gesture that silently expressed his thoughts. Drake was our only hope. Suddenly the weight of the world was lifted from my shoulders, letting me breathe again. I wouldn't have to sacrifice myself to the Witches in order to save Evan!

"Told you we would find another solution," he whispered in my ear. Then he said to Drake, "All right then, get us out of here. I don't want to stay in this place one more minute."

All at once the door opened with a groan. I jumped as someone slipped into the cell and quickly closed it behind them. The delicious scent of freedom quickly faded. Evan stepped in front of me protectively. My heart did a somersault when I found myself looking into the newcomer's eyes.

"We meet again. Imagine that."

Hearing the sound of his voice rise from the gloom made me shudder. *Faustian.* Encircled by a black mustache and goatee, his lips curved into a smile that in the dim light made my skin crawl. Though the memory of Faust was buried deep inside me, it had never vanished. I could never forget the gleam he'd had in his eyes while he was torturing me. "So you ended up here as well," he said.

Evan kept me behind him. He was ready to spring into action, his muscles tensed and his sharp eyes trained on Faustian.

"Not for long," I replied icily. "I'm only passing through."

"I know. That's why I'm here."

Evan and I looked at each other, confused.

"He's with me," Drake explained.

Evan shot his brother a glance, looking hesitant. "You sure he—"

"He's on our side. It's okay, you can trust him," he repeated, not a shadow of doubt in his voice. "He's the one who brought me here. He saw them taking you to the dungeon, recognized you, and came to find me. Evan, I can't get you out of this place alone. My powers are gone and I'm too weak. He, on the other hand . . ."

"I indulged in a little treat before coming here." Faust raised his eyebrows and headed for the window.

Evan and I stepped aside to let him pass. The treat Faust referred to must have been the Witches' little games, meaning he'd fed on their blood. When we passed through the Witches' temple of pleasure I'd had the vague impression I recognized someone. It must have been him.

Before our wary eyes, Faustian bent the iron bars and turned to look at us as I slipped the sleeves of my dress on and covered my shoulders. "Well? What are you waiting for, a letter of recommendation? Hurry, we don't have much time. If they discover me they'll fry my brain."

"Why are you doing it, then? Why run such a risk, and for us, of all people?" I asked disdainfully, still not sure I could trust him. After all, Evan was the one who had killed him and sent him to Hell.

Faustian looked me in the eye, his expression suddenly serious and tinged with sadness. "There's nothing they can take from me that I haven't already lost." He ran his hand down his neck and seemed to relax. "I understand your misgivings but believe me, I don't resent the two of you for anything that happened. In fact, I was asking for it."

"You couldn't get out of it. It wasn't your choice," Drake said, his voice charged with urgency, "and they realize that." He stared first at me and then at Evan.

Faustian stepped toward us, the dim light from outside illuminating his face. "I was following orders, that's true, but what I did to you *was* my choice." He offered me his hand. I stared at it for a long moment, then looked him in the eye again.

"This is my chance to make amends, if you'll allow me."

I nodded slightly without taking my eyes from his, but couldn't bring myself to shake his hand. I was afraid that if I touched it the past might come back to haunt me. He let his arm go slack at his side.

Evan took me by the waist and lifted me up to the window through which Drake was looking in. I grabbed hold of the bars and Drake pulled me up toward him and out. Even the toxic air of Hell smelled fresh and wonderful after the cell, but I was instantly anxious to see Evan again, to have him at my side and never let him go. I still couldn't be sure it wasn't a trap.

"Get him out, Drake! Get him out!" I begged, but quickly realized there was no need to ask: seconds later I saw Evan at the window. He jumped down beside me and hugged me as though he too had been afraid of never seeing me again.

"You're not coming?" Drake asked Faust.

We looked up at Faustian, but he shrugged. "I wouldn't know where else to go. Besides, there's nothing lacking here."

"There's a cave just past the thicket where we met if you change your mind."

"I'll keep that in mind in case something goes wrong," Faustian replied, not taking his eyes off Drake. "Now go or they'll discover you."

"But what if they discover *you*?" I couldn't help but ask, suddenly worried he might betray us.

"They won't learn anything about you, if that's what's worrying you. I know how to block off my mind—mine and others'. You know that for yourself." I remembered with a shudder how Faustian had kept the others from finding me after he'd kidnapped me. There was no need for him to remind me. "I don't have all my powers any more, but I'll be able to keep them at bay," he added.

"What will happen to you?" Evan asked.

"I'll manage somehow. There was only one Witch standing guard at the back of the hall. I covered my hand with a piece of cloth, pretending to bring you food. I don't think she even noticed me. In fact, this might sound strange, but she seemed to be *pretending* not to notice me."

Anya. It must have been her. My heart warmed at her millionth attempt to help me.

"My friend, that stuff they're giving you must have some pretty nasty side effects if you actually think a Witch pretended not to notice you," Drake joked. "Now get going and be careful. It's not bad having somebody on the inside."

Evan gave Faustian a silent nod of gratitude. "Thank you," I whispered through the semidarkness, "and good luck."

Above us, Faustian winked at me before twisting the bars back into place. "You'll need that more than I will."

I turned and hugged Drake tight, pouring into the gesture all the pain of those months spent without him. The nightmare had begun when we thought he'd been the one ordered to kill me. Though we'd discovered at the very end that he'd actually never betrayed us, we still didn't know the full explanation.

The instant I let go of Drake, Evan took my hand and squeezed it. "Let's get out of here." He smiled at me and joy and hope filled my heart.

"Come on," Drake said in a low voice. "The place I live isn't far away." He turned to look at us, his face unexpectedly bright. "Stella's waiting for us."

DRAKE

"Stella?" Evan asked, voicing what we were both thinking. "Am I understanding you right? You mean *your* Stella?"

"That's the one," Drake replied, a new light in his eyes.

"There are a lot of things you need to explain to us, Drake."

"We've got all the time in the world. Right now we'd better not make her worry."

Amazed by the news, we followed Drake into the mouth of a cave and crossed a dark, foreboding passageway. Evan kept his arm wrapped around my waist reassuringly. I heaved a sigh of relief when we saw a faint light at the end of the tunnel.

The light came from the same luminous rock I'd seen in Xandra's hideaway and later in the underground caves. Drake noticed me staring at it and explained that it was very hard to come by. It was foelstone, a luminous substance that hardened in contact with the air secreted by a ferocious animal. I thought of the glowing cocoons I'd seen in the spider's lair and shuddered.

Drake said Stella had also discovered that Dakor venom—which polluted everything in the area—was highly flammable, and she'd come up with a way to extract it from the spring inside their cave. For a long time she'd used it for heating, to make weapons to defend herself, and also to purify the water. That was how she'd survived.

The room we were in was small but looked comfortable. It seemed to have everything necessary: a table carved out of the rock, two small chairs that stood next to each other, a rudimentary hearth and, in the back, just beyond the spring, a large bed covered with thick furs. Of Stella, however, there was no trace. Evan and I exchanged a look, suspecting that Stella was actually a figment of Drake's imagination, a companion his mind had created to cope with his solitude.

Drake, though, looked around, pensive. "She must have gone out on reconnaissance," he said, a hint of concern in his voice. "I'm sure she'll be back any minute."

Evan and I looked at each other again. He rested a hand on Drake's shoulder. "Hey, bro, you sure you're okay?"

At first, Drake looked at Evan as though he was insulted, but then he smiled. "Yeah, why shouldn't I be?"

Evan shrugged and looked away, embarrassed. Was Drake delusional? "You've been here alone for such a long time . . . I mean, you know . . . It must have been rough on you."

"Absolutely. You can't even imagine. This place can drive you nuts." Drake sat down on a rock outcropping and shook his head. "Fortunately I found my Stella, otherwise I don't know what I would've done. And now I've reunited part of my family! You have no idea how much I missed you guys."

Evan rubbed his neck, embarrassed. "You still have to tell us what happened," he said, probably to avoid talking about Drake's mental state. After all, it was easy to imagine how hard it must have been to suddenly be hurled into that infernal place. I had experienced it for myself and understood his need to seek refuge in a beloved—albeit imaginary—figure. Once he was home, his mental state would stabilize and we would all remember the experience as nothing more than a bad nightmare.

"Just to be clear," Evan continued, subtle sarcasm in his voice, "that wasn't you who kissed Gemma, right?"

"What?!" Drake turned to stare at him, shocked by the question, and Evan's laughter filled the cave.

"Nothing, never mind." Evan looked suddenly relieved, as though a weight had been lifted from him.

"Sounds like I'm not the only one with lots to tell," Drake joked as he started a fire.

"The thing is, I'm not exactly sure when the other guy took your place."

"Hold on." I looked at Evan, a new doubt gripping me. "How did *you* know it wasn't the real Drake? We all thought it was him. We only found out the truth when it was too late—by then you were already gone."

"It's true, I believed it too. I believed it for a long time," he admitted. "During one of her guard-duty shifts, Anya told me what had happened."

"Sorry about that," Drake said as a tiny flame ran along a groove carved into the floor, warming the cave. "It was partly my fault. He caught me off guard and I couldn't stop him. I wanted to warn you but they don't have phones down here—can you believe it?"

I smiled at his carefree tone. I'd missed Drake so much.

"I'm the one who needs to apologize," Evan said. "I should never have doubted you. When I found out the truth, I couldn't believe I ever had."

"There was no way you could've known, and you were right to protect Gemma. I would've done the same thing in your shoes. I'm the one who should have been more alert. I just wasn't expecting an attack. It had been months since anyone had come looking for her and I figured they'd given up. I made the mistake of letting my guard down."

"We all did, so don't feel bad," Evan said.

"Hey, look where we all ended up. You have no idea what I've been through. The guilt and all the worry about what could happen—I knew what that bastard intended to do, but I couldn't help you or warn you. It all happened so fast. Simon and I were down in the workout room training and, like always, I was kidding him about his twisted relationship with Ginevra. She wanted his company during a race that day, so in the end I had to give in. You know what G is like—she always has to have her way. So Simon went to be with her and I started working out alone. I'd just activated an awesome exotic scenario—complete with hot girls cheering me on—when Simon came back. Or at least I thought it was Simon."

Bitterness suddenly filled Drake's face. He couldn't have known it wasn't really his brother. He ran his hands over his shaved head, his gaze lost in the memory. As he spoke, the images of that fateful day filled my mind so vividly I felt as if I were personally witnessing the scene:

"What, back so soon? Your girlfriend give you permission to play with me a little longer?" My laugh echoed off the walls of the workout room, but Simon was strangely serious.

"Something like that," he said.

"Don't worry. This'll be quicker than you think."

"We'll see."

"I'm all yours, bro." I smiled.

We were circling each other, ready to attack, but it was like something about him had changed during the minutes he was gone. I couldn't put my finger on what because he was pretty much ignoring my banter—he just kept staring at me like he was studying me or something.

"Go ahead, gimme all you got . . . or are you waiting for her permission to do that too?" I said to provoke him.

That was when Simon struck his first blow. It was so brutal it knocked the air out of my lungs. I realized something definitely wasn't right.

"Whoa, a little cranky, are we?" I said. He ignored me and continued to attack, barely giving me a chance to defend myself. He was way overdoing it. "Wow, you mean business today. Guess blondie didn't wear you out enough last night?" No response. "C'mon Simon. Is it something I said? Awww, I didn't mean to hurt your little feelings!" I zigzagged to dodge his attacks that were destroying the virtual forest around us. One of his blows grazed my ribs and I stared at him, shocked. I suddenly got serious and asked him, "Can't we talk about it?"

I didn't even see it coming: Simon lunged at me and I ended up sprawled on the floor. My eyes bulged from the excruciating pain fogging my brain, and when I looked down to check out what was causing it, I saw a knife sticking out of my ribs.

Simon had stabbed me. No—not Simon. I realized it couldn't be him. "Who the hell are you?" I stared at him in horror as my body started to lurch and spasm: the knife must have been poisoned. Whoever that bastard was, he'd thought of everything.

Simon's face vanished and the Subterranean showed me his real appearance. "Nothing personal—I just needed a way to become part of the family and get close to the mortal girl. She's so safe here in your fortress, watched over 24/7. I had to come up with something."

"They'll—" A shudder kept me from continuing and rage boiled up inside me as I realized I was dead meat. "They'll never let you near her!" I hissed, my teeth clenched and my body wracked with tremors.

"The poison must have already fried your brain if you haven't figured it out yet: that's why I needed you. As I see it, Gemma is as good as dead, though I'm curious to get to know her a little better. Maybe I'll take my time before killing her."

"They'll hunt you down."

"I'm not afraid of anyone."

"If you kill her, there's nowhere you'll be able to hide from Evan. He'll find you and show you no mercy." I coughed, my sight growing blurry.

"What a shame for him that he'll never find me." I looked up at the Subterranean and flinched at the sight of my own image. *"Because it won't be* me *he'll be hunting down."*

"Next thing I knew, here I was," Drake concluded. I rubbed my arms, unable to stop trembling after hearing his side of the story. "Using my appearance, he'd come into the house and stolen the poison from Ginevra's room. There was no way I could've known the blade was poisoned. He'd planned everything to take my place—that way he could get near Gemma and you guys wouldn't be able to track him down because you wouldn't know what he looked like. When I woke up, I was at the Castle."

"How did you manage to get out of there?" asked Evan, who had listened to the entire story with his elbows on his knees and his head in his hands.

"When I first got here, they gave me an ultimatum: surrender to them or resist and be tortured. The first option had its perks, so I decided not to put up a fight, hoping they'd give me a little breathing room. I'd seen other Subterraneans walking around the Castle wherever they wanted, and I figured it would be a good way to plan an escape. Usually they don't keep any of them under surveillance. After all, if there's no reason for them to rebel against the Witches there's no reason for them to try to escape either. On top of that, their minds are constantly monitored by those harpies. The really hard part was pretending to be subjugated by Kreeshna, the Witch who was supposed to have claimed me back in the day. As you know, when a mortal with the blood of the Children of Eve dies, a Witch comes to tempt him. If he gives in, she becomes his *Amìsha*—she owns his soul and has more privileges with him than her Sisters. In a sense, he becomes her property. Witches are spoiled brats. When they fail to claim a Subterranean's soul they'll stop at nothing until he's theirs."

"Is that why Devina considers you her property?" I asked Evan in a low voice.

It was Devina who centuries ago had had Evan killed and tried to steal his soul, but failed. *The redheaded woman.* Suddenly I realized she'd been sneaking into my dreams for a long time—even before Evan died. When the Witches had come to me in my dreams, their aim had been to awaken the Witch nature hidden inside me. *Her* goal, on the other hand, had been to make me understand she was going to take him from me.

"Exactly. To Devina, Evan is hers, just like I was Kreeshna's. For some of them the pursuit verges on obsession, at least until the Subterranean finally succumbs. Then in most cases they forget about him. Anyway, the first chance I got, I escaped from the Castle. There are so many Subterraneans who've surrendered that often the Witches don't even bother to go looking for the few who disappear. Still, I'll bet Kreeshna is still out hunting for me. She always looked at me like she wasn't convinced I'd really given in to her. I knew I was taking a serious risk by going back, but when I heard about you guys being there I didn't think twice. So now, tell me about you." Drake looked at Evan. "How'd you wind up here? I imagine the Subterranean used the same trick on both of us?"

"Something like that," Evan said vaguely, but Drake insisted on hearing the details. Evan slid his hand behind his neck, thinking out loud. "I took Gemma to see Eden, and when we got back Ginevra and Simon came into my room, talking about racing. That must have been right when the other Subterranean was attacking you. And it was my transgression that must have triggered the hunt for Gemma."

"Of course!" I exclaimed. "While you guys were out I went to the kitchen to get something to eat. Drake surprised me there but I could sense something strange about him." Drake shook his head, confirming my suspicion: it hadn't been him.

"After he got rid of you, he took your place and tried to seduce Gemma before attacking her," Evan mused.

"Which would explain your weird question about me kissing her."

"Yeah. I couldn't get over it—I was devastated. I thought you'd betrayed us, so I threw the fake Drake out, but he attacked us. We should have figured out right away it wasn't you because of how he was avoiding Ginevra. He was afraid of being discovered by her. She could have read his mind or at the very least known from the sound of his voice in his thoughts that he wasn't really you."

"So he killed you in battle? That's hard to believe. He must have—"

"No," I cut in. "Actually, I was the one who killed Evan."

Drake closed his mouth and looked back and forth between us, stunned.

"He outsmarted us," Evan explained, taking my hand. "He tricked us all, and by the time we figured it out it was too late."

I hung my head, overwhelmed with remorse.

"Who's hungry?" The unfamiliar voice filled the little room. Evan stepped in front of me protectively.

Drake shot to his feet and swept the girl up in a hug. "Guys, meet Stella."

Evan and I exchanged a fleeting glance as Drake squeezed Stella again as though he hadn't seen her in days.

"Easy does it!" she said, breathless. "I was just out hunting."

Drake rested his forehead against her, his reproach sweet: "You know you're never supposed to go outside without me."

"I survived for decades without you and I have no intention of dying now. Besides, I imagined Gemma would be hungry!" Stella held up the game she'd caught and Drake smiled at her tenderly.

"Actually, she's not all wrong," I said, hunger twisting my stomach into knots.

Drake took Stella by the hand and led her over to us, beaming.

"So you're Stella—and you actually exist," Evan blurted.

Drake frowned, looking confused. "Huh? What do you mean?" Evan tightened his lips and shrugged nonchalantly.

"We thought some wild animal had eaten your marbles," I joked, and we all burst out laughing. I could barely remember the last time I'd heard the sound of my own laughter. Out of the corner of my eye I looked at Evan, his face illuminated by the firelight, the tattoo standing out on his arm, the golden skin of his bare chest . . . With him there, everything was so simple. The meat even tasted better. The food Ahrec had caught had merely filled the void I'd had in my stomach, but this time I savored each bite because every worry had vanished and in my heart the sun was shining again.

"What about you, Stella? How did you end up here?" I asked as we were eating, unable to imagine why her soul had been damned to Hell. She seemed like a warrior. She had dark skin and exotic charm, and her cheerful nature instantly made me think of a female version of Drake.

"I ran away from my Subterranean," she replied breezily.

Evan couldn't help but laugh. "What do you mean you ran away from your Subterranean? Now there's a first!"

"She sure is something, isn't she?" Drake wrapped his arm around her shoulders and she leaned her head on him. "She refused to leave me. I was still in the war back then and had no idea she'd been killed."

"A woman offered me protection. She asked me what was dearest to my heart—but there was no need to tell her. She *knew*. It was you. She promised I would see you again if I went with her, and I believed her."

"A Witch," I was quick to say.

"Yes, but I didn't know that. She used deception to corrupt me. At least that's what I thought for a long time."

"I'm sorry," I murmured. For some reason I felt I owed her an apology.

"You shouldn't be. I'm grateful to her now. If she hadn't done it, my Drake and I wouldn't be together again."

"Actually, now that you put it that way . . ." I looked around the bare cave walls. "How do you pass the time here? I mean, when you're not busy getting gnawed on by ferocious animals."

Drake and Stella exchanged a complicit glance and I blushed. "We have everything we need here." I was sure Drake was going to crack a joke, but instead he caressed her cheek. It was a side of him I'd never seen before.

"I saw you in the Cowards' village," Stella suddenly confessed. I frowned. "I'm sorry for what they did to you. There was nothing I could do to help you."

I'd been right. The village had seemed to be populated by humans, and that was probably how they preserved some of their humanity. They were too cowardly to kill, but they hadn't thought twice about serving me up to the Indavas in order to save themselves.

"That's okay," I reassured her. "I understand."

"She ran back to tell me what had happened," Drake added. "She didn't know you. Word had spread that you were wearing a Dreide around your neck, but we couldn't have known it was you, of all people."

My eyes shot to Evan's. He was also staring at me, probably wondering what Drake was talking about. Hiding a smile, I shrugged and showed it to him. "This is what Ahrec wanted from me. I was only teasing you before," I explained in a low voice, grinning.

He raised a surprised eyebrow.

"You must be tired," Stella said with concern. She picked up a strange brush that looked like it was made with blunted porcupine quills and began to run it through my hair. "You can take a bath, if you like. Our well is safe, and it's always clean."

"It's true. Every day we use Stella's invention to draw water from the spring and purify it—which leaves us with fresh poison that we turn into fuel, weapons, and food. The rock already filters out most of the poison, but we still need to completely purify the water to get as much as we need."

"It was so brave of you to decide to come here and save Evan. I can imagine what you must have gone through. You must be exhausted. Why don't you lie down on our bed for a while? It's not very comfortable but—"

"Actually I've never been so awake in my whole life. What do you say we start walking? The medallion will help get us out, but first we need to reach the crest above the river, at the source of the waterfall."

Evan moved closer to me and whispered sweetly in my ear: "Do you feel up to it? If you want, we can wait a while longer until you've rested."

"What I want is to get of this place," I said readily. I took his hand and looked him in the eye. "With you."

"What about the baby? Wouldn't it be better for him if you conserved your strength?"

I shook my head. I couldn't wait to get out of there and forget that nightmare forever. "Don't worry about him. Ginevra put a protective spell on him before I left." I stroked my belly and Evan looked into my eyes. "He's safe." I smiled, reading the sweetness in his gaze.

"A baby?!" Drake boomed. "No way, guys! Seriously?" He strode over and suffocated us in a warm embrace. "I'm gonna be an uncle and you don't even tell me?!"

I smiled at him and Stella clapped her hands, full of enthusiasm. "That's wonderful! Congratulations!"

Evan and Drake high-fived, clasped forearms, and gave each other friendly slaps on the back. "Who would of thought?!" Drake exclaimed, still astonished.

"Yeah," Evan said. "I still can't believe it myself."

"Guys?" I was forced to interrupt them. "You'll have all the time you want for congratulations later on, but right now we'd better start walking. It won't be easy to reach the portal," I warned. I was eager to get home as quickly as possible.

"I agree," Evan said. "Simon and Ginevra will be so happy to see us all together again!"

Something in his words made Drake's face darken. "I'm afraid you're going to have to say hi to them for me."

Evan and I looked at each other in alarm. "What do you mean? Aren't you and Stella coming with us?" Stella went to Drake, took his hand, and rested her head on his shoulder.

"Drake, what's going on?" I gasped.

"Sorry, sunshine." He shrugged sadly. "Stella can't leave this place. We've seen other Souls try it. They get disintegrated on the spot. She doesn't have a human body to go back to, which means she has to stay here. And I have to protect her. My place is with her."

Evan and I continued to stare at them, helpless and unsure what to say.

He smiled. "All things considered, it's not so bad down here." He slid his arm around Stella's waist and gazed at her tenderly. "I've got everything I need."

"Drake—"

"I left her once—I'm not going to leave her again." His voice was so determined I couldn't reply.

Evan approached his brother and clasped his fist in his, chest to chest. "You sure you're going to be okay?"

Drake nodded. "When I found her she was on the verge of losing her humanity, and I would have met with the same fate. Finding each other again saved us both. We're safe here. We hunt for game so we don't hurt anybody. We live a private life—socializing around these parts isn't a good idea. Besides, I'm hoping to run into my Subterranean impersonator one day so I can give him the warm welcome he deserves."

"We'll never forget you. Your absence is going to leave a void in our lives, but I would do the same if I were in your shoes."

"Sooner or later we're bound to meet again, bro, don't you think?"

"Yeah, just don't count on it being sooner!"

I walked over to hug Drake and a teardrop escaped my control.

"I'm going to miss you too, sunshine. Hey, don't be sad for me— I've never been so happy before."

"I understand," I murmured, nodding.

"Good luck, bro." Evan hugged him, clapping his shoulder.

"Good luck. Be careful and keep a low profile. And every so often tell the little guy who's on the way about old Uncle Drake!" He winked at me, making me smile through my tears. "But now, get going. I'm sure Simon and Ginevra are worried about you guys."

I hugged Stella too. Evan took my hand and led me out of the cave. I turned around to give them one last look. I couldn't believe I would never see Drake again.

Evan squeezed my hand, drawing my gaze, and I smiled at him. I knew exactly what he was thinking, what he was trying to tell me. It didn't matter where we were—Heaven or Hell—as long as we were together. Deep down, I knew Drake had also found his happiness in Stella.

TOWARD FREEDOM

"Do you think Anya's noticed we're gone? She said she would be back in two hours. How long do you think it's been?"

Evan kissed my temple and squeezed my hand. "I don't know. When I'm with you time doesn't matter any more—it disappears along with the rest of the world."

I smiled. I'd forgotten how Evan could free my heart of all its agony. "I still can't believe I found you." It was like a dream. I held Evan's hand tight, afraid he might disappear, but his warmth was so real my heart continued to skip beats. For months I'd believed I'd lost him and my world had turned black. The pain was still vivid, and part of me would preserve the memory forever. But now he was with me again, his hand in mine. Every time his silvery eyes sought mine I felt like I was flying. Even if it were a dream, I thought, I would want to live in it forever and never wake up, because the real life I'd endured without Evan was too painful. It seemed impossible that the nightmare was over and that we would soon be home together.

"I always told you you were brave." Evan touched his thumb to the tip of my nose. "But I had no idea *how* brave. Until now, I was always the crazy one—but you fought your way through *Hell* to come get me."

"You're wrong," I said. "I came here to escape the hell I was living in day after day without you."

I'd faced dangers Evan couldn't even have imagined, but my biggest fear had vanished the second I'd discovered he was still alive. And I had done it. My heart leapt at the thought. Despite everything, I had found Evan. Nothing would ever come between us again.

"I can't help thinking about how insane and dangerous your plan was," he said reproachfully, his jaw clenched.

"Aren't you the one who always said we needed to experience emotions to the fullest, no matter how crazy they were?"

"Yes, but not without me. If something had happened to you I wouldn't be able to bear it. I'm the one who's supposed to protect you, not the other way around."

"I would never have left you here alone, not even if it meant having to stay here myself. When I lost you something broke inside me. I thought I would never heal. But then I found out you were still alive and the wound healed, because nothing and no one could have kept me from coming to find you."

Evan stopped in his tracks, pulled me against him, and held me tight. My body clung to his, feeling every muscle. He breathed into my hair, pouring out all the tension he'd accumulated. "I've lived for over three centuries, but the last months without you were the longest, hardest ones of my existence," he whispered, touching his lips to my ear. "I'll never let anyone separate us again."

"As long as I live—whether it's a day or eighty more years—the only thing I want is you by my side," I told him. Nothing else mattered to me.

Evan moved his head slightly, stirring my hair. "Not even death will be a threat to us any longer." Puzzled by his reply, I leaned back to look him in the face, and his silver-gray eyes narrowed on mine. "I've thought it over and I think there's a solution that will end all our problems. I could go on protecting you forever, but I don't want your life to be constantly in jeopardy—I can't bear it. No one's going to hunt you down again."

"What are you talking about, Evan? What's your plan?" I stared at him eagerly.

"I spent a long time thinking about how to solve the problem. I came up with the answer before I died, but I didn't have the chance to tell you. Ambrosia. It will give you eternal life."

"The forbidden fruit?! Evan, are you crazy?! Do you have any idea what that action might trigger? Haven't you thought about the consequences?"

"I don't care. To hell with rules and consequences!" he growled in exasperation. "I can't lose you again—not a day from now or even a hundred years from now." His gaze grew tender on mine as he stroked my cheek. "I want you with me, Jamie." He leaned in until we were forehead to forehead, his gray eyes on mine. "This time forever."

"Evan . . ." I couldn't let him take such a foolish risk for me—not without knowing what might happen as a result. "They might punish you." I was almost pleading. He didn't seem to be leaving me much choice.

"I don't care." He shook his head, his forehead still resting on mine. "I don't care," he repeated in a whisper. "I never want to lose you."

"I have the seed of evil inside me," I reminded him. "I can't go back to Eden. That's how they found me the first time."

"You're not one of them and you never will be. Ambrosia is the divine fruit—it'll sever all your ties with them, cancel every trace."

"Are you sure about that? How do you know they won't separate us to punish us?" A cascade of doubts filled my head, but Evan tenderly brushed his thumb across my lip.

"Everything's going to be fine," he whispered against my mouth. "I promise. Everything's going to be fine, Jamie. Trust me."

I nodded and then his lips were on mine, banishing every other thought. Heaven, Hell, Witches, Subterraneans—all the barriers shattered and everything blended together as I lost myself in Evan's embrace. The forest whirled around us and I forgot who I was.

"Let's find a place to rest," he said in a low voice, separating his lips from mine.

"I don't need to. I'm not tired," I lied, but my face gave me away.

"There are some caves down there." He took my hand and guided me toward them. "You might not be tired, but my powers are gone and I wouldn't mind a few hours of rest." He smiled, but this time I suspected he was the one lying.

I followed him because actually I wasn't sure myself I could keep going much longer. Sleeping for a little while wouldn't change anything. We'd already walked for hours, staying beneath the thick treetops to avoid being seen, but this time we never lost sight of the river. I realized how difficult our lives might become if we did.

"Here, this looks perfect," Evan said as we entered a small cave. I peered around through the darkness and suddenly realized all my fear had vanished because with Evan I finally felt safe.

He sat down on the ground, his back against the wall and his arms resting on his knees, looking authentically tired. I sat down between his legs, curling up against him, my back against his chest. His arm encircled me, making me feel protected. Suddenly my eyelids grew heavy and I had to fight to keep them open.

"Sleep." He interlaced his fingers with mine, filling me with warmth. "I'll be right here when you wake up." Evan rested his head against the wall behind mine and, as if by magic, every part of me surrendered to sleep.

"What was that?" I bolted awake, gasping for air, my heart racing at the spine-chilling murmur that had woken me.

"Shh . . . it was just a nightmare." Evan ran his hand over my head and I calmed down. He was still there. "It's nothing. Just a bad dream." He kissed my forehead as a shiver carried off the remnants of the dream.

I raised my head to look at him and he smiled at me. Then I heard the murmur. "There it is again!" I said in a low voice, the blood draining from my face. Evan pricked his ears and scanned the darkness of the cave.

It hadn't been a nightmare. I'd heard the sinister murmur of mingled voices. His muscles tensed, telling me the noise had reached him too. "How could you have heard it in your sleep?"

"It seems my senses are sharper here in Hell."

He cautiously got up and gestured for me not to move. "Evan," I whispered, but he held a finger to his lips, peering through the darkness.

"You're right. Someone's here. I heard it too."

"Let's get out of here," I begged him, but he continued to advance cautiously toward the sound. "Evan," I urged, frightened. We had no idea what kind of creature might be lurking in that cave and I had no intention of finding out. But he seemed undaunted and determined.

"Let's just go, please?" I joined him and the murmur grew stronger.

"Stay back," he warned in a low voice, turning a dark corner.

"This is no time to go snooping." I took his hand. He turned to look at me and seemed to understand.

"All right, let's get out of here," he agreed. I nodded and gave a sigh of relief.

Just as we headed toward the mouth of the cave, something grabbed Evan by the shoulder. We spun around and a scream escaped me at the sight of the hideous faceless creature before us. Reacting instinctively, Evan knocked its head off its shoulders with one swift blow. The creature fell to its knees, let out a deafening shriek that echoed through the cave, and vanished. Alerted by the first one's cry, an entire group of the creatures that were huddled up as though in prayer in a corner of the cave, whipped their heads around toward us.

"Run!" Evan ordered. A shudder ran down my spine, but he'd already grabbed my hand and pulled me outside.

"I told you we should have ignored it!" I said, my breath coming in gasps. Maintaining my speed, I turned around and saw the group of creatures spilling out of the cave in pursuit. They moved in fits and starts as though following us based only on our scent. "They're following us! Run! Don't stop!"

"What the hell are they?!" Evan exclaimed without slowing his pace. He cursed under his breath.

"Zombies!" I screamed into the wind as a shiver ran over my skin.

"How do you know that?!" he asked, surprised.

"It's not like I took a bus tour to the Castle," I shot back, rolling my eyes. "Did you think braving the terrors of Hell to save you was a joyride?" Evan shook his head, both concerned and impressed. "The river, Evan! We've got to follow the river! Don't lose sight of it or it'll be the end of us!" I shouted, panicking.

"Damn it!" Evan yelled, looking back at the zombies. "Faster! They're gaining on us!"

I took another quick look behind me and trembled. Tattered clothing dangled from their lacerated, blood-spattered bodies, and their unnatural gait alone gave me the creeps. Their faces—deformed by their total lack of humanity—consisted of two small, closely set cavities that served as nostrils, and wide, threatening mouths. I held back a shudder at the thought that they used them to devour their prey whole, like snakes.

"Evan!" I shouted, terrified by how close they were. Something occurred to me and I let go of his hand. Still running, I searched my satchel, trying not to trip in the process, and pulled out the canteen full of poison-tainted water.

"What are you doing?!" Evan shouted. "Keep running, Gemma!"

My hands trembling, I turned to the closest zombie and splashed some of the water in its face. The creature jumped and pounced on me, knocking me to the ground. I wailed in horror, but in seconds it exploded in a cloud of dust. I coughed and covered my mouth to avoid breathing in the toxic ashes. Evan raced back and helped me to my feet.

"There are too many of them! We'll never make it! We've got to shake them, Gemma, run! Run!" Evan shouted. "We need to get out of here, and fast!" I looked around frantically for a way out. We could have jumped into the river, but the current would have swept us away.

And fast . . . Evan's words triggered something inside me and suddenly I heard Ginevra's voice in my head: *It's called a Phœbus. Only use it if you really need to escape, and fast.*

I searched the satchel again, but my hands couldn't distinguish between the objects. At last my fingers closed around a small crystal cylinder. My heart leapt.

"Don't slow down! Run!" Evan called to me. I pulled out the Phœbus and raised it to my mouth. A high-pitched whistle cleaved the trees. "What are you doing, Gemma, trying to hypnotize them?!"

Looking over my shoulder, I saw that the zombies were bothered by the noise and slowed down, but after a moment of confusion, once the echo had faded away among the leaves, they resumed their hunt. "I don't understand. Nothing happened," I said wearily. All at once the sound of galloping hooves shook the earth beneath our feet. I looked up and saw something in the distance.

"What the—" Evan's surprised words hung in the air as I let out a hopeful cheer without slowing down.

"It's Ginevra's horse! It's coming to help us!" I exclaimed, panting. A huge stallion was galloping toward us at breakneck speed.

A low curse escaped Evan. "It's not going to get very far unless it can navigate that current!" My eyes went wide. He was right. I'd been so happy the horse was coming to our rescue that I hadn't noticed it was on the other side of the river.

"What do we do?" I asked, panicking.

"We jump into the water," he said. "I don't think those zombies can swim."

"They wouldn't try—the river's full of poison. Infernal creatures are afraid of it."

"It's perfect, then."

"No! We can't get in, either. It would kill the zombies, but it would burn you," I said, still running. "Besides, the current is too strong. It'll drag us away."

"Then you'd better find a way to stop him too," Evan said, pointing at the horse that looked like it was about to jump into the river. "I don't think Ginevra would be happy if we killed her steed."

"No!" I shouted, but the stallion leapt into the void.

Evan and I froze at the river's edge, our eyes locked on the animal. At the last possible moment, it unfurled a pair of wings, leaving us open-mouthed.

"Oh my God." I couldn't find any words.

"That is not a horse," Evan stated, looking stunned.

"Definitely not," I whispered without taking my eyes off the mighty beast that had soared into the air before our amazed stares.

With a clatter of hooves, the stallion landed on the shore a few steps from us. From its mouth issued a sound that made me think of a prehistoric animal. I blinked with fascination at the magnificent black angel with outspread wings. Now that he was close to us, I realized he wasn't exactly a horse. His face wasn't long and his features were more like a lion's. On his head were three small horns made of some sort of black crystal that looked like a magical diadem. His neck was long and mighty, his body muscular and strong. He had large hooves with talons on them, and his tail also ended in a claw. His skin was so black and shiny it looked like a suit of armor, and his wings were as broad and powerful as a dragon's. Thinking about it now, I realized I'd seen the Witches riding the same beasts through the air over the Cowards' village, but the dim twilight, along with my panic, had kept me from taking in their features.

The animal shook his head and let out a long call: an invitation to snap us out of our frozen state. I turned around and saw that the rest of the zombies had almost reached us. Crouching with their noses low to the ground, they scurried along as swiftly as spiders.

Evan took my hand and led me to the stallion. He tried to leap onto its mighty back, but the animal threw him off with a neigh of disapproval. "He doesn't seem to like me," he muttered.

"Hurry, Evan! They're almost here!"

He tried again, but the creature refused to be mounted. "He won't let me. I think he wants *you* to guide him."

"What?! I don't know how to fly that thing," I said, confused.

"Come on, Gemma!" he urged anxiously. "There's no time for a crash course. Get on!"

Snapping myself out of my daze, I climbed up onto the creature, who this time stood still. The instant I stroked his coat, which was soft—unlike what I had imagined—I felt a subtle chemistry between us.

"Think I can get on now too?" Evan asked ironically.

I gave him my hand and helped him climb up behind me. Just then, a zombie lunged at us but our steed opened its jaws and let out a cry so shrill it was barely audible. The zombie dissolved in a cloud of dust.

"Thank you!" I cried in surprise.

The creature shook its mane. Evan shouted for me to hurry. Unsure of what to do, I tried nudging the animal's side with my heel and he set off at a gallop. Evan whooped with joy as the zombies disappeared behind us. "This thing is awesome!" he exclaimed, as excited as a little boy. "Why didn't you think of this before?"

"Ginevra told me to use the whistle only in an extreme emergency," I shouted over the hoof beats.

Evan rolled his eyes. "Like those zombies weren't a big enough emergency?"

"Okay, so maybe I kind of . . . forgot I had it?" I was forced to admit.

"Shit. Go! Go! Go!" Evan shouted, suddenly panicking.

"What is it?" I looked over my shoulder. Evan didn't need to explain. The zombies were on all fours now, bounding after us with incredible speed. It was as though they'd evolved in a matter of seconds, adapting to the conditions demanded by the hunt. In all likelihood, those beings hadn't seen food in months. They looked like ghoulish gorillas thirsty for blood. *My* blood. "How the hell did they do that?!" I screamed.

"Where did they come from, a Steven Spielberg movie?" Evan shot back, disgusted by the sight of them.

"Evan! Look out!"

One of the zombies had leapt up behind us and was about to land on Evan but disintegrated in the air not a second too soon.

"What just happened?" I said, astonished. Evan had carbonized him with a wave of his hand.

"I'd like to know that myself. I'm probably not as out of shape as I thought!" He gave a dismissive laugh.

"So why didn't you think of trying that before?" I mimicked him teasingly.

Evan looked over his shoulder and cursed. "Damn it! They won't give up. Don't they ever get tired?!"

The bizarre creatures were gaining on us, leaping from one tree to the next with frightful agility. "We'll never lose them," he warned. "You've got to make him fly, Gemma!"

"I don't know how!" I cried. The stallion continued to race along the river.

"Talk to him! Maybe he can understand you," he said. Seeing the derisive look on my face, he insisted, "We'll never find out unless you try!"

"Okay," I said, unconvinced. I looked down at the big black lion running like a mighty war machine under us. "Fly!" I shouted, spurring him on with my legs.

Nothing happened. "It didn't work!" I turned and saw Evan laughing. Nudging him with my shoulder, I protested, "Hey! I only did what you told me to!"

"I know," he said, still grinning, "and it was hilarious."

"At least one of us is having a good—" I shrieked at the sight of another zombie lunging at us.

Our mount noticed in time and dodged it at the last second. The zombie splashed into the river. I watched with disgust as it emerged, its huge mouth frozen in a howl and its burnt skin dissolving in the water.

"This is no time to kid around," I murmured, becoming serious. It was wonderful to hear the sound of Evan's laughter again and that particular tone he used to tease me, but we had to focus and find a way to get out of there or we would end up as those zombies' next meal. I stroked our steed's back and a strange tingle rose up my arm as though his energy had flowed into me. I closed my eyes, the comforting sensation flooding through me. *Come on, Argas, take us away. We need you—*

"Wa-hoooo!" Evan's victory whoop brought me back and I opened my eyes.

"What is it?" I exclaimed with a start, clinging to Argas's back when I saw the ground rapidly becoming more distant beneath us.

"You did it!" Evan said excitedly. "Let's see if you guys can fly now too!" he shouted at the zombies who had halted, watching us as we rose into the sky. One of them took a giant leap toward us, but Argas's barbed tail suddenly burst into flame and blasted the thing into oblivion with a single blow.

"Did you see that?!" Evan exclaimed.

Dazed, I blinked as the air lashed my face. *Argas.* I didn't know why I'd called him that. The name must have been buried in my soul and crept through my thoughts like an ancient instinct.

Evan rested his chin on my shoulder and a shiver spread through my body. The tension slid away. The zombies were growing smaller, receding into the distance. I heaved a sigh of relief. We'd done it— though I had no idea what had just happened.

"You did it! But how?" he asked, smiling.

"I don't know. I simply . . . thought it." I stared at Argas, soaring majestically across the sky. With every wingbeat I felt a quiver inside. It was crazy, but I had the impression I was part of him, as though there was some invisible connection between us.

"It's amazing!" Evan murmured, fascinated.

I stroked Argas's back and he let out a soft nicker of pleasure. "Yes," I whispered, "it's amazing." I smiled and closed my eyes. *Take us away from here,* I whispered, lightly touching Argas's mind. He responded with an almost imperceptible whinny. I opened my eyes and a sly smile curved my lips. "You'd better hang on tight!" I warned Evan.

"What?" he shouted over the wingbeats.

Without warning, Argas swerved sharply, forcing Evan to grab hold of me. I burst out laughing. "Think it's funny, do you?" he asked, hiding a smile.

"It's time for me to start making fun of you!" I teased. His laughter rang out in the sky, joining mine. Suddenly everything was wonderful. I had found Evan and we were flying toward home together. Soon the nightmare would be over. Even the landscape that scrolled away behind us was free of that ominous shroud of darkness that had terrified me for days. Magically, it wasn't scary any more. Beneath us, the forest extended infinitely, dotted here and there by villages. Who knew what other terrible creatures were lurking there or how many bloodthirsty Souls and infernal beasts prowled the forest, but seen from above it all seemed so distant. I felt free, safely out of reach. Towering mountains challenged the sky that loomed over everything in its eternal twilight. As far as the eye could see, the river snaked across the land like a venomous Dakor, occasionally thundering over cliffs in broad waterfalls. I held my breath as Argas flew over an erupting volcano. A liquid that looked like molten crystal burst into the sky, filling the air with shimmering golden reflections. *Poison,* I thought instinctively.

Then I saw it: Mount Nhubii. Tall and majestic, it watched from afar, awaiting our arrival. "Evan, look!" I cried, full of enthusiasm. The enormous waterfall plunging from the summit seemed to descend infinitely.

I couldn't believe it was all about to be over. It felt like centuries had passed since its waters had dragged me there. But I'd challenged everyone and everything and ultimately accomplished what I'd come for. I'd risked it all for Evan, and soon he and I would be home. A tear of joy escaped my eye and flew into the air as, behind me, Evan held me tighter.

"I told you, Jamie." His whisper caressed my neck. "Nothing can ever separate us."

A shiver running beneath my skin, I closed my eyes and snuggled my neck against his head, smiling. We flew over the waterfall and my heart filled with hope. At last I could see it, the highest point: freedom.

"That must be it, over there!" I shouted to Evan, pointing at a majestic stone circle protected by the mountains' ragged peaks.

"Why do I have the impression I've seen that somewhere before? It looks like Stonehenge. What is it?"

I tilted my face toward him and smiled. "Our road to freedom." It was exactly like Ginevra had described it: a more complete version of the stone circle in England. "And this"—I pulled the medallion out of my dress and showed it to Evan—"is our return ticket. It'll take us home."

Evan unleashed a mighty laugh that filled the air around us. Argas joined in with a whinny of satisfaction.

"Well, what are we waiting for?! Let's get out of this place!" I closed my eyes, a smile on my lips, and concentrated on Argas.

Following my thoughts, the animal flew in circles and made a running landing. I spurred him on to keep him moving, my eyes never leaving the Dánava, and as though we were one being he obeyed, galloping straight toward freedom.

All at once a wild squeal from Argas sliced through the twilight like thunder in a cloudless sky, piercing my bones. I lost sight of the Dánava and suddenly found myself on the ground. It all happened so fast I didn't have the chance to wonder why Argas had suddenly thrown us. Dazed, I held my head, trying to regain my bearings, when a voice stopped my heart, clutching it in its icy talons.

"Going somewhere?" Devina leaned over me and grinned, her expression excited, ravenous.

"Gemma!" Evan cried, and my heart ached as he ran toward me.

"No!" I screamed. With a wave of her hand Devina sent him crashing into a tree. The branches writhed and twisted around Evan's body, pinning him in place like steel straps. I raised my eyes and glared furiously at Devina. "Let him go!" I snarled, but all she did was throw him a scornful glance as she picked something up from the ground.

"This looks familiar." I shot her a defiant look at the veiled accusation against Ginevra. "Did you honestly think you would get very far using *this*?" She dangled the Phœbus over her palm and then clenched her fist. The whistle shattered. "I've always said you weren't very bright. You were free again and you might even have made it if you hadn't called for his help." Argas uttered a disconsolate grunt, almost as though he felt guilty. "Your calling Ginevra's Saurus led me straight to you." *Saurus.* So that was what the Witches' steeds were called.

She was right—I'd been a fool. Ginevra had warned me that the whistle would draw attention. Once again, I had ruined everything. Devastated, I watched Evan struggling to free himself, his fiery gaze locked on Devina's.

Coiled around her arm, Devina's Dakor hissed. I stared at the serpent, hopelessly drawn to him, but then my eye fell on the whip Devina was holding. I pictured her lashing Evan and a blinding rage built up inside me, but she just laughed and stroked my cheek with her lethal weapon. "Isn't she *magnificent*?"

I cried out from the pain. *Poison.* All she had had to do was touch her whip to my face and it made my skin burn.

"That is what you must call her from now on."

"You named your whip?" I said with a mocking sneer.

"It's made from Molock hide. I killed the beast myself without using magic." In a veiled threat she slowly traced a circle around my neck with the whip, then showed me the handle, which glimmered in the twilight. It was carved from the same black crystal as Ginevra's Phœbus. "You continue to hide your thoughts from me, but I *know* you're attracted to it. It's the most precious substance in Hell. We once brought it to your world to study the effects of its purification. You can still find rare fragments of it on Earth, but this is of a purer, more resistant quality. The Castle itself is built of this material. Only our magic is capable of destroying it. But I see you also have a piece of it." Using her whip, Devina raised my butterfly necklace, but I jerked away. "Witches yearn for Heaven and the material it's made of: diamonds.

They're our most irresistible temptation, but here they lose their light. They absorb the black magic and turn into carbonado, the substance of darkness. Such a terrible punishment."

I looked at my necklace and my eyes widened. She was right. The little diamond Evan had given me had turned black. When I looked up again, I found myself staring straight into the eyes of Devina's serpent. They were the same color as his Witch's: liquid amber.

"I must admit it's been amusing, but I'm tired of playing with the two of you. Sophìa will be back soon, we can all feel it." Devina narrowed her eyes and came closer, forcing me to step back. "Can't you feel it too?" she whispered, her eyes locked on mine and her voice suddenly hypnotic. She twisted her hand and a stabbing pain shot through my belly.

"Gemma!"

The pain prevented me from reacting to Evan's voice. The wound throbbed under my fingers: the mark of Sophìa. I forced my eyes open, defying the pain, but the only thing I could hear was her voice. "Can't you feel it inside you?" Devina whispered.

"Gemma!" Evan's voice was muffled and distant, as though a wall had risen around her and me, isolating us from everything else.

"It's the Power. Don't fight it, Gemma. Everything will make sense." I felt at the mercy of her words, as though nothing else mattered.

"Don't listen to her!" Evan's shout slammed into the wall separating us, shattering it.

Devina's expression turned bitter and the wound in my belly burned again. "Why do you insist on renouncing it?" She turned to glare at Evan. "Tsk. In order to be with *him*?"

Evan howled in pain and my heart constricted in my chest. I shot her a fiery glare. "I was about to say it was to avoid being like you, but that would have been my second answer."

Devina bent down and tore the medallion from my neck. "You won't be needing this any more." I continued to glare at her. "We'll see how witty you are when I take you to see Sophìa. Now move." She yanked me forward and I collapsed on the ground, on the verge of tears. Devina forced me to my feet, but I broke free and ran toward Evan, crying his name as he writhed in his prison.

"Gemma!" The tears blurred my vision but I continued to run. "Gemmaaa!"

354

My attempt proved as useless as it was desperate. A sharp pain shot through my temples and I crumpled to my knees.

"Gemma!"

I raised my hands to my head. It felt like it was on fire. I struggled to look at Evan. He fought so desperately against the branches that bound him like chains, it seemed he would uproot the tree. Then the pain clouded my vision.

I'd reached my limit. I'd found Evan, but Devina had torn him away from me, once again denying us our freedom. It couldn't be true, it couldn't really be happening to us. I was imprisoned in a nightmare from which I couldn't awake, a nightmare with no end.

"Evan . . ." I murmured, my cheek pressed against the ground. And together with my whisper, it seemed my life was being torn away from me.

I had no idea where my mind had wandered; I couldn't even feel my body any more, beyond the vague impression that I was lying on a slab of ice. My only certainty was the emptiness in my heart, the undeniable feeling that something had been torn out of me, leaving behind a dark hole.

A loud noise jolted me awake and I found myself lying on a floor, my palms and cheek pressed against the cold stone.

"About time." I blinked wearily as Devina strode into the cell. "At last you're awake. Don't get your hopes up—you're not going anywhere this time, not unless you learn to fly."

I glanced up at the tiny slit of window and realized what she meant. We must have been very high up, in the tallest tower.

"It won't be long now. Sophia is almost here." It sounded like a threat, and I pictured the evil grin on her lips. "You would have been better off being a good girl. The Empress doesn't care for betrayal."

I struggled to my feet so I could look her in the eye and for the first time realized there was someone else with her. A prisoner. "Evan—" I could barely speak. My heart trembled, surrendering to the hope that it might be him, but the prisoner didn't move or speak, shattering my dreams.

"Where is Evan? What have you done to him?" I screamed, overcome with desperation. "Did you leave him there to die?" I rushed at Devina, tears in my eyes, but she grabbed my wrists and overpowered me. "You can't have left him there to die!" I screamed, on the brink of madness, but Devina shoved me to the ground, unperturbed by my agony.

Beside her, the prisoner let out a strange grunt, drawing my attention. Unlike the Witch, he seemed upset by my tears. I stopped to look at him. The torch outside the door cast a shaft of light onto his face, revealing gruesome scars. I flinched and stepped back, frightened, as my last hope that it was my Evan shattered into a thousand pieces. He withdrew, hiding his face under the hood of his long cloak, as though ashamed. It couldn't be him. It was just another wretched creature spawned from Hell. My longing for Evan began to feel like a physical pain: the agonizing need to have him beside me.

"I'll be back soon." Devina's icy voice echoed off the cell walls. She shoved the prisoner by the shoulder, knocking him to the ground. He crawled as quickly as he could into the darkest corner, dragging the chains shackled to his ankles behind him as Devina turned back to me with a sneer on her lips. "Meanwhile, enjoy Gromghus's company. I picked out his name. It means 'monster' in our language. It suits him, dost thou not agree?"

The door slammed shut. I burst into tears and huddled in another corner. It was over. This time it was all over.

EVAN

33

POISONED THORNS

"Sorry, did I keep you waiting?"

I heard the Witch's voice and looked up at her, furious. My attempts to break free from the branches trapping me had drained every ounce of my strength, but if looks could have killed, Devina would have been burnt to cinders in a split second.

She came over, rested one hand on my chest, and stroked my face with the other. "Did you miss me?" she whispered near my lips.

I turned my face to avoid looking at her, filled with loathing for that creature who could have single-handedly ruled over all of Hell as its unrivaled queen of cruelty. "Where did you take her?" I hissed. Devina scrutinized me as though trying to grasp my essence, then pulled back and smiled, a dangerous gleam in her eyes. "Where did you take her?!" I screamed with all the rage in my body.

"Calm down." Devina circled me, her eyes fixed on me, as I seethed with hatred. "In a way, we're on the same side, you know. Why do you think no one came close to Gemma for five whole months? We were the ones protecting her. At least, some of us were." She leaned her face close to mine, her accursed Dakor hissing as it anticipated my taste. "Actually, let's say all of us except *me*. You were protecting Gemma, but without our help you wouldn't have stood a chance—let alone your family, after you died. To protect her we eliminated more Subterraneans than you can imagine.

"I bet you're still wondering why your disobedience went unpunished. They could have denied you access to Eden because of what you did. You wouldn't have had any way to eat of the Tree and you would have died a slow death that ultimately would have condemned you to eternal oblivion. But that didn't happen, and here you are now." She touched her nose to my ear. "Do you want to know why?" I glared at her in contempt and she laughed. "What, you haven't figured it out? There was no legitimate order for Gemma's death. It wasn't her fate. *She wasn't supposed to die.* They could never have denied you access to Eden because the cause of your desertion would have given away their deception. The Màsala wanted only to prevent her transformation. They knew she was going to become one of us."

"That will never happen!" I shouted, jerking against the branches trapping my arms.

She laughed louder. "Your willpower is captivating, I must admit, but it will get you nowhere, don't you realize that?"

"Do what you want to me. But *leave Gemma alone!*" I snapped, still glaring at her. I knew what Devina wanted from me. I'd never been willing to give it to her, but if Gemma was in her hands, I would do anything to save her.

She flashed me a mocking smile. "I'll do what I want to you all right, but the Empress will see to the girl—it's none of my affair now. This, on the other hand, I'll keep as a memento." She yanked the dog tag from my neck and stared at me with a strange light in her eyes, like she had special plans for me. "You're still splendidly intact." She let her ravenous gaze slide down my body, still imprisoned by her magic restraints. "A pity. I'd hoped that with you tied up here someone would have taught you the lesson a fugitive deserves." She smiled, amused. "Maybe easy prey isn't enjoyed around here. The hunt is always enticing for a predator, dost thou not agree?"

I shot her a defiant look, wondering what she meant to do with me, but she went on, a mocking smile still on her lips. "But then again"—she glanced at Ginevra's Saurus, which, to my surprise, had protected me the whole time, keeping the Damned that wanted to attack me at bay—"traitors are lurking everywhere. You never know who you can trust these days. A Witch's Saurus protecting a Subterranean? Tsk!" She raised an eyebrow, her expression stern. "That means I'll have to take matters into my own hands once again."

An agonizing burning sensation engulfed me from head to toe, plunging me into the center of my very own bonfire. I gritted my teeth, struggling to withstand it. I'd never felt such intense pain before, not even when Devina had tortured me. It felt like the skin was being flayed from my body, like the scars that marked me everywhere were lengthening, wrapping around me like tentacles, tearing me apart. The venom from all the bites and lashes she'd inflicted on me was moving, coursing through my veins. I clenched my fists until the pain subsided, leaving me drained. All at once the branches of the tree released me from their grip and withdrew. I fell to my knees, devastated.

"You could have been at my side for all eternity." The pain had been so overwhelming I'd forgotten Devina was even there. It felt like I was in the center of a tornado of fire. "I had great plans for us. But now I wouldn't know what to do with you."

With effort, I raised my head and she peered down at me, grinning a demon's grin. "Gemma's going to choose to join us rather than stay with you."

Her words made me shudder because some part of me grasped the threat. My muscles were still twitching beneath my filthy, torn, threadbare clothes. I could tell something about me had changed—and not in a good way.

"Not even she will want you near her now." I looked at the backs of my hands and cringed with horror, instantly covering my face. "Because you're a monster. Gromghus—that's the perfect name for you." Devina laughed, her evil voice echoing through the twilight. She cracked her whip and the air around her thickened into a mirror and then shattered into reflective shards. She kicked a piece of the glass toward me and I scrambled for it like a hungry man for a piece of bread.

I looked at my own reflection and my world ceased to exist. I was a monster. Devina had turned me into a hideous monster, one that Gemma would rightfully be afraid of. My body was covered with deeply gouged scars that snaked from my chest in all directions, running over my arms, my neck, my face . . . I touched my head and to my horror discovered no trace of the thick hair that had covered it. My skull was completely bald and deformed by furrows. I clenched my fists and charged at Devina but froze, terrified by the sound of my own voice. Clasping my hands around my throat in horror, I found that I could only grunt like a wild beast. I stepped back, shocked and defeated by the terrible truth: Devina had made me a monster.

"Not so tough now, are you?" she said with smug satisfaction. I gripped the shard of glass so hard blood oozed from my palm. "What a shame I won't see you in action again in the Opalion! How I adored it when you ripped your adversaries' heads off with your bare hands . . . I can't wait to see the face Gemma makes when she sees your new look."

I cringed and took a step toward her to beg her not to do it. Looking her in the eye, I took her by the shoulders. For just a second I thought I saw a glimmer of compassion in her amber eyes, but then she said, "You're right—I'd better not let her know what I've done to you.

After all, she'll be my Sister soon." She smiled, pleased with her plan. At her words, I stepped back, defeated.

"Don't make that face. Gemma will be better off if you can't explain it to her, dost thou not agree? If she found out who you really were she would stay with you, but only out of pity. Is that what you want for her?"

Her voice pierced my heart like poisoned thorns. "No one would want to be with you of their own accord. Let her keep the memory she already has of you. Once she joins us, I'll grant you the gift of allowing you to stay near her—though there's no guarantee you'll always enjoy seeing her, especially when her lips are on those of her Claimed. She'll be transformed and you'll remain at her side, serving her, watching her with other Subterraneans she's enslaved. And she'll never know you exist. But you'll have to make do with that—after all, one can't have everything. Here." She threw me a long cloak to cover myself with. It unfurled in the air, blocking out her image momentarily before falling on the ground in front of me. "You're a monster now, don't forget." Devina laughed at my utter defeat.

The idea that Gemma might be afraid of me was unbearable. The very thought was devastating. Devina was right—my appearance would repulse her. What future could I ever offer her by choosing to stay with her? By *forcing her* to stay with me? No, I couldn't allow it. I would continue to love her, to watch her in silence, but I had to stand aside. Gemma would never find out what had happened to me.

We had lost. I *felt* lost. Even if I found a way to explain to Gemma what Devina had done to me, I couldn't ask her to make such a huge sacrifice. My only choice was to give her up.

Give us up.

A FINAL FAREWELL

I cringed when I saw her lying on the ground and my heart withered because I couldn't run to her. I had to hide. I couldn't let Gemma see the monster I'd become.

"At last you're awake." Devina's icy voice broke the silence of the cell. "Don't get your hopes up—you're not going anywhere this time. Not unless you learn to fly," she warned, discouraging any possible thought of escaping Gemma might have had.

I'd tried to fight back on the way there, but Devina had forced me to follow her to the Castle's tallest tower. She could have thrown me into any other cell and left me there to die—it didn't matter to me— but her cruel imagination had inspired her to lock me up in that particular one, together with Gemma, inflicting on me the torture of having to look at her without being able to reveal my true identity.

"It won't be long now. Sophìa is almost here," Devina said. "You would have been better off being a good girl. The Empress doesn't care for betrayal." She glanced at me, but I was distracted by Gemma's movements as she struggled to get up. It took all the willpower I had not to run to her. Instead, I clenched my fists at my sides until they bled and focused on the pain.

"Evan . . ."

Hearing her whisper made my heart ache. I squeezed my eyes shut and forced myself not to move a muscle. Discovering what I had become would devastate her. I didn't want to deprive her of the hope—the *illusion*—that I had managed to escape. I didn't want to steal from her the memory she had of me. Of what I'd once been.

"Where is Evan? What have you done to him?" Her voice broke with frustration as she lashed out at Devina. *She didn't recognize me.* The knowledge triggered both relief and disappointment inside me. "Did you leave him there to die?" Gemma screamed, rushing at the Witch in desperation. I closed my eyes so I wouldn't see it. "You can't have left him there to die!"

That wasn't supposed to happen. Gemma wasn't supposed to believe I was dead. I would have to find a way to reassure her and make her believe I was safe. I would stay at her side so she wouldn't suffer, but without letting her know who I was.

Devina grabbed her by the wrists and threw her to the floor. A groan escaped me, drawing her attention, and I was ashamed. It was the grunt of an animal, the sound of a monster. As if mocking me, the torchlight touched my face just as Gemma turned in my direction. Her look of curiosity and hope transformed into one of horror. I hated Devina for how those dirty games amused her. Though I had already imagined Gemma's reaction to my face, her shocked, frightened expression was still a stab to the heart.

Gemma pulled back, cringing, and the world fell to pieces at my feet. I quickly covered my face with my hood so she wouldn't see me any more and huddled under the cloak. In the hundreds of years I'd lived, I'd never felt such pain or such a sense of loss. Gemma was right there in front of me but I couldn't have her any more.

"I'll be back soon." Devina shoved me like a rag doll and I tripped over the chains on my ankles. "Meanwhile, enjoy Gromghus's company," she told Gemma with a sneer before turning and closing the door behind her, leaving us alone in the dark.

Together, but hopelessly alone.

I didn't even try to react. I had lost everything, irrevocably and forever. My only concern was that Gemma might look at me again. I was afraid she would recognize me and want to stay with me anyway. Devina was right: I couldn't ruin her life; I had to let her go. Defeated, I scurried back into the darkest corner of the cell, hiding from her eyes—those big, wonderful eyes I would never have the chance to look into again. Eyes that would never again light up for me, never again probe my heart—because I wouldn't let them. I would have to cherish in my heart the memory of her gaze on me as I'd once been. I would fight so that at least wouldn't be taken from her. I would continue to love her forever though she would never know it.

The sound of her weeping in the silence of the cell broke my heart. I'd deluded myself into thinking the worst was over, but hearing her cry renewed the pain, making it unbearable. Seeing her so fragile, defenseless, and hopeless devastated me. Each gentle sob, each tear, felt like losing her all over again, infinitely. The heartache was more agonizing than the physical pain I'd undergone during the transformation or any other torture they'd ever inflicted on me. I tried to ignore her, covering my ears with my hands, curling up against the wall, but I couldn't. I could bear the burden of my own pain for eternity, but I couldn't stand the sound of hers. I couldn't bear to hear her cry. After everything she'd endured, it was clear she couldn't take it any longer. She was on the verge of collapse.

Overcome by the power of my love for her, I moved closer. She had her head on her knees and didn't notice me, even when I reached out to touch her. But then I realized my nearness would bring her no comfort, so I moved back, hoping she hadn't noticed anything. My chains rattled, though, betraying my presence.

Gemma raised her head, alert. "Wait." I instinctively covered my face, hiding it under my hood, but she insisted. I could feel her gaze on me in search of answers. "You don't mean to hurt me, I can tell. At least let me see who you are." She reached out and pushed my hood back onto my shoulders. Her expression remained frozen. I desperately covered my face again and a hostile snarl rose from my chest, echoing in the cell, mocking me. It felt like I was hearing it for the first time: the sound of a beast. When the echo faded, Gemma's weeping returned to torment me, filling the air. What had I done? I'd frightened her. Out of fear of her seeing me, I'd reacted like a monster, aggressively. Maybe that was what I'd actually become. Was it possible that Devina had transformed more than just my appearance? I couldn't stay near Gemma if there was a possibility of my hurting her, if I couldn't control those terrible new instincts.

I flinched when I felt her hand rest on my knee. I'd been so overwhelmed by grief, I hadn't realized Gemma's weeping had stopped and she'd moved closer to me, drawn by my desperation. I grabbed my hood and pulled it well down over my face.

"You don't want me to see you?" she whispered, as though afraid of frightening me. My breathing accelerated at the gentle sound of her voice so close to me. I hadn't dared hope she would speak to me again. I shook my head slowly, keeping my emotions in check, and she understood. "Who are you?" she asked kindly.

I almost lost myself to despair when I tried to reply, because I had no words. How I wished I could shout *It's me! I'm here!* and embrace her and promise her nothing would ever separate us again, but it would be a selfish gesture, because Gemma didn't deserve to be with a monster. I shook my head again helplessly and hid behind my new mask.

"You can't speak?" she asked. A groan of dismay escaped my throat as I huddled there. "Gromghus. Is that your name?"

I was forced to nod.

"I'll just call you Gus. After all, who we are isn't important in here," Gemma said wearily. "We've all been defeated. Everything is lost . . ." She looked down. Hearing the sadness in her voice, I involuntarily reached out and took her hand to comfort her. When Gemma saw it, ruined by scars, she flinched imperceptibly. I began to pull it back, but she stopped me and held it in her own. I'd never known anyone so brave. For all she knew, I could have been a beast ready to devour her, yet she hadn't let herself be frightened by my appearance. She thought of me as a poor creature spurned even by Hell. A creature that, like her, was at the mercy of Devina's cruelty. Much as I longed to, I couldn't look her in the eye. I could never have stood to read on her face the only reaction I feared more than fear: pity. Gemma pitied me.

She stroked my hand again and I fought the desire to pull her to me and never let her go. Being able to touch her skin again filled me with a painful warmth full of nostalgia for everything we could never be again. I closed my eyes and pretended for just a second that nothing had changed. I stroked her palm tenderly like I always did, suddenly realizing it might be the last time I would ever touch her skin, clasp her hand in mine, feel her so close to me. The two of us alone in a dark cell, prisoners of an impossible love, bound to a cruel fate that, despite all our efforts, had vanquished us.

I'll love you forever, Jamie. That emotion filled my head, my heart, my soul, until they overflowed. Everything inside me was screaming out my desperation because I couldn't tell her who I was or feel her lips on mine one last time, tell her I would love her forever. I couldn't wish her farewell.

Gemma slowly raised her head as though she'd sensed my pain and her eyes met mine. Emotion hit me like a hurricane and I couldn't look away. Her gaze lost itself in mine and for an instant I forgot everything else. Slowly, I raised my hand and tucked her hair behind her ear, an instinctive gesture I couldn't stop myself from making, driven by my desperate longing for her. My hand lingered on her skin, barely touching it, and she started, as though a shiver had run through her. For a single egotistical second, I hoped she'd understood, but the delusion vanished when I saw her eyes resting on my wrinkled, scarred hands.

She looked up, her eyes going wide. She hadn't recognized me. She was only afraid of me. The pain ran me through like a sword.

A loud noise made both of us jump. Devina threw open the door and burst into the room like a demon come to execute us. "Sophia awaits you," she announced sternly to Gemma. Their Empress had arrived. Her expression lit up with a cunning smile when she saw that Gemma and I were so close together. "You come along too," she ordered me. She waved a hand and I fell at her feet. "It will be amusing."

To my surprise, Gemma rushed at her in my defense but Devina shoved her away and yanked on my chains, laughing. "You made friends with the monster, I see," she said with a sneer.

Devina crushed my hand against the hard rock and from my chest came a snarl that made Gemma pull back in fear. I felt dead inside. I had just proved Devina right: Gemma would always be afraid of me. Furious, I lunged at the Witch but before I could attack her she tore off my hood to humiliate me. I wanted to throw myself on Devina and tear her to shreds, but the fear that she might reveal what I had become forced me not to defy her. Instead, out of love for Gemma, I would let her tyrannize me. I backed up and quickly put on my hood in a desperate attempt to cover myself. It was a feeling I'd never experienced before: I couldn't fight back, I could only hide. Revealing myself to Gemma would condemn her to being with a monster, and I couldn't allow her pity for me to ruin her life. I'd always been a soldier and, like a soldier, the time had come for me to withstand torture rather than give the enemy what they wished.

"We've already wasted enough time. The Empress doesn't like to be kept waiting." Devina pushed me out of the cell and Gemma stepped around her to follow me, her face proud and fearless. Two Witches appeared, though, and inserted themselves between us to escort her while Devina, behind me, forced me to keep my distance. She took every chance she got to mock me in front of Gemma, who from time to time would peek over her shoulder, making me hide my face under my hood. No torture during my imprisonment had ever been so unbearable and Devina was perfectly aware of it. As if we were in a terrible dream, Gemma walked in front of me, ignoring my presence, and I continued to follow her, desperately aware that I could never reach her again. I'd lost her.

We crossed through dozens of rooms, each more bizarre than the last. Some were furnished with cages and other threatening-looking instruments for the Witches' games. Many looked like gardens full of branches from which Dakor peered out everywhere. By then I'd been in the Castle long enough to understand that it was a sort of academy where the Witches trained, entertained themselves with their slaves, and tortured those like me who rebelled against their dominion.

After walking down a long hallway we finally reached a massive door that opened on its own as the two Witches escorting Gemma approached it.

"Don't try anything funny. Stay here and don't move. I'm not done with you yet," Devina said, shoving me inside and leaving me in a corner of the room with two of her Sisters. "You two, keep an eye on him."

Gemma glanced at us but continued to the center of the hall. It wasn't particularly large compared to the other rooms in the Castle, but there was something eerily fascinating about it. I could see a dark opening in the ceiling and directly beneath it on the floor, a shining semicircle containing the Witches' symbol. Large, dark branches snaked up the walls, twisting around themselves all the way up to the ceiling. A majestic throne stood proudly at the far end, glittering like a black diamond. Its back was tall and had sharp points like cathedral spires.

The Witch seated on the throne watched Gemma approach. I'd seen her a few times before. Her icy gaze was magnetic and her hair was long and raven-black except for the locks that grew at her temples, which were as pearly as moonbeams and gave her a venerable, regal air. She wore a majestic black gown that flowed into a wide train made entirely of black butterflies and flower petals of the same color. Lilith, worshipped by her Sisters and disciples, better known as Sophia, the bride of God and Empress of the Underworld. Coiled around her arm, her Dakor hissed. It alone sent shivers down my spine with its lapis lazuli eyes identical to its mistress's. A thin crown of black butterflies that barely touched her forehead was woven into her hair like a diadem. She stood and turned slightly, and I noticed that her dress opened behind her shoulders, leaving her back completely bare. The butterflies were fluttering all over her, creating an incredible effect.

I looked around and noticed for the first time that there were butterflies everywhere: on the broad windows, the walls, the ceiling. From time to time, one of them rose from Sophia's gown and fluttered around her as she silently contemplated it.

Unexpectedly, Sophia's gaze came to rest on me, then darted to Devina, vaguely amused. It must have taken only a second for her to realize what had happened. Only Gemma was unaware of my presence now. And those who wished to claim her as their Sister did nothing but ridicule her.

"Naiad, it is a pleasure to have you here with me," Sophìa said to Gemma, her hypnotic, imperious voice filling the hall, a glint of satisfaction in her eyes at having obtained what she wanted.

Gemma, who had crossed the room with her head held high, never taking her eyes off Sophìa, stared at her defiantly.

"It is unkind to take one's leave before being received, is it not?" Sophìa asked maliciously, referring to our escape. The other Witches bowed their heads in reverential respect for the Empress. "Perhaps you do not care for my Empire of Darkness?" She raised an eyebrow and awaited Gemma's reply.

It was promptly given. "I certainly can't say I was given a friendly welcome."

Sophìa smiled at her boldness; Gemma was in the presence of the devil incarnate yet didn't seem the least bit intimidated. "There is something you were perhaps not told. *No one* leaves my realm without my permission."

"Then I ask for your permission."

Sophìa laughed out loud. "You are daring. That is why I am so fond of you. If you wish to receive my permission, however, you must give me something in return." The Empress stroked the feline at her side— a large, fierce-looking panther. "Bring him in," she ordered, her gaze fixed on Gemma as though studying her in detail. She seemed amused.

I stared at them in silent surprise as I wondered who else Sophìa meant to receive. Drake? Stella? No. Neither of them. When I realized what Devina had in mind, my heart trembled and turned to ice, then stone, and finally ash.

An identical copy of me—of who I'd once been—was escorted into the room by a Witch. He stopped in front of Sophìa, not far from Gemma. His chest was bare and the dog tag Devina had torn from me after my transformation hung around his neck. I was shocked to notice that Gemma was staring at it, suddenly looking disoriented. They looked at each other for a long moment, making me wish I was dead, but neither dared speak before the Empress. Devina would finally have her revenge for my rejection of her.

"You came here to take him back. You are brave, but that comes as no surprise. What fascinates me is how you succeeded in hiding your true intentions from me." Gemma continued to stare at her without replying. "My dear Ginevra betrayed us once when she decided to leave us, and now she's betrayed us again by allowing you to come here and defy us."

"Ginevra has nothing to do with it!" Gemma said angrily. "It's me you want. Leave everyone else out of this."

Sophia smiled. She'd hit the bullseye. "You are correct. And I wish it to be clear that unless I receive what you intended to offer me in return, I shall not grant you permission. Not with him."

No! I tried to break free from the Witches guarding me, but they held me back. I knew what she was asking: she wanted Gemma to agree to join them in exchange for freeing the man she believed to be me. They were tricking her!

"You are free to go," Sophia challenged her. "He, however, remains with us." The impostor who had taken my place played his part, struggling in the Witches' grasp. Devina smiled and cast me a look of smug satisfaction.

"Remain here, and he may go," the Empress continued. "You are much more precious to us than you are to him. It's simple. The choice is yours."

I had to find a way to stop her. It was a trap. Sophia was actually leaving her no choice; Gemma would never leave on her own. She would sacrifice herself, believing she was saving me, but instead it would all be in vain.

I was desperate. I couldn't let Gemma give in to the Witches but I had no way to stop her. Selfishly, I'd thought I could continue to have her near me, keeping my true identity a secret, but I'd never stopped to think of what it would mean if she decided to stay with them—or me, in my present guise. I didn't want Gemma to transform. I wanted her to escape from this terrible place and never return, even if it meant giving her up forever.

"I can't."

I jumped, emerging from my torment, when I heard Gemma's firm refusal. She'd remained silent, reflecting on the proposal, and must have reached the conclusion that, despite everything, joining them would be madness. I would lose her, but Ginevra and Simon would take care of her and the baby, and just knowing they were safe would have to be enough for me.

"I won't agree to become one of you." Sophìa stared at her, a smile on her lips as though Gemma had said just the opposite. "Not while I have Evan's child in my womb."

It hit me like a bucket of ice-cold water. I realized why Sophìa was so calm: Gemma hadn't entirely refused her offer, and the Empress must have read that in her mind. "I'll do it. I'll become one of you," Gemma continued.

A snarl escaped me, drawing their attention. I struggled in the Witches' grip in spite of their accursed serpents that were coiled around their arms, hissing angrily. I didn't care any more if Gemma discovered me so long as I could manage to stop her. The Witches held me back and I realized Gemma was staring at us, her eyes brimming with regret. She seemed to be struggling to hold back tears. Almost as if forcing herself not to look, she bowed her head. At the end of the day, no matter how much she might pity me, I wasn't her problem.

She raised her head and I could hear renewed determination in her voice. "I will agree to let you transform me, but on certain conditions." Meanwhile, the other Evan was silent, a puppet in Devina's hands.

"Ah!" Looking vexed, Devina stepped forward to stand between Gemma and Sophìa. "She's not yet one of us and she already wants to dictate the rules!" The Empress shot her a glance that silenced her on the spot, then looked back at Gemma, prompting her to continue.

"I propose a deal: the transformation will take place only after the baby is born. I ask for three days after the birth," Gemma proclaimed. Sophìa narrowed her eyes. "What are three more days to you?" Gemma insisted.

The Empress nodded. "Granted. We have waited for centuries. Three more days will make little difference."

But Gemma wasn't finished yet. "My son must not be involved."

"That I cannot guarantee. Your son was conceived from the seed of a Subterranean, yet a part of us also dwells within him. How great that part may be we do not know. It is a situation we have never encountered before."

"I'm not willing to negotiate."

"I shall promise you one thing," Sophìa said. "He will be the one to choose. You have my word."

"Your word means nothing if you use deception to make him choose like you've done with me."

"No tricks. We shall leave him free from all constraints."

"No dreams or apparitions?"

"We shall not influence him in any way. You must realize, however, that if he offers to join us of his own free will, naturally we will not refuse that alliance. Besides, one day you might also wish for him to be here with you."

Gemma stared at her for a long while, studying her as if she too were able to read minds. "Time will tell. But I have one last condition. I came all the way here alone, journeying through Hell battling your creatures. I'm not willing to leave here all alone."

Devina snorted and I glimpsed the hint of an evil smile on her face. "Of course! Take your slave with you, by all means. I have no need of him." She contemptuously shoved the impostor, who tripped and fell into Gemma's arms.

I stared at them, petrified. Their eyes met and my heart shattered into a thousand pieces. Even the possibility of loving her from afar was being torn away from me. Gemma would transform and I would have to live with the knowledge that *he* had taken my place in her heart.

"Not him."

I started and looked up at Gemma. She extricated herself from the impostor and her eyes swept the room until they rested on mine. "I'm taking Gromghus with me."

I blinked, paralyzed, as she ran to me. I closed my eyes and held her tight. It seemed unreal and I didn't want her to slip away. Leaning back, I looked into Gemma's eyes, ashamed of my hideousness. She lifted her hand and caressed my cheek, but I pulled away. Her eyes filled with tears.

"Evan," she whispered. Hearing my name on her lips again caused a pang in my heart. "What have they done to you? My love."

A tear slid down her face and I wiped it from her cheek. I attempted to speak but had no voice, so I tried to tell her with my eyes what I was feeling: a love that had no end.

"I'm sorry. I'm so, so sorry. It's all over now," she whispered comfortingly. "I'm taking you away from this place."

Sophia's laughter rang through the hall, breaking the invisible cord connecting our eyes. "It would seem your little trick failed, Devina," she said contemptuously.

Though she struggled to hide it, Devina looked livid. "Could you really still love him with such a repulsive appearance?" she asked scornfully, voicing the torment I felt in my heart.

Gemma smiled at her. "I don't expect you to understand what love is. You could have turned him into an insect and I would have continued to love him. Love isn't in the eyes, but in the hearts of those who are capable of experiencing it."

She looked at me and I stood taller. "When I thought you were dead, all my hope vanished along with you. I just wanted you back, whatever it cost. I'd already lost you once—I wouldn't be able to bear it again," she said, gazing into my eyes. Turning toward Devina again, Gemma said, "I don't care what he looks like, but I don't expect you to understand the depth of such an emotion, so I won't waste any time explaining it to you."

Devina snarled with frustration and vented her anger by attacking the Subterranean with my appearance who no longer served her purpose. He doubled over in pain and crumpled to the floor, unconscious.

Sophìa laughed. "I played along with your little game, Devina, though naiveté is not usually one of your weak points. Did you really believe it would be so easy to deceive her? She *is* one of us, after all." The Empress's face showed her derision.

"Not yet—she's only half Witch! Why are you listening to her?!" Devina growled, furious that her plan had failed. "Kill the baby and get rid of that worthless servant! That way she'll have nothing left to live for and will choose evil! I can do it for you." In the blink of an eye, she shot across the room and grasped Gemma's belly.

Don't touch her!!!

The howl filled my head, trapped by my inability to voice it, as I lunged at Devina to stop her. She noticed my movement and a sudden thunderbolt hit me in the chest, knocking me all the way to the other side of the room.

"Evan!" I heard Gemma's stifled scream in the distance, but the pain left me reeling, forcing me to the floor. I knew my face was exposed, but didn't have the strength to cover it or even get to my feet.

Meanwhile, Devina held Gemma captive, preventing her from coming to me. "Sophìa, listen to me! You have no reason to give in to her whims when you can take what you want and give her nothing in return."

"No!" Another voice rang out, fierce and authoritative. It took me only a second to identify it. I turned to look at the Empress and saw Anya at her side where the panther had been a moment earlier.

"Sophia, don't listen to Devina. If you do what she asks, Gemma will never forgive you."

"After the transformation she won't even remember it!" Devina shot back, trying to convince the Empress, who was listening closely to them both.

Anya ignored her and focused all her attention on Sophia. "I've seen their love. It's strong. The venom won't be enough to rid her heart of the longing for revenge. Listen to me, I beg you. Devina is afraid someone will steal her place." She turned to her Sister and shot her a piercing look. "The truth is she wants to prevent Gemma from becoming one of us. She's trying to hide it, but I know it's true. Sophia," she continued, her voice low and respectful, "you have what you wished for. Let him return to how he was and give them time to say goodbye."

"Why should I undo the spell? He means nothing to me."

"But *she* means something to you. Devina only transformed him out of spite because he rejected her advances while you were gone." Sophia looked at Devina. I remembered when Sophia had ordered Devina not to try to seduce me, but Devina had deliberately ignored the command. Witches were protective about their claims to Subterraneans, and Devina had never gotten over the fact that she hadn't been able to make me hers.

"There's no point in leaving him this way. It only gives Gemma another reason to hate you," Anya continued. "Give them a little time. What difference can a few months make? They'll soon pass and then Gemma will belong to us for eternity. Why continue to make her suffer when she's already decided to follow you? It's only a matter of time before she joins us. Consider it your gift to her."

Sophia looked at Gemma as she reflected on Anya's suggestion. Finally she nodded, forcing Devina to release Gemma, who immediately ran to help me up. I raised myself up on my elbows as Sophia spoke again: "Your advice is always wise, Anemone. I shall ignore the fact that you helped them to be together. However, I shall not follow your suggestion in its entirety; I will grant them both their freedom, but the slave will receive no additional favors from me. That is all I am willing to concede."

"I don't care," Gemma said, to everyone's surprise.

I stared at her in shock, hope rising in me. Her eyes told me she *truly* didn't care what I looked like. It would be difficult, but maybe she might find some way to still love me.

Sophìa smiled at her, fascinated by her reaction. "Naiad, never have I doubted your strength or your courage, yet today you remind me of a lesson long faded by time: the eyes of love see beyond appearances, just as those of the heart see beyond betrayal. I accept your terms and grant you both permission to return to your world, but do not forget that you belong to us. It is only a matter of time. You will have three days after your child is born and then we will come for you. You will comply with these conditions under pain of death—your own and that of all those you love: your child, your precious beloved, your family. No one will be spared, and their souls will be ours."

"That won't be necessary." Gemma stood up and looked at Sophìa with a determined air. "I will keep my promise."

"Then I shall see you soon." Sophìa locked eyes with Gemma, the words sounding like a threat. "Anya, Devina, escort them to the portal." When Devina opened her mouth to protest, Sophìa glared at her. "That is an order," she said sternly. "You have already caused enough problems. Do not make me regret my magnanimity."

Devina stared back at her defiantly but dared not speak. All at once the air crystallized in front of her, creating a mirrored passageway.

Anya smiled at Gemma and me as she guided us to it. Suddenly the contours of Devina's body faded before our eyes, a black panther appearing in her place. She lashed out with a menacing paw, challenging us to move closer, but in a flash Anya assumed the same shape and barred her way with a fierce growl that echoed off the walls. The two panthers faced each other, displaying their lethal claws that I knew from experience were tipped with Dakor venom, just like their fangs. A red patch on one paw distinguished the amber-eyed panther from Anya, a graceful black feline with a sharp emerald gaze. This sort of transformation in the past must have been what gave rise to legends, prophecies, and superstitions about black cats.

Sophìa put an end to their quarrel, urging us through the mirrored passageway. Gemma and I took a last look back and I saw the satisfied smile on her cunning face. Gemma had sworn an oath—made a pact with the devil—sacrificing herself to save me. But I would find some way to break that pact.

A second before the large hall disappeared behind us, I saw Sophìa rise from her throne. Keeping her eyes on me like a threat, she spread her arms wide. The sleeves of her gown fanned out into butterfly wings. She brought them back to her sides and rose rapidly into the air, disappearing through the hole in the ceiling.

"Here." Once again in human form, Anya smiled at me and opened her hand. On her palm was the dog tag she must have taken from the impostor. "I think this belongs to you." Looking at her, still stunned, I took it and put it around my neck with a nod of gratitude.

"That's all I'm able to give back to you. I'm sorry," she said softly, clearly upset she hadn't convinced Sophìa to change me back to normal. "You have to be careful," she warned us, casting me a glance. "Now that Gemma has agreed to join us, the Màsala will stop at nothing to prevent her transformation. Sophìa would rather have seen you transform right away, to avoid possible risks—we already lost one Sister in the past—but she decided to give you a little more time. It must have been a difficult decision for her."

"It's thanks to you that she agreed to my conditions," Gemma said.

But Anya shook her head, looking concerned. "That's not the point. What I'm trying to tell you is to remain alert. We'll try to help you, but it won't be easy. Be prepared for confrontations with far more Subterraneans than you've faced up to now," she said gravely. I nodded in silence, hoping my intense gaze would communicate to her my commitment to protect Gemma even at the cost of my own life.

While Devina paced irritably across from us, Gemma ran to embrace Anya. "Ginevra was right about you," she said.

"Tell her I haven't forgotten our promise. But now hurry, before Sophìa changes her mind."

The glass portal had taken us directly to the Dánava, and Anya led us to the center of the two rings of stone. She moved away, tossing Gemma the strange serpent-shaped medallion that Devina had torn from her neck.

Gemma stared at it, unsure of what to do. All at once the relic let out a hiss and stirred. Gemma and I watched as the tiny serpent came to life and slithered across her palm. It coiled around her finger in a gentle caress, then dropped to the stone beneath our feet and aligned itself in the symbol carved in the rock.

Lightning split the sky and the twilight thickened as the air began to churn. Gemma's dark hair lifted and rose into the air, whipped by the harsh wind howling around us. She looked at me warily and my hand slid into hers. I wished I could speak to her, but I would have to content myself with simply drawing her to me. The wind had grown so violent, though, that I couldn't even embrace her. I looked up and saw blurred figures like black ghosts whirling above us, creating a dark vortex, a barrier inside the stone circle. I finally managed to wrap my arms around Gemma, but the vortex swept us up and wrenched her away from me.

"Evan!" Gemma shouted, trying to be heard over the howling wind. I roared, holding on to her hands with all my strength as the cyclone flung our bodies through the air, the wind trying in vain to separate us. The spirits spun around us with increasing fury. No—they weren't spirits. I could see them clearly now. They were huge butterflies. They filled the air, surrounding us, then merged into one another, condensing into a pool of black water into which we plunged. I screamed in pain, my body on fire.

"Evan!!!" Gemma cried. My sight clouded and the current tore me away. Gemma continued to call my name and I fought to emerge from the furious whirlpool and find her, but it was useless. *Gemma . . .* The whisper filled my head as my strength abandoned me. It was as if the water was draining all my energy.

"Simon, quick! Pull him up!" I felt someone grab me by the arms and drag me out of the boiling cauldron. I forced my eyes open and Ginevra's face filled my field of vision. "Gemma . . ." I gasped, begging Ginevra to help her. Then I collapsed at the water's edge and everything went black.

A caress brought me to my senses like a soothing balm that instantly healed every wound. I opened my eyes to see Gemma leaning over me, her big dark eyes on mine.

Ashamed, I felt the impulse to cover my face because the current had torn away my cloak. I still couldn't bear the thought of Gemma staying with me out of pity, but I would have to learn to live with that overwhelming burden.

"We're home," she said softly, caressing my face.

"Jamie . . ." The whisper traveled from my heart to my lips and I jumped at the sound of my own voice. Gemma smiled at me and I bolted upright, touching my face in astonishment, my heart racing with the hope that the rest of me had also returned to normal. I held up my hands and saw smooth skin. Looking into Gemma's eyes, I saw she was still smiling. I couldn't believe the Witch had changed her mind. "But Sophìa said—"

"Anya must have convinced her after all," she said. I pulled her against me and crushed her in my arms.

"Hey!" Ginevra slapped Gemma on the shoulder, a huge smile on her face. "What took you so long?" Gemma looked at her, her face filling with the memory of her odyssey. "That was the longest five minutes of my entire life!" Ginevra said teasingly.

Gemma relaxed, relieved. "Was I really gone only five minutes?"

"That's how much time elapsed between one portal and the other," she explained. "In Hell there's no time."

"Then it was the most intense five minutes of my entire life too." Gemma looked at me and a smile lit up her face, smoothing away all signs of her torment. I couldn't even imagine everything she'd gone through in Hell during her quest to find me.

I raised my hand to her cheek and stroked it. "It's over," I whispered, but her image doubled before my eyes.

Someone propped me up. "Quick, he needs to eat of the Tree." *Simon*. I hadn't noticed he was there. I hadn't even noticed I was on the verge of passing out. He slung my arm over his shoulder and picked me up as Gemma fixed worried eyes on me.

"Don't worry, I'll be back soon," I mumbled, my eyes locked on hers as I vanished. Gemma's answering smile made me feel I was in Heaven again.

Our Hell was over. No one would ever separate us again.

GEMMA

THE SUN WITHIN

Framed by a snowy backdrop, everybody in town was gathered around the lake, forming a multicolored patchwork that moved to the hypnotic rhythm of Lana del Rey's *Young and Beautiful.* The music filled the night.

On the drive back from the airport, I watched them through the car's tinted windows and thought of the emptiness I'd felt in my heart when my friends had invited me to that concert. All I'd been able to think about was Evan and the fact that I would never see him again. Only one day before, the most I could have hoped for was to momentarily assuage the immense pain by spending a night out with friends, pretending that the snow that had frozen my heart would one day melt. Today, my heart had begun to beat again. No sun could ever warm me more than the realization that Evan was with me.

It felt like an eternity had gone by rather than just a handful of hours. The world seemed to have stopped during my odyssey through Hell and held its breath as it waited for me to bring him back. I hadn't slept a wink during the flight home, despite slumber's attempts to envelop me. Evan had slipped his hand into mine and hadn't let go. Part of me still feared it was all an illusion, that his presence there was one last island on which my mind had sought refuge before sinking into the depths of madness. I didn't want to fall asleep, afraid my Evan wouldn't be there when I woke up.

When I paused to reflect on everything I'd faced, it seemed impossible that I had actually done it. And yet Evan was beside me. I could feel the warmth of his breath. Against all odds, I'd brought him back. It had been a mad, arduous endeavor, but I'd done it. And despite all my fears, deep in my heart I'd always known that no Witch and no creature from Hell could ever keep me away from him.

I didn't want to waste a single minute of our time together.

"It's yours. I brought it in case you wanted to call your parents." Simon, behind the wheel, handed me my phone, though I hadn't even noticed it beeping. I'd sealed myself in a bubble where the only things that existed were Evan and me and my hand clasped in his on the back seat of the BMW, waiting for our months-long journey to come to an end.

Simon had already told my parents that Evan had been found—that the car accident had left him with amnesia, unable to contact us—and that we hadn't been able to track him down until he'd finally regained his memory. When I entered my PIN, eighteen missed calls lit up the display and an envelope icon blinked above. I opened the most recent of the twelve texts Peter had sent me over the last few hours.

Where are you?

I stared out the window, watching the crowd. Beside me Evan squeezed my hand. I was supposed to have gone to that concert but I'd been busy with something far bigger. I rested my head on Evan's shoulder and my heart smiled as I read the reply I'd instinctively written.

I went through hell but I'm finally back in heaven.

EPILOGUE

"What happened to all the snow?" I asked Evan, raising my voice to be heard at the end of the path, where he'd gone ahead on his bicycle. The vague suspicion that winter had stopped just for us occurred to me, making me laugh.

Evan jammed on the brake and skidded over the damp forest floor. "It must have melted when it saw you." This time he was the one to laugh at my awkward attempt to dodge the flying dirt as I pedaled behind him. "Besides, it's not safe to ride your bike if the ground is slippery, don't you agree? We can't risk your falling!" he said, looking amused as he teased me. That must have been one of the things he'd missed most during our separation—teasing me. He was wearing black cyclist's gloves that left his fingers bare and had tied his long, overgrown hair into a samurai ponytail. *He looked so sexy . . .*

"You thought of everything," I shot back, trying not to let him see me blush.

A week had gone by since our return from Yucatán and Evan had had all the time he needed to recover and regain his powers. That meant that even if I had fallen, my chances of ending up on the ground were zero, so Evan must have had something else in mind. When he'd woken me that Saturday morning, his eyes full of childlike enthusiasm, his suggestion that we ride our bikes to the lake house hadn't seemed so strange. But the closer we got to the shore, the more convinced I was that Evan was up to something.

It hadn't snowed for two days. The sun shone high in the sky, casting its light on the lake's icy surface. The leaves stirred in the breeze while the snow melted on the damp ground right before our wheels, clearing a path like a theater curtain rising on a play performed only for us. Only small patches of snow scattered here and there in the forest watched us, silent spectators of our newfound love. The scent of the woods was intoxicating. At last I could smell it again.

"Wait for me!" Struggling to keep up with Evan, I tried to curb his enthusiastic race through the trees as he popped wheelies and spun around like it was an obstacle course. "You still haven't told me what we're doing here," I reminded him when we'd reached our hideaway.

His carefree laughter echoed through the trees as he rode back and came to a skidding halt in front of me, a smile in his eyes. Dropping his bike close to the edge of the lake, he tossed his gloves to the ground and, after helping me off my bike, took me by the waist and lifted me into the air, holding me close. I slid down his body and the forest spun around us as his lips fused with mine.

"I love you. Will that do for an answer?" he whispered against my lips.

"It would if I didn't know you well enough to recognize that strange smile."

"What smile?" he replied teasingly.

"The one you're trying to hide right now!" I retorted, and he kissed me again.

"Nothing gets past you," he whispered.

"Glad you finally noticed," I said sardonically.

"If I really have no choice but to give in to your insistence"—he took my hand and led me to the shore, looking at me out of the corner of his eye—"I hear the Snowball Hop is coming up soon." He raised an eyebrow, a half grin on his lips, sat down at the water's edge, and pulled me down onto his lap. "I'm officially claiming every dance on your dance card. Think you can scare up a Victorian dress by next Saturday?"

"No more dances, please. The last prom I went to didn't end up among my fondest memories," I reminded him.

Evan smiled—he'd probably been expecting me to say that. "This time it's going to be different." He drew me closer, his words sounding like a promise. "Want to take the risk?"

"The only risk I'll be running is not being able to fit into the dress any more. Ginevra has a couple of them in her wardrobe, and my guess is that the theme of this year's hop isn't a coincidence."

"I wouldn't snub vintage dresses if I were you. You were so sexy in Hell with that outfit on." He raised an eyebrow and I thought back to when we'd made love in the prison cell. God . . .

Evan laughed, guessing what was on my mind. Blushing, I replied quickly, "At this point I'm afraid I'll have to make a few alterations." I looked at my belly, which over the last week had begun to swell.

He smiled. "I'm sure you'll be gorgeous," he assured me, and I almost lost myself in his dark eyes.

"I'd better be, otherwise I'll look horrible next to you!" I said, grinning. His expression became serious, and I knew he was trapped in past torment.

"Did I say something wrong?" I asked cautiously. Something in my words seemed to have upset him.

"Would you really have still loved me if I'd stayed a monster?" Sadness darkened his face as he waited for me to answer, but I had no doubts.

"My eyes could never see you as a monster"—my hand slid to his chest and rested on his heart—"because it's your heart that joins me to you. We're bonded together and no spell could ever change how I feel."

What I said seemed to reassure him only partly, as though something in him was still afraid he might lose me. "Will that always be true? No matter what happens?"

The question hung between us and Evan looked into my eyes as though searching them for my answer. I realized he was referring to my transformation, but once again I had no doubts. "*Antar mayy as.* I'll always love you, Evan. It couldn't be any other way." I rested my chin on his shoulder and felt his chest against mine as he held me close. No transformation could destroy my love for him. "Of course, I can't deny I would have missed the sound of your voice—but then again, you wouldn't have been able to tease me any more." I gave him a sly smile.

Evan smiled tenderly and put his mouth to my ear, making me tremble with emotion. "Well, I'm afraid you'll have to put up with me for a long time, because I'm going to make sure you never have a reason to miss *any* part of me. *Yatha tvam mayy asi,*" he whispered, sending a tingle over my skin.

I closed my mouth and swallowed, gazing into his eyes. They were so close to mine I risked being trapped in them. "It will be sweet suffering," I murmured against his mouth.

"When did you realize the other Evan wasn't me?" he asked softly. I watched his lips move, hypnotized. When my brain had processed the question, I looked up at him and smiled. I'd been waiting for him to ask me that for a while. "I recognized you when we were in the cell."

Evan looked at me in surprise. I could see him trying to figure out whether or not I was serious.

"Your gestures made me suspect it, when you . . . you stroked my palm with your thumb," I said with difficulty. The memory was still so vivid in my heart. I'd spent such a long time thinking about his caresses, yearning for his touch, that it would have been impossible for me not to recognize it. When he had touched me, a tingle had spread from his fingers and touched my soul. "At first I wasn't sure." Through his shirt I slowly stroked the scar that ran down his right forearm, losing myself in the memory. The marks left on his body by the poison would never fade, a constant reminder of Devina's cruelty. There was nothing in the world that could make me want to become like her. "It seemed impossible, but then I looked into your eyes and every doubt vanished. I realized it was you, but I thought it would be better not to let Devina know. I had to make her think her plan was working, at least until I was with Sophia."

Evan continued to stare at me, surprised by my revelation. He didn't realize the most incredible part was yet to come. "And, I heard your thoughts," I confessed all in one breath, and waited for his reaction.

"You . . . what?" he asked, stunned.

I shrugged, smiling. "I heard your voice in my head. You called me Jamie. No one else calls me that, so there was no doubt it was you."

"You can really read minds?"

My confession had astonished Evan more than I'd expected, but I couldn't tell if he was pleasantly surprised—or scared. Evan had always conveyed his thoughts to me, but in Hell he'd been without his powers, whereas mine had begun to develop.

"I can't control it yet," I said regretfully. "I don't know when it's about to happen." Actually, the only two times I'd read someone's mind were both right after being in the presence of Witches. My body must have sensed the bond and activated the powers hidden within me. "I suppose that'll happen once I've transformed."

Evan stiffened. "You're not going to transform," he said, his voice firm, his gaze commanding.

I stared at him, unable to reply. I didn't want to shatter his illusions because deep in my heart I nurtured the same hope. Instinctively, I pushed up the sleeve of my sweatshirt and began to fiddle with the black hair tie around my arm. Now that I knew what it meant, I should have taken it off, but it was something that had always been part of me.

"We'll keep it from happening." Evan's gaze softened on mine. He kissed my forehead and I closed my eyes, surrendering to our very own utopia. "We're part of each other, Gemma. We need to fight to make that true forever. *Samvicaranam. Samyodhanam.* Remember?"

"Stay together. Fight together," I translated. No one was going to separate me from him. I would fight against everyone—even myself—but we would stay together.

Sitting on Evan's lap, I stared at the lake, my gaze sweeping to the distant horizon where the snow and ice gave way to the colors of a clear sky full of hope. My fingers instinctively clasped the pendant I wore around my neck. The diamond sparkled once again; the evil that had darkened it in Hell had been purged. Would I, in the same way, also manage to emerge from the darkness? I didn't know what would become of me, but one thing was certain: all I wanted was to stay with Evan and our baby.

Seeming to sense my thoughts, he pulled me more snugly against his hips and held me tighter. Then he slid his hand under my sweatshirt and stroked my back, following the shiver he'd caused. He was so close his lips brushed mine with every movement.

I stroked his ear with my nose and took a deep breath, inhaling his scent. "Evan, would you do something for me?"

"Anything. Whether it's permitted in this world or forbidden."

He rested his forehead against mine and my fingers played with his hand, stroking it and drawing imaginary symbols, then moving onto his forearm, tracing the marks tattooed there. Evan let me study them.

"I'd like you to give me a tattoo. I want to have those words on me so I can remember this moment—remember the two of us—whenever I read them." *After my memory has been obliterated*, I thought, but didn't dare say it out loud. I needed it. I was more afraid than ever before of losing him again. Afraid of myself, afraid of the transformation.

His forehead still touching mine, Evan took a deep breath and slid a hand behind my neck, holding me tight. Then, slowly, he held the other one near my face, offering me his palm as I continued to stroke his arm. My fingers slid up over his wrist until they mirrored his. Palm to palm. A burning sensation stung my thumb and spread down the side of my hand, but I didn't take my eyes off Evan. Our gazes remained locked until the pain subsided and he smiled against my lips, brushing his nose over mine.

Clasped in Evan's lap, I turned my head and smiled in amazement. Our palms were still suspended between us, and along the inner side of my right hand was engraved in elegant writing:

संविचरणम्

The mark rose to my thumb, encircling it twice. But it wasn't the entire phrase I'd asked for; on Evan's left hand was another tattoo that lined up with mine, completing it.

संयोधनम्

He'd given himself one as well, uniting us even in that small gesture. The phrase could be read in its entirety only when we joined hands. "*Samvicaranam*," Evan whispered, running his thumb over the writing on my hand. *Stay together.*

I looked him straight in the eye and brushed my finger over his new tattoo to seal the vow. "*Samyodhanam.*" *Fight together.*

"For eternity." Without taking his eyes off my face, Evan interlaced his fingers with mine.

I looked at the tattoo and my breath caught in my throat as I understood for the first time the meaning of the symbol Evan had created for us. If we held our thumbs apart, each of us had a simple oval that came to a slight point on the outer side, but when we interlaced our fingers my oval joined with Evan's to form the infinity symbol.

"Did it hurt?" He looked at my face warily. Inside me a thousand different emotions struggled to prevail, and the winner would probably be tears.

"Yes—it made my heart ache. It's wonderful."

Evan had given me the tattoo I'd asked for, but only half of it; he would keep the other half. Now, along with the mark of the Children of Eve on his forearm, he carried on his left hand *our* symbol, the symbol of our bond and our battle. We had grown to know each other through our shared battle, and we would continue the struggle together. Fate had given us no peace and we knew we might never achieve it, but we would continue to fight for all eternity—whatever it took—to stay together.

My eyes shining, I stroked his tattoo and moved my hand to the mark of the Subterraneans. Then I slid it up his arm to his shoulder where, beneath his black cotton shirt, I knew there was another one of the lash marks left by Devina, the Witch who might one day be my

Sister. I ran my fingers over it, promising myself I would never become like her. Now I too had left my mark on Evan—a mark that spoke of love, not of death and destruction, like hers. Never would I want to be like Devina. That possibility might be what frightened me most about the thought of transforming.

"You know . . ." Evan had watched me as I reflected, but for some reason he was smiling. He swept a lock of hair from my face and reclaimed my hand. "Devina left me with a lot of scars, but one of them hurt her more than it did me. Inadvertently she gave us a gift, because now you're also in my past."

"What? What do you mean I'm in your past?" I laced my fingers with his, sealing them in our own special infinity, and snuggled against his chest, playing with the dog tag around his neck.

"I remember having a memory of you the night before I died in 1720."

I stared at him in astonishment, my hands on his chest. "Did she implant that memory?"

"No, I did—to remind myself that you're my fate."

I found my smile again. How had I been able to be without Evan for so long? My heart ached at the mere thought. "And it had an effect on the present?"

"Exactly. I have new memories now. In one of them, I'm telling my mother about you. In a way, it's almost like I introduced the two of you." I thought I might burst with emotion and he smiled, seeming happier than ever. "And it couldn't be any more perfect, because actually"—he lowered his voice to a murmur—"I didn't bring you all the way here to invite you to the dance."

I pulled back to look Evan in the eye and he offered me his hand to help me to my feet. "Before coming to wake you up this morning I went to see your parents at the diner," he said.

"To see my parents?" I stared at him, puzzled. "What for?"

"This time I wanted to do things properly." Evan stepped closer and my heart raced. "This place is full of us, don't you think?" he said softly, resting his forehead on mine. He opened his hand and showed me the little silver case he'd been hiding in his palm.

I swallowed, staring at the little box as it slowly opened upon his command. "Evan," I murmured, but he took my wrist, making me tremble, as his ring slowly slid onto my finger.

"Marry me, Jamie," he whispered with incredible tenderness. "It's all I want." His dark eyes probed mine and I wished the moment would never end.

"It's all I want too." The words flowed directly from my heart. I closed my eyes as a feverish heat swept over me, filling my mind.

Evan's lips tenderly touched mine again and again, playing hide and seek, sealing his vow and testifying to our love. "Should I take that as a yes?" he murmured, smiling against my lips. He squeezed my hands at my sides as I bit my lip, pretending to be thinking over his proposal.

"Couldn't you tell already?" I smiled, unable to help it.

He lifted me into the air and spun me around as his laughter filled the forest. "Come on, quick!" He took my hand, led me to my bike, and climbed onto his own. "I want the whole world to know!"

Smiling at his enthusiasm as I followed him, I stopped to look at the little ring on my finger. My heart was still pounding with emotion. I looked up at Evan who was zigzagging through the trees, freestyle.

"Hey! Where are you going?" I called after him as he charged up the rugged terrain.

Evan whipped his bike around and skidded to a halt in front of me. "Wherever I go, I'll always come back to you."

EXPIATION

THE WHISPER OF DEATH

One great sacrifice will end it all—but can true love ever be forgotten?

Prepare yourself for a journey with no return.

How can you look forward to the future when you know your days are numbered? Gemma has asked herself that every night since making her fateful pact with Sophìa, queen of the underworld. Three days after giving birth to her child, Gemma must return to Hell and be transformed into a Witch, erasing her past and surrendering herself to Evil. This is the price she's agreed to pay in exchange for bringing Evan back to life and ensuring the safety of their child. Evan, however, refuses to accept her agreement. He's convinced that together, they can overcome this new challenge. His deepest fear is different: he knows the Angels of Death will do everything they can to kill Gemma before she becomes a Witch. Pursued by unrelenting danger and dark secrets, Evan and Gemma ready themselves for the ultimate bloody battle to defend their love.

How far will you go to save the person you love?

ACKNOWLEDGEMENTS

I can never thank my husband Giuseppe enough for staying by my side with such dedication throughout this dream of mine, for supporting all my decisions, and for all his precious advice. Thank you. You're my rock. Infinite thanks go to my son as well for being my reason for living.

Once again, huge thanks to my parents for teaching me to love (and for all the chores they help me with when I'm too busy!). Thanks to my mother, who despite my protests always has her purse full of *Touched* saga bookmarks to give out to people, and to my father as well, who even today can't hear about my accomplishments without shedding a few tears. I'm grateful to my entire family for the enthusiasm they've shown.

Endless thanks to my brilliant translator Leah Janeczko who makes it possible for you to read my books and to my American editor Annie Crawford for her accurate revision of the text. She has been more than an editor to me and I trust every one of her suggestions. Working with the two of them for the English editions of my books has been an amazing adventure that I will never forget.

I thank Saverio Sani, professor of Sanskrit at the University of Pisa, for his truly precious transcriptions in Devanagari. Special thanks to Alex McFaddin and sweet Rhiannon Patterson for their indispensable information about Lake Placid. Be forewarned: I'll never stop hounding you for more!

Thanks to the singers whose voices inspired the finest scenes between Evan and Gemma: James Blunt, Lana Del Rey, and Hans Zimmer.

Thanks to all my Witches and Subterraneans all over the world. The English journey has been amazing, and I'm so proud to have found such passionate fans. I've received so many incredible, inspiring emails and messages. It's thanks to you that the *Touched* saga has become a bestselling series! I still can't believe that many English readers tried to read *Brokenhearted* in Italian because of their eagerness to know Gemma's fate. I can't thank you enough for your enthusiasm about this series! I would love to mention you all, but that would be impossible. However, please know that the thanks you deserve are written on my heart.

Indelible thanks to Meghan Haithcox and all the other readers who had quotes from my books tattooed on them. That's so exciting to me! From my heart I thank all of you who have written to me and all those who may write me in the future. Feel free to contact me through Twitter and Facebook or email me at touchedsaga@gmail.com—I will do my best to personally reply. I'm always happy to read your opinions and exchange thoughts. And please visit the saga's official website at www.touchedsaga.com for all the latest news, games, and polls.

Finally, there's one person I want to thank with all my heart, and that person is you. I don't know your name but I'm very grateful to you for dedicating a bit of your time to Evan and Gemma's story and their great love.

Here we are at the end of another journey—one that led Evan and Gemma all the way to Hell and back. It was an odyssey that many readers waited for with patience and affection. For this reason, my heartfelt thanks go out to all the readers of the *Touched* saga who have followed Evan and Gemma's story with enthusiasm and passion right from the start. I can never thank you enough. The wait was long, Gemma's journey to bring Evan back was fraught with danger, but I hope you all experienced a bit of their emotions.

Until our next adventure with Evan and Gemma!

THE AUTHOR

Elisa S. Amore is the author of the paranormal romance saga *Touched*. She wrote the first book while working at her parents' diner, dreaming up the story between one order and the next. She lives in Italy with her husband, her son, and a pug that sleeps all day. She's wild about pizza and traveling, which is a source of constant inspiration for her. She dreamed up some of the novels' love scenes while strolling along the canals in Venice and visiting the home of Romeo's Juliet in romantic Verona. Her all-time favorite writer is Shakespeare, but she also loves Nicholas Sparks. She prefers to do her writing at night, when the rest of the world is asleep and she knows the stars above are keeping her company. She's now a full-time writer of romance and young adult fiction. In her free time she likes to read, swim, walk in the woods, and daydream. She collects books and animated movies, all jealously guarded under lock and key. Her family has nicknamed her "the bookworm." After its release, the first book of her saga quickly made its way up the charts, winning over thousands of readers. *Touched: The Caress of Fate* is her debut novel and the first in the four-book series originally published in Italy by one of the country's leading publishing houses. The book trailer was shown in Italian movie theaters during the premiere of the film *Twilight: Breaking Dawn—Part 2*.

Sign up for the TOUCHED saga newsletter at:
http://eepurl.com/bR8EuT

Find Elisa Amore online at www.touchedsaga.com
On Facebook.com/TheTouchedSaga
On Twitter.com/TouchedSaga
On Instagram/eli.amore
Add the book to your shelf on Goodreads!

Join the Official Group on FB to meet other fans addicted to the series:
facebook.com/groups/251788695179500

If you have any questions or comments, please write us at
touchedsaga@gmail.com

For Foreign and Film/TV rights queries, please send an email to
elisa.amore@touchedsaga.com

***

If you enjoyed this book, consider supporting the author by leaving a review wherever you purchased it. Thank you.

BCPL
Baltimore County
Public Library

CPSIA information can be obtained
at www.ICGtesting.com
Printed in the USA
LVOW12s1801080817
544250LV00002B/246/P